SNAFU
·.· HUNTERS ·.·

SNAFU
·.· HUNTERS ·.·

Edited by Amanda J Spedding & Geoff Brown

Cohesion Press
Mayday Hills Lunatic Asylum
Beechworth, Victoria
2020

SNAFU: Hunters
Amanda J Spedding and Geoff Brown (eds)

REISSUE 2018 (Print 2020)

•.•

Cohesion Press
Mayday Hills Lunatic Asylum
Beechworth, Victoria
www.cohesionpress.com

CONTENTS

Apex Predator - N.X. Sharps & Tim Marquitz 1

Two Birds - Evan Dicken 24

Non-Zero Sum - R.P.L. Johnson 41

Only Stones In Their Place - Christine Morgan 69

That Old Black Magic - James A. Moore 101

Ngu'Tinh - D.F. Shultz 151

Warm Bodies - Kirsten Cross 182

The Bani Protocols - Rose Blackthorn 211

Hungry Eyes - Seth Skorkowsky...238

The Secret War - David W. Amendola 262

Outbreak - V. E. Battaglia 285

Droch-fhola - Brad C. Hodson 304

Bonked - Patrick Freivald..323

Also From Cohesion Press

<u>Horror:</u>

SNAFU: An Anthology of Military Horror
– eds Geoff Brown & Amanda J Spedding

SNAFU: Wolves at the Door
– eds Geoff Brown & Amanda J Spedding

SNAFU: Survival of the Fittest
– eds Geoff Brown & Amanda J Spedding

SNAFU: Hunters
– eds Amanda J Spedding & Geoff Brown

SNAFU: Future Warfare
– eds Amanda J Spedding & Geoff Brown

SNAFU: Unnatural Selection
– eds Amanda J Spedding & Geoff Brown

SNAFU: Resurrection
– eds Amanda J Spedding, Matthew Summers, & Geoff Brown

SNAFU: Last Stand
– eds Amanda J Spedding & Geoff Brown

SNAFU: Medivac
– eds Amanda J Spedding & Geoff Brown

COMING SOON

SNAFU: Holy War
– eds Amanda J Spedding & Geoff Brown

APEX PREDATOR

N.X. Sharps & Tim Marquitz

Target confirmed. Operation Mousetrap is a go." The crisp, mechanical voice of the commander cut through the headset. "You will link up with local assets and infiltrate the mining camp. Eliminate the rogue and dispose of any evidence. Our presence in the area cannot be exposed. Do you read me, Sergeant?"

"Yes, sir."

"Don't underestimate the target, Sierra. He might well be an older model but you know damn well no one survives long in this line of work without a few tricks up their sleeve. Memphis out."

Staff Sergeant Sierra growled under her breath after the comms went silent. She knew well enough what she was up against and didn't need Memphis's warning. Sierra was no cub to be led about by the scruff. She turned to her pack, huddled tight in their drop seats, awaiting orders.

"We've got the green light." Wide, toothy grins met the announcement. She gave them a moment to revel in it before holding her hand up to quiet them. "Now bring it in, we're almost there."

Sierra led her pride in prayer as the suborbital insertion craft began the re-entry sequence. The six women asked not for forgiveness, nor did they beg salvation. Instead they entreated upon their Goddess that their aim be true, their guns functional, and their blades sharp. Sierra felt the pressure of gravity reasserting its hold but disregarded the gentle creak in her bones while the pride lifted their voices in unison to praise the Mistress of Dread, the Lady of Slaughter, She Who Mauls.

The commandos brought the prayer to an end with a roar while the insertion craft banked to port, indicating glide and circle sequence. Aware that a single flaw in the craft's stealth package would invite interception by Chinese surface-to-air missiles, Sierra had her pack concentrate on performing a final account of their gear in case they needed to drop early. They did so in contemplative silence. This wasn't their first suborbital insertion but death was never far from the thoughts of soldiers such as these. The goal was always to provide the Goddess sufficient sacrifices to spare the pack any losses. The Lady of Slaughter cared not who met their end upon the field, only that she earned her rightful blood-price in battle.

Staff Sergeant Sierra scrutinized her pride as they went about their business. To her right sat Sergeant Charlie, eyes scanning her wrist-screen, checking for deviations in the signal. Charlie was the pride's dedicated micro-drone operator, acting as the eyes in the sky. While all of the women were capable of utilizing the quadrotor, named Horus, Charlie was by far the most gifted operator. Horus was *her* child.

On Sierra's left was Corporal Foxtrot, the squad's designated marksman. Foxy held a rifle scope up to her eye, peering through while making a series of adjustments. Across the aisle sat Specialists Juliet, Tango, and Victor, fighting against seat restraints to tighten the straps on their battle rattle. Sierra offered a sympathetic nod at seeing the stiffness in their postures, the budding frustration in their eyes. Despite the layers of thermal clothing and ballistic plating that covered the women Sierra knew they felt naked without their weapons in their hands; procedure demanded all small arms be secured to prevent them from becoming airborne hazards during descent.

The women sat in barely restrained excitement – a trio of killers desperate to be about their work. Staff Sergeant Sierra knew her sisters on a primal level. Her enhanced senses accentuated their peculiarities, processing the scents and sounds that identified each as surely as any fingerprint or blood sample.

"The LZ is hot. I repeat, the LZ is hot," came the voice of the insertion craft's pilot over the comms. "We've got SAMs incoming."

Sierra scowled as the craft juked to avoid the inbound missiles. She heard the pilot launching chaff to distract the radar guidance and ground her teeth together, reminded once more that the shuttle was unarmed due to payload restrictions. She hated their reliance on the man piloting the craft. Modifications aside, he was not one of them, not one of the pride. And now that the stealth approach had proved ineffectual, her sisters' lives were in the hands of the First Lieutenant's nerves and augmented reflexes; a situation far from ideal. A near miss on the starboard side a moment later sent a shudder through the fuselage and confirmed Sierra's doubts.

"Staff Sergeant, we are approaching the LZ but you've got to unload on the double. I've ditched the SAMs but this area is crawling with hostiles and I want to get the hell out of Dodge," announced the First Lieutenant.

"Roger that." Sierra cut the link on the comms before her fury bled through. It did no one any good to antagonize their ride home. Her lips peeled back to reveal a feral smile of dominant canines and sharpened incisors. "You heard him, ladies, we've got a date with the Mistress of Dread and she will not be kept waiting."

The commandos roared, releasing their restraints and snatching the weapons and packs stashed above their seats. The starboard flank of the insertion craft peeled away with a metallic hum, exposing the pride to a blast of piercing wind. It was bracing after the warm confines of the shuttle. Sierra crouched before the opening as Foxy led the deployment. As soon as the craft leveled the corporal leapt through the door, weapon leading the way. The pride followed with Sierra bringing up the rear.

Foxy hit the ground first and shouldered her rifle, scouring the LZ for hostiles. She found one almost immediately. The report of her rifle announced the death of an enemy combatant hunkered on the ridge even before Sergeant Charlie touched down behind her. The other commandos followed in sequence, dropping into crouches to return fire as rounds zipped through the air to clank off the shuttle's hull and peck at the ground around them. Sierra waved the First Lieutenant off and, without delay, the insertion craft shot away with a surface-to-air missile on its tail.

Sierra joined her fire to that of the pride, sending carbine rounds at the rocky outcropping shielding an unknown number of hostiles. The commandos spread out and increased the tempo of the fusillade, causing the enemy to hunker down in the face of withering fire. Charlie, given a reprieve, pulled Horus from her pack and spread his stabilizers, bringing him online. The quad-rotor zipped into the blistering mountain air with the faintest of hums.

In no time Horus's sensor suite generated a real-time evaluation of the field and beamed it directly to the wrist-screens worn by each member of the pride. Appraising the display showed them everything they needed to know regarding the battle zone.

"We've got eight shooters armed with assault rifles and a single belt-fed spread out on the ridge above. The approach is steep but Horus has highlighted a more accessible path we could use to flank them," Charlie told the group.

"Charlie, Foxtrot, Juliet, Victor, keep them occupied. Tango, follow me," Sierra ordered, scrutinizing her own wrist-screen for the flanking path.

In unison, Sierra and Tango shrugged out of their packs, slung their firearms, and dashed across the broken terrain, devouring the distance in a fast and low stride while their sisters provided cover fire. The mountain air was thin and clawed at the back of Sierra's throat with every breath but it was the least of her concerns. Gunfire from the ridge resumed as the pair reached the mouth of the pass. They paused there to catch their breath. The belt-fed opened up and Tango flinched on reflex though the two had yet to be seen. Sierra grinned. No amount of combat experience ever fully settled a warrior's nerves.

Another look at the wrist-screen told the Staff Sergeant the enemy had spread even further along the ridge in an effort to counter her people, making their task all the harder. Sierra prayed the Goddess remember the sacrifices of her sisters and keep them from harm. She unslung her carbine and took point, trading speed for discretion on the ascent. Farther down the mountain Foxy's rifle spoke, silencing the enemy machine-gun emplacement. Sierra swept her aim from side to side as she advanced, confident Tango would catch anyone she might miss in her advance.

They found the first hostile precisely where Horus indicated he would be – kneeling behind a boulder and fumbling a reload. Sierra sent him sprawling with a trio of 5.56 rounds, painting the rocks with his blood. She and Tango sniffed out the next soldier on their own as Horus met with some unknown interference, the target blinking in and out at random. They spied the hostile peeking out of a shallow recess in the mountainside, firing and ducking back under cover to avoid the quadrotor's scanners. Sierra and Tango lit him up the next time he materialized. He slithered back into his hole, his life draining away.

The commandos resumed their advance along the trail, heads on a swivel and sniffing the air to find the six remaining enemies. Nictitating membranes shielded their large, sensitive eyes allowing them to absorb more light than human standard, providing an unparalleled view of the environs. Their mobile ears swiveled and rotated, tracking for any signs of danger that might have eluded the quadrotor.

'Hostile MG active, hostile MG active, hostile—'

A peal of thunder erupted forty meters up the ridge, interrupting the urgent missive from Horus. Sierra and Tango dropped and narrowly avoided the high caliber penetrators directed at them. The machine-gun scythed into their earthen cover, spitting a rain of stony splinters over the prone commandos.

"Suppress that damned gun," Sierra demanded over the comms.

The staccato of gunfire intensified as the pride renewed their suppressive fire. The belt-fed redirected its attention back down the slope to silence the barrage and Sierra took advantage of the opportunity and raised her head for a look.

"Specialist, what's your condition?" she asked.

"Pissed myself a little, Staff Sergeant, but am otherwise intact."

Sierra chuckled despite herself. Modified they may be but the pride were still fundamentally human.

Tango shook her head. "Might not want to laugh too hard, Staff Sergeant. It looks like you took some shrapnel. You're bleeding through your pants leg."

Sierra grunted and reached for her calf, feeling the lacerations she hadn't noticed. They stung at her touch but she diagnosed them as superficial. She grinned. Better a little blood than wet panties.

'Four hostiles headed your direction', Horus said through the implants in their ears, which kept them in contact even if the rest of their comms broke down.

Sierra glanced at the wrist-screen, viewing four thermal signatures through the drone's sensor suite. She snapped her carbine up in time to catch the first combatant in her optics. Cross dot merged with silhouette and jacketed lead punched through yielding flesh. Momentum carried the combatant backward a short distance, rifle clattering from his hands. The three other hostiles took notice and ducked back, stopping short of entering the Staff Sergeant's line of sight.

"I'll keep their heads down. You go pay a visit and share the good word of our Lady of Slaughter."

"My pleasure, Staff Sergeant," Tango replied with a purr, rising to sling her carbine.

Sierra released a burst of rounds to discourage curiosity as Tango set to scaling the rocky incline. The staff sergeant watched as Tango crawled up and over, disappearing behind the jagged rise. The belt-fed proceeded to spit certain death downrange. When Horus confirmed Tango was perched above the three hostiles exchanging shots with the Staff Sergeant, Tango unsheathed the Kukri from her thigh and drew the .45 from her hip holster.

"On three," she subvocalized to Sierra through the comms.

One.

Two.

At three Sierra ceased fire and watched with amusement as Tango dropped into the midst of the hostiles. *Death from above.* The specialist struck with knife and pistol in a savage, whirling sequence worthy of the Goddess's praise. Blindsided, the combatants died without struggle, major arteries severed and critical organs punctured in the blink of an eye, the walls of their makeshift cover painted in wet and dripping crimson. Tango ran her tongue along the flat of her knife, no doubt savoring the copper sacrament.

Sierra rushed by at a near sprint. "Vicky is hit," she said between breaths.

Tango sheathed her knife and followed the Staff Sergeant, swapping pistol mags on the fly. They closed in on the last two enemies in the battle zone, snapping off shots as they navigated the uneven footing. Hollow points from Tango's .45 connected with the nearer of the two, expanding upon penetration and disrupting soft tissue. The machine gunner pivoted, hefting the belt-fed to fire along the path they tread, finger jammed against the trigger in desperation.

From there on, the trail offered no further concealment for Sierra and Tango. They unloaded on the gunner the instant they broke cover. Several bullets found their mark, hammering into the hostile's torso, but he remained upright. Staggering, he braced to continue his stream of fire. Sierra let go of her carbine and drew her sidearm, expecting the 7.62 to shred her before she could get another shot off.

To their mutual astonishment the gunner's head cratered in a puff of red mist and gray pulp and he crumpled in a heap of ruined flesh.

'All threats neutralized. Battle zone clear. Initiating patrol sweep', Horus broadcast.

"Sorry, Staff Sergeant, you were taking too long," Foxy said over the comms, "Thanks for setting up the shot though."

"That was your handiwork?" asked Sierra.

"Affirmative."

Sierra thanked her and got back to the business at hand. "How's Vicky?"

"Alive," Specialist Victor answered over the link. "MG winged me but the weave deflected the worst of it. Hurts like a mother but I've suffered worse."

Sierra breathed a sigh of relief. The pride was intact. "In that case haul ass up here and bring our packs," she ordered.

"Yes, Staff Sergeant, on our way."

Sierra kicked the belt-fed away from the dead gunner and knelt to examine him. He was considerably larger than the others and he must have been ugly even before Foxy evacuated his brain pan. His torso bore seven entry wounds but barely a dribble of blood at each. Sierra probed his chest, validating her suspicion. The gunner had a sub-dermal ballistic weave of his own. He was a mod like she was, though a poor imitation of the meticulous care and state-of-the-art technology that had gone into crafting her own body.

"What do you make of these combatants, Specialist?" she asked.

"Collateral damage," replied Tango over by the gunner's associate.

"Elaborate."

Tango dropped to her knees, opened the corpse's mouth and set to prying a tooth out.

"They're armed with cheap AK variants, wearing rags, and I'll bet my favorite knife that big fella you're poking has black market mods all through him. This guy here does too."

The tooth popped out and she stowed her trophy in a vest pouch. "They aren't People's Liberation Army and they're definitely not Eight Immortals Group, which means we probably just killed our contacts who were supposed to help us infiltrate the mining camp. Blue on blue," Tango finished.

"Blue on fucking blue," cursed Sierra, though she couldn't bring herself to be disturbed by what they'd done. The pride had defended itself and that was all there was to it. "Something spooked this lot."

"Care to take a guess?" asked Charlie.

"I've a good idea."

Sergeant Charlie and the rest of the pride crested the ridge right then. Foxy and Juliet passed Sierra and Tango their rucksacks. Vicky sat on a boulder and clasped a hand to her side where she'd taken a glancing blow from the MG. Tango inspected the damage, prodding the torn skin meant to cover the now visible ballistic weave. The move elicited a yelp from her patient. Vicky shoved her aside and slapped a length of duct tape on the wound.

"We don't have time for all that. I got this from Horus."

Charlie consulted with Sierra, sharing a video clip on her wrist-screen. Horus hovered dozens of meters over the ridge, showing a clear view of the ravine on the other side. The drone's optics scanned the topography for several seconds before highlighting patterns the quadrotor's programming deemed as aberrations. Horus zoomed in, magnifying the anomalies: bodies, five of them.

"Let's take a closer look," Sierra said.

"I should properly dress your leg first, Staff Sergeant." Tango gestured to her wound, concern apparent in her eyes.

Sierra grabbed the roll of adhesive from Vicky, ripped off a strip, and applied it to the lacerations on her calf. "After our little shootout these hills are going to be crawling with hostiles. We have zero time to waste. Juliet, you're on point. Foxtrot, you bring up the rear. Everyone else, fall in."

Without further discussion the pride struck off, summiting the ridge then sliding down the scree on the other side. They traversed the ravine in a staggered column while Horus patrolled the sky and sought out potential threats. From the tail Corporal Foxtrot kept her eyes peeled to complement the drone's electronic vigil. Sierra gave her a grateful nod and waved the rest of the pride on. The day Foxy relied wholly upon plastic and silicon was the day she dug her own grave and placed herself in it.

Juliet located the first body, or at least fragments of it. The pride gathered around a human reduced to bloody ribbons. Shell casings punctuated the red ruin but Sierra could tell this wasn't the work of a gun or even a knife. The destruction visited on the carcass bore animalistic qualities, gouges from tooth and claw.

"Do you smell that?" Juliet asked.

The kill was fresh and the cold had helped preserve the spoiling meat but the copper tang and voided bowels bouquet of death smothered the senses. Though somewhat masked by the heady perfume Sierra recognized the spoor of another predator. She assessed the scent, connecting it with the sample shared by Memphis during the mission briefing. The sample contained pheromones collected and catalogued so that mods could distinguish friendly mods from others on the battlefield.

Tango beat her to the punch. "The rogue was here."

Sierra nodded.

Charlie move alongside. "Staff Sergeant, Horus is tracking two scouting parties headed straight for us and they've got a drone of their own."

"Initiate Snipe Hunt Protocol," Sierra answered.

"Already on it." Charlie tapped a series of commands on her wrist-screen, activating Horus's electronic warfare package, designed to shut down enemy drones and jam their sensors.

"Our quarry was careless enough to leave a trail for us to follow. Juliet, lead the way."

Again the pride set off, loping across and out of the narrow gorge. They passed more evidence of the rogue's presence along the way – bodies like burst melons, ravaged and discarded. Accustomed as the pride was to death they still found the overkill distasteful. It bespoke a lack of restraint, reinforcing the necessity of terminating the obsolete mod responsible.

Despite the irony of her position Sierra refused to feel shame for their role in hunting down and dispatching older mods. The unstable operators presented a liability to the Apex Program and, by extension, the security of the United States. She felt no kinship with the quarry, they were a breed and multiple generations removed. The rogue was obsolete, nothing more than a prototype. Sierra and her sisters were the future.

'Patrol deflected. Proceed freely', Horus transmitted after they'd traipsed along for a quarter of an hour.

Sierra called the column to a halt. "Charlie, send Horus ahead to reconnoiter. I want to know what we're walking into."

"Yes, Staff Sergeant."

"Foxtrot, Tango, you're on overwatch. Stay frosty."

"Roger that, Staff Sergeant," Foxy and Tango said in harmony, hustling off to take up elevated positions.

"Juliet, tend to Vicky's wound."

"That's not necessary. I'm fine," the solider answered.

"Stow it, Specialist, that's an order. Might as well let Juliet kiss your boo-boos while we get our bearings and have a few minutes. I've got my own to deal with."

Sierra sat and took a slug of water from her canteen. She removed the medical kit from her ruck before taking another swig of water. Rehydrated, she peeled back the adhesive stuck to her leg, revealing the gouges in her bloody pant leg and the subsequent lacerations in her calf. She pulled off a glove and began extracting the slivers of rock embedded in the skin with her retractable claws. Once finished she sprayed anti-bacterial over the cuts, covered it in gauze, and fastened it all together with a fresh strip of duct tape.

"Check your screens. You're gonna wanna see this," Charlie called out.

Sierra tugged her glove back on and viewed the live feed streaming on her forearm display while Horus recorded, the quadrotor suspended above a city in tumult. An inferno raged, engulfing the stacks of shipping containers that had been converted into residences. Figures in riot gear bearing the Eight Immortals Group device battled in the streets against men in drab jumpsuits and hard hats trading fire with automatic weapons.

Sierra watched a rebel wind-up to toss a Molotov cocktail only for it to explode in his hands, intercepted by a lucky bullet. The improvised incendiary consumed the man and those standing nearby. A mass of jumpsuits overwhelmed a detail of riot troopers on the main thoroughfare as the chaos expanded.

Those few with guns used them as clubs but the majority, armed with little more than rocks, took turns pummeling the EIG contractors. Sierra snarled at being forced to watch the combat from a distance though she knew she didn't want to be involved. Her priorities lay elsewhere.

On the screen a bulky armored personnel carrier turned the corner farther up the avenue. Several rebels retreated down back alleys or hid in domiciles but most persisted to assail their victims, oblivious to the approaching threat. The remote weapon system mounted atop the APC rotated to greet the crowd. Fifty-caliber tracer rounds lanced through soft targets, causing the mob to crumble under the pitiless barrage. The weapon system ceased firing a few moments later, the field transformed into an abattoir.

"Recall Horus," Sierra told Charlie. "I've seen enough."

If the rogue's trail didn't take any drastic deviations it would lead the pride right into the rapidly deteriorating situation at Ming Resources' No. 4 Extraction Site. Memphis explained during the meeting how the escalating tension between the state-sponsored company and its workers in the territory had boiled over. The Eight Immortals Group had already stamped out insurrection at another mining location in the province but the violence was spreading. Trusted informants belonging to Memphis listed No. 4 as the next most likely to revolt, and they'd been right. And as of four hours ago it was the last known location of the rogue mod they'd been sent to eliminate. The two circumstances were not a coincidence.

"Orders, Staff Sergeant?" Charlie asked.

"Regroup, we're moving on."

"We're going to just walk right into a war zone?" Juliet raised an eyebrow, barely visible through the eye slot of her balaclava.

"Nothing can be allowed to impede the mission. If anything the fighting will serve to conceal our presence. We can use the noise to our advantage."

"And if the rebels attack us again?"

"React with extreme prejudice. Miners, EIG, PLA. Kill 'em all and let She Who Mauls sort 'em out."

12

The pride continued on without another word being spoken. Tracking their quarry into an active warzone was far from ideal but there was no alternative. The good news was that the rogue's trail was unmistakable. Now that the pride had a fix on him it would be nigh impossible for him to shake them. Mental state deteriorating, the mod hadn't given any consideration to masking his path but that was generally how things went with these types of missions. The difficulty wasn't in finding the rogues but putting them down.

The commandos made good time, reaching the outskirts of the extraction site before nightfall. They paused at the edge of the city to develop a feel for the situation before circling around the conflict in pursuit of their quarry. Rebel miners fought on in the waning light, ill-coordinated yet invigorated at having shed the blood of their oppressors. Outnumbered, the EIG contractors responded with superior firepower and training. Armored Personnel Carriers delivered shock troops to the areas of heaviest resistance and the battle spilled through the city without regard.

Any drones launched by the EIG were promptly struck from the air by miners compensating for poor accuracy with sheer volume of fire, the darkening sky streaked with tracers. Charlie set Horus to patrol above the reach of small arms fire to keep him from being spotted but the downside was that he could only provide limited support in the impending hunt. It was an inconvenience, if only a minor one. Even were they to be stripped of all weapons and gear Sierra knew her pride could overcome any foe they came across.

From the smoky shroud of gunpowder to the metallic tang of spilt blood, a multitude of odors vied for dominance. Sierra inhaled, spending several moments isolating the rogue's spoor amid the muddle of battle and fixating on it.

"We hunt," she said once she had locked on.

The pride dispersed into formation, the move as familiar to the commandos as breathing. Sierra locked onto their prey's trail and followed it directly into the extraction site. Charlie and Juliet prowled at the Staff Sergeant's left wing while Victor and Tango took her right. The four of them spread out placing several city blocks between them and the Staff Sergeant, casting as wide a net as possible with which to encircle the rogue and prevent him from slipping away. The sound of gunfire rattled around them as they advanced. Foxtrot trailed behind the squad, climbing from one elevated position to another as the pride pierced deeper into the haphazard stacks of shipping container and prefabricated buildings that made up the ragtag city.

The women crept through narrow alleys and broad avenues, dodging squads of Eight Immortals Group contractors and mobs of miners alike, both bent on racking up a body count. The battle diminished as daylight leeched away but pockets of intense fighting remained, scattered throughout the city. Black market night vision and low-light mods had allowed the miners to meet the EIG on a more level playing field but they were still losing. The pride came across mounds of their bodies scattered at nearly every turn.

The latest corpses they encountered, however, hadn't been laid low by EIG rounds. These had the mod's distinctive mark all over them. The slaughter matched that of the bodies they had found earlier. Four miners, weathering the riot in the presumed safety of a freight box, had been caught unaware by the rampaging mod and rendered down to scraps. Sierra drew in a deep whiff of the dead miners and seized upon the scent of the rogue's winding trail intermingled with the carnage. It confirmed they were closing in on him. Sierra knelt and dipped her fingers into the rent flesh of a headless torso to see how long it'd been since the rogue had passed that way. The pitiful remains were rapidly cooling but still retained some warmth. In the frigid mountain air that meant only one thing. The rogue was nearby.

"Contact, engaging Immortals!" Juliet barked over the comms.

Sierra snapped her wrist-screen to eye level and got a bearing on Juliet's location, Horus dipping lower to provide better detail. The specialist was less than a hundred meters away but separated by a row of stacked containers, pinned between two converging fire teams of EIG. Charlie, nearer to Juliet, had immediately turned to render aid and Sierra watched the pair work to extricate themselves. Two Apex Program mods against eight Immortals was a fair fight by anyone's standards but the pride never fought fair if they could help it.

"Converge on Juliet," the Staff Sergeant ordered, bounding across to the tower of corrugated steel and scaling it with leonine finesse.

From her new vantage point Sierra observed three contractors closing in on Juliet's makeshift shelter while a fourth hemorrhaged blood into the compacted dirt. From the meager protection of a flame-gutted bulldozer Juliet traded rounds with the Immortals, slowing their approach. The fire team farther down the lane, which had been maneuvering to catch her in a vice, had run afoul of Charlie's arcing blade. She slashed through their ranks with surgical precision, severing vital arteries and sending Immortals shrieking to their deaths.

Sierra joined her fire with Juliet's, designating a target and placing a tight grouping of rounds center mass. The EIG contractor's forward momentum faltered; he stumbled to one knee but did not drop. Sierra howled at his defiance. The Immortals were clearly heavily armored but it was possible they'd been modified with subdermal ballistic weaves of their own. She took note and adjusted her aim, delivering a series of shots to the man's face.

The Immortal dropped without a sound but the Staff Sergeant was already transitioning to the next target, no time to appreciate her handiwork. Juliet stole the next kill from her and together they wore down the final fire team members with a barrage of deadly hail. As soon as the last Immortal in her sights fell Sierra turned her attention to Charlie and watched as Tango and Victor joined the melee against the other troops, hacking the last of the EIG soldiers apart from behind.

"Hurt?" Sierra asked, returning her focus to Juliet, noticing the woman's labored movements when her sister stood. Sierra dropped down off the corrugated steel to the hardpack below and approached her subordinate.

"Cracked a couple of ribs it feels like. Nothing major," Juliet replied with a wince.

Sierra nodded, offering up a sympathetic smile for the specialist's grit, her fingers unconsciously surveying the damage to Juliet's side. She hopped on the comms. "Foxtrot, has our little skirmish drawn any scrutiny?" She stopped her examination of Juliet's armor when no reply came from the pride's marksman.

"Corporal?" she queried, an icy pall washing over her.

Sierra's wrist-screen placed Foxy's icon 350 meters south of their current orientation. That was well beyond the regulated spacing she was expected to maintain. Sierra glared at her screen again, almost demanding it show something different. The locator remained steady, and Sierra felt bile rise in the back of her throat as Charlie, Tango, and Victor wandered over from claiming trophies and set up a perimeter.

"Sergeant, bring Horus down to Foxy's location. I want eyes on her now!"

Charlie didn't argue, but Sierra knew the risks of having the quadrotor descend for an active sensor sweep and tapped a set of commands into her wrist-screen as Charlie did. Still, Charlie commanded it to do just that despite the frustration she must have felt. A sea of worry churned in Sierra's stomach as Horus reported to its new stationing and Foxtrot failed to materialize on the wrist-screen. The quadrotor scanned a jumble of shipping crates turned mass graveyard for victims of a clash from earlier that day but no patterns emerged that might tell Sierra where the soldier had gone.

"Switch to thermal," Sierra ordered, the words rumbling out.

Horus did as commanded and two human-shaped heat signatures bloomed on the display: one sprawled out across the ground and another, much larger than the first, fled the scene.

"Horus, tail the moving signature." Sierra knew right then what had happened. Her heart pounding against her ribs she sprinted off in the direction of the stationary thermal sign. "Do not lose it whatever you do, you hear me?"

Horus complied, abandoning its circuit and boosting away to keep pace. The pride followed in the Staff Sergeant's wake, abandoning caution in a reckless dash to the location of Foxy's icon. A figure chanced crossing the route ahead, only for Sierra to light it up without pause. It proved to be an innocent bystander, an unarmed miner seeking shelter from the battle, but Sierra felt no compassion for the man, her attention fully focused on finding her sister. The memory of the incident was gone from Sierra's mind before they'd even passed his crumpled form four strides later.

The rogue's scent reemerged from the char and stink of the city, filling Sierra's nostrils as they neared Foxy's marker. *That does not bode well,* Sierra thought, grumbling at her own negativity. She needed Foxy to be alive but deep inside she knew otherwise, and it made her sick. The area was littered with the wreckage of bodies. They were primarily rebels but the clash hadn't been entirely one-sided as evidenced by the twisted metal carcass of an Eight Immortals Group APC.

"Charlie, Juliet, break off and find Foxy. Tango, Vicky, you're with me."

Juliet and Charlie obeyed without question, angling off to find their missing sister. Sierra, Tango, and Vicky maintained a fix on the rogue, whose movements suggested severe mental degradation. He changed direction seemingly at random, weaving in and out of buildings and makeshift residences without any obvious tactical purpose. Horus drifted along in the target's wake, reestablishing line-of-sight whenever the rogue broke from concealment until the three commandos were able to corner him in a two story pre-fab.

Sierra surveyed the building from her vantage point across the way. The cheaply built structure had weathered the rioting unscathed, much to her surprise, but it explained why the rogue mod had chosen it to settle in. Thermal scans peered through the roof, showing the pre-fab to be devoid of all life save a single pacing blur of warmth: their target. Sierra let out a slow, quiet snarl beneath her breath at seeing the mod's signature light up. They had him at last.

"Charlie, what's Foxy's status?" Sierra asked over the comms, desperate for good news. She crouched behind her firing position, eyes never wavering from her sights.

"KIA, Staff Sergeant. He… he butchered her."

Sierra had been prepared for the worst but the confirmation still hit like a howitzer. She swallowed against the nausea that welled up inside her, tamping it down with controlled fury.

"Staff Sergeant, she's missing… parts," Juliet added, the Specialist having a hard time getting the words out. "It looks like the rogue's scavenging mods."

Sierra stared at the pre-fab, upper lip peeled back and teeth bared. Most targets were executed with clinical detachment, their death nothing more than the job she was assigned to do, but this one was different. Sierra decided to make an exception for this senile old fuck who'd killed her sister.

"We've got him surrounded," she told the pride. "If you double-time it there might be a piece of him left for you when you arrive."

"We've got a problem, Staff Sergeant!" Juliet screamed in her ear. "Foxy's comms implants are gone."

"How observant of you," a gravelly voice said over the line. "But don't worry, I left something in exchange for your sister's ears."

"Get out of there!" Sierra roared.

Simultaneously she felt the *whump* of explosives detonating nearby, then another, and saw the pre-fab wall disintegrate before her eyes. A hulking form emerged from the whirling smoke and debris. There was no time to identify the rogue, though she knew him by his grotesque musculature and unkempt hair, mission details standing out in her mind. He moved with a speed that belied his size and he fell upon Vicky before either she or Sierra could deflect him. The Staff Sergeant pivoted away from the door, searching for a clear shot as the rogue engaged Vicky, the two in tight.

The specialist was unable to bring her rifle to bear, so she went for her sidearm as she struggled for space. Sierra felt a flash of feral joy as the woman pulled it loose of the holster but Vicky never got the chance to put it to use. The rogue backhanded it from her grasp and sank his pronounced canines into her neck. Vicky fought on, peeling skin from his torso with her retractable claws but it was clear she was losing. Sierra stumbled as the rogue wrenched free of Vicky, the twisting motion of his jaw tearing a section of the woman's vertebrae out through her neck. Sierra howled at the volcano of blood erupting from her sister, the specialist's eyes already glossing over as she went limp.

The rogue cast Vicky's body aside only to be met by a hail of gunfire, Sierra's finger heavy on the trigger. He shielded his head with an oversized forearm and charged forward, enduring the punishment to close the distance between them. Sierra altered her aim, shooting at his knees in hopes his joints would be less reinforced and she could bring him down. The rogue persevered despite the barrage of lead tearing through his legs. He barreled into her and ripped the carbine from her hands. She stumbled back in surprise at how easily he'd disarmed her but he gave her no opportunity to recover, clubbing her across the face with the rifle. She raised her arms in instinct to guard against a follow-up attack but he thrust the stock of the gun into her stomach, dropping her to her knees with a *whuff* of escaping air.

For all Sierra's training, conditioned to withstand such violence, the force of the attack had caught her off guard. He bashed her with the rifle again and sent her crashing onto her back. The rogue stood over her, frothing at the mouth, claws poised to deliver the killing blow, when a long, curved blade bit into his neck from behind. He reared up with a roar like erupting thunder.

Tango yanked the knife from the wound, twisting it on the way out for good measure, and struck again but the rogue caught her wrist on the second swing. He reeled her in and punched her in the face over and over again with his free hand, breaking her nose and flattening it across her face as the cartilage compacted.

Sierra drew her pistol and squeezed the trigger, hitting the rogue in the side of the head. There was a metallic *clang* and

Sierra followed her shot with another, catching him high in the cheek. The rogue huffed and whipped Tango around by the wrist, flinging her into Sierra and fouling her next shot. In the second it took the Staff Sergeant to adjust her aim their attacker had fled.

"Horus, pick him up," Sierra groaned. She heard the whisper of the quadrotor complying somewhere above her.

Tango scrambled to her feet, oblivious to her busted nose, and offered a hand to Sierra. Once she was steady, the Staff Sergeant looked to her carbine only to find the barrel bent and stock shattered.

"Here." Tango unslung her own gun and handed it over. "I'd much rather cut this bastard anyway. Seems to work better."

"Vicky?" Sierra asked, though she knew she'd regret it.

"Dead."

Sierra nodded, having presumed as much. She accessed the comms and opened a private channel to Charlie and Juliet, avoiding the frequency the rogue mod was tuned in on.

"Sergeant? Specialist? Do you read me? Charlie? Juliet?"

No reply came. She waited a few seconds and tried again. The result was the same: a chilling nothingness. The explosion she felt must have been a bomb the rogue left behind with Foxy's body. The world dropped out from beneath Sierra. The loss was too great for her to contemplate. Never before had the pride suffered such casualties. They might well be nothing more than assets to the higher ups, evidenced by the names foisted upon the women, but to Sierra they were much more than that. They were her family. And now they were gone.

"It's just us," she managed to spit out, the words bitter on her tongue.

"Then we make sure he pays." Tango held her blade out, her fury evident.

"She Who Mauls will not be left wanting." Tears stung Sierra's eyes but she denied them. There would be time for sorrow but first came revenge.

'Subject has entered mines, line-of-sight lost', Horus broadcast.

The two surviving members of the pride raced toward the mine. Away from the miasma of the warzone the rogue's spoor was so distinct Sierra could almost see it piercing deep into the mountain. The two shed any extraneous gear at the entrance, preferring to travel light – only guns and ammo and blades. If they failed to bring the rogue down now there would be no need for any of the rest.

Before they slipped into the mine, Sierra armed the self-destruct mechanism built into Horus. If they failed to return before its battery ran critical the quadrotor would detonate, erasing any evidence of their presence in the area. Likewise Charlie, Foxy, Juliet, and Vicky would decay at a hyper-accelerated rate as their cores melted down to prevent any of the Apex Program breakthroughs from falling into enemy hands. It would be a sad end to the pride's existence, but a necessary one.

"Let's finish this," Sierra told her one remaining sister.

The pair forged ahead into the darkness, Sierra trusting her nose and ears to guide them to their target. The narrowness of the tunnel was suffocating, pressing in from all sides to envelope the commandos. Even the sounds were smothered by the close confines. Wooden beams set in the walls at regular intervals kept the ceiling from caving in. Glass from busted fixtures crunched underfoot. Intact lights were few and far between, bare bulbs dangling from the rafters. They moved deeper and deeper, expecting an ambush at every turn but the rogue surprised them by making no attempt at hiding.

He stood partially illuminated under a flickering light fixture. Long gray hair tinged yellow by the poor illumination draped over a face more canid than hominid. Thick blood bubbled from the gash in his neck and oozed down his bare chest. He was a monstrosity in form and spirit. Lips split in a feral grin at seeing them and Sierra unloaded without hesitation. Every bullet found its mark but he shrugged it off with nothing more than the barest of backward stumbles, regaining his footing without issue. He held a hand up, waving the sisters on.

"Let's finish this," the rogue told them, his sneer coated in blood and arrogance.

The Staff Sergeant dropped her rifle and brandished her Kukri, more than willing to oblige. Together she and her sister attacked. Sierra went low and Tango high. For every wound the women made on their adversary he returned it twofold. His fists were sledgehammers, brutal blows crashing into the sisters, stealing their strength and pounding flesh. His knees and elbows and feet darted like serpents to take advantage of any opening. Above all else Sierra and Tango avoided his clutching fingers. They understood that were he to grab hold of them it would mean their lives. Still they fought on, pushing him deeper and deeper into the depths of the mine.

As they battled, the sisters using speed to counter the mod's advantage of strength and constitution, Tango landed a strike deep into the meat of the rogue's bicep only to have her blade lodge in the bone. She lost her grip when he knocked her backwards. Sierra closed on him then, dragging her blade across the rogue's femoral artery but he kicked her into the wall and proceeded to stamp down on her knife hand. She felt her wrist fracture and screamed in agony as her blade slipped loose of her fingers. He shattered it with his heel and backed away with a lopsided grin.

"I'm impressed, little kitties. You've done well," the rogue told them, yanking Tango's knife out with a flourish, "but not well enough." He let loose a rumbling laugh, the sound echoing through the darkness, seeming to go on forever before finally fading. He held up the blade and inspected it, testing its balance, and then dropped into a crouch with his new acquisition gleaming out in front. "Shall we continue?"

Weaponless, injured, and flagging, Sierra glanced at her sister and whispered a farewell with her eyes. They stood no chance of defeating the rogue with only their claws and teeth but his arrogance had offered Sierra an opportunity she could not deny.

Before Tango could grasp what she intended, Sierra murmured a prayer to She Who Mauls, shoved her sister aside, and leapt at the mod. The rogue grinned and welcomed her close only to realize his error when Sierra ducked low at the last moment and crashed into his legs, taking them out from under him. Her momentum carried them forward…

…over the lip of the shaft that had preserved the rogue's laughter a moment before, dragging it out and warning Sierra of the endless fall that lay just beyond the darkness.

She howled as the blackness enveloped them. Sierra would soon meet the Goddess but she'd do so with a smile on her lips, her sister alive in the tunnel above. That was a victory she was willing to die for.

TWO BIRDS

Evan Dicken

Nothing but death dwelt on Mount Kuchisake, at least that's what Izō hoped. An arrow skittered through the branches over his head, followed by a shout from farther down the hill.

"Halt, or the next one will be through your neck." A thin-faced samurai in ornate armor drew another arrow from his quiver.

Izō dodged behind a nearby juniper before the man could take aim, smiling as the shot rattled through the trees before disappearing in the scrub off to Izō's left. Although deadly on open ground, the tall, lopsided horse-bows favored by the samurai would be next to useless on the densely-wooded hill.

After a few ragged breaths Izō was off again. He might not have to fear arrows, but a veritable flock of Akechi clan soldiers scrambled up the broken incline behind him, spears waving like windswept reeds as they sweated in their armor. Mostly ashigaru footmen, hardened veterans of Lord Nobunaga's campaigns around Kyoto, they were far more dangerous than the samurai who'd led them into the woods after Izō. Armored and on horse-back he might have picked the spearmen apart, but exhausted, hungry, and armed only with a broken katana, Izō didn't fancy his chances. Fortunately, if the legends about Kuchisake were true, he might not need to fight.

Izō grinned. Two birds with one stone.

Branches whipped across Izō's exposed face and arms, tearing more holes in his once fine kimono. His pursuers called to one another, their excited shouts like the yips of hunting dogs. Dirty and bleeding as he was, Izō must have appeared a far cry from the fierce, hawkish man scowling from the wanted signs the invaders had plastered across the province. He grit his teeth against the shame. Lord Hatano would be mortified to see one of his generals brought so low, but Lord Hatano was dead – betrayed and murdered after Nobunaga promised him safety in exchange for surrender.

There had been a time when the anger burned through Izō, growing until he thought it must surely consume him. Many times he had considered simply charging Nobunaga soldiers, killing and killing until they cut him down – wasn't it a samurai's duty to follow his Lord into death? But time had banked the flames and now Izō's fury came cold and canny. Nobunaga and would pay for what he'd done. Izō vowed that when he met Lord Hatano in the Pure Land, it would be with news that the great betrayers would never see their ambition realized.

The ground began to level off and Izō paused, hands on knees, to catch his breath.

A glint to the left caused him to throw himself aside just in time to avoid the sweep of an ashigaru's spear that would have sent him tumbling. There were two of them – more clever or experienced than the rest, they must have run ahead while Izō dodged their commander's bow fire.

"Surrender, and you won't be harmed," the lead spearman said between gasps. Both men were red-faced and puffing from the headlong sprint. Izō would've been able to wear them down if he had the time, but every moment brought the rest of their squad closer. He needed to act quickly.

"You got me." Izō raised his arms, letting his blade dangle loose in one hand.

The ashigaru relaxed a fraction but kept their spears pointed at him. That moment's hesitation gave Izō the chance he needed, and he lunged, letting his sleeves dangle so the spears pierced the fabric. As the points slipped past he twisted his sleeves to bring the spear hafts close enough to grab. The first spearman tried to wrench his weapon from Izō's grasp, but instead of resisting Izō let the force of the pull drag him forward, tangling the man's weapon with his fellow's. The ashigaru's surprised shout became a grunt as Izō drove his elbow into the man's face. Slipping his arms from his robes Izō grabbed the straps of the ashigaru's armor and wrenched him off balance. One of the man's flailing arms caught Izō a stinging blow to the face, but he only grit his teeth, sweeping the man's legs. With a pained grunt the ashigaru crashed down amidst the foliage to tumble bonelessly down the hill.

There was no time for thought. The other ashigaru had freed his spear from Izō's shirt, and it came flashing in, quick as the beak of a hungry stork.

Izō leapt back, almost tripping over the uneven ground.

The ashigaru glanced after his fallen comrade then glared at Izō through narrowed eyes, his hate sharp enough to etch glass. "Bastard."

It was a look Izō knew well – he'd worn it for years. He smirked, hoping to stoke the man's anger.

Get a bird mad enough, it might not even see the stone.

The other Akechi soldiers were close enough Izō could hear their labored breathing, deep and hoarse. He feinted at the ashigaru then leapt back; the man's spear pierced the air where Izō's head had been a moment before. Again, his foot caught on something hidden amidst the underbrush, this time he sprawled backward, the impact jarring the blade from his hand.

Izō felt about on the ground as the ashigaru lunged with a triumphant cry. His fingers closed around something smooth and round like a river rock, but strangely light. The spear darted down and Izō squirmed to the side, bringing up the rock in hopes of deflecting the blade. With a hollow thud the strike tore Izō's meager defense from his hands, and he scrambled back, stomach tensed against the expected bite of steel, but the blow never came. The ashigaru stared at the end of his spear, which transfixed not a stone but a human skull.

Casting about, Izō realized what he'd thought to be roots and fallen branches were actually bones. Broadleaf shrubs grew through shattered ribcages, weeds and spreading ferns conceal-ing piles of disjointed legs and arms. Finger bones and loose vertebrae skittered like loose gravel as Izō pushed to his feet.

With a disgusted grimace, the ashigaru shook the skull from the end of his spear. The brush behind the man trembled and several Akechi samurai stepped into the clearing, followed by a score of spearmen. All of them looked out of breath, but none were the source of the deep, hungry panting that filled the clearing.

Izō was unable to keep from smiling. It seemed the legends about Mount Kuchisake weren't exaggerated.

Sometimes, if you found the right birds you didn't even need a stone.

The thin-faced samurai stepped forward, puffing as he brushed leaves and twigs from his silver-chased armor. "Akai Izō, please, we must speak–"

The samurai stared quizzically at the thick, glistening tentacle that had stealthily descended from the canopy above to coil about his waist. He had time for a tight, chagrined frown then was dragged up into the shadowed forest canopy, struggling like a carp at the end of fisherman's line.

Even tired and frightened, the Akechi soldiers were still veterans, and Izō had to swallow a momentary flash of respect when they didn't scatter like frightened sparrows. The ashigaru drew up into a ragged phalanx, bristling with spear points.

"Did Nobunaga ever tell you what I did for Lord Hatano?" Izō kept his voice low and conversational so as not to draw the creature's attention. "I held the rank of general and yet I commanded barely a dozen men."

The creature was a jagged shadow, little more than the rustle of leaves marking its quick movement among the tangled branches. One of the ashigaru jabbed into the darkness and had the spear wrenched from his hands.

"You're a long way from Kyoto. The mountains in these parts are wild, full of all manner of terrible things. My Lord couldn't have them wandering into his villages, killing his people, *my* people." Izō hunkered down, careful to keep his movements slow. Mountain oni were voracious but stupid. Like birds of prey they were attracted to sudden movements and shiny objects. "Unfortunately, you're not my people."

The oni reached from above, threading the spears to pluck a black-bearded warrior from among the press. Izō caught a glimpse of long, sinewy arms, segmented and muscular like the body of a worm, then the man was gone, a single shriek the only sign of his passing.

Black blood rained from above as ashigaru stabbed up into the trees, stippling the soldiers' faces like ink from the brush of a careless artist. The oni's pained snarl was met with cheers from below, but the Akechi warriors' success was short lived as the creature dropped down among them.

It was perhaps twice the size of a man, its boneless body like a festival drum corded with rings of glistening pink muscle. It had no eyes or ears, only a mouth, wet and toothless, yawning wide at the bottom of its body. Things moved beneath the oni's rubbery skin, the vague outline of bodies struggling within the creature like flies caught in pine sap. Legless, but with five tentacles radiating out like the limbs of a starfish, the oni flailed about, entangling men and weapons.

To their credit, the ashigaru stood firm. Too close to bring their spears to bear, they hammered at the oni with the butts of their weapons, but with no bones to break or organs to crush, the spears did little damage. One of the soldiers turned to flee, only to be knocked flat by a whiplike blow from one of the oni's long arms and dragged howling into the thing's mouth.

As satisfying as it was to see his enemies destroyed, the sight conjured a sour tightness in Izō stomach. While it was true Akechi warriors had brought death and subjugation to Hatano lands, they hadn't murdered Izō's lord. The Akechi were but one of many clans sworn to Nobunaga. These men were soldiers, loyal to their lord just as Izō was to his. He grimaced as the oni swallowed another shrieking ashigaru, its body ballooning grossly as the man joined his comrades within. But for a twist of the wheel Izō might have been among them.

The trouble with killing birds is that you have to be sure they deserve it.

Izō sighed, shaking his head – no warrior should die like that, no matter what monster they served. He searched the undergrowth for his blade. Although scarred and broken, there were yet powerful enchantments bound to the steel – the work of Emperor Jimmu's famed Yamato smiths, passed down through millennia to protect the people of Japan.

A glimmer caught his eye and he stooped to see his sword had fallen amidst a small pile of teeth. Izō bowed his head in a brief prayer for forgiveness before retrieving the blade. Lord Hatano would be avenged, but not like this.

Izō crept around the clearing, careful to present as small a target as possible. Fortunately, the shouts and struggles of the Akechi kept the oni occupied, although from the look of things it wouldn't be for long. Barely a half-dozen ashigaru remained.

While every oni was different, Izō had hunted ones similar to this. The thing's arms were long and quick despite their size and its mouth was at the bottom of its body. Like a hawk, the thing was made to swoop down on its victims. Izō scowled at the nearest tree, not looking forward to what he needed to do. Unfortunately, the best way to surprise a bird was from above.

Sliding his blade between his teeth, he climbed, the rough bark scratching his hands. Izō had never fancied himself a climber, but the trees were sturdy with many thick branches spaced closely together – well suited to an oni that relied on surprise. He edged out over the battle, almost losing his grip on the branch as he took the knife from his mouth. Only five ashigaru remained below; their hopeless cries mingled with the oni's happy gurgling. Sweat stung Izō's eyes, and he blinked it away.

Looking down at the creature, Izō regretted not having committed seppuku after his Lord was murdered. Dying would've saved him a lot of trouble.

He dropped from the branch, jaw clenched against the scream that threatened to burst forth as he plummeted toward the oni.

It was just as terrible as he'd imagined.

The thing's flesh was like cold seaweed, slick and slimy with mucus. Izō could feel the Akechi warriors within, struggles growing weaker as they slowly suffocated. His blade hissed like a sword fresh from the forge as it bit into the oni's flesh. The creature bucked and shuddered, bludgeoning Izō with its heavy arms. Bright flares streaked across his vision as the oni caught him a ringing blow across the head, but he hung on, bringing the blade down again and again. Pale, stinking blood spurted across his hands and face, and Izō clamped his mouth tight against the flood of bile. Even so, the oni would have thrown him had not the ashigaru recovered enough to drive their spears into the thing's arms, bracing against the shafts to pin the flailing appendages to the ground. They wouldn't hold longer than a few moments, but a few moments was all Izō needed.

He drove the Yamato blade deep, using his weight to drag it down the thing's back. Black veins spread from the wound, the rot of an injury left untreated for days. The thing gave a shriek like a kettle on the boil and Izō saw one of the ashigaru go tumbling as it wrenched an appendage free.

The tentacle coiled around Izō's leg. He scrabbled at the oni's back, but the flesh was too slick. He slipped along, expecting to be slammed against tree or rock, but came to a sudden jarring stop as something caught his arm. Izō glanced down to see a pair of hands reaching from inside the long gash he'd opened in the oni's flesh. As the creature tugged, Izō saw arms, shoulders, then a thin, scowling face emerge from the wound.

The samurai had lost his helmet and his hair was slick with viscera, but his expression was resolute as he clung to Izō's arm.

"Get my men out," he said through clenched teeth.

Izō gouged at the oni's side, barely able to keep hold of the sword, let alone aim his strikes. A gout of black blood heralded the emergence of several spearmen. They slumped to the ground, gagging and coughing, slick as newborn foals.

Izō felt his shoulder pop with a sharp twinge as the samurai and the oni continued their bizarre tug-of-war. He slashed at the thing, sawing with all the finesse of a peasant butchering a tough joint of meat.

"I can't hold you." The samurai's voice seemed to come from far away. "Give me the blade."

Izō's gaze crawled down to the sword, then back to the man's straining face. Doggedly, he shook his head then brought the Yamato blade down, driving deep into the creature's body.

The oni shrieked and Izō was ripped from the samurai's grip. There was a moment of heady weightlessness before he crashed to the ground, rolling twice before fetching up against a tree with a teeth-rattling thud. Pain blossomed bonfire-hot along Izō's back, but he paid it no mind, focused as he was on drawing in gasp after shuddering gasp of the sweet forest air.

He could hear the oni howling, each furious bellow growing weaker and weaker as it thrashed around the clearing. After what seemed like an eternity, the creature fell silent, its cry disappearing into familiar coughs and groans of battered men. Wincing, Izō sat up and flexed his shoulder, surprised not to feel the sharp stab of broken bone. It seemed he'd earned some nasty cuts and bruises in the tussle with the oni, but nothing that would cripple him. He'd recover.

If the Akechi soldiers didn't kill him first.

Izō looked up as a shadow fell over him, meeting the samurai's gaze. The man looked as bad as Izō felt; the man's armor black with blood and a large bruise purpling his left eye. A few ashigaru milled behind him, leaning on their spears as they limped about, battered but still very much alive.

The samurai raised an arm, the Yamato blade glittering in his fist.

"Steel shines ever bright." Izō smiled as it caught the light. "In battle, only men are tarnished."

They were as good last words as any, he supposed. In a way, it would be fitting for Izō to die by a blade that had killed so many monsters.

"Thank you for saving our lives. You should've let me finish the thing, though." The samurai knelt, drew his own sword, and held it out to Izō. "Here, it will serve you better than this dull, broken knife."

"If it's all the same to you, I'd prefer my blade." Izō ran his tongue over his teeth. "I've a fondness for broken things."

"As you wish." The samurai shrugged, holding out the Yamato blade. "One old sword is the same as any other, and broken ones are easy enough to find nowadays."

Izō took the blade, still wary despite the samurai's gratitude.

"I am Akechi Mitsuhide, and I've come a long way to find you." He offered Izō his hand. "We must speak, but first I thank you for saving my life and the lives of my men."

Izō made a sour face. Mitsuhide was the general tasked with pacifying the Hatano lands. He'd also been the one that had negotiated Lord Hatano's surrender. "Had I known you were Nobunaga's lapdog, I would've let the oni have you."

"Then I'm glad you didn't" General Mitsuhide's smile cast the gaunt angles of his face into harsh relief. "I regret the chase, but I needed to capture you."

"You shot at me."

"Only a warning. I asked you to stop first."

"You *shot* at me."

"Sorry, it usually works." Mitsuhide shrugged. "Come, our camp is not far from the mountain. You have my word you won't be harmed."

"Wouldn't be the first time you guaranteed the safety of one of my clan."

Mitsuhide gave a pained wince. "Your lord's murder casts a shadow over us all."

"Some shadows are darker than others."

"If I were going to kill or capture you, why not do it here? You're hardly in a state to resist."

"I might surprise you," Izō said.

"Please, come and talk."

"We can talk here."

"So be it." Mitsuhide gave a pained hiss as he sat across from Izō, one hand pressed to his ribs. "They say you kill demons."

Izō snorted then nodded at the oni's cooling corpse. "Is that what they say?"

Mitsuhide glanced at those ashigaru who'd managed to stand. "See to the wounded."

Nodding, they limped away, and Mitsuhide leaned close to continue in hushed tones. "Do you know the name *Dairokuten Mao'ō?*"

Izō snorted. "The Demon King of Six Heavens? Isn't that what the peasants are calling Nobunaga?"

"There is truth to the name." Mitsuhide gave a nervous shake of his head. "Nobunaga was always cruel and paranoid, but it has grown worse. There's a shadow about him. He lets his soldiers ravage the countryside, burns monks and priests in their temples. Several of his generals spoke out against the atrocities, and he had them executed. Then there was the betrayal of your lord."

Izō's grimace was not only for the pain in his bruised ribs.

"You must believe me when I say I didn't know he would murder Hatano in cold blood. More than that, he *laughed* as your lord was beheaded."

"So Nobunaga is vicious and dishonorable," Izō said. "Many lords have done far worse and not been demons."

"There's more." Mitsuhide glanced over his shoulder, as if to even continue might draw his lord's wrath. "The last time I was in Kyoto, I was passing his chambers late at night and I heard him muttering. Lord Nobunaga is oft given to speaking to himself, so I thought little of it until I heard another voice answer. I swear he was alone in his room, but more than that it was the *sound* of this thing – like wind blowing through a graveyard. I consider myself a brave man, but it was as if I was a child lost in the dark. I swear by my ancestors that what I heard speaking with Nobunaga that night was not human."

Izō sucked air through his teeth. Nobunaga's rise to power *had* been almost uncanny. Powerful as they were, no spirit or oni could've engineered such victories as the Oda clan had won. Sometimes, men with ambition and cruelty often turned to pacts with dark forces to realize their grand desires. If Nobunaga had truly dragged some demon from the twisted labyrinth of *Jigoku* it would be no mere oni or hungry ghost, but something ancient and unspeakably evil.

"All the creatures around Kyoto were killed centuries ago. We have no hunters, no warriors skilled in combating these things. I didn't know where else to turn." Tears glittered in Mitsuhide's eyes. "If Nobunaga become ruler of Japan, I fear it will become a living hell."

"You would betray your lord?"

General Mitsuhide straightened. "I would save him."

Izō shook his head. How could he have missed this? He'd gotten so caught up in vengeance that he'd lost sight of what were birds and what were stones.

"I'll need some new clothes, a few good meals, and no questions from you or your men."

"Yes, of course. Anything." Mitsuhide grinned. "I'd give you thousand broken swords if you wished."

"No need," he said with an almost regretful look at the dead oni. "I'm hoping one will do."

•　•

They crept like thieves through the darkness, faces masked, armor and weapons blackened, and swords muffled in their sheaths. The night was hot and humid, high summer in the city of Kyoto. They stuck to the back alleys, avoiding the frenzied buzz of conversation and laughter that filled the capital even in the small hours of the morning. Those merchants and drunks who happened to notice a score of armed men pass by quickly found other things to occupy their attention – nighttime killings were not uncommon under Nobunaga's rule, and those who spoke too loudly of them often found themselves next on the list.

"Our enemy is at Honnō Temple," Mitsuhide whispered. "My lord has always enjoyed despoiling places of worship."

"Guards?" Izō asked.

"A few dozen at most. Kyoto is Nobunaga's stronghold, he would never expect an attack here." Mitsuhide was grim. "My army is ready to march on the city should we fail."

"Let's hope it doesn't come to that." Izō gripped the Yamato blade more tightly. It had been forged in the ancient days to battle demons, but broken and scarred as it was Izō only hoped enough of the old spells remained.

The temple was little more than a dark blot amidst the gloom, gates locked and barred; a few guards lounged in wan light cast by a pair of lanterns hanging from the eaves.

Mitsuhide nodded to a pair of his men, who drew knives, but paused when Izō held up a hand.

"We'll go over the wall, there." He thrust his chin at a section that abutted a nearby building.

The soldiers looked to Mitsuhide.

"No questions, General," Izō said.

After a moment's hesitation Mitsuhide nodded, and the men stowed their blades.

The wall was twice Izō's height, the tiled overhang looming as they padded up, ropes in hand.

"Give me a boost," Izō whispered to the nearest man, who knelt and made a stirrup of his hands.

"All right, up and over. Careful you don't chip a tooth on the wall," the ashigaru lisped as he took hold of Izō's foot. Glancing down in surprise, Izō saw the man had pulled down his mask to show a grin, ragged where several teeth had been knocked out by a hard elbow to the face.

Izō winced. "Sorry about that back on Kuchisake."

"I'm grateful, actually." The man's smile grew wider. "Saved me from getting swallowed by an oni, didn't it?"

"So it did."

With a soft grunt, Izō leapt for the overhang, scrabbling at the tile for a sickening second before getting a grip on the wall. He dangled there, breath held and ears pricked for the shout that would mean the guards had heard.

None came.

He levered himself up and over the edge, suddenly aware of how exposed he was. Trying to hunker down he tied the rope off and lowered it, expecting any moment to feel the cold bite of an arrow in his back.

The courtyard was of tiled stone in the Chinese style, empty but for a pair of servants carrying a large teapot and tray of sweetened azuki buns.

Izō dropped to the ground, trying to time his landing so it coincided with the servants opening the door to the central temple. Light spilled from beyond the door, absent the sound of laughter or song that would indicate Lord Nobunaga was entertaining guests. He murmured a prayer of thanks to Lord Hatano and any other of his ancestors who were watching over him, then crept into the courtyard.

A few soft thuds behind and the Akechi soldiers joined him, weapons bared. They made it almost to the door before the call went up.

There was a shout from the gate, then the sudden flare of torchlight. Guards tumbled from outbuildings, unarmored and wild-eyed, but with swords and bows at the ready. The Akechi warriors turned to meet the oncoming rush, and the night was soon filled with the shouts of fighting men and the clash of weapons.

A young samurai rushed at Izō, bare-chested, hair streaming loose from his queue as he brought his sword arcing down. Izō stepped into the strike, reaching up to catch the man's forearm to rob the blow of its strength. Forming a hard ridge with his free hand he drove it into young samurai's jaw, then hooked his ankle and tossed him to the ground. Spears stabbed down like beaks of hungry storks, and Izō was forced to throw himself flat, scrambling toward the temple door. A hand hooked the strap of his breastplate and hauled him up.

"My men will hold the courtyard!" Mitsuhide shouted into his ear. "We must reach Nobunaga."

Together they stumbled for the temple and kicked the door wide. Shrieking servants fled before them, scattering bowls, trays, and lanterns across the woven tatami floor. Flames spread up tapestries and hanging scrolls to lick at the temple's heavy oak beams. In the midst of the chaos sat Oda Nobunaga, hands on his knees, his robes in perfect arrangement.

"Akechi Mitsuhide." Nobunaga's voice cut through the din like a thunderclap. "I expected this from the others, but you? I thought you were a man of honor."

"I served the man, not whatever creature sits before me now." Mitsuhide pointed his sword at Nobunaga. "I know what you are."

"Do you, now?" Nobunaga's expression of placid indifference might as well have been carved from basalt for all the emotion it betrayed.

"And you've brought a hunter." Nobunaga stood, arms folded in front of him as he looked to Izō. Izō thought he saw a flash of surprise in the demon's eyes as it noticed the broken blade in his hand. "One of Hatano's dogs, I see. That old sorcerer might have proven troublesome. Which reminds me, I never properly thanked you for bringing him to me, Mitsuhide."

At this, the general leapt forward, katana transcribing a tight arc to Nobunaga's neck. The blow simply stopped, the sword neither rebounding nor shattering. Rather, it was as if Mitsuhide's blade had become mired in the air a hairsbreadth from the demon's neck. The general strained and tugged at the sword to no avail.

After watching Mitsuhide for a moment, Nobunaga brushed the blade away like a bothersome fly. The general stumbled back, only to be hurled flailing into one of the temple pillars by a casual flick of the Nobunaga's hand. Mitsuhide groaned and rolled to his side, gasping like a landed fish.

"Don't mistake me for a fool." Nobunaga turned to glare at Izō, who had been edging toward his back, blade held like an icepick. "I'm not some petty mountain lord, ready to sell his soul for a castle or a handful of rundown villages."

The fires dwindled, flames tumbling over and around each other like frightened rats trying to escape a locked room. The sounds of the battle outside grew faint, lost within a stifling curtain of silence. Glancing back, Izō saw that the shadows had spread to swallow the door, the featureless void beyond empty of even the memory of fighting men. A strange keening filled the air. High and tongueless, like the whine of a thousand, thousand insect wings it bored into Izō's head, spinning his thoughts into a tangled snarl.

Nobunaga spread his arms. "I am a king, a conqueror, a god. What man, what monster could be my equal? To find my peers I am forced to consult with the Lords of *Jigoku!*"

Izō walked as if into a high wind, head down, eyes closed. In his hubris, Nobunaga had summoned no mere demon but one of the Yama Kings, and in doing so opened a path. The buzzing void that had filled the temple was like an icy hand around Izō's heart.

Hell was coming to earth.

Nobunaga stepped forward to catch him by the throat, lifting him from the ground as if he were full of wind. Desperately, Izō looked to where Mitsuhide lay. The general was on his hands and knees, but didn't look in any shape to come to Izō's aid.

He could hear them now, voices on the demon wind, the low, hateful cries of those banished to *Jigoku* in the ancient days.

Nobunaga's face was close, the madness in his gaze like the eye of a swirling vortex. "Why settle for Japan when I could be a king of heaven and earth?"

Nobunaga tightened his grip and darkness threaded Izō's vision, black spots spreading like silkworms on a mulberry leaf. Pressure built behind his eyes even as the world seemed to slip away. Izō's arms felt as if they were made of stone, the strength to lift his sword almost more than he could manage.

The blade crept closer to Nobunaga's side, its jagged, rust-spattered tip trembling like a trapped blowfly.

"Ah, that won't do." Nobunaga glanced down, then grinning, slapped the sword from Izō's hand. "Steel is only as strong as its wielder."

A shadow moved behind Nobunaga, staggering, limping, little more than a blur in Izō's fading vision. It stooped to pick something from the ground.

"You murdered my lord," Izō whispered through lips that felt cold and wooden, desperate to keep Nobunaga's attention.

"I've murdered *a lot* of lords."

Izō grasped Nobunaga's wrists as General Mitsuhide rose up behind his lord, stabbing the Yamato blade deep into the demon's neck. The pressure on Izō's throat relaxed, and he drew in a great shuddering breath. With a shriek of disbelieving rage, Nobunaga tried to turn, but Izō clung to the lord's wrists, holding them fast with what little strength remained.

Nobunaga shrieked and strained, but the terrible vitality had abandoned him, and he stumbled to one knee, dragging Izō and Mitsuhide to the ground. Heat and sound rushed back into the chamber, fire crawling up the walls to the renewed sounds of combat from outside. The high wail stuttered and died even as Nobunaga slumped to the ground, eyes wide and disbelieving.

The ground trembled, a low and rhythmic vibration like the beating of a great, yet distant drum.

Izō tugged at Mitsuhide's shoulder. "We need to go."

The general blinked at him.

"Hurry, before the Yama Kings collect what is owed."

They staggered to their feet, kicking free of Nobunaga's robes. Censers and bits of mortar rained from the ceiling, the heat of the fire enough to tighten the skin on Izō's face and singe the edges of his robe. A thin wail came as they stepped through the door, and Izō glanced back to see Nobunaga, one pale, quivering hand extended, his eyes terrified and pleading.

There was the hint of dark shapes amidst the smoke, circling like carrion crows, then the flames rose up, and Oda Nobunaga was lost from sight.

Coughing, Izō and Mitsuhide stumbled into the courtyard. Fire had spread to the temple outbuildings and was already creeping along the walls. The battle had shrunk to a few small knots of struggling men, most having been driven out by the heat. At Mitsuhide's hoarse call the survivors of his strike force formed up around them to help push through the knot of gawkers at the gate and into the night beyond.

Shouts chased them down the street and into a nearby alley where they stood panting, hands on knees, the strange glow of the fire lighting up the night sky.

"Strange, I always end up with your sword." Mitsuhide held the blade out to Izō, who took it with a tired, but satisfied grin.

"What now?"

"I suppose I'll have my army move into the city. Nobunaga's death will cause a lot of unrest, many will be vying for his position. I could use a man who can think on his feet. Lord Hatano is avenged, perhaps you would consider–"

"I think I've had enough of high politics." Izō wiped the soot from his face. "I'm headed back to the mountains... things are simpler out there."

Mitsuhide bowed then clapped Izō on the shoulder. "Thank you."

"I never could have done it alone." Izō returned the bow.

"Nor I."

"Two stones, one bird." Izō snorted, coughing for a moment before bursting into a full-throated laugh. Mitsuhide's confused smile only made him laugh all the louder.

Sometimes, proverbs made no sense.

Non-Zero Sum

R.P.L. Johnson

Sealed inside his suit and strapped inside a Stryker armored vehicle that was itself trussed up like a Thanksgiving turkey in the belly of a C17 Globemaster transport plane, Adam Blake thanked his lucky stars he wasn't claustrophobic. Then again, given he'd probably be coughing his lungs out onto the desert sand within forty-eight hours, maybe a little honest phobia wasn't such a bad thing.

He passed the time reviewing their mission briefing, even though he'd had all the details memorized an hour ago. It helped to occupy his mind and stop his thoughts from wandering back to that image that had dominated every television channel for the past four hours – the mushroom cloud rising up over the Arizona horizon.

Sergeant Blake was part of the Marine's Chemical, Biological Incident Response Force, as was every man in his team. *Almost every man*, he corrected himself. Even though his team was cobbled together from half a dozen squads – volunteers all, single men with no dependants – he had a nodding acquaintance with all of them. But the two new additions, he didn't know them at all, not even in passing, and they weren't the kind of guys you forgot in a hurry.

The younger man, the one that had been introduced as Burrows, was obviously a spook – CIA or NSA probably. Not that Blake held that against him. Whoever he was, he had volunteered for a one-way mission in service of his country and that had to count for something. Like the rest of them he wore the loose-fitting JSLIST protective suit over his battledress uniform, but his bore no name or rank insignia. It was also suspiciously new, as if the man was modelling it for the cover of the Marine Times.

The spook's buddy was never going to grace any magazine covers. Blake guessed he must be pushing seventy, and age had dried him out like leather stretched over knotted wood. His JSLIST was new too, but he wore it open at the throat and Blake could see the old combat jacket beneath. It bore the name Carroll on faded name tape. Blake was pretty sure they hadn't used that camouflage pattern since Vietnam. As well as the old man's dog tags, the chain around the thick neck held half a dozen medallions of various saints and a big pewter crucifix.

The old dude carried a bolt action rifle that looked every day as old as its owner. The wood stock was worn smooth from decades of use, but the barrel and the upper receiver looked freshly blued. The damn thing was huge.

Blake's pride and joy was a 1969 Pontiac Judge; he guessed that the exhaust on the old muscle car was bigger than the barrel on that rifle, but it would be a close run thing.

The old man caught him staring at the weapon.

"Many elephants where you're from?" Blake shouted above the roar of the plane.

The old man smiled. "Not any more," he said.

"That thing standard issue back in your day?"

"Son, this is a modified 600 Overkill. It'll send a nine-hundred grain bullet downrange at twenty-four-hundred feet per second. 'Standard' is not the word I'd use."

A nine hundred grain bullet! The rounds in Blake's M4 weighed only sixty-two grains.

The noise from the Globemaster's engines rose in pitch as the big plane fought for altitude.

"Hold onto your lunches, Marines," said the pilot's voice over the intercom. "We're going to climb above the worst of the cloud. No point getting cooked before we get to the drop zone."

Yeah, plenty of time for that later. Blake knew this was a one-way mission. Even the aircrew on the Globemaster were taking a hell of a risk getting this close to the cloud. But they needed data; they needed to know who had done this to them, and that meant sending in the Marines from the 'BIRF.

Their best intelligence so far had concluded the bomb had come in by truck from Mexico. The target had probably been Phoenix, although so far every terrorist cell that had claimed responsibility had been dismissed as mere attention seekers. Thankfully, the complexities of maintaining a thermonuclear device had proved to be too much and the bomb had detonated prematurely in the Sonoran Desert.

They had caught a break, for sure, but it was still a devastating breach of security. They needed to know who had done this and whether they had the capacity to do it again, perhaps more successfully.

The engine note changed again. They were decelerating, getting ready for the drop. Deploying a Stryker by airdrop was unusual. Dropping the big, eight-wheeled vehicle with its crew and passengers inside was unheard of, but this was a special case. Their time on the ground was limited and precious. To maximize their mission time they were going to drop right through the cloud and land as close to the hypocentre of the explosion as they could. The Stryker's thick armour and self-contained atmosphere would give them some protection as they plummeted through the thick smog of radioactive particles thrown up by the explosion.

Blake heard the rear door open and the noise, which had been deafening before, became ear-splitting.

"Drogue chute deployed," said the Loadmaster over the 'com and the Stryker started to quiver like a racehorse in the stalls. Blake pictured the little chute fluttering behind the open rear door of the Globemaster. Its job was to pull the main chutes, all eight of them, out of their sleeves.

"Brace yourselves people," Blake shouted above the din. "The next one's going to be a real kick in the ass."

"Primary chutes deploying in three… two… one…"

When the primaries opened, Blake felt like someone had driven the Stryker at full speed into the side of a cliff. He was thrown against his harness by the sudden deceleration as an acre of parachute yanked the Stryker out of the back of the speeding plane. He couldn't see out, but the dirty sunlight that slanted in through the hardened viewing slits scythed around the inside of the cramped vehicle as it spun.

This isn't right. They shouldn't be spinning like this. He felt a momentary stab of fear as the steel cage and everyone inside it plummeted toward the desert that was still a mile below. It was stupid; they'd all be dead soon enough anyway, but dying in a botched airdrop would mean they had failed. It would mean they would learn nothing about the attack, at least not without sending more men to their deaths. He remembered the billowing, radioactive cloud rolling upwards and outwards like a cancer eating up the sky. Blake took the fear and twisted it into anger, a cold resolve.

The Stryker swung like a pendulum until down became somewhere closer to where it ought to be. They were still spinning, but they were level and Blake could feel the deceleration pressing up through his boots as the giant chutes slowed their descent. They were safe, for now.

"Ooh rah!" he shouted and his team answered, even the old dude. Only the spook stayed silent.

From somewhere at the back a voice mimicked the cry of a child at a county fair. "Again… Again!"

• • •

Even with eight chutes, touchdown was hard.

Although their Stryker was a reconnaissance vehicle and carried more instruments than armaments, it shared the eight massive all-terrain tyres and rugged, armored chassis of its more aggressive cousins. Despite that, they hit the desert like a fifteen-ton sledgehammer.

Blake unstrapped and made his way up the narrow aisle to the front cabin where their driver, PFC Kareem Lyons was already gunning the Stryker's Caterpillar turbo-diesel power plant to life.

The cabin was even more cramped than the troop transport bay behind. The driver and navigator sat in front of twin steering yokes staring through narrow viewports at the swirling dust storm outside.

"Bearing, Sergeant?" Lyons asked.

Blake checked the GPS, but as he had expected contact with the satellites above was patchy at best.

"North forty-five degrees west," Blake replied, that should get them close enough. "Or as near as the terrain will let you."

Lyons nodded, gunned the engine and the Stryker lurched forward, rocking like a ship.

They drove for about twenty minutes while Blake and his team of specialists took readings from the mass spectrometer and Geiger counter. The explosion had created its own weather system: the rising column of super-heated air had built what the meteorologists called a thermal low, not unlike a tropical cyclone. With so much heat to dissipate, Blake guessed the dust storm around them would last for days, maybe even weeks. The swirling sand was also building up a significant amount of static electricity that was playing hell with their instruments. The radio was useless. They had a communications laser that could squirt data up to the satellite, but the bandwidth was limited and even that would probably be greatly attenuated by the swirling dust.

Blake started to weigh the alternatives. They would just have to collect as much data as possible and either hope for a break in the storm, or haul ass for its edge once the effects of radiation sickness looked like ending the mission.

"Sergeant, we need to stop for a moment." It was the spook, Burrows.

"Sir, we're still several clicks from the hypocenter."

"I'm aware of that, Sergeant. Now pull over."

Blake knew not to argue, although looking out through the cabin's toughened-glass ports he was damned if he could make out the reason for it. The dust storm still raged. He couldn't see more than twenty feet in any direction but what he could see was just Arizona scrub. The readings on the spectrometer hadn't spiked and the shallow valley between sand dunes they were traversing had been an unremarkable shithole even before the detonation.

"We're going out," Burrows said. "Ready the airlock."

Burrows sealed his suit and pulled the bulky mask down over his face before pulling the hood of his JSLIST suit tight around it. His old companion was already suited up and standing at the rear door with that equally ancient elephant gun.

Blake gave the order and the collapsible airlock – little more than a thick rubber tent that folded out from the Stryker's rear hatch – was erected. The two men entered and closed the armored hatch behind them before unzipping the outer door and stepping out into the dust storm.

Blake followed them on the video camera built into a hardened pod on the outside of the hull, panning it around with a tiny joystick built into the console until he had them both in frame.

"What the fuck are they doing out there?" Blake muttered.

Carroll, the old man, was easily recognizable as he towered above his much slighter CIA handler. The man took something out of the thigh pocket of his suit – it looked like a metal snake. When Carroll unwrapped it, Blake saw that it was a long length of motorcycle chain, the sort of thing greasers used to beat the crap out of each other back in the sixties. The chain was crimped together at its ends so that it made a circle. Carroll spun it around and then cast it into the dirt with a flick of his wrist so that its rotation pulled the heavy chain out into a perfect circle.

When it landed in the dirt, Carroll took a second to sprinkle it with some water from his canteen before sitting inside the circle, cross-legged like some goddam Indian guru. He pulled some more objects from his pocket and laid those out against the perimeter of the circle in front of him.

The dust storm and the camera's shitty resolution meant Blake couldn't make out any of the objects. He did notice that Carroll kept that big rifle close at all times.

"Williams, you reading anything?" Blake asked.

PFC DeShawn Williams manning the spectrometer

shrugged. "I'm reading plenty," he said, "but it's all the same shit I've been seeing for the last five miles."

What the hell were they doing? They had pin-pointed the center of the explosion seconds after the bomb had detonated. They knew exactly where it was and even in the storm, they knew exactly where they were in relation to it. If there was anything to find, any tell-tale concentration of residual elements that might give some clue as to the origin of the bomb then their best chance of finding it was miles away.

This was needless exposure, and as for the old man singing Kumbayah in the dirt, Blake started to wonder if they hadn't all had more of a radiation dose than they thought.

"Okay Sergeant, we're done here," said Burrows over the com. Even at such short range, his voice sounded distant and scratchy.

"Roger that, sir. Readying the decontamination shower now."

"No need for that, Sergeant."

"Sir, I can't let you back in without decontamination. The dust on your suit would contaminate the whole vehicle."

"I know that, Sergeant. We're going to hitch a ride on the outside. I need you to continue toward the hypocenter."

They continued across the desert, stopping half a dozen times for the old man to throw his chain in the dust and rest his old bones inside the circle. Sometimes, after performing their little ritual, Blake got new orders: either a new direction to take or an instruction to take readings on the mass spectrometer. Blake tracked their progress on his map, it was painfully slow. Their path picked a meandering line in a rough direction about two points west of the center of the explosion. At this rate they would be testing the limits of their air reserves before they even reached their goal.

The rest of the team was growing impatient too. They all knew theirs was a one-way mission. They had to feel like it meant something; that their sacrifice wasn't going to be in vain.

Blake did his best to keep them focused. "Williams, get on the periscope," he ordered. "Keep an eye out for any survivors."

"Survivors? For real?"

"We're still outside the kill zone, Private."

"Sergeant's right, DeShawn," said Lyons from the driver's seat. "At Hiroshima they found survivors just a few hundred meters from the hypocenter."

"This wasn't no fuckin' airburst, man. This was a bad-ass truck bomb. Anyone inside a few hundred meters would have been atomized. We're probably driving through a cloud of your 'survivors' right now."

"Contact right!" shouted Lyons.

"Halt!" Blake ordered while DeShawn Williams panned around with the short periscope on the Stryker's roof.

"Contact, my ass. There ain't nothin' out there."

"What did you see, Marine?"

"A person, I think. It was real quick. They looked like they were crawling… like they were on all fours."

"What's up?" asked Borrows over the 'com. "Why have we stopped?"

"Sir, we have a possible survivor. Lyons saw–"

"Where?" This time it was Carroll. "Tell me exactly what you saw."

"It was only for a second," Lyons said. "Something moving in the dust storm."

"Williams, you stay on that scope," Blake ordered. "Fernandez, Howard, you're with me. Prep the portable decontamination shower and get a spare suit ready. If there's anyone alive out there I want to get as much dust off them as possible and get them inside a suit and breathing clean air."

"Roger that," said the two marines in unison.

After buttoning up their JSLIST suits and checking each other for breaches, they stepped out through the airlock into the radioactive storm. Blake made his way carefully around to the right of the Stryker, where Lyons had said he had seen his survivor. The wind was almost strong enough to knock him off his feet. It was like being sandblasted; all he could see was the swirling brown dust, and his ears were filled with a sound like static from countless tiny impacts.

"Williams, do you have eyes-on?" Blake asked over the 'com.

"Negative, Sergeant."

"Roger that. Switch to thermal, see if that helps."

"Switching to thermal imaging."

Blake scanned his surrounds, but could see nothing except the swirling dust until Carroll and Burrows advanced around the Stryker's nose – both had their rifles raised. Blake imagined what the Stryker would look like to a survivor, let alone the five strange figures, armed and masked with bulky re-breathers. Whoever was out there would be scared shitless.

"Lower your weapons," Blake said over the 'com.

"Son, you'd better get back inside," said Carroll. His voice was deep and calm, like the measured tones of a news anchorman.

Blake ignored him. "How's the thermal camera looking, Marine?"

"Still sketchy. Wait… I got a signal but it's moving too fast. Doesn't look like— Holy shit!"

Blake caught movement at the edge of his visor – a flash of white cutting through the swirling storm, then it was on him.

It rode him down to the dirt. Hands clawed at him, gouging and ripping at the tough rubber of the JSLIST suit. A flailing limb caught his re-breather and knocked his whole mask upwards so the heavy rubber seal was across his eyes. He tasted dust. *I'm exposed!*

He pushed upwards, trying to free himself. Around the obscuring mask he caught fragments of his assailant: a white, hairless head with a terrible wound where the eyes should be – a wet crater above a mouth that was too wide and filled with broken ridges of what might once have been teeth. Long fingers encircled his throat. He wanted to gag from the sand in his mouth but he couldn't muster the breath. The sand got inside his mask making the world dark… or maybe it wasn't the sand.

The sound of a shot cut through his foggy senses. The weight and pressure left him and he sucked in a great gulp of air only to cough it back out as the sand hit the back of his throat. Blake rolled to his knees, hacking and spluttering. Then someone was at his side squirting water into his mouth and yelling at him to spit. He managed to clear his mouth while the boom of Carroll's big calibre rifle echoed around him. Specialist Howard slapped an oxygen mask over Blake's mouth and he took his first clean breath. His head cleared enough for him to cleanse and re-set his own mask.

When he turned around Carroll and Burrows were standing over the body of the survivor.

"What the hell were you thinking?" Blake yelled. "You just shot a fucking civilian."

They both looked back at him, inscrutable behind their masks.

"Look at it, son," Carroll said.

Blake ignored him. "Some goddamn farmer or hitchhiker manages to ride out the shockwave from a nuclear blast, poor bastard, and then you come along with your big-ass elephant gun and blow half a dozen holes through him. What the fuck do you think we're doing here?"

"Just look at it."

Blake dropped his gaze to the body sprawled in the dirt. It was naked, clothes burned off, Blake guessed. It lay sprawled at an unnatural angle – the legs bent back as if on broken knees. How could it have moved so fast with injuries like that? It was impossible and yet it had happened.

"Jesus!" Howard said from somewhere behind Blake. "What could do that to a person? The blast? The heat pulse? Dude's fucked up."

"It's not a person," Carroll said. Burrows shot a glance at the man, but said nothing.

"What do you mean?" Blake asked. "If it's not a person then what the hell is it?"

"Careful, Carroll," Burrows said.

"What does it matter?" The old dude said, "they're all dead anyway. The least we can do is let them die knowing they done some good."

Blake looked at the thing again. The knees weren't broken,

they bent backwards like a dog's hind legs and the wound on its face wasn't a wound at all. The fleshy crater that took up most of its 'face' above the gaping mouth was pink and ridged with frills of tissue like the inside of a bat's ear. But whatever it was, it didn't look damaged. It was meant to look like that, like some kind of a cross between a giant nostril and a radar dish.

"You know what happens at the center of a thermonuclear explosion?" Carroll asked.

Blake thought of the twinned horrors at the heart of a thermonuclear bomb: the first fission explosion was terrible enough, but it was only a detonator, a way of driving the pressure high enough to cause fusion and unleash the terrible forces that powered the Sun itself.

"I know the basics."

"No you don't. Plenty of people thought they did, thought they understood the physics, and maybe they did up to a point, but they never stopped to think whether something else was happening. Something beyond physics... something metaphysical."

"What are you talking about?"

"The concentration of energy at the center of the explosion is too much for the universe to handle. For a fraction of a second, it's actually enough to rip a hole in the fabric of space and time. It tears a hole in reality itself."

"Bullshit!"

"That ain't even the crazy part," Carroll said with a shake of his head. "You see ours ain't the only universe. We're not the only game in town and when the hole opens, it allows things to cross over. When there's a loss of life in this reality, like those killed in those nano-seconds when the hole exists, it's like there's a kind of suction. It's like opening a door on a plane at thirty-thousand feet. There's a difference in pressure. Loss of life in this universe pulls life across from the other side: new life... different life."

"I still say bullshit," Blake said, glancing between Carroll and Burrows. "Next you'll be telling me that's where Godzilla came from – just stepped through one of these holes at Hiroshima."

"That was just an A-bomb, not thermonuclear, not powerful enough. Good job, too. That many lives lost... who knows what might have come through. Look," Carroll said, as he calmly wiped the receiver of his rifle with an oiled rag. "I know this sounds hard to believe, but look at that thing and tell me it's from this Earth. I hunted these things for twenty years, ever since the Bowline tests in '69. Usually, what comes through is no bigger than a jack rabbit. We try to minimize the loss of life but we can't clear every bird and mosquito out of the test area so there's always some negative pressure. Hell, even the bacteria in the soil have life energy, and there's more biomass in soil and rock than you'd think. But there hasn't been much call for guys like me recently, not since the test bans."

"So let me get this straight," Blake said, trying to make sense of what he'd heard. "You're saying these terrorists smuggled a nuclear weapon across the border and when it detonated and killed them it sucked this... this demon through from another dimension?"

"That's about the size of it."

"Sergeant..." said Williams from inside the Stryker.

"So we're not here to gather intelligence about the bomb. We're... Ghostbusters or some shit."

"No. You can gather all the intel you like. This was still a terrorist attack on US soil and you need to do your job. I'm the Ghostbuster."

"Sarge, you need to see this," Williams repeated.

For the first time Blake noticed the ring of steel in the dust, Carroll's motorcycle chain and the small collection of items he'd placed inside its perimeter. One of the items was a candle – four inches of white wax like the kind kept in kitchen drawers across the country in case of a blackout. This one was stuck into the sand and despite the swirling dust storm it was still aflame.

"What is it, Williams?" Blake said into the 'com.

"Another thermal trace, Sergeant. Bigger than the last one, and hot."

"A vehicle?"

"I don't think so."

Blake noticed that although the candle didn't seem to be affected by the storm, it was certainly being affected by something. The flame wasn't burning straight up, nor was it guttering in the wind. It was horizontal. A little finger of flame pointing northwest."

"Williams, what's the bearing on that heat trace?"

"Northwest, Sergeant. About fifty yards and closing."

Carroll focused on the flame then looked out into the storm following its point. The man reloaded the Overkill with a handful of its massive rounds.

Blake heard something above the roar of the wind that set ice in his veins. He unsnapped the quick-release buckles on the sling of his M4 and raised the carbine to his shoulder.

A shadow raised itself against the back of the swirling dust – grey and huge. Carroll's Overkill boomed in a steady rhythm. Blake wanted to see what it was before he started shooting.

Then he wished he hadn't.

The creature was enormous, taller than the Stryker and massively muscled. Like the smaller creature Carroll had killed, it lacked anything Blake could call a face. The blunt head with its wet crater of a sense-organ sat between hunched slabs of muscle that banded its shoulders. Twin ridges of bone, halfway between horns and blade-like plates, ran back across its brow from above where the eyes would have been on any Earthly creature, to meet at a central ridge that ran along its back.

Blake flipped his M4 to fully automatic and began to fire at the creature in short controlled bursts. Howard was doing the same, even Burrows joined in as a hail of lead rained down on the creature. They couldn't miss, not with a target this big, not at this range. And yet it kept coming. They had already thrown enough lead at the thing to shred a bull elephant, but it hadn't even slowed.

It charged, forcing them to scatter or be trampled under its massive, clawed feet.

"Williams," Blake shouted into the 'com. "Get on that .50 cal. now!"

"Sergeant, there's no airlock on the top hatch, the Stryker will be contaminated."

"Do you see that fucking thing? Forget the rads, if we don't stop it none of us will live long enough to get cancer."

Blake slid into the dust under the angular nose of the Stryker, switched magazines and kept up his fire at the creature. *It must have hide like steel plate.* The storm of 5.56mm rounds didn't seem to bother it at all. Only Carroll's huge calibre rifle seemed to have any effect.

The creature lashed out at Burrows with a huge hand. Its fingers were almost human, except the central pair was fused into on massive digit, the nail overgrown into a six-inch claw.

It caught Burrows on that terrible hook, lifting him off his feet and flinging him away like a child's toy.

The effect on Carroll was dramatic. He stopped shooting and just stared at where Burrow's body lay in the dust, the dead man's guts drawn out along the furrow his carcass had carved in the sand.

Carroll stepped backward into his steel circle and sat, his rifle lying silent across his knees.

"Keep shooting, Goddamn it!" Blake shouted at the man but Carroll ignored him.

The creature turned on Carroll, swiping one huge arm around, clawed fingers scything through the air.

Blake expected to see Carroll's body ripped in two, but the creature's arm never seemed to make contact. It slashed and swiped at Carroll, but its blows were deflected as if by an unseen wall that extended upwards from the ring of steel around Carroll's feet.

Blake heard the clang of the Stryker's top hatch being flung open and Williams opened up on the creature with the roof-mounted machine gun.

It roared in pain and anger and turned its attention from Carroll to this new threat.

"Watch out!" Blake yelled as the creature charged the armoured personnel carrier. Howard was crushed between the fiend and the steel wall of the Stryker as it slammed into the Stryker's side. It lifted all four wheels on its left side off the ground, and fifteen tons of steel pivoted upwards. The creature roared again, its huge claws digging into the thick rubber of the Stryker's all-terrain tires and lifted. The vehicle – their home and only safe haven in the radioactive storm that swirled around them – toppled first onto its side then turned full turtle onto its roof.

Williams screamed as he was crushed half in-half out of the remote weapons station on the Stryker's top.

The airlock ripped away from the rear doors and two suited soldiers stumbled out. The creature lashed out, picking them up with one swipe of its massive arm. One, Blake couldn't tell who, slammed into the side of the upturned Stryker with bone-crushing force while the other was flung a dozen yards.

The creature turned back to Carroll and charged, trying to skewer the man on the thorny plates of its head. Whatever it was that had held the creature back before held firm again. It grappled against an invisible wall; clawed hands tried and failed to find purchase on the mysterious barrier.

Now that Blake knew what to look for, he thought he could see the barrier in the swirling dust. A column of still, dust-free air surrounded Carroll, and the old man sat at its center with hands pressed against the sides of his head like a child wishing the world would go away.

Damn him! Carroll had a shield and the most effective weapon against this brute and all he was doing was cowering in fear.

Carroll had a shield… but maybe Blake could use it as well. While the creature hammered away at the invisible barrier, Blake sprinted past, keeping Carroll and whatever field the man had conjured between himself and the monster. Blake pressed his face to it and felt its strange, unyielding nothingness.

"Fight, damn you!" Blake shouted at Carroll, but the old man gave no indication of having heard him. It was as impenetrable to sound as it was to the creature's attacks.

Blake smiled as an idea formed. He hoped the barrier really was is impenetrable as it appeared. Taking out a grenade, he pulled the safety clip and, keeping his thumb mashed down on the spoon, he pulled the ring from the fuse assembly.

When he let go, the spoon sprang free, igniting the fuse. A wisp of smoke rose from the fuse assembly as it burned down toward detonation. With the fuse-delay of about four to five seconds, Blake was trusting his life to its accuracy.

He counted down the seconds:

One Mississippi...

Two Mississippi...

Three Mississip–

Blake stepped from behind the barrier, threw the grenade straight at the fleshy concavity of the creature's face and crouched back behind Carroll in one smooth motion.

The grenade detonated right in front of the creature's face, sending jagged shards of scorched metal casing through its flesh.

The front of the creature's head disappeared in a red mist. It collapsed forward, hung for a moment, slumped against the invisible column surrounding Carroll like a drunk leaning against a lamp post before sliding sideways and crashing into the dust.

Blake stepped from behind the barrier and fired a few shots into the bloody stump that was all that was left of the monster's head. The grenade at point blank range had done its work, as had the invisible barrier, protecting Carroll from the blast as well as deflecting the blast around Blake.

Satisfied it was dead, Blake went to check on his team mates. Lyons was alive and still strapped into the driver's seat of the upturned Stryker. Williams, Howard and Specialist Brad Hickman were dead, but Wyatt Pollin had survived being flung twenty feet by the monster's blow although Blake suspected he had a couple of cracked ribs and some torn ligaments in his shoulder from where he had failed to stick the landing.

Blake turned his attention back to Carroll. "Get up, Carroll!" he demanded. "Get up and start talking. I've got three dead marines plus Burrows, and a wrecked vehicle. No more secrets! What the hell was that?"

Carroll eventually raised his head then reached out a hand. The instant it passed above the encircling chain, the barrier disappeared – Blake felt it as rush of stale wind.

"Couldn't shoot," Carroll said. "Would've broken the circle."

"Fuck your circle, Carroll. What about the rest of us? What about fighting for your team? Your mission? I heard you in the Stryker when we dropped. 'Ooh-Rah'. You're a marine. Since when do marines run and hide like that?"

"You don't understand," the man muttered.

"Enlighten me."

Carroll stared at the body of Nathan Burrows sprawled in the sand. "It doesn't matter now. I'm a dead man."

"You knew what this mission was about," Blake snapped. "We're all dead men."

"Not me," Carroll said with a shake of his head. "Burrows was going to get me out. That was our deal. One last hunt."

"Bullshit. Get you out? Out of where? You've already absorbed enough rads to kill you. Die here or die in a Navy hospital, what difference does it make?"

"You don't get it. I wasn't *going* to die. Burrows was going to get me frozen. Cryogenics, just like Walt fuckin' Disney."

For a moment Blake was taken aback. "Why?"

"Twenty years, I been huntin' those things. Twenty years of watching the tests and cleaning up afterwards and we never once cracked the walls of heaven. Never saw no cherubs, just those... things," he gestured toward the monster's carcass before taking a step toward Blake. "You see, I figured it out. There's no heaven, only hell. Just us and them. I've seen the truth. I know where we go when we die and I ain't planning on dying."

The old man was clearly crazy, but then so was this whole situation and unfortunately Carroll was the closest thing Blake had to an expert on this stuff, so he was just going to have to deal with the old man.

"Look, I'm sure whatever deal Burrows promised you is still on the table. We just need to complete our mission and get clear of this storm so we can contact base."

That wasn't going to be as easy as it sounded. Not without a vehicle. "Lyons! What's the news on the Stryker?"

Lyons came over shaking his head. "We could maybe right it if we had time. We can dig her out and try to roll her with the jack, but she's got two shredded wheels and the front axle is busted." He glanced back at the Stryker. "We could maybe remove the wheels from that axle and use them to replace the shredded tyres but that's a hell of a job in the field."

Blake nodded. "Okay. Better get started then. Everyone's going to have to pitch in. That means you too, Carroll!"

But Carroll wasn't looking at him. He was staring down at the candle that still burned despite the raging storm. Its flame was a brilliant white tongue of fire almost six inches long and pointing in the direction of the hypocenter. It seemed their mission was far from over.

* . *

They followed the direction set by the candle's flame. It was tough going. The JSLIST suits had not been designed with operator comfort in mind and they were weighed down with as much equipment from the Stryker as they could carry.

Blake almost had to physically carry Carroll too. The old man seemed truly terrified of dying. Once he had realized this was no normal hunt, his whole demeanor had changed. But the man realized being alone was no guarantee of safety either, so he had eventually agreed to come with them.

Blake tried to keep him talking, asking him all kinds of questions about his time at the Nevada Proving Grounds. It helped to lighten his mood somewhat and it was all useful information.

"What about that shield thing?" Blake asked. "How does that work?"

"It's called a circle of protection. It's a holy space. Things work differently inside it, like the candle."

"And the bad guys can't get in?" Blake asked as they trudged on.

"Nothing can get in until the circle is broken from the inside."

"Hey, Sarge!" said Lyons. "How do I get me one of those?"

"It won't work for just anyone, son," Carroll replied. "It takes practise and something to focus your faith on."

"The chain?" Blake asked.

"Chain, chalk… it doesn't really matter."

The storm grew stronger until pushing through the wind felt like trying to walk underwater. Then, without warning it was gone.

Something else disappeared too; the constant clicking from their portable Geiger counter. Just seconds ago it had been so fast that it had sounded like the white noise between radio stations. Blake had just tuned it out. Now it was gone altogether.

Blake looked to Pollin who was holding the small instrument. "Fault?"

"No, Sergeant, not that I can tell. Just no reading. Not even normal background radiation."

Blake spotted something glinting ahead; Howard had seen it too.

"What the hell is that?" the marine asked.

It hung, glinting in mid-air. It appeared to be metal – twisted and ridged like a section of spine from some metal beast.

"It's a crankshaft," Lyons said. "Part of one anyway."

He was right. It had been scoured clean and gleamed like it was freshly-milled. It hung impossibly in the air. Blake waved his rifle barrel above and below it and then to the sides, but there was nothing holding it up. It was hovering.

He looked to Carroll. "You want to fill us in on why gravity seems to have taken a day off?"

"Search me," Carroll replied with a shrug. "I've never seen anything like that before."

Blake reached out and carefully touched the crankshaft. It felt entirely normal and entirely solid. After his first tentative touch he wrapped a fist around it and pulled, but it wouldn't budge. He would have had more of a chance to right the fifteen-ton Stryker than to budge the floating crankshaft.

"There's more over here," Fernandez said. Blake looked over and saw a tiny metal leaf floating in mid-air – a piece of torn metal plate with viciously sharp and jagged edges.

"There's paint underneath," Fernandez said.

Blake peered beneath; in a hollow protected from the wind, some of the original paint remained.

They moved onwards through a cloud of suspended debris – not just metal, but also splinters of charred wood and what looked like shards of black glass fused from the Arizona sand itself.

The debris grew thicker, forcing them to weave through a three-dimensional maze of immovable particles until they eventually came to the source.

It was a house, or rather the remains of one. It seemed to have been caught mid—explosion. The troupe faced the back wall of the property. It was still relatively intact; the door was fixed in its frame, hanging open. A rear window hung like a shattered cloud just outside its frame. The front of the house was just gone. Through the open door Blake could see the front rooms standing open to the street, its contents pushed against the walls as if a great broom had swept through and cleaned the room furniture and all.

To the left and right other houses defined the edge of a dirt road.

"What the hell is this place?" Pollin asked.

"Ghost town," Fernandez said. "I saw one on Sixty Minutes. There're ghost towns all over this county, old mining towns just abandoned after the silver dried up. Nothing else out here worth staying for, so folks just up and walked away."

"Not everyone," Lyons said, pointing to a car beside the house. Like everything else, it had been frozen at the moment of the explosion. The car stood almost upright in a permanent, impossible pirouette around one of its front wheels, but apart from that it looked to be fairly new and in good condition. It was certainly better than any abandoned vehicle should be after years in the desert.

"Looks like someone set up here. You think it was the terrorists?" Blake asked.

"Drug runners more like, or maybe organised people smugglers," Fernandez replied.

Blake glanced at Carroll and noted the look of alarm on his face. "Carroll, you got any idea how much energy it would take to freeze a town like this?"

"The energy doesn't *freeze*. The life force gets replaced." Carroll's frown persisted. "At the moment of detonation, when the forces are strong enough to tear open the portal between dimensions, any life extinguished here gets replaced from over there. That's it. There is no freezing." He shook his head "I've never seen anything like it. This is something new."

"Man, that is so not what I wanted to hear," said Lyons.

"Okay," said Blake. "Here's how this is going to work. We sweep the town. You know the drill. We're still on the clock and no matter what we've seen today, remember how this all started. Some asshole tried to drive a nuclear truck bomb into downtown Phoenix." He pointed to the old man. "Now Carroll here is going to do his thing and we're going to do ours. I want any intel bagged and tagged. I want samples and I want a vehicle. We're going to have to get outside the radius of this…" he struggled to find the words. "Of whatever the fuck is happening around here and we're going to do our jobs and get that intel back to HQ. Everyone got that?"

"Ooh rah!"

The marines pressed forward through the shattered building. It seemed to have been occupied fairly recently; Blake noted clothing and food that still looked fresh, all caught at the same frozen moment in the midst of the explosion.

He spotted movement out the street and dropped, making his way through the shattered room on his belly.

The main square of the old ghost town was a shattered bramble of broken shards of wood. Every building looked to have burst outward, growing up and away from what must have been the center of the explosion that had turned the buildings around the square into a crown of thorns.

But that was nothing compared to what lay at its centre.

A fused circle of black glass surrounded a central pit that glowed with otherworldly light. It flickered like the reflection of something constantly in motion. Across the surface of the black glass lay a twisted skein of tendrils. So dense were they, it looked like the floor was carpeted with black worms. Each was no thicker than Blake's thumb, but so long their ends were lost among their tangled brethren.

They spread from the central pit, crawling up the walls of nearby buildings like ivy. Only there, at the farthest perimeter of the writhing mass could the tips of the tendrils be seen waving in the air like the fronds of some unimaginable sea monster. In some places they had fused together into sheets of motile tissue, flat and tough as dry kelp washed up on a beach.

Blake followed them back to the pit. From his vantage point he couldn't quite see inside – he was glad. What little he could see hinted at something vast moving in the darkness beneath.

Other creatures surrounded the pit, and Blake counted half a dozen of the swift moving creatures – like the one Carroll had killed – as well as two of the big Stryker-killers.

"It's the portal," Carroll said in disbelief.

"What?"

"I've seen pictures from the tests. High-speed photography at the moment of the explosion. The portal looked like that," Carroll said, pointing.

"But it's supposed to be closed," Blake shouted. "You said it was only open for the instant of the explosion!"

As he said the words, Blake knew the door between worlds was still open because the loss of life here had been much greater than in any mere test. This had been a town once – undocumented and off the maps, and probably the base of some smuggling operation – but still a concentration of life energy. When the bomb had gone off it had allowed something big to gain a foothold in this world. That many-tendriled thing that flowed from the portal like a mass of mating snakes was caught between two worlds, keeping the portal open.

"We need to get out of here," Carroll said. Pale, his eyes darted left then right, and the man wore every one of his six-ty-plus years on his haggard face. This was way more than he had signed up for.

"You hang in there, Marine," Blake said, but the old man was right. This was more than they could handle. He had no idea what the powers-that-be could do about a portal to another dimension, but that wasn't his problem. The biggest contribution he could make right now would be to get this information back to the outside world.

Movement out of the corner of his eye.

A creature was crawling up the wall. No bigger than a possum, its many-jointed legs told Blake exactly where it had come from.

"It's okay," said Lyons as he drew his knife from the kydex sheath slipped to his chest rig. "I got this one."

"Wait!" Blake hissed, but it was too late.

Lyons slammed his knife into the creature, pinning it to the wall, but the thing wasn't about to go quietly. It screeched and thrashed against the blade that pinned it to the wall, smearing black blood against the timbers.

"Fuck!" Lyons shouted. He grabbed the thrashing monstrosity and pulled his knife out ready for another blow, but the creature was too strong. It twisted out of his grip with desperate strength and skittered away out onto the street, still screeching.

"We need to move, *now!*" Blake ordered.

There was a heavy thump as something landed on the ceiling above them, then another.

Blake looked up. Half of the shattered room was open to the sky and peering over the lip of the lattice of ruined joists were two of the demons, their cratered faces tracking Lyons and Blake like radar dishes.

"Contact!" Blake shouted and fired up through the boards. No need for subtlety now. This would have to be a fighting retreat.

The hail of bullets should have shredded the timbers, and torn into the creatures above, but Blake had not accounted for the unnatural strength of the stasis-locked structure. His rounds just stopped as if they had hit armored plate, and fell as squashed mushrooms of lead to mingle with the brass of his spent shell casings.

One of the creatures jumped down, slamming into Lyons who still had his knife out. The marine stabbed the creature again and again, but it seemed to have no regard for its own safety. It ignored Lyon's blows and concentrated on delivering its own. It clawed through his JSLIST, talons snagging on the tough MOLLE webbing of the man's chest rig.

Blake didn't dare shoot for fear of hitting his squad mate, and watched in horror as the monster's mouth opened impossibly wide and closed on Lyons' head, crushing mask and skull beneath.

Pollin and Blake opened fire at the same time, both knowing their teammate was dead and both wanting to exact revenge on his other-worldly killer.

The second creature landed in the room, but Fernandez was ready for it. He fired at point blank range. Rounds chewed into the creature, but it seemed to be made out of spring steel and Kevlar. Fernandez' rifle finally clicked down onto an empty chamber, but the creature was still very much alive. It swiped at him, raking clawed appendages across his throat like a quartet of switchblades.

Blake kicked the creature and grabbed Fernandez by the hood of his suit, hauling the marine toward the back of the house. He expected the creature to come leaping back, but although it screeched in fury, no attack came his way. He checked over his shoulder; the creature squirmed in mid-air, clutching at a sliver of timber protruding from its chest. Blake's kick had impaled the creature on a fragment of the shattered structure like some alien bug in a collection.

He fired one handed, aiming for the sense organ at the centre of the creatures head. It thrashed once then was still.

The ground shook. The mass of writhing tentacles surged from the portal, and hidden in its fronds was another of the creatures. It wriggled free of the tendrils and took its first breath in its new world.

"It's no good!" Carroll shouted. "You kill one and another just takes its place."

A zero-sum game. Every scrap of life-energy lost on this side of the portal was immediately replaced from the other side of that bridge between worlds. It was like trying to bail out a boat that was already half sunk – for every bucketful of water emptied over the side, more just flowed in to take its place.

Blake knew what had to be done. There was no point killing the creatures on this side; they would have to cross over. Killing these demons on their home turf would have the opposite effect, sucking life from this world into the next.

Blake grabbed one of the bags they had brought with them from the Stryker. Inside were three half-pound blocks of C4 used for controlled explosions of enemy munitions.

"Get as far away as you can," he shouted and ran straight toward the pit. He made a mental tally of his remaining ammunition – he was going to raise hell. Those demonic bastards had no idea what was about to hit them.

He raced across the carpet of tendrils, and they squirmed underfoot. One of the bigger creatures started to lumber toward him, but it was too slow. Blake would reach the pit before it got near him.

The portal yawned in front of him, and for the first time he was able to look down into it… and the horrors it contained.

"We never cracked the walls of heaven," Carroll had said. *"Never saw no cherubs."*

No cherubs indeed, but surely no religion had ever envisioned a hell such as this.

The world beyond the portal seemed to be made of nothing but writhing tendrils. There was no other Earth, nothing so normal as a planet orbiting some other sun. This was a world of flesh – a twisted inter-weaving skein of black tendrils thicker than any jungle canopy. Other things moved within the darkness. The only light came from the flickering around the edges of the portal. Hundreds of creatures swarmed through the mass like clownfish through an anemone's fronds, making their home on the body of this thing that was their entire world.

Was Carroll right? Was this Hell? And what would happen to a soul that died there, as he knew he would? Blake had never been a particularly God-fearing man, and the day's events certainly didn't fit into anything he'd been taught at his childhood Sunday School. But he still believed there had to be more to the universe than this.

Blake knew in his heart that Carroll was wrong. The world was not a zero-sum game. There was somewhere else, somewhere they hadn't yet seen; somewhere that gave them strength and that powered the strange rites Carroll had used. *A holy space* – that was how Carroll had described his protective circle. Well what made it holy? Blake didn't know but he was sure the answer lay somewhere other than the charnel pit of a world beyond the portal.

Clutching the bag of explosives, he leaped into the portal…

…and hit a solid wall.

The heavy bag ripped from his grip and tumbled down into the darkness as Blake staggered to his feet, standing on nothing at all.

Something was blocking the portal. Something as unyielding as Carroll's circle of protection.

Of course he couldn't pass through. The life energy in the joined world was equal. If the titanic might of the world-creature beyond the portal couldn't pull itself through, then of course Mr and Mrs Blake's little boy wasn't just going to be able to jump across.

"Shit!" he swore. He had lost the bag. Far below he could see it caught in a particularly knotted tangle of dark fronds. He saw something open under it, something he would hesitate to cause a mouth but for which there existed no other word in any sane reality.

Blake unslung his rifle and fired.

His rounds tore through the closing teeth and into the bag beyond.

ONLY STONES IN THEIR PLACE

Christine Morgan

We ride!" cried Kjarstan. "We ride for slaughter, for wealth, and for glory!"

His men shouted in answer, voicing great cheers. They rattled spear-shafts on shields in a drumming wooden thunder. Their banner, a white sword on a triangle of red, flapped from the pole Kjarstan's nephew held aloft.

"Our king has sent summons!" Kjarstan went on, his stallion's hard hooves striking up muddy splashes from the soft, thaw-soaked earth. "He has need of us, those good and loyal, oath-sworn! Need of our sword-might, our strength and our courage!"

Heartier still were the cheers to greet this. Even the humblest of peasant-horses, seized from plow's purpose, tossed their heads and snorted like proud battle-steeds.

"Shake from your limbs the weight of this long winter's weariness! Rouse your blood and war-fire! When we are old men, white-haired and wizened, we may sit by the hearth-stones... those of us not yet then gone to gold-shingled Valhalla! For now, there are foes to be cut down and plundered!"

Oh, but their blood and war-fire *were* roused. They'd struck at Pedham with the ending of autumn, when the harvest was in, the livestock butchered, the smoke-houses and granaries full. Once they had taken the village, there'd been little to do but wait. Wait, tend their weapons, gamble, and talk.

Under such circumstances, even the best of men would grow restless. The simplest squabble, a dispute over dice or rivalry for a woman, an ill-spoken insult or ill-timed jest could flare into violence as an ember into flame.

Now, though...

Kjarstan grinned, teeth a broad flash through his face-plate and a blond bristle of beard. His mail-coat, helm, and arm-rings gleamed in the morning's thin light. It was a grey day and clouded, the land wet from recent rain and snow-melt, and the wind off the sea carried a damp, heavy chill ... but spring had come.

Spring had come, as had the summons.

The king's messenger went by ship around the headlands and along the coast, bringing word wherever allies could be found. But there were not ships enough to carry them all with their war-gear and horses. Kjarstan had sent Udr and Anbjorn, two of his own best warriors, back with the messenger as proof in good faith of his oath and intent; the others, almost sixty strong, would meet them again in a matter of days.

And then they would put an end to the armies of Gunnleif Guthnarsson. Gunnleif the outlaw, the traitor, the oath-breaker and kin-slayer.

"What say you?" Kjarstan asked his men now. "Are you rested and ready? Do your swords thirst and your axes hunger?"

Many throats as one bellowed back their affirmation.

"Will you see our foes flee before us, and fall to our fury?"

Again, they bellowed, and louder – so loud the skies shook.

"For Earl Kjarstan! Kjarstan and the king!"

"The king!"

"King Jorfyn!"

"For Thor, Tyr and Odin!"

"Death, death to Gunnleif and his craven piss-dogs!"

Yes, they were eager, they were rested and ready, and they would ride!

"We will have victory!" Kjarstan told them. "Victory and rich reward! Let us fatten our purses on Gunnleif's stolen silver! Let us earn generous gifts, our king's gratitude in gold! We'll drape our women in amber and jet, and bring jeweled trinkets as toys for our children!"

Further back, where hovels and thatch-houses huddled around a log-timbered hall, the surviving villagers looked on with dull, beaten eyes. They would be hungry in the weeks to come; Kjarstan and his men had feasted well from their larders, drained dry their ale-barrels, and depleted their stores.

But such was their lot. They were farmers and swineherds, not warriors. Those who'd fought back had been slain. These remaining could count themselves lucky enough. They still had their lives, their homes were un-burned, and some even had their families intact.

If, of course, a few young widows and daughters would not be staying, preferring to follow those whose furs and fleeces they'd warmed through the cold nights...

If, perhaps, a promising youth or two had decided to forsake farm and field in hopes of proving his worth alongside the men from the north...

Well, such it was and so it would be.

"And," Kjarstan said, slowly drawing his blade from its scabbard with a scraping hiss of metal, "we will make name for ourselves!"

His men roared their approval.

"Make name by action and deed, such that the skalds will long sing of us and see us never forgotten! To honor our fathers and theirs before them; to leave lasting legacy of pride for our sons and their sons and their sons' sons after!" He swept his sword in a shining arc.

"Kjarstan! Kjarstan!"

"To battle and slaughter and glory!"

"We ride, my war-brothers..." He tugged on the reins so his horse reared up high, fore-hooves lashing the air. Then he kicked his heels into the beast's side and set off at a gallop. "We ride!"

* • •

On groaning hinges, the door opened. Its draft flickered the candlelight and stirred dark wisps of hair escaped from the long plait hanging over Hreyth's mail-clad shoulder.

She glanced up from the table, where was spread a wolf's pelt with rune-marked bones scattered upon it. They were old, those bones. Time-worn and hand-worn, ivoried with age, shaped and polished. The runes set into them were blood-red, soot-black, and gold.

Egil stood in the doorway, his wide shape filling it. He was not a tall man, nor fat, but big just the same. Slab-thick with muscle, barrel-chested, brawny and strong. His leather coat seemed ever to strain at the seams.

"It's happened," he said. His voice was like that of millstones taught to speak – grinding and gritty, crushing the grains of thought into the flour of words.

Dread moved in her heart. Dread, but no surprise. "Where?"

"Along the high-hill river valley between Pedham and Langenvik."

Her fingers brushed through silver-soft fur as she swept up a handful of rune-bones and poured them, with brittle clicks and clatters, into their bag. The bag she tied at her belt, which held also a sheathed *seax* – her short but sharp stabbing blade.

"How many?" she asked.

"Fifty."

"Fifty?" At that, surprise did come, flavoring the dread, enhancing it the way salt enhanced the taste of a broth.

"At least."

Hreyth touched the ash-wood amulet of Yggdrasil, the World-Tree, hanging around her neck on a cord.

Fifty at least.

She looked at Egil, the craggy outcrop of his nose, the knotted jut of his jaw, the broken expanse of his brow. His skull was bald, scar-gnarled, and misshapen. When he gave over to his battle-rage, there was no warrior more ferocious and feared, and his sword Life-Breaker had sent many men to the corpse-halls.

But his eyes, meeting hers, shared her unease.

"We must be quick," she said, and reached for her cloak.

••

Kjarstan's boldness and boasting, his promises of war-plunder and wealth as they brought death to their enemies, had carried them well through the first days of their ride. They talked and laughed, joked and sang. Every man of them, they knew, would win glory and fame.

Too long had they sat idle, wintering in their seized hall, feasting and fucking and throwing dice. Too long since they'd felt the crisp wind on their faces, heard the ring of steel and the clash of shield-walls. Too long since they'd slashed and stabbed, hewn and hacked, heard the screams of their enemies, smelled the blood-stink and shit-stink of gutted entrails.

Oh, there was joy in it – joy in war, joy in slaughter and carnage. A joy and a passion and a fire like nothing else. Whatever delights a man might take from riches, from meat and mead, or in the arms of a woman… only when he confronted death could he truly be most alive.

And if he should be struck down? If he should be pierced by sword-blades or spear-points, cut by axes, fall and be killed? A man could hope for no better end! Who would wish to die old and infirm, weak and feeble? To die of sickness, or drowning, or foolish mishap? A man must die well to earn his place at Odin's table!

Away from the sea, into the high country, they rode. The coastline fell away behind them. Creeks tumbled down rocky clefts. Vales lay open, bleak and muddy, but beginning to green. Twigs budded. New grass grew. Snow lingered in the lee-shadows of ridges, dirty ice-patches un-reached by the sun. Now and then, hares scampered or a scrawny deer stepped. Once, they glimpsed a bear, lean and hungry, but not so hungry as to dare menace men and horses.

They made camp by night, building fires, setting watches, sleeping bundled in blankets and cloaks. Jugs of sour barley-beer they'd brought with them, bread and hard cheese, smoked fish. To those who'd come from Pedham, the few youths and women never before gone far from home, it was both a frightening and exciting adventure.

Soon, they reached the high-hill river valley, long and slope-sided as if scooped in a trench from the earth. Above it rose rugged peaks, white-topped the year 'round. The river itself, fed by many more rushing creeks, flowed fast and full. Stones and boulders littered the ground, strewn like pebble-pieces of some giant's game.

Clouds drifted in. The day, not warm to begin with, cooled and grew damp. Mists whirled in ghostly skeins along the water. The horses' breath billowed steamy vapor. Men and women pulled their cloaks more tightly around their bodies; beads like dew-drops collected on the fur trim of hoods.

The red banner hung limp and dispirited from its pole. Stefnir, Kjarstan's nephew, swiped moisture from his forehead and wrung it from his fair hair, then cursed as some trickled down the nape of his neck.

The talk, laughter, jokes and singing dwindled. Soon they went on in silence, a sodden silence broken only by the plodding squish of hooves, the creak of straps, and the faint jingle of mail.

The mists thickened. Or a fog rose. Or the clouds lowered. Or all of those, together and combined. The world turned to greyness, dreary and blurred. The snow-peaks vanished, the land lost its edges, the trees faded to suggestions, and the boulders became indistinct. The river, off to their left, was a liquid whisper more felt than heard or seen.

"Stay close," said Kjarstan, his voice both oddly loud and oddly muffled. "No one goes straying, no one gets separated."

So he said, but when each of them could only see a few horse-lengths to either side, such words proved less than reassuring.

"It will clear soon," Kjarstan added. "If it does not, or this Hel's-gloom worsens, we'll stop for a while and wait it out."

The horses trudged on, heads low, manes and tails dripping. Everything smelled of wet wool and leather. Unwelcome thoughts insinuated their way into minds. Hel, as Kjarstan had mentioned… Hel, goddess in whose bleak realm resided the miserable dead who had not won their way to Valhalla…

Someone did try to bolster their spirits with another song, but the sound of it was a dirge and was soon let trail away. The silence returned.

Stefnir gripped the banner-pole with a half-numb, clammy hand. His other held the reins, though slackly, his horse following that of Rikolf, just ahead.

How suddenly their moods had changed... how distant in memory seemed the smoke and hearth-fires and cheer of the hall... or the fervor of riding to battle... how far and distant and impossible...

His horse stopped. Stefnir saw that Rikolf's had stopped as well, though he could barely make out more than its hindquarters. Not even Rikolf's red cloak was visible.

From somewhere behind him came a sudden low gasp, or cough. Stefnir turned his head, but only grey fog and vague shapes met his gaze. He opened his mouth to call a question – was everyone all right? – but his skin prickled with unaccountable gooseflesh before a single word passed his lips.

With his knees, he nudged his horse a few paces forward, meaning to bring himself up alongside Rikolf. He would ask the older man before bleating like some frightened little lamb–

Rikolf's saddle was empty. His horse only stood there, head down, reins dangling.

A cry wavered out of the mist – a woman's cry – over almost as soon as it began. He heard a man's grunt, and a thump.

His nerves shrieked.

"What is it? Who's there?" he shouted.

No one answered.

"Kjarstan?"

There still was no answer.

"Anyone!?"

And still, no one answered.

The silence returned again.

The silence returned again, and was complete.

* * *

Kjarstan would not, would *never*, break his oath.

This, Udr Udarsson knew as well as he knew his own name,

and the names of his father and grandfather before him. This, he knew as well as he knew his own heart.

The very implication was an insult, the kind of insult only answerable by blood. To suggest Kjarstan had not only broken his oath but utterly betrayed his king and kindred by joining with that yellow piss-dog, Gunnleif? For that, even blood would not suffice.

Yet, when the expected day of arrival came with no sign of his banner… when a second day passed the same, and a third… when possible explanations for delay wore thinner and thinner…

What else were men to think?

Udr and Anbjorn told them what to think.

"If Kjarstan is not yet come as promised," they'd said, "it is because some ill fate or fortune has befallen!"

They, two of Kjarstan's best and most loyal warriors, had accompanied King Jorfyn's messenger to Langenvik as proof of intent. Their earl – their *friend*, and war-brother! – would not lightly cast them aside as hostages.

"On my life, I so swear it," Udr had said. "On my life and my sword."

"Both of which," a dour old lord called Olla had retorted, "will fast be forfeit if you are proved false."

"It is that misbegotten whoreson Gunnleif you should give blame," Anbjorn said. "If his dogs struck Kjarstan by surprise in the hills–"

Back and forth they had argued – Jorfyn's advisers voicing their doubts, Udr and Anbjorn their protestations. Finally, with harsh words about to turn to harsher blows, the king intervened. A small group of swift riders, he declared, would go out in search of Kjarstan's missing men. A dozen, no more. To seek sign or answer, and return with news.

"We will ride with them," Anbjorn had said.

"Madness!" cried Olla. "If they *are* to stand hostage against treachery, do not let them leave!"

"Do you say," asked Anbjorn, with a dangerous hush, "that we would turn against our own king?"

"I say," said the old lord, "that you would be loyal to your earl."

Anbjorn might then have struck him, respected elder or not, if Udr and Jorfyn's *skald* hadn't intervened.

Again, the arguments raged with much shouting, until the king decided *one* would go while the other stayed behind. It satisfied none, but mollified enough, and so the matter was settled. The king then had them draw lots. Udr was chosen to ride.

He rode with a handful of others selected by the earls and from the king's own guard. They set out for Pedham, back-tracking the route Kjarstan should most likely have taken. On rare occasion they ran across spies or scouts from Gunnleif's army, dispatching them with ruthless efficiency of sword and spear.

Now they had reached the high-hill river valley, and something was not at all right. A strange mood crept over them, a strange apprehension. Talk died away. Men tensed in their saddles and twitched alert at every bird-call or noise. More than one checked to see his blade rested loose in the scabbard, ready to be drawn.

Udr himself felt uncommonly jumpy; his sack tight, his skin crawling. Nothing he could see, hear, or smell gave any reason for such skittishness.

The valley ahead lay peaceful, dusted fine green from the new-growing grass. The river flowed smooth in its course, disturbed only by the silvery leap-flicker and splashing of fish rising to snap at skate-flies.

Still, his palms clutched, sweating at the reins as he guided his horse through the random scatter of stones. He found himself wishing the lots had drawn differently, with him the one to stay behind at the war-camp where it was safe.

Which was no sort of thought for a warrior… a wrong sort of thought in more ways than one… and he could not say why.

Further on, one of Jorfyn's men gave a shout of discovery. When the others neared him, they saw he'd found a horse. Udr recognized it as one of the horses from Pedham, wandering saddled and bridled but riderless among tall grey standing stones, nosing at the tender green shoots to graze on the new grass.

"It bears no wounds, nor bloodstains," someone said. "Where is its rider?"

"Look, there's another, by the river there, drinking."

"Riderless as well, with panniers and packs untouched."

"Why would they abandon their horses yet laden?"

"They did not abandon their horses," Udr said. "They must have been attacked."

"Well, if they were, why would the attackers not have–?"

"Here!" called another man, amid a jumble of stones. "See this."

They rode to him as he stood over a bright splash of crimson that Udr first took for blood then he recognized it as a crumple of cloth, white on red. A white sword on a red field, attached to its pole but lying forsaken on the ground.

Udr sprang down and bent to it. "Stefnir never would have let drop his uncle's banner."

"Then where is he? Where are they?"

"Dismount. Spread out and search."

They did so, anxiously, their former apprehension creeping again along their nerves.

"I see a shield." A man pointed. "And a spear beside it."

"Broken?"

"No, not broken, not so much as scratched."

Without any order given, they gathered together, forming a defensive circle as if in anticipation of attack. Udr shivered, and by no means was the only man to do so. The air had gained a sudden chill.

And when had the sunshine given way to this fog?

.

The war-camp of King Jorfyn consisted of tents and huts surrounded by trenches, thorn-brambles, and angled rows of stakes hewn to crude points. The banner of the king – three white serpents interlocked on a triangular green field – flew accompanied by the banners of other earls and battle-chieftains.

Njoth, Jorfyn's *skald*, brought Hreyth and Egil into the makeshift *wittan*-hall, where gathered the king and his advisers.

It was a small assembly, a half-dozen earls and war-lords seated on benches by a stone-ringed central hearth-fire. Apart from them stood a young man with a dark beard; he was unarmed and his posture declared his resentment of that fact.

The king himself – of middle years, greying but not wrinkled, hale and hearty – wore a tunic of green wool with white *wyrm*-work embroidery at collar, cuffs and hem. He held across his knees a scepter, a long whetstone below topped by a piece of whale-ivory carved into entwined serpents. His cautious, intelligent, war-weary gaze fell upon the newcomers.

Two other women were also in attendance. One, red-haired and curvaceous, sat near the king's side, nursing a babe at a plump, freckled breast.

The other, immense and imposing in shining battle-glory, stepped to block Hreyth's way. The sword strapped across her back must have measured four feet in the blade. Its grip-worn leather hilt proclaimed it was by no means just for show.

"I am Valhild," she said. Her helm hung on a strap at her side, leaving her bare-headed with myriad thin, close-woven blonde braids. A scar sliced her chin. "First among the king's guard."

"Hreyth of the Grey Cloak."

"So, you are the rune-witch Njoth's been going on about?"

"I am."

"Hmf. I expected some haggard old crone."

"It seems we are both of a sort to defy expectations."

"True enough." Valhild's gaze swept Hreyth's mail-coat, and the sheathed *seax* at her hip. She grinned. "Mine's bigger."

Hreyth smiled, touching Rook-Talon. "Mine gets the job done."

Valhild roared a laugh and clapped Hreyth on the shoulder hard enough to make her stagger. "I like this one," Valhild told

79

the king, then turned to Egil – she towered over him, but he did not back down. "And who's this?"

"Egil Einarsson," Hreyth said. "Or, Egil Splitbrow, as men call him."

"I can see why." Valhild inspected the scarred, fissured dent at the front of his bald, lumpy skull. "You must have a hard head."

Egil looked up at her, mouth unsmiling, eyes flat. "It gets the job done."

Again, the big woman laughed, louder than ever. She slugged him on the arm. The sound was like that of a mattock meeting a bull's carcass. "I like this one as well," she said to King Jorfyn. "You'll do worse than to put your trust in them, I think."

With that, she stepped aside and let them pass into the circle, where spaces were made for them on the benches. Further introductions were made. The angry, resentful young man apart from the rest was called Anbjorn, who followed Kjarstan, the missing earl.

There had not been much in the way of serious confrontation between their armies as of yet this spring. The sides were too evenly matched, neither leader wanting to risk a direct assault, neither having the numbers to make a proper siege. So, they sat across the bay and tide-plain from each other, with occasional scout-parties and skirmishes, negotiations, insults, raids, and harassment.

"Fifty men more or less," said Jorfyn, "may not seem like much in a war. But these are Earl Kjarstan's men of which we speak. Among the best, each worth any three of Gunnleif's."

"Any *five*," Anbjorn said, earning him not a few glowers.

"And in battles such as we face here," the king continued, undeterred, "every man counts. If Kjarstan had come as intended, we would have taken the town by now."

"But, if Kjarstan has joined Gunnleif," put in an old earl, Olla, he of the sourest, expression. "Those same fifty men, whether worth five or three, will slaughter us like wolves upon lambs."

Jorfyn raised a hand to forestall an argument. Or, rather, to forestall the rekindling of an argument that had already gone on far past its welcome – Anbjorn protesting his lord's loyalty, Olla doom-mongering, the others debating how those fifty men could turn the tide and which way, and so on.

"I cannot move against Gunnleif without knowing what's become of Kjarstan," the king said, addressing Hreyth and Egil directly. "I need him with me. More vitally still, I need him not against me."

"Your spies at the town?" asked Egil.

"Have heard nothing beyond that which we know."

"Would be hard to keep so many men secret."

"Agreed," Jorfyn said. "Regardless of where matters lie with his loyalty – which I have never before had reason to doubt – I cannot believe he could be with Gunnleif and we've no word of it."

"Nor would they have deserted," Valhild said, which brought fervent agreement from Anbjorn. "We're not speaking of Saxon farmers running back to their fields, or dirt-eating Britons skulking in the bushes."

"Then there's the matter of the riders we sent out," Jorfyn went on. "A dozen men, hand-chosen by myself and my earls."

"And Udr, my war-brother," Anbjorn said. He shot Olla a look like an arrow. "Unless you think Udr betrayed them, led them into a trap."

"They have not returned," said Olla, uplifting his palms as if that itself proved enough.

"I've told you, something happened to them. Something strange."

The old earl scoffed. "Armies of men don't just disappear. It isn't as if they were at sea, where they could have been sunk, lost, and drowned, ship and all."

"Folk do vanish," said Njoth, the *skald*. He was lamed, absent a leg at the knee, getting about on a stout wooden crutch. "Not only at sea."

"My grandmother would tell me of farmsteads, or villages, or whole halls abandoned," Jorfyn's wife said, lifting her babe and patting its back to draw up a milk-burp. "As if overnight, leaving work half-done on the loom and unfinished meals upon the feast-tables."

One of the other earls nodded. "Mine would tell me of travelers venturing into dark forests or over high passes, never to be seen again."

"But not," Olla said firmly, "whole armies out of thin air! Grandmothers' tales? We'll be talking of dark-elves and *seidr*-magic next!"

"Aren't we already?" Hreyth asked. She rose and moved near the glowing hearth, turning in a slow circle to let them all see the strangeness of her mis-matched eyes – one blue as the fjords, one amber-gold. "Is that not why I'm here? Your king's *skald*, in his wisdom, sent for me because folk *do* disappear, or worse."

No one answered. Only a few – Valhild, Anbjorn, Njoth, and the king most among them – could long withstand her gaze.

"We may think we are mighty, with our kingdoms and oaths, our laws and law-speakers," she went on. "We forget there are older places, and things, of this world."

Njoth nodded vigorous support. "If they trespassed on a giant, a dwarf-cave, a troll-den... if they woke a dragon from its slumber... disturbed a grave-barrow..."

"There's no knowing what they might have unleashed," Hreyth finished for him. "And whether it will be satisfied with whatever it's already done, or will come looking for more."

• •

In the town was the army of Gunnlief Guthnarsson, whose banner – a snarling yellow dog on a triangle of black – waved from the top of the walls. Shields hung there as well, round shields painted half black and half yellow. Spears leaned ranked against the ramparts, an iron-tipped forest.

But no one came out to challenge or follow as their company of eight rode from Jorfyn's war-camp beside Langenvik's broad bay.

With Hreyth and Egil were Valhild, of course, and Anbjorn, and four other warriors chosen by the earls.

The day was brisk and clear, the wind off the sea sharp as a blade's edge. Eventually, as they rode amid idle conversations, a burly swordsman named Atli asked Egil what someone always seemed eventually to ask.

"Does she lay with you?" he whispered. "Is she your woman?"

He no doubt intended discretion, but Hreyth's ears were keen. She hid a smile as Egil made his usual growling reply.

"Ask such again, and my fist will give answer."

There was then a moment of cautious, considering silence. Then one of the others – called Thrunn – mentioned he'd heard it likely they'd see a rainy spring, and his friend Osig replied that a rainy spring meant a fair summer, and so the subject was safely changed.

Valhild, who'd also heard the exchange, grinned wryly at Hreyth and made more distance fall between their horses and those of the men. "Will *your* fist give answer if I ask you the same?"

"Oh? Have you an interest?"

She snorted. "Not in you. I only fight and drink like a man."

Hreyth's eyebrows rose.

"He seems tough," said Valhild, as if by way of explanation.

"The toughest."

"But that wasn't my question."

Hreyth released her reins with one hand, and made a fist – a rather small one. She looked at it, then looked at Valhild, and chuckled. "To what end, breaking my fingers?"

"You might land a lucky blow."

"I'll not chance it. As for the question beyond the question, Egil was brought orphan to the hall before I was born, and is as a brother to me."

Again, the big woman snorted. "*There's* a story told often enough. If I'd a sack of silver for each lovestruck fool I'd seen crying over his mead because of some girl who held him as brother or friend…"

"Tyr's truth in *that*," Hreyth agreed, rolling her eyes. "But, in this matter, it is as I say."

"Very well, then. How came he by his distinctive scar?"

"When he was brought orphan. His village fell under attack. His family was slaughtered, he himself injured and left for dead, only a child. My mother tended him, took him in. She was a healer… of sorts." She frowned; speaking of her mother was not something she often did, or found pleasant.

Most folk, realizing as much, let it pass. Not so Valhild.

"Of sorts?"

"She brewed potions. Both helpful and… otherwise. They say she poisoned her husband."

"Did she?"

"I believe so. I was too young to know at the time. I remember he beat her, and they hated each other, and when he died, his kin accused her of murder."

"Your mother murdered your father?"

"No," she replied. "That's why her husband beat her."

"Ah," Valhild said, nodding in worldly-wise comprehension. "What of your true father, then?"

Hreyth shrugged. "Of him, I can say only what was told to me, and it sounds the most terrible arrogance."

"I like terrible arrogance."

"You would."

"Don't make *my* fist give answer!" Valhild hefted hers, the knuckles callused, a design of Thor's hammer marked into the skin with needle and ink.

They both laughed.

"As I was told it," Hreyth said, "during a long year when the men and their ships were away a'viking, a stranger visited the hall. A lone wanderer who wore a grey cloak and a strip of cloth bound over his lack of an eye. He sought to discuss *seidr*-magic with my mother, staying three days and three nights as her guest."

"And when he was gone...?" Valhild made a rounding gesture in front of her belly.

"And when he was gone." Hreyth mimicked the gesture.

"A one-eyed wanderer in a grey cloak, eh?" She whooped, drawing the attention of the others. "You're claiming Odin All-Wise himself –?"

"I do not claim so, only say as I was told, and I warned you it sounded a terrible arrogance."

Just then, Anbjorn signaled urgently. "Tracks," he said. "Hoof-prints. They must belong to Udr and those who rode with him."

"Let us investigate," said Valhild, testing how her great sword rested in its scabbard. She winked at Anbjorn. "Remember, if you're leading us to some trap or our doom, I'll cleave you from crown to crotch."

"I assure you," he told her earnestly, "I've not forgotten."

• • •

They crested a rise and beheld the broad river-valley, green and peaceful, dotted with dark, coarse boulders and smoother grey standing stones. No carrion-crows circled, no scavengers roved, no stench of decay reached them on the mild spring breeze.

All that moved was the rippling current of the water, shining like glass; a few fish leaped, a few birds flew. Here and there, horses grazed.

Horses... many still saddled and bridled... the buckles glinting in the sun... other glints and flashes of metal showed from the grass... as if from sword-blades or bright-polished helms.

"I see no corpses," Valhild said.

"I see no one at all," added Osig. "They aren't here."

"But they *were*," Anbjorn said. "I know these horses. I know this gear. That's Kjarstan's war-stallion! And, there, his banner, by those stones! Stefnir would never have let it fall so long as his arm held strength."

"Unless they fled," said Inglar.

"They did not flee!"

"What, then? Did they surrender? Were they taken, meekly, without a fight?"

"I'll give *you* a fight, you–"

"Come and try–"

Valhild nudged her horse between them, a one-woman shield-wall with a dangerous scowl. "Settle it later," she said. "Or *I'll* settle it now."

There were no corpses, no indications of struggle, only wandering, riderless horses; shields and spears and a banner-pole as if carelessly cast aside, dropped swords or cloaks simply strewn here and there among the random scatters of stones.

"*Could* they have..." Thrunn trailed off, as if unable to bring himself to utter the words.

"Vanished?" Egil suggested.

"Pff, vanished," muttered Inglar, then subsided as he caught Valhild's look.

"They *were* here," Thrunn said, in a slow but solid sort of reason. "Now they aren't. So, they must have gone somewhere."

"Then, Freya's tits, *where*?" Anbjorn flung up his arms in frustration.

They dismounted, one by one, warily. Hreyth last of all swung down from her steed. This was not what she had expected to find, no monster's slaughter-yard, no grave-barrows or rock-hewn giant's halls. Some other mischief seemed at work here, a subtler magic, *seidr* or sorcery.

"Someone lost a boot," Osig said.

Anbjorn held up a helm, undented, undamaged. "This is Udr's. He had it from his father. He wouldn't have left it, not while he lived."

Atli stooped to a twinkle in the grass and came up with a jeweled brooch in his hand. "And who, winning such a battle, would walk away without taking plunder?"

"This was no battle," Egil said. "There's no blood. Not a drop to be seen."

"The king sent skilled warriors," Inglar said. "Are we to believe none of them so much as wounded a foe?"

"Or fought foes that did not bleed," Anbjorn said.

Osig eyed him dubiously. "Every living thing bleeds. Man, beast, or monster."

"And men plunder," said Atli.

"Living *or* dead, men plunder," Egil agreed. "And beasts devour, and monsters do both."

"But, whatever did this, did neither." Valhild frowned, shaking her head. "I don't like it."

Hreyth unfastened her cloak as the others continued their search. She spread the heavy grey-wool cloth on the ground and laid the wolf pelt upon it.

"It's as if they *did* vanish, plucked from their very saddles as they rode." Anbjorn turned his friend's helm over and over in his hands.

"And from their very boots?" Thrunn glanced uneasily around.

"While leaving the horses untouched?" Inglar added. He had not joined in the searching, but stayed near Hreyth, watching her.

For those questions, none of them could offer answer.

Onto the silver lushness of the wolf's fur, Hreyth cast a fistful of rune-marked bones from the bag at her belt. They landed with rattling clicks, some atop others, runes showing blood-red, soot-black, and gold. She studied them, the patterns of them, the arrangement they'd made, their meanings and messages.

Earth-Smoke-Man-Stone-Breath-Change-Theft-Danger.

She rose slowly, gaze sweeping over their surroundings. The peaceful river valley, green with new grass... its sloped sides curving up toward rugged, rocky peaks... the spring-blue sky overhead now gone pearly-pale... skeins of mist lingering in dark fissures and clefts, wafting in curls around the bases of the many tall and scattered standing stones...

The stones.

The standing stones, akin to those erected by the Old People of half-forgotten days, but these not towering huge and set in henges with altar-slabs and crosspiece lintels.

These, of smoother texture and lighter hue than the rocky peaks above or crag-ridges and dark boulders jutting from the earth; these were each at the most not much taller than a man, and of a random, straggling-line order... but for the cluster, almost a ring, near to where Anbjorn had found his war-brother's helm...

The stones.

An apprehensive silence had fallen, creeping with the same soft, insidious stealth as the fog seeping from the shadows. When she spoke – "The *stones!*" – her words came louder than intended, a sharp cutting of that silence. Everyone started, some gasped, and several hands went to hilts.

"By Odin, woman!" Inglar thumped a fist against his chest, as if to correct his heart in its cadence. "Are you trying to shock us to death?"

She turned her gaze upon him, and judging by the way he blanched, whatever Olla's man saw in her mismatched eyes made him regret his choice of words.

"*Stanvaettir,*" she said.

"What?" he asked, scowling at her.

Egil's own eyes widened beneath his scar-creased brow. "Creatures of the deep earth."

"Breath-stealers," Hreyth said. "They draw out the life of men, transform them, and leave only stones in their place."

Another silence fell, this one filled with dread and understanding. Even Inglar, hand still held over his heart, showed a reluctant, dawning comprehension.

"Are you telling us," Anbjorn began at last, his voice low but shaking, "that these... these stones all around us... are... my earl, my war-brothers, my friends?"

Before she could reply, a whirring rain of arrows smote into their midst.

One struck Thrunn in the shoulder, piercing through his mail-coat. He shouted with mingled pain and surprise. Another nailed Inglar's wrist to his torso; he fell back, uttering a strangled cry. A third grazed Valhild's leg, slicing the leather and the skin beneath.

"Shields!" the big woman bellowed.

Egil raised his, stepping in front of Hreyth as another volley flew. Arrows thunked into heavy limewood or buried their iron heads in the grass.

Atli and Anbjorn raised their shields as well, overlapping their rounded edges, forming a line to either side of Valhild and Egil. Thrunn, swearing ferociously, ripped the arrow from his shoulder and joined them. Blood gushed from his wound, coursing over and dulling the shine of his mail and his bright silver arm-ring.

Blades sang from their scabbards. The nearest horses, no longer placid, whinnied and ran, stirring whorls and eddies in the low, rising ground-mist.

"Inglar?" called Valhild.

"Down but living," Osig said, crouching beside the wounded man, then seizing his other wrist as he reached for the protruding arrow-shaft. "Don't pull it! You'll just die all the sooner."

Inglar coughed. Red bubbles burst on his lips. He fumbled at an awkward angle with his left hand for a spear, unwilling to face death without a weapon in his grasp.

"Gunnleif's yellow-dog bastards!" Atli peered through a gap in their small shield-wall. "Behind the ridge by that broken boulder... fifteen, maybe twenty."

"Outnumbered *and* they have archers," said Valhild. "The gods must have thought we needed more of a challenge." She eyed Thrunn's blood-soaked mail. "How's your arm?"

He grimaced. "Still attached, and it's only my left." In his right hand he held a short-handled ax with a wide, sharp double-blade.

"They'll be coming for us," she said, after another flurry of arrows struck their shields.

"Let them come."

"Then why aren't they?" asked Anbjorn. "They've stopped shooting."

"No sense wasting arrows on limewood," Osig said.

"Come on, you ass-sniffing curs!" Atli shouted at their foes. "Fatherless bitch-whelps! Come and fight! Come and die!"

"They're afraid," Egil said.

"They should be," said Thrunn.

"Not of us."

"They *should* be!" he repeated.

"They suspect something," Hreyth said. "They know something is wrong here."

From behind the ridge came a man's voice. "Drop your swords and surrender!"

"Fuck your sister!" Atli retorted.

"We want to talk!"

"*We* want to fight!"

Anbjorn nudged Atli with an elbow. "They might know what happened."

"They might shit amber, too, but I wouldn't bet on it."

"Enough," Valhild told them. She lowered her shield enough to poke her helmed head up over it. "Talk, then!"

"We're looking for some missing men."

"As are we, but there's no one, only horses."

"Do you take Ulfvir Sneasson for a fool? We know Earl Kjarstan was coming this way."

"We've not found him, either."

A pause followed, no doubt marked by hasty conference behind the ridge. Then the man – Ulfvir – spoke again. "But *we* have found *you*."

More bowstrings twanged, more arrows flew. So did a hurled spear, which struck, shaft quivering, in Valhild's shield.

"So," said Atli as they hunched behind their limewood wall. "We talked."

"You didn't tell them about the stones," Hreyth said.

"You didn't finish telling *us* about the stones," Anbjorn said. "*What* about the stones?"

"Forget the god-fucked *stones*!" Valhild ducked a second spear then hefted her great sword, its long blade sheened silver in the fog-dimmed sunlight. "Stand ready!"

Gunnleif's men charged with their yellow-and-black shields held high, weapons drawn, uttering full-throated war-cries. As they came, Egil and Atli stepped forward and met the first two with a tremendous crack of wood and iron.

Then the battle was upon them.

Thrunn reared back and flung his ax; it spun whickering through the air and caught a brown-haired man squarely between the collarbones. Valhild's sword swept in a deadly arc. Her foe shield-turned the blow, leaving his body exposed, and Anbjorn sank his blade deep into the man's belly.

Ulfvir, the leader of the enemy, the one who'd said he wanted to talk, wore the shaggy yellow-brown pelt of a dire-hound for a cape. Its forepaws were knotted at his neck and its head, still with skull and jawbone and muzzle of snarling teeth, jounced on his shoulder as if snapping to bite. He, like Thrunn, carried an ax. Unlike Thrunn, he did not throw it, but brought it down in a furious slash that cleaved Atli's shield into kindling – and Atli's arm at the elbow.

Atli screamed even as he thrust his sword at the dog-pelted man's face, but missed, and stumbled to a knee with his stump gouting crimson and the fingers on the severed portion twitching and clenching convulsively in the grass. Ulfvir again lifted his ax, meaning to take Atli's head, but Egil bashed his shield's boss into the man's chest, making him stagger.

A younger man, lean and lithe and quick, darted around his companions, perhaps thinking to get past Valhild and Anbjorn, and strike from behind. But Valhild, for all her size, was almost as quick as him. She side-kicked, shattering his kneecap, tripping him. He went sprawling near Hreyth, who gripped her *seax* two-handed and seated it hilt-deep in the small of his back, the blade's edge grating against his spine.

"You were right," Valhild said with a grin. "It does get the job done."

"We haven't time for this," Hreyth told her. "We'll disturb the *stanvaettir*, and end up stones ourselves!"

"You're the rune-witch!" Whirling, Valhild swung in another great slicing arc, shearing mail and leather like thin cloth, opening a foe's torso from shoulder to hip so that his entrails bulged obscenely from the gore-purple cut. "Think of something!"

The chaos and clangor filled the world. Sounds rang, echoing strangely in the gathering mist. War-cries and death-cries trembled the air. Osig fell with his thigh slashed to the bone, the blood a torrent. Anbjorn dodged a sword-thrust then went reeling from a helm-cracking blow to the head.

Think of something. She was the rune-witch; she must think of something.

Inglar had somehow gotten to his feet, despite his right arm still arrow-pinned to his body. He'd shed his shield and picked up a spear in his left hand, and now ran at their enemies, shrieking like a *berserk* out of legend. He ran at Ulfvir, the dog-pelted leader, who'd retreated already from Egil's relentless defense of the stricken Atli; Ulfvir scrambled back further, his courage deserting him in the face of Inglar's ferocity.

Another of Gunnleif's men moved to meet Inglar's charge. The spear-point rammed through yellow-and-black painted wood, splintering both shield and shaft with loud cracks, fouling them entangled and useless. Still like a *berserk*, Inglar ignored the man's desperate sword-strokes. With another enraged shriek, he flung himself full on his foe. As they crashed together to the ground, Inglar tore free his arrow-pinned arm from his chest – the dark jet of heart's-blood leaped in a fountain – and buried the arrowhead in the other man's throat.

The mist roiled, the mist churned.

Hreyth ducked the wild swing of a black-bearded man's blade. She heard Egil shouting, and Valhild's war-cry as the big woman's great sword claimed another quick kill. Hreyth heard screams and insults, and Ulfvir demanding their deaths. She saw bodies writhing in pain amid motionless corpses.

She saw the mist, a thick fog now, not rolling in from the sea or river but issuing like cold smoke creeping and seething across the earth. Wisps flowed down from fissures in the rugged rock-ridges, and a billowing undulation from the broken boulder's wide rough-edged cleft.

Stanvaettir, she had thought, but she had been wrong.

A black-bearded man swung again, hilt-first for her temple as if meaning to stun her senseless. Hreyth caught the blow with her left forearm – she felt the snap reverberate all the way to her toes – and Rook-Talon's sharp, sturdy blade stabbed up through the man's beard and chin-underside, scraping teeth, cleaving tongue, to impale his brain through the roof of his mouth.

He collapsed in a violent, blood-vomiting gurgle. Hreyth wrenched Rook-Talon loose, the *seax* dripping. She tried to raise her left hand to swipe the scarlet mess from her face but it would not obey her. She blinked, shaking her head frantically, clearing her eyes.

With one, that of blue, she saw only what anyone would – the fog, wafting thick to surround them.

With the other, that of gold, she saw more.

Things *moved* in the mist, shapes and forms, lines and symbols, dancing like *wyrm*-work embroidery, a glow of strange colors pulsating the way embers waxed and waned through a coating of ash.

Not *stanvaettir*, no.

Something else. Something bigger, something more.

And it was coming, coming for them. Caring nothing for which lord, king, or earl they might serve.

The others, friend and foe alike, did not notice. Their sole concern was the battle, fiercely fought and costly on both sides.

Think of something, rune-witch, think of something!

Rune-witch.

She spun. There, undisturbed amid the combat and carnage, was her grey cloak, laid out on the ground with the wolf-pelt spread upon it. No one had trampled or trodden upon it. The rune-marked bones seemed faintly to flicker with their own inner light. The air above and around them was clear. Even as she watched, tendrils of eddying mist wafted near to the bones then curled away.

"Gather!" Valhild bellowed, standing over Anbjorn – whether he was dead or merely unconscious, Hreyth couldn't say. "Gather, fall back, and shields!"

Those who could, did. Egil all but carried Atli, who had bled to a whey-water pallor from his severed arm. Thrunn came limping, fending off two warriors, many small wounds making him resemble a hound-harried boar near the end of the hunt.

For Osig and Inglar, there was no question; they had gone to the mead-benches of Odin's golden hall. Gone, but with glory, and far from alone. If Ulfvir had led twenty, he'd lost more than half. But he, and his remaining men, looked largely unhurt, and still outnumbered the paltry defense of Valhild, Egil, and Thrunn's three-shield wall.

Hreyth could have picked up Anbjorn's shield and joined them, for what little good it might have done. Instead, she ran for her cloak through the thickening mist. It swirled about her legs, made her mail-coat glisten silver, and cooled – chilled! – her flesh.

"I'll take your heads back to Gunnleif in a bag," snarled Ulfvir. "We'll set them in a row and piss on them in turn."

"You'll have to come get them," Valhild replied.

"With pleasure," he said. Yet he and his men hung back, hesitant to again throw themselves against the formidable strength of Valhild's and Egil's swords.

"Hreyth?" Egil spoke with low urgency.

"I'm here."

For a terrible moment, she felt the fog congeal dense and heavy against her skin, weighing on her limbs like damp wool, and she thought she was too late. But another step brought her into the clearness. She bent and seized the edges of the wolf-pelt, scooping its contents into a bundle as best she could with one hand.

"What's happened to the sun?" someone asked, one of Gunnleif's men, anxious.

"Never mind the sun," Ulfvir told him. "Kill them, or I'll bring *your* heads back to Gunnleif!" He raised his sword, and howled. "*Kill them!*"

As they howled in return, emboldening their spirits to renew battle, Hreyth ran back to the close cluster of her companions. She let go an edge of the wolf-pelt, casting the rune-marked bones in an arc at their feet and hoping it would be enough.

Then Egil swept her behind him, and their small shield-wall braced for the overwhelming charge.

* * *

The overwhelming charge did not come. It ended in a dark whorl of mist, a chill breeze, a shiver, and a sudden hush.

Hreyth, who had closed her eyes in wincing anticipation, opened them. Valhild cautiously lowered her shield. The others did likewise.

At their feet lay the rune-marked bones. Around them, already, the mist was lifting, dispersing, giving way again to mild spring sun and clear blue sky.

In front of them, mere paces from their line, several tall grey shapes jutted from the earth at canted, slanted angles. By some, shields painted half yellow and half black had fallen. By some, swords and spears.

Crumpled at the base of the nearest was a dire-hound's shaggy pelt, knotted at the forepaws.

No one spoke. Their throats worked as they swallowed, their mouths faltered at forming words, but no one spoke.

The dead, those slain in the battle, were as they had been. Unaffected. So too were the horses, nosing in the grass. Atli barely clung to life, and Anbjorn was little better.

Of Ulfvir, and his men...

Only stones left in their place.

Valhild found her voice first, looking at Hreyth. "Your runes protected us?"

"I hoped they might."

A nod, and the firm squeeze of Valhild's big hand on Hreyth's mail-clad shoulder, conveyed her thanks. Then she stepped toward the group of stones, though made no move yet to touch.

"Wh-what happened to them?" stammered Thrunn.

"The *stanvaettir* stole their breath," Egil said.

"Not just *stanvaettir*," Hreyth said. "Another power."

"And it did this?" Valhild indicated the valley. "All this?"

"With each theft, growing stronger. Growing hungrier, more ravenous."

"How do we kill it?"

"Kill it?" Thrunn gaped. "How?"

"That's what I'm asking," she told him. "Can it be killed?"

"I don't know," Hreyth said. "Perhaps."

"If not?"

"If not," said Egil, "this valley won't contain it long."

Hreyth thought of farm-steads and villages... of Jorfyn's war-camp and Gunnleif's forces at the town – two armies, and more men arriving every day in answer to the summons of their earls.

"It emerged from those fissures in the rock, and that broken boulder's cleft," she said. "There must be something under us, underneath the ground. A cavern, pit, or tunnel."

"A lair," said Valhild with a grim smile.

"My runes stopped it once. If I can find where it came from, I might be able to block its way and trap it in the earth."

The grim smile widened. "Well then, what are we waiting for? It's gorged itself and gone to rest; let's finish this before it wakes again."

Egil shook his head. "We cannot all go. We have injured men."

"And the king must be warned," Hreyth said. "Gunnleif, too, for that matter; they'll have greater worries if this evil descends."

"You heard them," Valhild said to Thrunn. "Get horses. Take our wounded, and the bodies of our dead, and ride for Langenvik."

• •

Egil bound Hreyth's arm with two sticks, and strips cut from her cloak. "You're hurt," he said, tying more of the grey cloth into a sling. "Are you certain?"

The pain *was* considerable. It gnawed the way the wicked squirrel Ratatoskr gnawed the bark of Yggdrasil as he ran up and down its great ash trunk, but she could not let it dissuade her.

"I work the runes. It must be done."

Valhild approached, settling her helm securely in place. "Thrunn's off," she said. "Gods willing, Anbjorn and Atli survive the journey, and the tale be believed when they get there."

"Gods willing, we survive our journey as well." Egil donned his own helm and helped Hreyth to her feet.

"What a tale we'll have to tell if we do!" Valhild clapped him on the back. "Over mead-bowls in the king's feasting-hall! Hailed as heroes, shining with silver and gift-given gold, our names long remembered in saga and song."

"And if we don't survive?" asked Hreyth, clutching her bag of rune-marked bones in her sling-bound hand.

The big woman laughed. "Then I trust you'll put forth a good word to the All-Wise All-Father for us, so that even if we do not fall in battle, we'll still tell our tale over mead-bowls in *his* feasting-hall!"

They'd left their three horses loosely tethered with some that had belonged to Ulfvir and his men, and proceeded to the rocky ridge from behind which the first hail of arrows had come… and from fissures in which Hreyth had noticed the curling, coiling, issuing mists. The broken boulder reared there, cracked nearly in half to reveal a narrow crevice running throat-like into the earth.

Its wound looked recent, perhaps frost-made over the past winter, perhaps sundered by tremor-quakes as Ymir stirred in his giant-god sleep. Scree and shards gritted underfoot at each step, stone chips and flecks sifting loose as they passed.

"I go first," Egil said in a tone brooking no argument.

Hreyth followed him, and Valhild brought up the rear. The way was narrow indeed and grew narrower still, until Valhild could not even have drawn her great blade. Her shoulders and Egil's scraped the rough passage walls. The air was cool, heavy with moisture. Thin shafts through the rock let in weak threads of sunlight; otherwise, they went in a deepening darkness.

Until Hreyth, with one of her mismatched eyes, again glimpsed the waxing and waning strange glow, etching lines not unlike runes themselves in the misty shadows opening ahead.

Here was a roundish cave-chamber of tapering formations, joined columns, and shallow ridge-lipped pools where drips plinked and rippled. At the heart of it brimmed a well – a well rich with power, *seidr*-magic.

This, yes, this was the source of it. This cousin to Mimir's Well, where Odin had made sacrifice in exchange for knowledge. This well, which drank rather than quenched, which took rather than gave, which stole and consumed rather than bestowed.

Across its glass-black surface, images seemed to whirl and flow… images, visages, spirit-faces; bodies drifting, floating weightless as if in liquid, trailing hands and limbs and hair…

"Do you see them?" she whispered.

"I see only water," said Egil.

"As do I," Valhild agreed, adding, "What do *you* see?"

"Later. I'll begin setting the runes. Be ready."

"For what?" Valhild asked, eyebrows lifting.

"I wish I knew. But, if anything comes up from the well, hold your breath."

Their expressions suggested they found this scant comfort, and Hreyth felt the same. Held breath against a power such as this? A power that had drawn life from so many men, leaving only stones in their place? Dotting the river-valley with them, silent standing warnings of an incomprehensible danger; and she had come, a young rune-caster of uncertain parentage, armed with little more than her witch-queen mother's lore…

But she *had* come, and as she'd told Egil, it must be done.

She reached into her bag of rune-marked bones – old and worn smooth, ivoried, rolling and clicking beneath her fingers. One by one, she brought them out and set them in a ring around the well's rim.

The spirit-fraught glassy surface heaved in a sudden, terrible bulge as her circle neared completion. Hreyth sprang back, gasping. Her heel caught on the lip of a shallow pool. The last rune-bone clattered to the cavern floor.

Mist plumed from the well, wreathed her hand, gloved it, wrapped her arm, and pulled. It was insubstantial yet solid, mist made iron, iron made mist. It had her to the elbow, to the shoulder, to the throat.

From somewhere sounding far away, she heard Egil call her name, and Valhild shout a battle-cry.

The gasp she'd taken, she held. Struggling to do so, locking jaw and mouth, lungs already throbbing with a burning ache. The mist engulfed her head and chest.

She felt a tug at her belt – Egil, anchoring her with one hand as he groped along the floor for the fallen rune-bone. His boots slid as he, too, was inexorably pulled toward the hungry well.

Then came a violent, striking crash – metal on stone, steel on stone, the steel of Valhild's great sword-blade, hewing and hacking at the cave ceiling's formations. Sparks flew. Again and again, the strong steel struck, until stone cracked and shattered. Huge fanglike chunks of rock, some broken off in pieces and some at the root, smashed down.

The solid mist released abruptly. Egil and Hreyth pitched backward. As his free arm flailed, she saw the rune-bone in his fist and grabbed for it.

A heap of rubble filled the well, mounded there like some crude and makeshift cairn. Valhild stood astride the pile with her sword-hilt in both hands and the blade poised for a downward thrust.

Around the well's rim, the rest of the rune-ring was – by god-miracle, praise Odin! – undisturbed. Hreyth slid the last bone into place. The rune upon it flashed an almost blinding gleam that raced around the circle in a line like fire.

The chamber's air changed with an odd, pressuring pop. The cave walls shook; more rock-chunks fell from the ceiling and water sloshed over the lips of the pools. There was, for a moment, the sense of a vast, gusty sigh, an exhalation from the very lungs of the world.

The sense of *seidr*-magic dwindled to a fading echo, then was gone.

Hreyth released her long-held aching breath. Her gaze found Valhild's in the gloom, then the familiar crags and outcrops of Egil's scarred features beside her.

They had done it. They had lived. They had won.

Tales over mead-bowls, feasting-halls, hailed as heroes, shining with silver and gift-given gold, names long remembered in saga and song.

Through the half-collapsed passage, they picked their bruised and battered way back to surface and sunlight. The high river-valley spread green and peaceful before them, horses grazing in the new spring grass.

But, although the spell had been broken, it had not been unmade… and where so many brave men had once been, still remained only stones.

THAT OLD BLACK MAGIC

James A. Moore

We didn't find him. He found us.

We'd just loaded up on supplies, as much as we could at any rate, and we were headed out into the field. Somewhere along the way, the new guy was just there.

He was a slick sleeve. Not a bit of rank to him, but no one in their right mind would have looked at him and called him green. He was too old, for one. I was twenty when we met. I have to say he was ten to fifteen years older than me. New soldiers, those fresh from basic, they don't look that way and they don't move that way. He wore the same combat boots as everyone else, but he almost never made a noise when he walked, and I never heard a single sound that startled Jonathan Crowley.

Sergeant Marks took one look at him and scowled. "How long have you been here?" He looked at the man's uniform and spotted the nametag exactly where it belonged. "Crowley! You listening to me?"

The man looked at him and nodded. "I'm not deaf the last time I checked."

That was about all it took for the sarge to grab him by the arm and haul him out of the ranks. Being of sound mind and wanting to keep our bodies as close to that state as possible, we ignored the action and kept walking. Smart people don't piss off their sergeants.

Twenty minutes later Crowley and Marks got back into the ranks. Not a word was said, but from that moment on, Crowley was one of us. He did his job, he took care of his equipment, and he kept to himself. I have never much trusted a quiet man. It seems to me that a man who keeps to himself is either full of too many dark thoughts or too many secrets, and I'm not so sure there's much of a difference.

I think with Crowley it was dark thoughts.

Normandy was done.

We'd stormed the beach and done our best and paid a price that no one dared think about. It's been decades and I can tell you with complete sincerity that when I close my eyes and the weather feels too much like France did, I can count on nightmares to come into my sleep and hunt for my soul. They are hungry dreams, too, and they sniff in every dark corner of my mind and under every hidden memory while they seek their prize.

What part of France were we in? Who knew any longer? I didn't. How long had the war gone on? Too long.

I missed my home. I missed my family. I missed Jenny, even though she'd already sent me a letter that sounded a lot like she was looking to move on. I was young, but maybe not completely stupid. I knew what was written between the lines even though I was trying hard not to see those ugly, unwritten words.

According to the captain, we were in France and not far from Luxembourg. You couldn't have proven it. All I saw was hills and trees and from time to time a field that had maybe once been planted with something to seed and was now growing a variety of muds. Frozen muds, mostly, as the weather had gone cold and we woke in the morning with frost on the ground and spent the days trying to stay warm.

Infantry. Love that word. It says so much if you've been a foot soldier. We were well armed. We had a little food left. We were getting colder every day as autumn snuck in and changed the remaining greens to differing shades of orange and yellow and blood red. I kept hearing that we had the Germans on the ropes, but all I saw was more of the same, and every time we turned around we were ducking back into the woods because this was not our territory, much as we were planning to take it back.

It was just past the point when we should have been walking any longer. It was dark, pure and simple. The only lights were coming from a building that was too far away to identify. We went for it anyway, because there comes a point where any shelter would be better than none and there was a chance that they would be friendly. Yes, we had tents. Not a one of us said a damned thing about trying to pitch them.

Lester was walking next to me. Desmond Lester was a good egg, kept his calm and did what he had to in order to get through the day. He didn't smile much, he didn't talk much, but he was also reliable. If something needed doing he did it. Four times in the months we'd known each other he had taken the lives of other people. Some of the guys cried when they killed, some of them grinned and made marks on the butt of their rifle or bragged. Lester just did what he had to do and plodded on, his lean face drawn and tired but his eyes alert.

He was the one that stopped me moving and pointed them out.

Them.

The ghost dogs and their ghost master.

Since then I've heard they're called the Wild Hunt, or Wotan's Hunt, or *la Chasse d'Artu*, depending on where you are. I guess that last one was the best because it was the French countryside. Whatever name you want to call them, they were terrifying.

So what's so scary about a bunch of dogs? I had a friend of mine ask me that when I was a few beers too many into my night and my tongue was looser than usual.

I looked at him for a long time before I could answer. It's hard to find the words.

The dogs themselves were the sort most sane people would be wary around. They were big animals, lean and hard and hungry. You could almost feel how hungry they were. They were hunting for fresh kill, and they intended to have it. I have seen men look at women that way and known they were trouble. I have seen addicts looking for their next fix with that same sort of starving desperation. Now and then, in moments of weakness, I still look at a shot of whiskey that way. I haven't had a drink since, well, since I got drunk enough to swing at my wife if I'm being honest. I can never forgive myself for being that angry and that weak. But I also knew a big part of both those feelings came from the bottle and I made myself stop. Jenny forgave me. I know that. I have never forgiven myself. Every time I've ever had that thirst for the bottle I remember the fear in her eyes when I cocked back my fist, and the rest is easy.

But I was talking about the dogs. They had that sort of hunger and there was nothing like mercy in the snarls drawn across their muzzles. I couldn't say what sort of dogs they were. They were black and they were shaggy and they leaped and heaved their way through the air and above the trees.

And behind them came their master, riding on a massive beast of a horse. I was raised around horses. I know them well enough and I've ridden them all my life. Never in the whole of my existence have I seen the like of that steed. It was as black as the night and carried the man on its back with ease. The hooves of the thing ran across the sky, but each time they struck where ground should have been, I swear I saw a tiny flash of lightning and I heard a ghostly rumble of thunder. The breaths that snorted from that stallion's muzzle were storm clouds waiting to be born, and the winds that moved in the animal's wake were sure to let those seeds grow. I could feel the menace that came from the thing and knew that the passing of its form would lead to disaster.

The rider himself was worse. He crouched low over the neck of his mount, his face thrust forward as if he, like his hounds, scented the air for fresh trails to hunt. One hand held to the mane of his horse, the other held a great hunting bow that rattled against his side with each stride of the charger beneath him.

How long did I stare? I couldn't say. It felt like hours. I'm guessing about six seconds in reality. Sometimes it feels like that after the fact. When you're in it, everything happens so quickly, too quickly to think if you want to survive. When it's done, you can look at what happened and you can examine it a thousand times and your mind makes it bigger I think. Except with the Wild Hunt. I don't think my mind could ever make that bigger than it was. When the hunt had run past, both me and Lester stared after it and then stared at each other with wide, wet eyes.

Not a word was spoken. We agreed not to talk to anyone else about it, but I can say this, we were more alert after the passing of that spectral huntsman.

Looking back, I think that night was the first time I ever saw Crowley smile. Crowley was a plain man. That's the only way I can put it. He was as average as any one I have ever seen in my life. If you put him in a crowd of a hundred people, he'd fade from view. I believe that, because mostly I can't remember much about him. Brown hair, brown eyes, lean build and average height. There was nothing at all about him that stood out.

Except when he smiled. I can barely remember his face, I already said that, but, oh, my, I can remember that smile. His mouth didn't grin. His lips peeled back into a feral wolf's snarl that tried to hide inside a smile. His smile was bright and sunny and promised a hundred painful ways to die. I was still reeling from the vision of a hunting pack running across the sky, but I remember his smile standing out even then. I can look back and remember the bloodied shores of Normandy beach and the bodies that floated in the water as we tried to make our way first to shore and then, somehow, to safety, and I am chilled. I can remember the night I saw the Wild Hunt and I am humbled. I remember Crowley's smile and I shiver. I guess that's all I can say about that.

I almost asked him if he had seen the hunt too, but I didn't. In the end that damned smile of his scared me too much.

There wasn't much to say after that. We just walked on, moving as quietly as a dozen men can when walking down the road in the darkness of the night.

The lights turned out to be an inn at the edge of a crossroads. I'd like to say we came upon a quiet scene but that would have been a lie.

We came upon a scene of violence.

Seems to me that one of the biggest problem with that war was the bullies. I don't care what country they came from there were some folks just seemed to need to show how much in control they were, how much they could do and what they could get away with. Me? I was raised to believe we were supposed to help people, not hurt them.

There was a gathering of people standing around the small inn at the crossroads where we'd seen lights. It was a small place, the sort that I guess has been around for just about forever. The road wasn't much and the fields were ruined, but once upon a time there must have been crops and I reckon the inn had been new. I couldn't tell you the name. I never did learn French when I was over there. Hell, according to most of my teachers I never even really learned English, but I suppose I caught enough of that one to get by.

In any case, the inn was lit up by lanterns and there was a small gathering of people outside it, looking at what had been done. They shivered and I think it was more than the cold that chilled them.

There were four bodies. They were situated together, their heads close enough that, if they'd been alive, they could have whispered to each other. Each pointed in a different direction on the compass, and each was naked. Someone had taken the time to carve their bodies with hundreds of runes. By the blood on the ground it had happened there and I'm guessing they were alive when it happened.

All of us looked. Most of us stared and more than a couple of the guys crossed themselves. What was done to them was blasphemous.

Crowley shook his head and said, "Flayed. They were still alive when it happened." At odd intervals along their corpses strips of flesh had been peeled back, twisted over themselves several times, and then stuck back into the flesh of the people they'd been peeled from. I was grateful for the darkness. We couldn't see the worst of the damage for the shadows.

Crowley turned to one of the locals and started firing off questions in French. Not a one of us knew he spoke the language, because, of course, he never volunteered that knowledge.

We all listened in, though I suspect most of them were as ignorant as me as to what was said.

Crowley's face was an open book. He was angry. He was disgusted.

When he'd finished his interrogation he looked directly at the captain and shook his head. "Nazis. They came here yesterday morning and took over the inn. When the sun rose this morning they started working on the people here. The Innkeeper, his wife, his son and a girl who nobody here seems to know." He gestured to the smallest of the corpses. I guess she was maybe eight or nine years of age. His voice was harsh, his expression was worse.

"Why would they do anything like this?" The captain was as shocked as the rest of us. He stared at the bodies as he spoke and his eyes seemed incapable of drinking in the details. He looked, but I don't think he saw much of anything. I was in the same boat. It was easier to look at Crowley than to deal with what we were seeing.

Crowley didn't much seem bothered. He squatted close to the bodies and started looking them over carefully. It only took me a few seconds to realize he was reading what was written on their bodies.

"What does it say?"

"It says, 'shut the hell up so I can read this.'"

I listened. I outranked the man, being as I'd made it all the way to corporal, but that didn't matter.

He studied the writings on the first body, even going so far as to lift the legs and arms to see if there was more written that might be hidden in the bloodied mud, when the young girl's corpse sat straight up and looked right at him.

The voice that came from her bloodied mouth never belonged to a child. It was low and deep and loud and spoke words I had never before heard. The sound of them chilled me almost a much as the source.

I backed away, and I know most of the others did too. Several of the villagers got the right idea in my mind and ran for their homes. They had that advantage. My home was over an ocean away.

Crowley spoke back, nearly spitting his answer.

She yelled louder, until he could barely be heard. Her chest did not move. She took in no breaths. Her words came out of a mouth that offered no steam in the cold of the night, when every other person who'd spoke showed their heat with every uttered word.

She came closer to Crowley and he stayed his ground, not looking worried about the approaching shape at all. He stood. I remember that. I also remember wondering why he wasn't screaming and running, because about half the squad broke ranks and started doing just that before the sarge called them back.

The dead girl kept screaming, obscene noises that hurt me to hear and that made my stomach lurch. I don't know what she said. I don't know that I ever heard a language that could make a person sick, but she was doing it.

Crowley started speaking in low tones, exactly soft enough that I couldn't make out any words clearly, and with each word he spoke the dead girl staggered backward as if struck. She stopped speaking and turned to screaming instead, holding her arms in front of her face as if to ward off savage blows, and perhaps she was, because the flesh on her arms rippled, peeling away from her bones, blistering and then burning into dust and ashes though there was no heat. The rest of her body soon followed suit, and in a space of ten seconds, her remains were gone, drifting away on a harsh wind that affected nothing else.

When she had vanished into nothingness, Crowley rose from his squat and shook his head. And he was smiling. His eyes looked almost feverish and his smile was broad enough that I feared it might actually split the skin of his lips.

A moment later he sobered and shook his head.

"I'm not sure what the Nazis summoned, but whatever it is, it doesn't want to be found."

He was speaking to the captain.

The captain did not answer. He stared at the spot where the little girl's body had been standing on lifeless feet, and trembled.

I understood exactly how he felt.

Per the captain's orders, we left the area, walking for another mile or more before he decided we were far enough away to safely make camp.

We left the bodies where we found them.

When we started walking. Crowley stayed behind for a while. No one questioned his decision. I don't think anyone dared.

。

The deaths haunted us. We were in a war zone. We had all of us been shot at and either wounded or killed other people. I was twenty or so, as I recall it, but just like most of the guys with me, I didn't really act it. We were too busy worrying about whether or not we would live to see home to goof around. Most of the time we had to scout out towns before we could consider entering them, because as much as we might have wanted to claim we were winning the war it didn't feel that way. There were Germans everywhere and they seemed to be in control of nearly every town we encountered.

Through all of that, the deaths haunted us. They weren't acts of violence in a kill or be killed situation. They were slow, methodical murder.

Everyone was on edge, except, of course, for Crowley.

He seemed more alive than he had been, more vibrant and more vital as if finding those massacred shapes had somehow made his world a little brighter. I won't say he had a spring in his step and he sure as hell wasn't whistling, but he moved differently and seemed lighter on his feet.

And he smiled all the goddamn time. Not always a full smile, not always bright and sunny, but it was like that nasty grin of his was lurking just under the surface and you could feel it there, waiting to pounce.

We managed two days of peace and quiet before things went south.

Early morning on the third day we were walking and we were doing our best to be quiet in the early-morning light of a cloudy day when a rifle shot blew the helmet right off the captain's head and took half his brain with it. I remember looking at his helmet as it bounced across the dirt road and looking at the bullet hole right through the front of it and thinking that it shouldn't have been there, and that there shouldn't have been hair and red sticking to the inside of it either. I didn't really register that he was dead; I just looked at the damned helmet and tried to understand what had gone wrong.

I would have died right then, but Crowley was there and he hauled me backward and threw me into a ditch right around the time something blew a crater in the spot where I'd been standing.

"Pay attention!" He roared the words at me and moved, crouching low and grinning as he moved across the road and looked toward the woods about fifty yards away.

They were there. You couldn't see them, but the flash from their muzzles let us know they were trying to kill us.

A bullet took Lorenzo in his chest and blew out his back. That was bad because Lorenzo was a good guy. It was worse because that same bullet also took out the radio pack Lorenzo was wearing. Just that fast we were cut off from any possible assistance.

Fifty yards away, and I swear to you that Crowley was looking at them. His eyes scanned the woods too intently. He took his time as the ground let off puffs of dirt where bullets came too close and as the rest of us tried to find a good position to shoot from while keeping ourselves intact.

I had trouble looking away from Crowley. I yelled at him to get to cover, same as he had yelled at me, but he either didn't hear or didn't care. Instead he stayed where he was until he spotted whatever it was he was looking for and then he ran straight for the woods.

I thought it strange the sarge didn't yell until I saw the man slumped in the road, both hands on his stomach and a dark stain marking his jacket and shirt alike.

Januski moved to help the sergeant. I looked back to Crowley.

I saw a bullet pound into his jacket along the shoulder. I don't think it hit him, I didn't think it then, either, but it blew the epaulette off the jacket as he charged, his long legs cutting the distance quickly.

He took the time to fire at the enemy. I give him that and nothing more. He did not duck. He did not dodge. He seemed utterly unconcerned about whether or not he lived.

All we could do was try to offer him covering fire or watch him die. I chose to offer as much help as I could and every time I saw a muzzle flash I aimed at it.

Crowley ran hard and fast and made the woods as quick as any track star I ever did see.

We couldn't fire when that happened. We might have hit one of our own.

I can only tell you this. There was an explosion over in those woods that was large enough to shake the few remaining leaves from the trees and to split an old oak in that copse in half. After the explosion the gunfire slowed and then stopped.

Except for the sounds coming from Sergeant Marks as Januski tried to patch him up. There was an awful lot of silence. I don't think I can explain how worrisome that is when you're certain people are trying to kill you.

Crowley came out of the woods, hauling two men behind him. One man was struggling and thrashing, the other was either dead or unconscious and was being dragged along by his heel.

After about ten yards Crowley dropped the one who wasn't moving just long enough to beat the one trying to get away into a stupor. I could hear the punches from nearly forty yards away.

When the German stopped struggling, Crowley dragged his prisoners along with him.

They weren't regular soldiers. Their uniforms were all black and they were older men, not soldiers but officers.

Not just officers, but SS. Hitler's special elite according to what we'd heard. These were the guys the rest of the Germans were scared of.

Crowley scowled at us as he came back and threw the two men into the road.

The one he'd beaten on was breathing in rough gasps, and his face was swelling.

"Boys, I'm going to need you to keep a look out for a while."

"What happened to the rest of them?" Lewis was a good egg, but not so bright.

Crowley looked at the kid for a long while and then spoke as if dealing with a child who refused to learn. "I killed them."

"All of them?"

"Well, Lewis, I didn't leave them in the woods so they could come after us." A long pause while Lewis looked at him, frowning. Then, in an exasperated voice Crowley said, "Yeah, Lewis. They're all dead." He looked my way. "Is he actually this stupid?"

Lewis shook his head. "Hey. Don't call me names."

"Lewis?"

Lewis was a big man, easily six and a half feet in height and broad as a barn. "Yeah?"

Crowley smiled. Lewis flinched.

"Shut up and let me work here."

Lewis nodded.

Crowley dragged the first of the men in black off to the side and crouched over him, speaking softly in the cold air.

Listen, technically I was supposed to be in charge at that point. I knew that wasn't going to happen. I knew it and I accepted it. I was a grunt. I was there to fight and to take back what the Nazis had stolen, but I preferred not to lead. I didn't want that many lives on my conscience.

Crowley spoke to both of his captives while we listened without any idea what was being said. He spoke to them in German. I didn't understand a single word and if anyone else did they hid it well. I say he spoke. What I mean is he interrogated. That's the only way to put it. He never touched them, but I could see them flinch when he talked, and I could well see the fear in their eyes. The second one actually cried while Crowley questioned him. At the end the man fell back and openly sobbed. I have no idea what Crowley said or did to cause that.

When he was done he pointed to the two men he'd dragged with him and said, "I'm done with them. Do what you want."

He looked right at me as he said it.

"I. What?" It wasn't my best moment.

"Corporal." He pointed to my two chevrons. "You're in charge. Your sergeant is dying, your captain is dead." Those brown eyes looked at me and I nearly cringed. "That means it's on you."

"Well, the sarge is still alive."

Crowley looked at me and spoke slowly, softly. The expression on his face was one of barely repressed anger. "He's dead. He won't make it through the day. There's no one around to help him. I would, but I have other things to take care of."

"What? Where are you going?"

"Leiber and Dunst over there," he jerked a thumb at the Germans, "told me what I needed to know. Now I'm going to go find the man who committed those murders and make him tell me what he summoned."

"Summoned? What are you talking about, Crowley?" I was doing my very best not to panic. I need to clarify this: I did not want command. I wanted to survive and get home and that was all. Two little patches on my sleeve did not make me a good candidate for command.

"I really don't have time for you." He spoke under his breath, but the way he said it, I knew he didn't much care if I could hear him. "Okay. The four people that got killed? They were sacrifices. Their lives in exchange for summoning something to help the Nazis win the war. I want to make sure that doesn't happen. It's what I do. So, I'm going to hunt down the bastard that did the summoning. I'm going to kill him. I'm also going to stop whatever the hell he brought through. I don't know what that is yet, but the Wild Hunt showing up told me there was some bad news coming our way. That's why they showed in the first place. The only time the Wild Hunt appears is to warn people that something truly deadly is drawing near. You just have to know how to listen and what to look for."

"Well, what do you look for?" I wanted to beg him to stay and take command. I needed that. I wasn't ever going to be ready.

That look again, like he was talking to a deeply stupid person who simply would not listen. "You look for corpses laid out in a sacrificial cross. You look for corpses cut and marked and used as a beacon for things that should never be allowed into this world."

I flinched a little, and he took mercy.

"Listen, kid. I need to go take care of the bad things that are coming. You need to take care of your people and try to get help for the sarge." His tone remained patronizing and I felt my teeth lock down on each other. I wasn't annoyed. I was angry.

"Miller!"

The eldest of the privates looked at me. "Yes, Corporal?"

"Get everyone on the road. Try to find help. See what you can do to keep the sarge alive. Tie up those two bastards and haul them with you. Me and Crowley are going to take care of some business with the Nazis."

Miller nodded as did Nunnally and Januski who went back to patching up the sergeant as best he could. He wasn't a medic. We didn't have one any more, but he'd worked on a farm all his life and had taken care of more injuries than anyone else in the squad.

Crowley looked at me. "You think you should be coming with me instead of caring for your squad?"

"I think if you're really doing something like taking care of whoever killed those folks, you might need back up."

"I don't." He didn't sound cocky when he said it.

"You're getting it anyway." In hindsight, that was maybe the dumbest thing I ever said.

Crowley stared at me for what seemed like a long time. Finally he nodded. He also smiled.

"Fine. Try to keep up."

A moment later he was cutting back across the field he'd stormed to get to the Nazis in the first place. He didn't quite run but it was close. I did my best to keep up.

We moved hard and fast and I managed to keep pace, but I'd be lying if I said it was easy. Truth of the matter is, I think Crowley actually slowed to let me keep up with him but I can't prove that. It was just a feeling. I think that maybe he cold have run as fast as a Jeep moves if he wanted to.

That copse of trees was the first obstacle. I saw several dead German soldiers in that cluster of trees. Most of them had expressions or horror on their faces. All of them were broken in ways that made no sense to me. I don't think I had but a few seconds to look at them as we were going past. I know Crowley never gave them a second glance. I also know that image of their bodies has haunted me for decades.

Past the trees were more fields, most of them burnt out and blown apart. Crowley moved through them at a trot and I had no choice but to follow.

We kept that pace until we ran into a small town that had been utterly destroyed by the war. I can't say for sure who destroyed it, but I like to tell myself it was the Nazis and that we could never have done any such thing.

I said it was a small town, but I think that's wrong. There were a lot of buildings, or rather there were remains from a lot of buildings. Mostly there were shattered pieces of walls and foundations and the burnt-out husks of what had likely been homes and churches and a few communal structures.

The only thing that had not been destroyed was a cemetery at the edge of what had been the town. Headstones rose from the ground, a crop of remembrance to those who had passed before.

When we got close, Crowley raised a hand and beckoned for me to slow, to approach with caution. Not a word was spoken then, but I listened anyway.

The ruined town had unsettled me. I had seen combat. But mostly we'd managed to avoid civilized spots and stayed to the countryside. It was safer, you see. The remains had jarred me.

All I could think as I passed through them was that there had been people there once. There had been families and they'd had lives and lived them as best they could and now all of that was gone. Either they were dead or the Germans had taken them. I did not know which, but I suspected the former.

The cemetery was worse. There was a feeling of menace there. The fine hairs on my neck rose as we approached and my skin felt almost feverish. There was something here. Something bad.

I said the cemetery was untouched and that was a lie. When we got closer I saw the truth of the matter. Each headstone had been marked. It wasn't a big thing, but it was there. Someone had cut each marker with a rune. Crowley stopped and studied the first one and then moved on. The same mark on each piece, two jagged s marks, like stylized lightning. I remembered that symbol on the lapels of the of the black-garbed Germans – the symbol of the SS. But a stroke mark cut through each of those symbols.

"What do they mean?" I asked Crowley, fully expecting no answer.

"Either it's a sign that someone doesn't like the Nazis or it's a name. Hard to say."

"A name?"

He sighed. "A name. A sigil representing that name. Or, someone doesn't like the Nazis."

"What kind of name?"

"If I knew that, sweet pea, I'd have told you." I contemplated the fact that he'd just called me 'sweet pea' but decided to let it go. Crowley scared the hell out of me.

Maybe it was my fault. Maybe if I hadn't distracted him, Crowley would have noticed the one mark that was different. It was almost the same but three small dots had been added into the broken SS symbol and Crowley had been looking at me as he passed it.

As soon as he moved past, the symbol glowed, and the air *thrummed;* a single low note vibrated across the whole cemetery and Crowley looked around, frowning.

My sense of unease increased and my stomach turned and lurched. My mouth watered and I thought for certain I would vomit all over my shoes.

I never got the chance. Instead the ground quaked under me and I fell on my ass in the dirt as the headstones bucked and threw themselves to the sides. Something was moving under the ground and it pushed everything above it around with ease.

The earth shrugged and then let out a moan of pain. I was there when my daughters were born, and when my son struggled before dying in the process of being born. I heard the sounds my wife made. They weren't all that dissimilar to the sounds the ground offered up as it split and gave birth to a hellish thing.

I do not know about life after death. I'd certainly thought about it before. When you are swimming in bloodied waters and bullets are hammering the people around you and slashing the waves, the afterlife kind of becomes a thing you consider about as often as you blink.

None of my thoughts on the subject ever came close to what ripped itself from the cemetery. It knitted itself from the remains of the dead, clothed itself in the mud and the roots and the insects that feasted on the lifeless remains of a whole village.

There was a system to it. I remember thinking that even as I watched the demon heave itself from the groaning, whimpering ground. The bones and flesh of the dead tried to make themselves fit into a pattern that made sense, I suppose. The bodies tore themselves apart even as they ripped from the ground. From the smallest toe bone to the femurs, those bones collected in twin columns, rose from the ground like weeds stacking themselves into a misshapen mockery of legs. Mud and roots and blades of torn grass formed the muscles over a structure of bone, leaving much of the collected pillars of muck-crusted remains exposed.

Above that more skeletal remains crowded themselves together and pushed into a colossal form. It was not human, but it aped that form. A golem crafted from bone and filth, a giant with a head built from a cluster of skulls mashed together like grapes crushed in an angry hand.

It did not stand still as it was born. Like a living thing it writhed and squirmed. Like a monstrous, bloated deformed toddler, it staggered on clumsy legs and screamed its outrage to the world.

I screamed, too. Nothing in my life, not the war, not even the spectral forms of the Wild Hunt had ever prepared me for watching that abomination tear itself from the funereal womb.

That lump of a head was not a proper shape, but it hinted at what should have been. The deep cuts and broken earth formed a rudimentary face, hollows where eyes should have been, a bulge in the general shape that mimicked eyebrows. A gash for a mouth. That head turned and looked, the whole of the shape seeming to look toward me and then toward Crowley.

The thick, brutish appendage that closely mimicked an arm and a hand, swept up from the thing's side and crashed into Crowley, swatting him as easily as a grown man might slap aside an infant.

Crowley grunted and rolled through the air, his face battered into a new form, his body very obviously broken.

I did the only thing I could in that situation. I raised my rifle, took aim, and fired at the thing. My aim was good. Bone and muck snapped away from the shape in a small fountain, for all the good it did. I may as well have stabbed at a rock. One leg rose, ripping free from the earth in a cascade of severed plants and crushed headstone.

The shape came at me and opened its mouth; a low noise pumped from that opening, a wet sound that made me remember the bodies that never reached the shore at Normandy Beach.

I fired again with no noticeable effect, but to buy me time to stand. I stepped back, looking around for any possible weapons that might be more useful, when Crowley came at the bone heap.

Crowley's face was bloodied. His clothes and his flesh covered in smears of mud. He should have been dead. I'd seen him hit by the thing and knocked aside as easily as a man struck by a runaway car. I'd seen his leg bent at an impossible angle, flopping as he rose higher into the air and then struck the ground.

There was blood on his face, but there were no wounds. There were shreds ripped from his uniform, likely spots where the bony ridges of a hundred jutting fingers had scraped cloth and then flesh away from the meat underneath. But there were no wounds.

Crowley was intact as he moved between me and the grave thing. Alive and smiling. He was enjoying himself. Madness!

The bone thing moved forward raising both malformed arms over its misshapen head.

"You should run! Now!" I knew Crowley wasn't talking to the beast.

Instead of listening I fired three more rounds into the thing. Bone exploded. Mud blossomed away. If there was pain, if there was injury worth noticing, it gave no sign.

Crowley turned toward me, an angered expression on his face. I could see the anger in his expression. I could tell the anger was because he was worried about whether or not I would live through the fight.

The anger faded and his eyes flew wide.

"Drop!" I didn't question him. I simply listened and flopped to the ground like a sack of rocks.

Just in time to watch the dead thing explode. I saw the streak of smoke. I saw the whole shape stagger a step to the left as something slammed into it. I watched the left side of the body bulge. Expanding outward in a sudden flare of fire.

That almost face took on a shocked look as the center of the beast exploded. Had it been alive the creature would surely have died. Instead it fell forward and caught itself on arms built from a hundred corpses as it bled mud and decay.

The world was still there, but my ears rang with a painful note. Debris covered me and my left arm was screaming at me, burning just below the elbow where the meat of my forearm was thickest. Blue afterimages eclipsed my vision, but I could see well enough to make out the shapes of soldiers coming at me from behind the veil of ghost shadows.

I checked my arm; a fragment of bone cut into the muscle. It was old, weathered and dirty, a part of the beast.

The bone golem tried to rise and Crowley stepped back and hurled a lump in its direction. Grenade. There was no doubt in my mind.

I dropped again as the creature exploded into several thick lumps.

Detritus flew everywhere. Muck and burnt, shattered bones, rocks, roots and squirming insects both intact and torn apart, arced away from the monstrous remains and scattered across the ground and both of us.

I have heard it said that in moments of stress the world slows down and I don't think that's really true, at least not for me. I think we simply take in so many details that in order to understand them we must focus on them so harshly that the world seems like it's slowing. All I can say with any certainly is that the events did not seem slow to me. They were overwhelmingly fast. Only in hindsight could I clearly see what happened.

As the thing convulsed and exploded I saw something in the distance, a red shape. I did not see it clearly, and I did not see it well, but I remain convinced that I saw it, and that what I witnessed was not added later by my imagination. I saw it even as I was raising my arm to cover my face and protect my eyes.

I stared at the ruined thing and breathed hard. I wanted to look away but it was damned difficult. Crowley did not have that problem. He was looking back the way we'd come and he was scowling.

I finally looked that way as the rest of my squad came toward us. They were the reason we were alive. Crowley couldn't have defended us at that time, I think. I know that I was getting nowhere.

Miller looked at me and shrugged. "Radio's fried and Sarge is dead. We followed you."

All I could do was nod. While that was going on Januski looked at the bleeding wound in my arm and pulled out what was left of his medic bag. I don't imagine there was much after all he'd used on the sergeant, but he managed to find some gauze and a white powder that burned like hell while it allegedly disinfected my wound.

Crowley scowled as he looked around, trying to find out where to go next, I guess. He didn't just look. He sniffed the air, examined the ground tasted the soil and finally nodded to himself.

"Good luck fellas." He started gathering his things.

While he did that Nunnally let out a few choice words and backed away from the remains of the cemetery thing.

The dregs were moving, slowly sliding toward each other, bugs and bones and everything else. Nunnally bumped into Crowley as he was backing away and Crowley sneered at the remains.

I don't know what he said. I don't want to know. The words made me feel feverish and I could sense the power that came from them. All I know is that the effects were immediate. The bones in those moldering heaps caught fire. Some of them popped like firecrackers and others blazed hot and then hotter still until the light from them was nearly blinding; like flash paper thrown by a stage magician. And then they were gone, burned away into nothing more than fine ash that drifted up into the air and scattered with the wind.

Without another word Crowley started walking.

I followed him and my squad followed me.

Of all the things that went wrong in that war, that was the worst. My squad followed me. I thought I was doing the right thing following Crowley. I was so very wrong.

* • *

I'll say this for him. Crowley did his best to discourage us without ever saying a word. He had a talent for scowling, tsking, sneering and generally being unhappy with being followed.

I was not to be discouraged. We had no radio. We had no commanders other than me. Frankly, I was looking toward Crowley to get us out of the insanity in one piece. As plans go it wasn't much but it was all I had and I wanted nothing to do with being in charge.

So, yes, it falls on me.

We walked for two days without much of anything unusual aside from Crowley himself, who continued to hunt and stalk whatever it was he was searching for. He did not volunteer information.

Several times he left us behind, but I was good enough at tracking that I found him again, much to his disgust.

On the third day, as he was crouching low to the ground and staring at the way the dirt settled along the side of a narrow road, I asked him, "What are you hunting, Crowley?"

The sun was up, almost directly over our heads, and I remember him looking at me and shielding his eyes from the glare.

"Something made that thing we fought. The Nazis raised something with their sacrifices. I don't know what. I have suspicions, but whatever the hell it is, it does not belong in this world and I aim to remove it before it can do any more harm."

"How?"

"Same way it was brought here, I suppose. I'll find out what it is and then I'll get rid of it." I could have been asking a stranger about the time of day. The only difference was that I'd have been asking a stranger in a bad mood. I don't recall Crowley ever being in a good mood, really, except when he was fighting something. That was the only time he seemed genuinely pleased with his world.

I blinked back the wetness that stung at my eyes, hating what I thought of as weakness. Tears were for kids and for girls as far as I'd been told. I was nineteen and not wise enough to know any better. "How do those things exist?"

"You mean the monsters or the Nazis?"

"The thing that came from the ground. The red shape I saw. The people all cut up."

"What red shape?" Crowley's eyes instantly narrowed and his lips twitched.

I hadn't thought much of the form in the distance. It was there, but like the monster made from the ones of the dead I was doing my best not to think about it. There wasn't much to say, but I told Crowley just the same.

He nodded his head and then rolled his shoulders. "Well, that might make this a bit easier." The look he shot me said otherwise and I felt a flash of shame because I had not told him about what I had seen earlier. There should have been no reason for my worries, but there was a pervasive sense that I had let the man down, as if I had been asked by my teacher to go to the chalkboard and then completely botched a simple question. Crowley was like that.

When I was done with my brief description he stood and very slowly, carefully, scanned the area around us. He took his time and his eyes got a far off look.

As he looked, Crowley spoke to me. He said, "The world is full of things you don't want to know about and even more that you never want to see. It always has been and likely always will be."

"So monsters are real?"

His smile was not a pleasant thing. "Oh, yes, and some of them are even of the inhuman variety."

I was puzzling that out when the first sounds came to us. They were distant, but not as far away as I would have hoped. Deep, throaty, rumblings came to us. Crowley frowned and I joined him. There are certain noises that stay with you forever, I think. Some of them are natural and some are not. This was a sound that lived in my nightmares for years, decades after the fact. This was the sound of a manmade monster.

There are folks I know who can tell you everything you ever wanted to know about every possible type of armament. There are kids in my neighborhood who, even today, can give you exhaustive details about the sort of fuel used, the number of rounds per second fired, et cetera. Here's what I can tell you: the Panzer IV tank was a terror to behold.

I can't quote the dimensions of the great, thundering thing that came at us from down the road. All I can say is that it was larger than life and I wet myself when I saw it. One thing to see a tank go by in the distance, or to stand by one of the vehicles that is on your side in a war. Quite another to have a vehicle like that aiming for you.

There were four of them on the road, dwarfing the road, tearing the shit out of the sides of the road with their vast treads. The ground shook. The air shook. Our bodies shook as the damned things came our way.

I froze. I freely admit that. I took one look at what was coming our way and all thoughts left my head. They shouldn't have, but they did.

All I wanted to do was hide. In addition to the tanks themselves, there were soldiers. So many, it seemed, that counting them all would be impossible. It was the perception, you understand. There were seven of us, including Crowley. Next to the tanks the soldiers seemed tiny, but they were there and we were grossly outnumbered.

We should have never stayed on the road. Around the same time we heard them, we could see them. More importantly, they could see us.

They did not check our credentials. They did not ask us to surrender. The Germans opened fire and a stream of bullets hit Januski and blew him into shreds.

That was enough to get the rest of us scattering. The tanks were scary as hell, but they also couldn't turn and run as fast as we could. The weapons on them could do a fair impersonation, however, and they vomited lead and flames at a terrifying rate.

The ground shook. From time to time it exploded. Dirt and fire were everywhere and I had the fortune to manage not getting hit by anything as I ran for all I was worth.

Nunnally was right beside me for part of the trip but he stopped after a hard fifteen yards and turned back to face the enemy. He was swinging his rifle around when they ended him. I saw him drop from the corner of my eye. I also saw his helmet move past me, bouncing and rolling, dented into a new shape and bloodied to boot.

I lived. For a while I thought I was the only one. I tried firing back, and I think I hit at least one of the krauts, but I'd be lying if I said I acted heroically. I ran, because against four tanks and what seemed like an ocean of soldiers, I could think of nothing else to do.

How far did I run? Far enough that my body shook with the exertion and my heart hammered madly against my ribs. Far enough that every breath in the cold, autumn air was a painful stitch in my side. Far enough that the Germans stopped chasing me.

I was huddled in the woods when I finally lost consciousness. I cried myself to sleep.

When the morning came around I was shivering violently in the cold.

I might have stayed in a deep sleep for a while but Crowley woke me with a boot to the side of my helmet. He didn't kick me. He just gave me a nudge.

I almost screamed when I came to, but the look on his face stopped me.

We didn't speak for a long time. Instead he simply handed me the dog tags from all of my squad and squatted nearby while I looked them over and considered the situation.

There were no more tears. I'd cried them all out.

"The last tank." His words startled me. He'd been quiet for so long that I'd almost forgotten he was there.

"What?" I looked at him and sighed. "What about it?"

"It had the same mark we found in the cemetery. That means I'm going after it."

"There are too many people." I shook my head. "Too many tanks. You'll never live through it."

Crowley sighed. "Rules and regulations. That's what there are too many of. The rules say I have to be asked for help. I can defend myself, but that's all. If you ask for my help, I can do more than you might believe."

"You want me to ask you for help?" Remember how I thought I was done with tears? My eyes gave off that same damned sting again and I shook my head. "What am I supposed to do here? Ask you to kill yourself?"

"Just ask for help. That's all."

I looked away from him for a moment and considered his words, wondering what would happen if I did nothing at all.

"Help me find the things they summoned. Help me kill them."

Crowley's smile was bright and chilling.

"Let's go hunting."

From that moment on my life became a series of exhausting maneuvers. Wherever the ones responsible had gone, they surely traveled by vehicles. We were on foot. I carried what I could, mostly extra ammunition and a few c-rations. Crowley hardly seemed bothered by the weight of what he carried, but I felt like I was sinking in the muck after an afternoon of rain washed the countryside. It was cold and I was miserable and all that mattered to me was not losing sight of Crowley as he moved along, looking at the ground and tracking his enemies even when I saw no indication there were tracks to follow.

We might have talked more, but he was too busy jogging along the roads and occasionally moving through fields.

When we stopped at last to rest I fairly collapsed. I was winded, dehydrated and dizzy.

"Still feeling good about following me?" Crowley's voice was surprisingly soft.

I shook my head. There were no words left in me right then.

"So, the thing you asked about. How these things can exist." Crowley shrugged. "There are other worlds all around ours. Most of them don't know we are there any more than we know they are, but there are exceptions. Think of it like radio waves if that helps. Everything out there moves in its own way, and you, me, everything around us, it all moves the same way. Something moving in a different frequency might see us. We might see it. Hearne the Hunter, and his pack, that is a case where now and again we see something. It bleeds over. Hearne likes to chase down disasters. What he gets out of it I don't know, but that's what he does. The thing is, we can only really see him when the disasters are big enough to make him come close. He's not a cause. He's a symptom."

Crowley didn't look at me while he talked. He opened a C-Ration, looked at the dubious contents and then started eating.

"Thing is, there are ways to make things from other places more in tune to our world. Call it sorcery, because that's what it is. You call these things and whether or not they want to come, they do. Sometimes the rules are specific and call for a particular demon or monster. Other times they just summon whatever is closest."

"Where do all these worlds come from?"

"Don't interrupt. It's rude." Crowley looked my way for a moment as he admonished me, but there was no venom in his words. They were merely spoken. "The thing to remember, and I mean this, is that sooner or later somebody always thinks they can work out summoning something to their advantage. They can't. What's happening now, is someone on the Nazi Party thinks they can use whatever they've summoned. They might be able to for a while, but it won't last."

I thought long and hard about what he'd said. He wasn't talking down to me, exactly, but he was simplifying and I was all right with that. I had a lot on my mind and I really couldn't devote as much to him as I should have.

"Want to say that in plain English?"

"Son, I don't know how much plainer I can get." He looked my way. "Okay. Someone's trying to summon a demon from Hell. That's a good analogy. And that someone wants to control the demon. It isn't going to work. Near as I can tell, the demon already got away."

"How do you figure?"

"Because if the demon was still under whoever's command, the damned Germans wouldn't be looking all over the countryside trying to find it."

"But the markings on the tank…"

"The markings are supposed to offer protection. Whoever summed the demon wants to stay safe. That's why I'm going after the tank."

"You can't take on four tanks by yourself."

"You've been dumb enough to stay with me, so I'm not really by myself." He actually managed to sound amused instead of insulted.

***

The morning brought snowfall.

It was a wet, hard snow and even the treads from the tanks were hidden away. Despite that Crowley seemed cheery enough.

"Why are you smiling? We lost their trail."

"Because if we have to stop, so do they. The snow's going to slow them down, and that means we can get closer."

"It still doesn't mean we can do much to them."

Crowley shook his head. "You're still thinking about fighting them as if we were ever planning to go in with guns blazing. That's not going to happen and it never was."

"Well, I never said…" I let my voice fade off. He was right. That was exactly what I was thinking. It was what I was trained for.

"We're dealing with necromancy and dark magic. That means there is no time to play fair." Crowley looked at me for a long time, and I felt like he was sorting through whether or not to tell me things he had kept to himself. "You get to stay back here for now. I need to look over where the tanks should be and I need to decide how to handle them."

I thought about arguing. In the end I just nodded instead.

Two minutes after he headed in the direction of the tanks – I was guessing about that, because I couldn't have told you where they were on a bet – I followed him. I told myself I wasn't going to leave a man to fight on his own, but the truth was that he'd got my curiosity boiling and I wanted to know more than I already did about the things he was talking about.

•˙•

The snow was hellish. I mean that. If I could have figured out which way was back I would have taken it. What had started as a heavy snow in the night became a full on blizzard. The sun was somewhere above me, but all I could see were thick, fat flakes of snow falling from the heavens. And trees. I normally found those before I ran into them.

The worst part, I think, was the way the snow danced. It was charming when I was at home and there was a heavy snow. But back then I knew where I was and I had the lights of the house and a hundred familiar landmarks. Here I was in the middle of the woods, possibly even a forest proper – and if you don't know the difference, I pray you find out under better circumstances – and all I could see were the shapes the snow took on as it twisted and whirled in the currents of a wind I barely felt.

The silence was another thing. I heard no noises worth noting, save an occasional sigh of the wind.

From time to time I'd stop and try to listen for something more, but all I ever got was the low, whispered sigh and the shivers as the cold sank deeper into me.

That continued on through the day and well past the time the sun set. In the complete darkness I had no choice but to stop. I settled myself under a natural shelter, several branches that crossed over each other and left me an area of relative calm. The snow still fell and tipped and tapped the canopy above, but there was still no wind and the silence lulled me for a while.

I wrapped up as best I could and tried to think warm thoughts. I couldn't make a decent fire, but I tried for a while before giving up.

Eventually, I slept.

When I came to I thought I'd been buried alive. I wasn't actually far off. The weight of the snow-covered branches above had crushed them lower to the ground, but as I grabbed at the first of them and rattled it back and forth a cascade of white plummeted down and the branches started to rise. Nature can provide sometimes. I'm lucky I wasn't buried under all of that snow forever. I'm lucky I didn't freeze to death. Lucky, lucky man. Sometimes I forget how lucky I was to live through that. Not just the blizzard, though that was part of it. I mean the whole affair.

The silence was a living thing by the time I stood and shook myself off. The most impressive noises I heard were my own breaths and the sounds of snow falling in loose trickles from branches shaken by my passing.

It was World War Two in France and the Germans were everywhere. I should have known that would never last.

I had made only a quarter mile of travel at best; heading in what I believed was as a southerly direction. Crowley was, I was certain, either dead or gone. I was deep in the Nazi-ruled section of the country and I did not want to be. So I was headed south. I hoped. The problem was that the sun was hidden behind clouds too thick to let me even really guess the time of day, and after a few attempts my compass yielded nothing but a constant, slow spin of the needle, I gave up and moved on.

Have you ever walked through snow that was waist deep? I was half frozen and I was shivering but working up a hard sweat at the same time. It was all I could do and all I could think about.

Until the thunder came my way.

I knew it wasn't real thunder, of course. It was the echoes of artillery fire blowing through the countryside and bouncing off the hills.

I stopped my forward motion and tried to decide where it was coming from. It didn't take long. I was walking straight toward it. The ground beneath me shook and my boot soles vibrated right along with it.

The tanks were close. I couldn't hope to know what had started them off. Maybe I was too cold to notice until they were close by. Maybe they had been stopped and had only just started moving again.

What I do know is that I heard Crowley's voice amidst the chaos and was drawn to it. He was dangerous, I knew that, but he was familiar and I was desperate.

I can't say I ran to his help. The snow was too deep. I did the best I could, pushing against a wall of cold and wet and trying simultaneously not to be spotted by my enemies.

The road came up abruptly. The tanks managed to force

their way through or over the worst of the snow with little effort, and each tank following after made the path that much clearer.

I pushed myself until I reached the trench the tanks had cut in the snow and fell onto the road in exhaustion. My muscles shook and my breaths came hard and fast and left my sides feeling bruised.

When I got up, I looked at the path of destruction in my way and I followed it. Several of the Nazi soldiers were dead in that trail, broken and bloodied and lifeless.

Each corpse told a story that I could follow easily enough. They were behind the tanks, that much was obvious. The first few bodies I found had cut throats or broken necks. It wasn't hard for me to imagine Jonathan Crowley moving behind them in the snow and killing them one by one.

The snow still fell, you see. Despite a night of sleep and a half-day wasted in an effort to move south, the snow still fell from a dark, leaden sky and didn't seem at all concerned with the deaths of a few Germans, but it made wonderful cover.

I counted ten bodies killed in quiet. I don't know how many died before I found the trail. I wasn't about to go back and count. All I know is that ten men died before anyone sounded an alarm. It was easy to understand. The snow was too heavy for anyone to notice much of anything. These days, they have all sorts of ways to track people without seeing them, but in the Second World War, you mostly used your eyes. Bodies fell and it wasn't long before the snow tried to hide them. By the time I passed the seventh body I reckon the first was already out of sight.

The tanks were moving and they were noisy, but they were barely silhouettes. I finally managed to reach the one at the end of the trail and Crowley was there.

The man was walking just behind the tank, letting the snow hit the monstrous thing and take the brunt of the force. He saw me and nodded.

He didn't seem at all surprised to see me, which was kind of a strange thing, as I hadn't expected to be there.

We couldn't risk being heard over the tanks. It wasn't likely, but sounds can carry in the damnedest ways. So we slowed a bit and walked on, following the thunder down the road.

"I was beginning to think you'd tried for the Allied side of France." His face was deadpan, but his eyes looked at me hard and I felt a blush coming on as I looked down at my feet.

"I thought about it."

"Get lost?"

"Something like that."

"I tried asking a few of the krauts what they were doing. They didn't know. The only one who has any idea is in the second tank. A captain named Rotenfeld. He's the one that committed the sacrifices."

I remembered the bodies. Every time I closed my eyes I remembered them. Rotenfeld had cost me a lot of sleep.

"What are we gonna do?"

"I have to get to that third tank in the line. It's slow going."

"So how can I help?"

Crowley smiled. "Make noise."

He handed me a pouch that was deceptively heavy. Inside it I found several grenades. They were German made.

The good news about grenades is they all work about the same way. It didn't take long to figure it out."

"Which tank?"

"Start with this one.' He pointed to the one closest.

Here's the thing, you put down a grenade, you need to run. They make a very big explosion for their size. I always kind of chuckled when I saw someone throw a grenade in a movie, because right up until the nineties or so, it seemed to me they didn't really get it. A puff of smoke wasn't all that happened. A body didn't flip through the air and land in one piece all that often and even if it did, it landed broken in the worst ways possible.

So I ran hard to place the grenade. I pulled the pin and tossed the damn thing in front of the tank, and then I rabbited back to the trail and dove for cover.

I got lucky on the first one. I blew the left tread off the damned thing. Tank with one tread is about as worthless a vehicle as you have ever seen.

Before they could even climb out the see what the damage was, I was throwing another grenade and thanking God Almighty for my pitching arm.

The second tank in line rocked back a bit when the grenade went off. It didn't seem to do much permanent damage, but I can bet safely the ears of those inside were hurting them at the very least.

I threw a third grenade that did even more damage to the tank closest me. But after that I had to run again.

The German soldiers were coming back to the end of the caravan and they were in a killing mood.

Here's the problem. The soldiers that came back my way weren't human.

I don't know just what they were, but they were covered in fur and half ran, half loped on all fours, and their uniforms were torn because they just plain couldn't hold all of what those poor bastards had become. They snuffled and growled and kicked at the tank a bit, and then they came for me.

There was no sign of Crowley. I'd done what he wanted and he'd moved on, looking for his chance to break into the third tank.

That just left me, and the pack of nightmares heading my way.

They came hard and they came fast. I guess you could say I got sort of lucky again, because whatever had happened to them left them not giving a damn about their rifles.

The first one I shot went down hard, a spray of blood flying from the back of that misshapen head.

The rest of them came at me in a fury and dove into the snow, heading in my direction. The waist deep snow, where I couldn't see them worth a damn.

The day was overcast, and that helped a little, but there was still a sun up there and the light from it made the snow glare up something fierce.

I could have tried hiding in the snow, but the way those things moved, I figured they were probably going by scent.

That meant I wasn't going to be able to hide very well.

I saw something moving a goodly ways off, and I didn't think, I just threw. The grenade landed on target, and a moment later I saw snow rising in an wave and at the center of that wave was blood and broken bone, and what looked like a German outfit.

I was still trying to figure out where the next one might be when it came out of the snow and hammered me to the ground. It let out a sound like a chimpanzee maybe, or one of those screaming monkeys. And while I was trying not to piss myself a second time those massive arms came down and smashed me flat.

I'd have lost that fight right away if not for the snow. The fool thing dropped me hard and fast and the snow was loose enough that I fell back and the snow collapsed on me.

No time for guns and too close for grenades. I pulled my bayonet knife. Those hands came for me again and grabbed my shoulders. The fingers were hot despite the cold, and the nails were thickened to the point where they cut my jacket sleeves.

My knife cut too. I thrust it straight in between those arms and was rewarded with a different kind of scream. The blade slipped into something solid and then skimmed along a hard surface and the thing jumped back, roaring, blood flowing freely from where I'd opened it's face, peeling back half the flattened nose and slicing a gash from the lower lip all the way down to the collarbone.

God, how it screamed. Even as it came for me again. I had only one move, really. It never let go of my jacket even when it backed away. All it did was haul me forward and so I stabbed again and again, and I think I was doing a fair bit of screaming myself until I realized it was down and I was standing over it, my arm warm from the blood of the damned thing that was bleeding out in front of my eyes.

You ever try to pull up a rifle while you're holding a knife? I don't know how I managed it to this day. Somehow the knife went back into the sheath and the rifle was lifted on its sling and I fired into the snow wherever I saw movement.

I couldn't give you details if I had to. I just know I burned through my remaining bullets, firing at anything that looked like it might consider moving in my direction. When I was done with that it was back to throwing grenades until I was out of them. I nailed that first tank another time and something inside it finally had the decency to explode in return. The shockwave knocked me on my ass again, but when I stood, there weren't any things coming for me.

The German at my feet looked human again, just dead as could be. Whatever had changed it must have left the body when he died. He was a kid, same as me and I'd ruined his face with my blade. Enemy or no, his family never did a thing to me, and I'd taken him away and mutilated him besides.

Of course, when he came for me, he was something else. I focused on that part and moved on. Sometimes you have to do that, I guess. The details of your life can eat you alive if you let them. Best to temper them with a little logic now and then.

I turned toward the tanks. I had taken on a mission to help Jonathan Crowley fight the bastard that had sacrificed people in the middle of nowhere, France. I intended to see it through.

In the distance I could hear the rumble of the tank engines, gunshots, screams. I could just make out the tanks through the shroud of snow. Much closer, I saw the red figure I'd seen before.

It was a thin shape. I cannot say if it was male or female. Despite standing on two legs the shape was too far removed from anything I could easily recognize. A long ribcage, broad shoulders muscled with thin, sinewy strands. The face was something between a skull and a horse, and had a thick head of hair that was darker but no less red.

It looked at me for a moment and then it came for me, moving over the snow, barely touching the frozen surface. It hissed at me as it came, and it reached out with one long-fingered hand that seemed to have too many joints on each finger.

I didn't try to escape. I was too busy being horrified.

Everything about the beast was red, from its long-toed feet to its eyes, to its straggly hair.

That had draped over its face as I started to pull back.

After that all I saw was red.

* . *

Jenny was next to me in the meadow.

It was that perfect type of summer day, when the wind blew softly and washed away the possibility of sweat. Before I left for the war she and I parked ourselves under a big old oak on the family property and we had a picnic. When it was done we talked about how we would be together when it was over, how it was necessary to fight against the kinds of savages that would attack our shores, how much we would miss each other. The list was endless.

While we talked we wound up laying together under that tree. She was nestled against me and resting her head on my shoulder and I couldn't see her face, but I could smell her sweet scent and I could feel a few wisps of her hair tickling along my jaw line and nose. I knew then I'd marry her.

It was like that again, only sweeter this time. She was comfortable and so was I. I wanted it to last forever.

So of course, it only lasted a few seconds. But I remember it so clearly, so intensively, that even after all of these years it felt more real than all the time I spent in the war.

* . *

I was lying somewhere. Jenny was gone and so was the homestead. It was a forest, but it didn't seem like the same one I'd been walking in and freezing my ass off in.

The trees around me were vast things, massive in a way I had never seen before. The ground beneath me was a soft, thick loam. Far above, almost lost in the thickness of the forest, I could see a blue slash of sky.

As I looked around I noticed two things at the same time. First, the red thing I'd seen before was there in front of me, perched on a fallen tree that had long since begun to rot away. Second, I was dressed in my birthday suit and nothing more.

I pushed myself backward across the ground, my bare feet digging deep and shoving my body away from the thing.

It was wet with red; it dropped the stuff from its eyes and even from the pores of its skin. The air around that beast fairly seethed with disease. Just looking at it made me feel like I was sucking in every kind of hellish infection that ever existed.

As I backpedalled, it jumped down from its perch and came for me, low to the ground, almost like a hunting dog, those red, wet eyes bleeding hatred.

"Why are you not mine?" I did not see that mouth move, I saw the heavy teeth, some fangs and some flat like a horse's, but I saw no lips to move and still the words filled me.

"I-What?" The words made no sense.

"All that I touch is mine to shape as a sculptor shapes clay and yet you are not changed. You do not obey me. Why?"

"What the hell are you?"

It swatted away my question like a man dismisses a pesky fly.

"Answer me! Why are you not mine?"

I looked around as quickly as I could. It was a quandary: I really wanted my weapons and my clothes but I didn't dare look away from the bleeding thing coming at me.

"I don't know!"

In my searches I realized two things: I wore no bandages but I was not injured, and I felt no pain. Actually, I felt nothing. Not an ache from sore muscles, no hunger, no thirst, not even the mulch and leaves shoved up against me as I backed away from the thing. I might have been a bit worried about that, but something with too many teeth was already coming at me and that sort of took all the worries away from the rest of my problems.

It didn't touch me. Instead it moved closer and loomed over me. Andrew Cartwright used to loom over me when I was in third grade and he was in sixth. I was very adept at knowing what looming felt like. The menace was real, but it didn't actually touch me.

Bits of rotted meat clung to those teeth. What I could only guess was dried blood mingled with the coarse hair falling from the thing's head, and matted fur to the chest of the beast, but even from only a few feet away I smelled nothing.

"What did you do to me?" Anger surged inside of me, not quite burning away the cold fear, but definitely drawing my attention to the thing coming for me. How could I live a proper life if I couldn't feel? Couldn't taste?

The red thing moved closer, loomed over me and roared. I heard it. I felt it. Whatever it was doing, it had the upper hand.

"You are not here! You are still in the snow, freezing. You will die if you do not answer my questions! I will leave you there, to freeze!"

"I don't know!" Fear aside, I was still angry and I roared my counterargument right back at him.

"What the hell are you? Why are you working with the Germans?"

The whole damned shape shuddered and jumped and shook with anger and it reached for me again, but this time it stopped maybe an inch from my face and I saw the claws of the thing scrape the air. I could see the way the pressure of contact with that air made the thick claws on those fingers bend instead of letting them touch me and I understood.

I don't know how he did it. I didn't begin to know why, but somewhere along the way Jonathan Crowley must have done something to me. I have always been a church-going man, but never been all that faithful and seeing what I had in the war already guaranteed I would never think much of God again. How could I? How could anyone be in a world where oceans were buried under the corpses of friends and enemies alike?

I didn't think it was my faith that saved me. I thought then, and I know now that it was Crowley. He had managed somewhere along the way to stop the monster screaming at me from touching me.

And that knowledge made me smile as broadly as he did when he faced a new threat.

"You can't touch me, can you?" I made myself stand and the thing glared at me and hissed.

I reached out to see if I could touch the beast and it stepped back, those red eyes rolling in the sunken sockets that surrounded them. There was no way I could read what that thing was thinking. It was too inhuman. But I could guess that it was furious.

"You can't touch me. You can't hurt me." I stepped toward it again and I drove the flat of my hand into the beast's torso and pushed with all my might.

I felt like I drove my hand into boiling oil, but the creature screamed as loudly as I did and then I fell back and landed in the bitter cold of the snowdrift.

I felt the cold. I felt the pain in my arm from where a bone shard had broken skin and where the wound was likely already starting to fester.

I nearly wept. Every pain, every discomfort, was a blessing after only a few moments of absolute numbness.

I was so happy I almost missed the thing coming for me.

I need to make this clear. I'm older now and I've lost a lot of my mass, but back then I was over six feet tall and I weighed in at a solid hundred and seventy pounds, if you added in all supplies I was carrying. That red nightmare was tall and skinny and if it weighed in at more than a hundred and twenty-five, then I will eat my hat.

It grabbed me by my arm. I felt the wound that Januski had patched up tear open under the pressure. I swear to you now, I felt the disease spill into that wound through my jacket, my shirt and my bandages.

And then it threw me. I said before that Crowley got thrown. I did too and I think I went further. I saw the tanks go by while I was tumbling through the air and screaming my fool head off.

I hit the snow hard and fast and sank into it. To this day I don't know what I hit. I just know it broke my arm in three places.

I have to guess I screamed. I don't clearly recall.

I got up. I don't know how, except that maybe it was adrenaline. I looked toward the area I'd come from and had no idea how I could have gone that far and lived. I know I was in shock. I also know the pain that was howling through my arm and my body probably helped keep me going.

I looked for Crowley, and I found him.

I can't say if the damage I saw was done by me or by something else, but the tanks were in horrible shape. The damage to a couple of them was definitely my doing. The other two? I don't believe so. The very first tank, the lead vehicle, it was on its side and billowing black smoke from every conceivable opening. The treads were broken, the underbelly of the thing bled oil and fuel and even as I watched it caught ablaze. I expected an explosion, but instead it just burned and the people inside of it screamed.

They screamed and I shivered.

The tank that Crowley had started for in the first place was a different case. It was still intact, but the hatch at the top was open and while I could not see what was inside the vessel, I could see odd lights. The sort of lights I had never seen inside a tank before, flickering and offering colors from every possible part of the spectrum.

In front of that I saw Crowley arguing with a man in a black SS uniform. The man held an ancient knife. I have to guess that it was ancient, because the blade was made form some sort of black stone and the handle was covered in old, cracked leather and dangled several more stone trinkets under it.

Crowley stared at that blade like it was a cross and he was a vampire. He didn't seem capable of looking at it for long without flinching. A man I had seen charge across a half a football field's distance in a hail of bullets. A man I had seen take on a monster made of rotting bodies and headstones and worse things. He looked at that knife with genuine fear in his eyes. And he looked at the man holding the knife with hatred. I would not want to face Crowley under the best of circumstances, but the anger he aimed at the Nazi should have burned him to the ground.

The Nazi was a thin man, even more gaunt than Crowley. He was pale and his skin was sweating. It was snowing. The air that came from my mouth with every breath was a fog, but the man was sweating. Dark circles rimmed his eyes and I had to think he was sick, like pneumonia sick.

As if to make my point, he coughed and then doubled over in a coughing fit. The only part of him that didn't move was the hand holding that knife out like it was a ward to fend off Crowley.

Crowley didn't move on him.

I did. I'd like to say I ran across the field and tackled the sick bastard that had killed those poor souls back at the inn, but the truth was I started slogging his way and cursing the lack of any real weapons on my body.

Not that there were many I could have used. My arm throbbed with every heartbeat and I had to take in hard, deep breaths to keep moving.

The good news was that the man in black kept trying to cough out his lungs.

Crowley looked at the man and seemed intent on trying to reach him, but he never moved forward. He just glared.

No gun, no knife. Not even a rock. I only had one arm to use, so I just pushed through the snow until I finally flopped onto the road I did my best to catch myself with my one decent arm, but the other one, the useless one, flapped around a bit, and every movement made me want to vomit or pass out or both.

I couldn't tell you how I managed to get to my feet. All I know is that I went for the SS officer and I slammed into him with all my mass. He was thin and feverish and coughing his fool head off until he was almost purple in the face and his eyes were bulging.

I wouldn't say I hit him all that hard, but it was enough. Down he went into the snow near the last remaining tank and he let go of his knife to catch himself. He let out a scream and coughed again and I reached down with my one good hand and grabbed his little knife and held it in my hand.

And while he was still coughing, I backed up.

And then Crowley smiled again.

By the time I'd made ten paces back, Crowley was on him. He hauled the coughing man off the ground by his jacket and screamed questions at him in German.

The man laughed and coughed at the same time, shaking his head. I don't think he could respond in any other way. I thought then and I think now that he was already dying from whatever sickness he'd taken into his body.

Crowley might well have shaken the wreck to death, but then the red thing came back.

It looked the same. It was red and wet and furious. It didn't even seem to notice me when it came charging through the snow, leaving red footprints as it moved.

Crowley stood his ground. He reached into one of his jacket pockets and brought out a handful of black powder. I don't know what he said or what he did, but when he opened his hand the dust moved against the wind and swirled into a stream that slapped the red thing in the face like a swarm of bees. It fell back into the snow and screeched. My ears throbbed from the sound.

The skin on the red thing burned. It blackened and smoldered and I watched the black patch grow, moving over the body as it rolled and hissed and shrieked in agony. The eyes of the thing blackened and it fell onto all fours before grabbing at the snow and trying to wash away whatever Crowley had done.

And then it jumped for the tank.

Crowley had been grinning before that, but he changed his mind when it started moving into the tank itself.

It did not climb the side of the tank and move through the open hatch. It dove for the metal and flowed into it like a man diving into water. The steel sloshed and buckled around it before becoming what it had been before.

"Damn it, no!" Crowley ran for the tank.

The tank squealed as loudly as the demon had and started collapsing in on itself. The metal crunched and screamed and bent, and the thing that had moved into it took it over.

That's the only way I can say it. The thing I'd seen earlier was pulled from the graveyard and it seemed like this was a similar notion. The Panzer didn't quite melt. It didn't grow hot or fall apart and rebuild itself into something else like the cars in that Transformer movie. It just sort of pulled itself together into a new shape.

I watched it with a slack jaw. I couldn't quite accept it. Or maybe shock was finally getting the better of me.

The German coughed and laughed and said something in his own tongue that I couldn't understand. He looked worse than before, but he was smiling.

Crowley stopped short as the tank stood up on two legs. There was no symmetry to the outside of the thing. It looked nothing like the red monster I'd seen before.

This thin was metal, and it was as lumpy and unfinished as the grave golem had been. There was a head. There was a rudimentary face. There were tank treads wrapped into the arms and head and chest of the monster. Gears that had been squashed like pumpkins were pressed into the thing. The arms didn't end in hands, but in clubs of more twisted metal.

It tried to hit Crowley. Like any sensible man, he tried to get the hell away from it. When that fist hit the snowy ground, the earth shook. I mean that. I remember when I was a kid there was a farm hand that was heavy enough you could almost feel a tremor when he walked past in a hurry. His name was Earl and he died of a massive heart attack while he was trying to get an old generator to work again.

I didn't think maybe the ground shook. I saw the snow ripple away from where the monster hit and I saw Crowley lose his balance and scramble back to his feet as the thing came for him.

The German said something else, his voice hoarse and crackling from whatever was broken inside of him. I looked away from the fight for a second and stared at that smiling face, and I lost my temper. Two steps brought me close enough to raise my heel over that bastard's head and to stomp down with all I had

143

in me. He stopped laughing and his temple got a dent in it.

I don't know what to say about Crowley. I guess part of me doesn't think he was human. All I know was he took a punch from that thing. He blocked it with his arm and instead of being crushed into a pulp, he actually deflected the blow. He got knocked back a dozen feet, and he landed on his backside again, but he took that blow and wasn't crushed. Hell, I'd stomped on the Nazi's head and likely killed him, and by all rights Crowley should have died when he caught that punch.

He got right back up, that smile of his wide and nasty, and his eyes as glassy and feverish as the man I'd just killed.

And he roared words at the tank-monster and it flinched back from him like he'd aimed a flamethrower at it.

Crowley walked closer to it, taking his time as the thing stumbled back, that rough, unfinished face screwing into a different shape and a noise coming from it that was like a thousand tortured cats screaming at the same time.

It came for him again, stomping down the snowy road and making that horrible noise as the metal of its body started to heat up. At first it steamed the air, and then it started glowing. Crowley stood his ground as it rumbled his way, and kept speaking, saying things that hurt my mind as much as the damned thing I was looking at did.

It tried to grab him, but Crowley danced past, taking a glancing blow from an arm that was red again, but not wet. No, it smoked and steamed and burned and as Crowley spun away I could see the fabric of his jacket catch fire from the intensity of the heat.

The blow was enough to throw Crowley again, but he didn't stop. He kept speaking and pulled off his jacket and dodged again as it turned to find him and then stumbled in his direction.

It might have hit him too, but by that point the entire shape was losing cohesion. It was melting and dripping and falling into fiery drops that burned right through the snow.

Crowley walked backward as it kept coming. It fell to the ground on its rough knees and then slumped forward, its arms still reaching for him.

Crowley kept talking, even as it collapsed completely, sloshing into a pool of white hot metal that faded under the level of the snow.

It finally stopped screaming.

I thanked God and trembled.

And then I passed out.

• •
•

When I woke up again I was in a house. It was a small affair, but it was warm and it was dry and I was on a bed.

I guess I must have gone back to sleep for a while, but when I came to again Crowley was sitting on a chair near my bed. He was clean and dressed in fresh clothes. I was clean too, and dressed in a pair of worn but comfortable long johns.

"How did we get here?"

Crowley didn't smile. "I carried you. Not really that hard to figure out, really."

"Thanks."

"You saved my life. I figured I owed you."

"I figured the other way around. You did something to me. Put a spell on me or something, but that red thing couldn't even touch me."

"Wicht. Or wight."

"'Scuse me?"

"It was a wicht in German, or a wight in old English."

"I have no idea what that means." I hurt everywhere and I was feeling a bit cranky, but I was also feeling mighty grateful. I outweighed Crowley by a good bit, but he got me away from all of that craziness. I had no idea how far he'd carried me. All I really knew was that I was safe, I was warm and clean and someone had even splinted up my arm nice and tight.

"It's a kind of minor demon."

"Minor?" I sounded dubious, but only because I was.

He nodded and then reached to an end table on his side of

my bed and offered me a cup of warm broth. Chicken soup never smelled or tasted so good. It was just the right temperature, too. I could drink it without burning the sin out of my mouth. "You keep that down, there's bread and cheese."

"Where are we?"

"Allied side of France. I have a few friends here. One of them is helping us, because I helped her once upon a time."

"You said that thing was a minor demon?"

"Ralf Rotenfeld was the man who summoned it. He's the fella you kicked in the head."

"What was he trying to do?"

"Win the war, I guess. Not the first time and not the last some jackass will try. Instead of summoning a major demon from the pantheons of hell, he got an inconvenience."

I know I must have stared like a fool. Crowley grinned at it. "'Inconvenience?'"

"You should try keeping up. Repeating myself is annoying." The words were said without malice. "That thing was a minor demon. He couldn't control it, because he couldn't figure out what its name was. Sometimes names have power. Not always."

"How did he even summon it?"

"That knife of his, I don't know where he found it, but that was… that was old and powerful."

"I dropped it."

"I found it. It's safe." He waved the notion aside. "In any event, it's gone now. Banished."

"What happens now?"

"You go back to the army and tell them that you encountered Nazis and lost your entire group."

"Where are you going?"

"Maybe you didn't notice, but I wasn't a part of your squad. I was just along for the ride."

"I sort of got that when you had your talk with the sarge."

He nodded. "Nice enough guy for a moron."

There was a long silence while I considered his words.

I was almost ready to drift to sleep when Crowley spoke

again. "Unless you're looking to get a section eight, I wouldn't mention the wight or me. It won't go well if you do."

"I have to report what happened."

"Nazis happened. It's enough. You have an arm with three breaks to it, and you have a bad infection in the other arm. Your feet don't look so good and if I had to guess you're going to lose a few toes to the frostbite." He was very direct. I listened on with a growing sense of horror. "Likely you're done with the war. You leave the right way, you go home a hero. You leave the wrong way and no one believes you, but they'll all say what a shame it was you came out broken." He stood. From my perspective he was very tall. "Your choice."

Crowley cut me a chunk of bread and a thick cut of cheese and I nodded my gratitude. While I was eating it he looked my way again and said, "I don't like to mention these things, but I have to. Don't go thinking about doing what Rotenfeld did. It won't go well. No matter who tries to win that way, it ends badly. Keep yourself clean is what I'm saying. I owed you. Maybe I still owe you, but don't push it."

He grabbed his supplies then. A small sack. Not remotely military issue. Then again, neither were his clothes.

"Where are you going?" I hated that I asked. I wasn't sure I wanted to know.

"Rotenfeld told me a few things. He didn't really want to, but I made him."

"I thought you said he was dead."

Crowley nodded. "There are ways to get answers." I could tell he was serious. My skin crawled at the notion. "Rotenfeld told me there are others working with Hitler to use sorcery to do their work. I'm going to look into that. So, time for me to head out."

Crowley left just that easily.

I never did hear what he did for Jacques and Madeline, the people who cared for me until they could notify an army squad heading by.

That's the whole of the story, really. I never saw Crowley again. We didn't exchange cards or any such nonsense.

He was right. I lost two toes on my left foot. I also lost a little of my strength in my arm. I wasn't so worried about that. I got away a lot easier than a lot of the soldiers did.

And you know what? I even got Jenny in the end. We reconciled. We married. We had kids and they've had kids and now there are even a few great-grand kids that come to see me around the holidays. I miss her every day. I guess I always will.

It's almost Christmas and the snow is falling. And that always makes me think of Crowley.

There's a strange thing going on in town lately. Not sure what it is, exactly, I just know that a few people have vanished, been gone a few days and then been seen by other folks who swear they looked like they were sickly and desperate. No one ever sees them up close, but they see them, normally moving around the river.

Last week I woke up from a dream of Crowley and I had the phone in my hand. I'm old, but as I like to say, I ain't stupid and I ain't dead. I looked at the call history on my phone after I woke and it said I made a three minute call to an unlisted number.

You get old enough, you can accept a lot of things. I figured I dialed some numbers on the phone when I was sleeping.

I felt that way until I got the call from an unknown number and answered it.

It was a short conversation. Crowley asked me if I was sure I wanted his help. I didn't even think about it. I just said yes and he said he'd see me soon.

That's why I wrote this down. See, I don't think Crowley will do me any harm, but I think l he'll come and see me and I expect he'll ask me a few questions. I expect I'll have to invite him into my house. That seems like one of the rules to me. I have to ask him for help. I have to invite him past the threshold.

And I reckon I'll have to beg him to leave my family out of whatever is happening.

My family. They're the ones who told me about the missing people coming back. They're the ones who keep me posted on the latest sightings of the folks that have been called "river people" by a lot of my neighbors.

So I'll answer his questions. I'll ask for his help and I'll invite him in, because I owe him that for saving my life.

And then I'll beg him not to meet my family or talk to them and I'll hope he still thinks he owes me one for saving his bacon back in the day.

Thing is, I've heard from a lot of my family. Most of them. But I haven't heard from Lincoln. He's my second eldest grandson. He's the one no one says bad things about, and who, sometimes, gets the strangest look on his face. He's the one I told this story to a long while back when he was young enough to sit on my knee, and he's the one who likes to haunt old bookstores.

Now and then Lincoln has shown me things he bought. When he was very young it was magic tricks and books on Houdini. Later it was an occasional necklace or ring he'd found. They always had the sort of images that weren't shown in polite society when I was a kid and everyone went to the same church.

Eventually he graduated up to tattoos. I never got heavy into the research after meeting Crowley. I didn't want to know, you see, but I read a bit. Here and there. Look carefully at my doors and windows and you'll see some very carefully concealed symbols that are supposed to ward off evil. Just in case, you understand.

I know enough to see that Lincoln is maybe doing things he shouldn't.

To hunt down something that he said was minor, Crowley cut down a lot of German soldiers. A whole lot.

I can't help but wonder what he'd do to get to whatever Lincoln might have called.

I can't help thinking maybe if I'd never told him all those war stories when he was just a kid...

Crowley should be here soon. He might be happy to see me. I know I won't be happy to see him. His voice was too young. I think, God help me, that the man I see when he comes here will be unchanged. I know that sounds crazy, but I guess if a man can heal from getting broken and beaten until he should be dead, holding back the years is probably not beyond him.

I think he will be young. I think he will be friendly. I think he will be smiling that damned creepy smile of his as he asks me polite questions and considers whether or not I'm responsible for what Lincoln has done with the old stories I told him. I expect whatever answers he wants, I'll give them to him. It's been a lot of years and I still keep hearing his voice and seeing the distant, cold expression on his face when he said, "There are ways to get answers."

I have never been that brave a man.

I pray he decides to forgive me.

Ngu'Tinh

D.F. Shultz

The creature was just a few paces away, slinking in Nathan's direction through the foliage. It looked like a ten-feet-tall praying mantis, only with smooth skin like a reptile, and a tiny, eyeless head. It moved slowly, hunting its prey.

Senses heightened by adrenaline, Nathan was acutely aware of his surroundings. The lapping of the nearby river; the buzzing of insects; a bead of sweat rolling down his temple. He felt the weight of the CAR-15 in his hands, the feel of his finger on the trigger.

Palm leaves quivered as the creature brushed past within arms-reach. He steadied the assault rifle; *how did I get myself into this shit?* Only a few days earlier he'd been safe on base, drinking with the rest of the team in their makeshift bar. There had been a lot of talk lately about casualties. Inside the repurposed army tent, Nathan listened to snippets of drunken chatter.

"Got him when we went to take a piss."

"Found 'em ripped to shreds."

"Just like the others."

"Disappeared in the trees. Not a goddamn trace."

There were a few other SEALs at the table with Nathan: Leon, Simon, Buck Williams, and the 'Professor'. They'd called him that since finding out he'd quit his PhD to join the squids. Bao, their translator, was also there. Nathan suspected Bao was the smartest man in the room.

"I heard it was alligators," said Leon.

"You mean a crocodile," said the Professor. "They don't have 'gators in Nam."

"The fuck's the difference?"

"It wasn't a croc'," Nathan said. "Prob'ly some VC guerillas. They know how to use the river and the trees."

"What about the bodies? They're all mangled like an animal got 'em."

"Sometimes the VC string men up to the trees," Nathan said, "keep 'em alive and pull their guts out."

"The screams help draw in men for an ambush," the Professor added.

An angry-looking marine walked up to the table. "It's not like that," he said. "We just find 'em torn up, pieces missing."

"God—" Simon shook his head. "Why?"

"My guess is intimidation," Nathan said. "They're trying to put us on edge."

"Bastards," Leon spat.

"They won't get away with this," Simon said through gritted teeth.

"That's just the thing, though," the marine said, bitterness edging into his voice. "We haven't been able to get authorization to do anything about it, and we don't have any actionable intel'. But we heard about you SEALs. Word is you might have the skill-set and operational freedom to track these guys down and take 'em out."

"Well if you're looking for a hunter," Simon said, "Nathan's your man."

"You know, it's funny." Nathan set down his beer. "I never was a big fan of hunting."

"I find that hard to believe," Simon said with a laugh.

"It's true," Nathan said, leaning back in his chair. "I remember the first time I took down a deer. My dad was there, congratulating me, patting me on the back. I knew how I was supposed to feel, but it's not how I felt."

"Sad you took out Bambi or something?" Leon asked, and the rest of the SEALs laughed. "You got a soft spot we don't know about?"

"Nah," Nathan lied, because that was part of it. "That deer was too easy to track, too easy to shoot. I never liked hunting animals. It just felt like cheating."

Leon laughed. "That's one way to brag. You should teach classes in that shit."

The SEALs looked back at the marine, who stood silent and unblinking beside their table.

"You want somethin'?" Leon asked.

"The name's Chris Donaldson," he said, and the others introduced themselves. "I never wanted to come to Nam, but I signed up when my little brother got drafted. Thought maybe I could keep him safe. His name was Bradley."

Bradley Donaldson. Nathan remembered the name. A young kid, 18-year-old marine. Two weeks ago they'd found his body by the river. What was left of it anyway.

Before Nathan could speak, they were interrupted by barking and yelling outside the tent. The SEALs leapt from their table and ran outside.

The chained guard dog, Rex, had got himself a piece of the pant-leg of a uniformed army officer. The man was sprawled on the ground, struggling to pull the fabric from the growling dog's teeth.

"Get this thing off me," he shouted.

"Down, Rex." Buck pulled the dog by the collar then offered the man a hand up.

"Sorry about that, Chief," Nathan shouted to the officer across the dirt clearing. "You wanna come inside for a drink?"

The man glared.

"What're you doin', Nathan?" Professor whispered from behind. "That's General Cain."

"General? But he's got one star."

"Those are army ranks, you dumb fuck."

Shit.

"You—" the General pointed at Nathan, "come with me." The man turned on his heel and marched towards the center of base camp.

The army was in charge of this region. The Navy SEALs were guests here, and it didn't seem like their presence was much appreciated by some of the higher-ups. Rex's attack on General Cain was probably not helping things – their makeshift bar was against regs, and Nathan's disrespect might've just solidified their reputation with the brass.

Nathan ducked into the General's office.

"I've heard all about you SEALs," General Cain said, sitting at his desk. "You're assassins."

"We're here to serve," Nathan said.

"We've got this area under control," the general said, his nostrils flaring. "We don't need any outsiders sneaking around at night, killing from the shadows. I want you all to sit tight and let us work."

"Understood." Nathan nodded, but with the casualties mounting from an unseen VC squad, Nathan doubted whether Cain really did have control over the area. "Permission to speak freely, sir?"

"By all means," the general said but Nathan doubted the man meant it.

"All the guys on the team will tell you they joined to serve their country, and it's true. But there's a lot of ways to serve your country, and they chose to join the SEALs. The real truth is they signed up for the action, and if you tell 'em they can't operate, there's gonna be a lot of pent-up energy they're gonna have to release somehow."

Nathan pretended he was talking about his men, but he was really talking about himself – he didn't come here for a vacation.

"Is that some kind of a threat?"

"Absolutely not. But these men have pushed themselves to the limit to come here. They've gone through hell, and more training than most people can imagine. It would be a shame to waste that talent."

Nathan could tell he wasn't going to change the general's mind. On the way out, the general added, "Get rid of that fucking dog."

Nathan brought the bad news back to the SEALs.

"What did you say to him?" Buck asked.

"Nothing," Nathan said. "He'd already made up his mind about us."

"So we're supposed to just sit around and jack off all day?" Leon asked. "What is this bullshit? And what about the VC? People are getting killed out there."

"I'm as pissed about it as you are," Nathan said, "but it's politics."

They were supposed to sit on their asses, so they did for the next few days. A few more bodies were found, mangled like all the rest, a look of terror frozen in the eyes of those who still had them.

It was midday when the Professor came running to Nathan.

"Nathan," he shouted, "we need you at the docks."

"What's up?" he asked, automatically reaching for his sidearm.

"It's Deacon."

Deacon worked on a special program with the SEALs, training freshwater river dolphins for underwater ops. Getting them to detect explosives, maybe even place them. The dolphins had better noses than any machine for detecting explosives, and they seemed to love the work.

Buck and Nathan ran to the docks and saw Deacon on his knees. In front of him lay the body of one of the dolphins, a former dolphin now, fileted just like the human victims.

"They killed Glenn," Deacon shouted, rage pulsing from the man. "Nathan, you hear me? They killed Glenn."

"How'd this happen?" Nathan asked gently, knowing he needed a calm Deacon if he was going to get to the bottom of this.

"I sent the three of 'em on a training run down the river. They've done it plenty of times before. But this time they didn't come back. When I went to find 'em—" Deacon stopped and looked at the dolphin pieces.

"And the others?"

"I only found Glenn." Deacon shook his head. "Rob and Billy are missing. Their trackers are offline."

"They could still be alive," Nathan said. "Maybe the trackers are out of range."

"What're we gonna do?" the Professor asked. "We gotta do something about this, right?"

"We're running an op," Nathan said. "Tonight."

Leon wrinkled his brow. "To look for a couple of fuckin' dolphins?"

Deacon's face flashed with anger, and he swung a hard right. Leon brought his arm up just in time, and the fist struck with a dulled slapping sound. Then punches were flying from both men.

Nathan held back Deacon, and the Professor stood between him and Leon.

"Cool it," the Professor said.

"Jesus," Leon shouted at Deacon. "The fuck's your problem?"

"You're an asshole," Deacon said.

Leon had a habit of pushing people's buttons, seeing what he could get away with, but now was not the time.

"We consider those dolphins part of the team," Nathan said.

"An expensive part," the Professor added. "Dollar for dollar, those dolphins are about four times as valuable as us."

"Besides," Nathan said, "I think it's time we secured the river."

"But what about the general?"

"Fuck 'im. We've got a job to do."

The team made their way back to the operations tent, cleared the table then laid out their intel, plotting the previous attacks and looking for patterns.

"How're we gonna find these guys?" the Professor asked. "The marines sweep the area constantly and they haven't found jack."

"That's just the problem," Nathan said. "They do these big daylight sweeps with forty-plus men. Anyone could hear 'em coming a mile away. But at night, with a smaller team-"

"So where do we look?" Deacon jumped in.

"They're taking the water." Nathan pointed to a river on the map; the attacks formed a rough pattern that traced along its course. "They've prob'ly got a camp upriver. We just need to sit tight around here and wait for 'em to pass by. We leave tonight. Try to get some sleep before then." Of course, none of them would.

They met at the docks in the dark of night. The team checked their weapons, loaded gear into the inflatable Zodiac then hopped inside. Nathan would've felt safer in a Mike Boat, but they had to keep a low profile.

Nathan was the point man; Buck the radio man. Their translator, Bao, was there just in case they grabbed a VC for interrogation. Leon and Simon were the coxswains. Deacon, Kyle, Bentley, and the Professor rounded out the nine-man team.

Nathan took a moment to size up his squad's killing power. His weapon was a CAR-15 with a 40mm grenade launcher and plenty of rounds, canister and high explosive. Bentley carried an M3 machinegun and a 7.62mm Chicom pistol. Deacon and Kyle each carried M79s with the XM-148 40mm grenade launcher attachment. They had about twenty of the soda-can sized grenade rounds between them: high-frag, buckshot, smoke canopy, and an experimental XM-463 stealth round. The Professor carried an SKS semi-auto rifle and a .38 combat masterpiece; very professorial. Leon and Simon carried Stoner 63 assault rifles. Most of the men had a KA-BAR and a couple of M61 hand grenades. Bao carried an AK47, and Buck carried the radio.

Just as they were loading into the zodiac, a shadow moved up from base. It was Chris Donaldson, the marine from the bar.

"What're you doing here?" Nathan asked.

"I'm coming with you."

"Like hell you are."

"I couldn't keep my brother safe, but I can still put a bullet in those VC *fucks*."

"You sure 'bout that?" Leon scoffed. "Last time I checked you jarheads weren't doin' so hot out there."

Donaldson faced off with Leon. "Either I'm going with you, or I'm going straight to Cain to let him know about your little operation."

"You threatening us, dip-shit?"

"Shut up, both of you," Nathan said. Heads turned towards him, and they waited expectantly for an answer.

"You're not really considerin' it, are you? He'll just get in the way," Leon said.

"Fuck you," Donaldson snapped. "I can hold my own." He turned to Nathan. "I need to do this. For my brother."

Nathan sighed. "Okay." It was a bad idea, but agreed anyway – a brother needs vengeance. "Just promise me something: don't fucking die."

"Someone's gonna die tonight," Donaldson growled, brandishing his M1 rifle, "but it sure as shit ain't gonna be me."

They took it slow out of the docks; picked up the pace when they were well down the river. The ride was a little less than two hours. Steering to the riverbank, they nestled the zodiac into twisting mangrove roots, concealed under dense overhanging branches – perfect spot for an ambush. Bentley and Kyle set the claymores upstream then waited at the river's edge.

Not too long after, they spotted a sampan coming down river.

"Should I blast 'em?" Bentley held up the remote detonator.

Nathan shook his head. "Not yet."

The sampan moved closer until revealing its sole occupant.

"Just one of 'em?" Bentley said.

"Could be a scout, maybe," Leon said.

"Put the detonators away," Nathan ordered. "Let's ask our man some questions."

They waited for the boat to close the distance, coming within a dozen yards of their riverside hiding spot.

"Hands in the air," Nathan shouted.

The team sprang from their positions along the river, weapons drawn.

"Tell him to get over here," Nathan instructed Bao.

Bao shouted something to the man, who paddled the sampan over to the riverbank. The SEALs grabbed the edge of his wooden boat and pulled it closer, and the man stood with arms raised, eyes wide – terrified.

"Ask him if he's VC," Nathan said.

Bao translated, and the man stammered something in reply. "He says he's not," Bao said. "He says he's a hunter. His name is Hiro."

"A hunter?" Nathan laughed. "Bullshit. What's he hunting out here at night?"

Bao relayed the question, and Hiro answered with two syllables that sounded like 'yeow kwai'. The way he said it, cold and stone-faced, sent a chill along Nathan's spine.

Nathan motioned to the man. "What did he say?"

Bao paused. "Demons."

"Demons? He really say that?" Donaldson said.

Bao nodded.

"Check his bag," Nathan ordered.

Kyle grabbed the large sack in the bottom of the sampan, pointed a flashlight inside then rifled through the contents.

Hiro glanced around nervously before speaking in a worried tone, the syllables rushing out.

"He says we're not safe here," Bao translated. "He said, 'the daughters of Ngu'Tinh are in the waters'."

"New tin?"

"Something like, 'demon fish'. A myth of Vietnam. Ngu'Tinh is a giant creature with hundreds of legs. It is said to eat fishermen." Hiro continued rambling while Bao translated. "He says Ngu'Tinh's daughters live here. Demon-spawn. The river is their feeding ground."

"Think I found out why he's so nervous." Kyle lifted a small vial of rosy-brown liquid from Hiro's bag in the sampan. "Heroin. He's got loads of it. Needles and powder, too."

"Drug runner for the VC?" Bentley guessed.

Nathan shrugged.

Kyle shone the flashlight on Hiro's face, revealing red blemishes all across his skin. "He's an addict."

There was a sudden flash of movement from the overhanging trees — a cracking, *thwipping* sound. Something large snapped down from the canopy and back up again; just a blur of motion, and Bentley was gone.

"Jesus," Simon shouted.

The SEALs scanned the motionless canopy, listened to the sudden silence of the forest.

"Bentley?" Nathan called into the trees.

A gurgling sound above.

Bentley fell back down. One piece at a time. Parts plopped into the water – three successive splashes. One landed in the sampan with a hollow, wooden thud.

"Fuck," Kyle yelled, stepping back from the severed arm. "Jesus, fuck!"

"God damn! Bentley!"

"The hell was that?"

"Anyone see it?"

The men trained their weapons on the canopy. Leaves rustled above. Something was moving fast, sliding through the branches.

"Squad, rapid!" Nathan ordered, and the forest erupted with gunfire. Nathan sprayed the canopy with his CAR-15, and his ears rang as his squadmates unloaded into the foliage.

"Ceasefire!"

The gunfire stopped. Silence, except for the creaking of broken tree limbs, a few branches falling and dropping into the water, some landing on the forest floor.

"Did we get it?" Buck asked.

"I don't see a body," Nathan said, "whatever it was."

"You don't think he was telling the truth do you?" Kyle motioned to Hiro. "About the demons."

The men glanced at the Professor.

"Of course not," he said. "Demons don't exist."

"I don't know about demons." Nathan kept his eyes on the canopy. "But I've never seen anything move that fast."

"There's a hundred-and-forty types of snakes in Nam," the Professor said, "and some of 'em are twenty-feet long."

"Just keep your eyes open."

The men scanned the trees.

Something heavy dropped into the water, splashing down an arm's length from the sampan. Nathan swung his weapon at the monstrous shape, just a silhouette against the stars. It was ten-feet tall, hunched, a four-limbed thing with a tiny head. The

160

creature had serrated arms that ended in points, like a giant praying mantis.

Nathan fired off a few rounds just as the creature snapped forward, pulled Kyle screaming from the Sampan, and dragged him under the water.

"Jesus!"

"Fuck!"

They scanned the water, weapons ready. Bubbles rose to the surface. Then pieces of Kyle floated up: arms, legs, torso... then his head. His dead face stared upwards, bobbing gently in the water.

"God! It got Kyle."

"Shit. Shit. Shit."

"What was that thing?"

"Wasn't a fucking snake."

"There it is," Leon shouted. A large ripple moved across the surface, darting left and right, retreating into the distance.

Nathan popped a high explosive canister into the 40mm attachment and levelled the barrel. He trained the weapon on the retreating ripple then fired. *THUNK*. The round struck the surface and exploded violently. *BOOM*. The blast sent a splash thirty feet in the air and lit the river like daylight. The shock-wave hit like a wall of wind, then a sheet of water fell across the men, and a wave surged over their feet.

Simon stared at the water. "You got it, right?"

"Maybe," Nathan said. "But we're not sticking around to find out."

"We're leaving?" Donaldson shouted. "We just found the enemy and you're gonna run?"

"I don't know what that thing was, but there could be more of 'em around. And right now we're engaging on their terms." Nathan glanced around. "Into the boat," he ordered. "Let's go."

Leon, Simon, the Professor, and Deacon moved into the Zodiac.

"What do we do about him?" Buck pointed at Hiro; the addict, motionless in the sampan.

"We'll take him," Nathan said. "He might know something."

Buck grabbed Hiro's arms to pull him from the sampan but the man struggled, shouting in Vietnamese.

"He says leave him here," Bao translated.

"I got that part."

"We'll take his stash," Nathan said. "I'm sure he'll be happy to come along then."

Buck grabbed Hiro's bag and tossed it to Nathan. Hiro screamed, and his head tracked the motion of the bag through the air into Nathan's waiting hand.

"Come and get it." Nathan dangled the bag at arm's length. Hiro leapt from the sampan into knee-deep water. He splashed forwards, lunging through the river to the prize of heroin.

For an instant, a terrifying sensation gripped Nathan. A penetrating tingle in the base of his skull. Primal instinct, subconscious awareness.

Nathan turned and dropped to a knee. He felt the rush of wind as a serrated limb whizzed past overhead – the arm of a creature that stood just a few feet away. Nathan pulled the trigger on his CAR-15, emptying the rest of the magazine into that monstrous green torso. The rounds blew through its body, exploded out its back, and turned its body into green Swiss cheese. The creature leapt into the canopy, oozing from its fresh wounds.

Nathan spun to screams and gunfire. His men were fighting two more of the green horrors. The sampan was painted with a coat of blood and chunks that used to be Buck. There was a flurry of gore where the creature's arms thrashed like a giant blender working its way over the corpse. The Zodiac was ripped up and deflated, most of its compartments slashed open, and half sunk into the river.

Deacon scrambled back to land, Leon unloaded his stoner, spraying wildly, and Professor fired off a few clean shots with his SKS. Donaldson stood his ground and fired with his M1, yelling like a mad man. Simon was spread across the top of the water in a five-yard radius.

Nathan reloaded and took aim, but the monsters submerged, disappearing into the water. Nathan and Leon provided covering fire, unloading into the river as the squad retreated to the forest. Nathan couldn't identify the voices shouting over each other in the chaos.

"Go, go, go!"

"They're in the river."

"Run."

"Wait," Nathan shouted.

"Are you crazy? Why?" Deacon shouted.

"It's Bao," Nathan said, moving quickly.

Bao lay prostrate beside the river, partly slumped over mangrove roots. His clothes were soaked in blood, two bullet holes in his torso.

"Shit," Deacon muttered.

"One of you fucks hit Bao," Nathan said, and took a knee beside Bao, who groaned, coughing up blood.

"How bad is it?" Deacon asked.

Nathan just shook his head. There wasn't much he could say.

"Maybe we can radio for an extraction?" Deacon said, sounding defeated.

Nathan motioned to what was left of Buck, their radio man, and the wrecked the sampan. "No radio."

"My guess is the jarhead shot him," Leon said.

"Shut up," Donaldson said. "I prob'ly just saved your ass."

"Like hell you did."

"Put a few bullets in that thing behind you," Donaldson said with a glare. "You would've known that if you didn't lose your shit."

"He's right," Deacon squared off with Leon. "Did you even fuckin' aim?"

"You're not gonna blame me for this. We're only here because of your stupid fucking dolphins."

"Fuck you."

"What?" Donaldson raised an eyebrow. "Dolphins?"

"You didn't know?" Leon asked. "He's a dolphin trainer for the Navy. They only set up this op' 'cause he lost a couple of his pets."

"Wait a minute. So you wouldn't come out here when they were killin' marines - when they killed my brother - but you'd come out here for a goddamn pet fish?"

"Dolphins aren't fish," the professor said.

"Shut up."

There was a flash of motion from behind, and Nathan felt a sudden tug. He turned, ready to shoot, or die trying. But it was only Hiro, the boatman The addict had a tight grip on the bag of heroin looped over Nathan's shoulder. Nathan wrestled the bag from Hiro's grip then shoved him back. Hiro tripped on a root and landed on his back.

"You tryin' to get yourself killed? I almost blasted you!"

Hiro spoke calmly, pleading, and motioned to the bag.

"I think he wants a hit." Deacon stated the obvious.

"Not really the time, is it?"

Hiro continued talking, a stream of unintelligible Vietnamese.

"Hey, I think Bao's tryin' to say something," Deacon said.

Bao groaned.

"What is it, buddy?" Nathan asked his wounded friend. "You should take it easy."

"He says-" Bao coughed. "If you let him have some he will help you survive." Leon stifled a laugh, but Bao continued. "He says he knows how to kill the demons."

"He might know something useful," the Professor said.

"The hell could he know?" Leon scoffed.

"He must live around here," the Professor said. "He could've learned something about those things, whatever they are."

"Let him have a hit," Deacon said. "Let's see what he knows."

Nathan hesitated then held out the open bag. Hiro rushed over and reached inside, pulling out a small straw and a tiny plastic bag with white powder before promptly inhaling the contents. He closed his eyes and twitched subtly, then his face relaxed.

"Are you supposed to snort heroin?" Leon asked.

"Sure," the Professor said. "You can snort it, inject it, smoke it. You can even eat it."

"Forget that," Nathan said. "We need to find out what he knows before those things come back. Bao? Bao?"

Bao was motionless.

"Christ." Nathan shook his head. "Sorry, Bao."

"Now what? Those things wrecked our ride," Leon said.

"We'll walk," Nathan said. "But first let's get away from this river. With those things in the water, we'll be safer moving through the forest."

They headed out in diamond formation. Nathan took point. Professor took rear security. Leon was on the left, Deacon the right. Donaldson took the centre, escorting Hiro. They marched a long time, deeper into the forest, without speaking.

"Hey Nathan," Donaldson said. "The boatman wants somethin'."

"He wants a fix," Nathan said.

"I don't think so."

Nathan stopped and turned. Hiro had a wide-eyed expression. He spoke urgently, fear in his voice, and motioned to the trees.

"What's up with him?"

"Prob'ly just freakin' out from the drugs."

"Probably not," the Professor said. "Heroin has a calming effect."

"You think he knows something we don't?" Donaldson's voice wavered.

"Nah," Leon shook his head. "He's just a junkie."

Nathan wasn't so sure. Fear crept along his skin, like the forest was watching him. "Keep your eyes open," he ordered. His heart beat hard in his chest, and he wiped a bead of sweat from his temple. "Something's out there."

"He's pointing at something," Donaldson said.

Hiro gesticulated towards the forest, an angle halfway between Nathan and Leon.

"What do you see?" Nathan squinted as he stared into the forest. A shape resolved, nearly imperceptible against leafy backdrop. A tall, slender creature stood just two dozen paces away, nearly invisible, seemingly made of glass. Its outline was only visible from the creature's gentle, hypnotic sway.

"Squad," Nathan said just loud enough to be heard. "Rapid, on my signal." He levelled his rifle. The creature cocked its head to the side then leapt into the trees. Nathan fired, bullets tracing the movement of the thing into the leaves. A hail of fire followed from his squadmates; bursts from Deacon and Leon, shots from Donaldson and the professor.

"Ceasefire!" Nathan ordered.

"Did we get it?" Leon asked.

"I don't think so." Professor shook his head. "No body."

"There was just one right?" Donaldson asked.

The men scanned the forest, listening intently. It was deathly quiet. No motion, except for the swaying of leaves in the wind.

"It was standing right in front of us. Shit, man, did you see that?" Leon's voice wavered.

"It was almost fuckin' invisible," Donaldson said.

"My question is," Nathan said, "how did he know it was there?"

The men glanced briefly at Hiro.

"Is it still around?" Nathan asked Hiro, waving towards the forest. "Is it still out there?"

Hiro seemed to understand. He squinted, ran his eyes over the forest, took a deep breath then pointed. Nathan looked towards the spot but saw only waving leaves.

"Ready," Nathan said, and the squad aimed their weapons.

"I don't see shit," Deacon muttered.

Leon frowned as he peered at the spot. "Where is it?"

"Grenades," Nathan ordered. Deacon popped a high-frag round into his XM-148, and Nathan loaded a high-explosive. "Fire."

The team unloaded. Two grenade rounds exploded in the distance, one blasting a sphere of destruction, the other sending a hail of fragmentation through the trees. They emptied their magazines into the forest.

"Ceasefire."

It was quiet, except for the reloading of weapons. Nathan plugged a canister into his 40mm attachment when something dropped from the trees. It landed forty paces away, crashed flat to the ground.

Nathan signalled to move, pointed to the spot, and the squad advanced in formation. Nathan reached it first, and saw a giant green body splayed on the ground. "We got it," he said over his shoulder, keeping his weapon trained on the motionless body. The others rushed forward; circled around the fallen creature.

"The hell is that thing?" Donaldson said, disgust thickening his voice.

"Whatever it is," Leon said, "we really fucked it up."

There were more than a dozen holes blasted through the creature's body. Its right arm was severed near the shoulder, and other limbs hung by strands of flesh. Pieces of the creature were scattered around where it fell, and the whole mess sat in a puddle of green liquid and innards.

"Looks like it's got scales," the Professor said. "Like a fish."

"That's not a fucking fish," Leon scoffed.

"No shit."

The Professor bent to examine the creature. He probed with the barrel of his SKS, running it against a series of large open slits on the creature's mangled torso. "It's got gills, too."

The creature twitched.

A flash of movement.

The Professor's eyes went wide, his jaw dropped open. The creature's remaining arm had plunged through the Professor's gut, emerging blood-soaked from the other side. The appendage withdrew, and the man slumped to the ground.

"Professor," Deacon yelled. He pulled his squadmate close as Donaldson and Leon unloaded into what was left of the green carcass, shredding it into sloppy chunks.

The Professor coughed up blood. "Shit," he managed,

through heaving breaths. "Must've been a reflex… Defence mechanism for the gills…"

"Take it easy, Professor," Nathan said. "We'll get you back to base."

"Bullshit," the Professor said. He was leaking badly from both sides of the wound.

"Guys," Donaldson said. "What the fuck is that?" He motioned with his M1 towards the butchered green monster. The pieces were vibrating. Minced remains of the creature, shreds of flesh and innards, oozed together, coalesced.

"Jesus," Leon said. "Is it still alive?"

"Is it… Is it putting itself together?" Donaldson said, staring in disbelief.

The creature slowly took form. It was a skeleton of goo first, oozing up from the ground, joined by pieces of green carcass.

Hiro shouted something and pointed to the bag in Nathan's hands.

"Now's not the fucking time," Leon shouted.

Hiro shouted back, insistent, pointing alternately to the bag and the monster.

"Maybe he knows how to stop it," Donaldson said.

Nathan opened the bag to Hiro, who reached in and rifled through the contents. He pulled out an ornate knife with engraved symbols along the blade.

Hiro made his way to the reanimating creature, took aim at the head, and thrust the knife. It entered the skull with a sickly crunch, and what remained of the creature turned instantly to dirt.

Hiro pulled the knife from a roughly head shaped mound of earth. "Iron," he said, with a thick Vietnamese accent. "Iron kills demon."

"Jesus Christ," Leon said.

"That thing," Donaldson started, "that thing really is a demon."

"Holy Christ, a fucking demon."

"Ngu'Tinh," Hiro said. "Yeow kwai."

The men looked to the Professor: eyes open, unblinking, silent.

"Goddamn."

"So this fucker knew along how to kill it," Leon said. He took a few aggressive paces towards Hiro. "Anything else you didn't tell us?"

Hiro put up his hands, stepped back, said something calmly.

"No use," Nathan said. "Can't understand each other anyway. Not without Bao."

"So now what?" Leon said.

"We get back." Nathan nodded decisively "Before any more of those things show up."

"How many you think are out there?" Leon said, peering into the trees.

"We saw two in the river. One in the trees," Nathan said. "So at least three."

"We should ask him," Donaldson said, pointing to Hiro. "He knows some English."

"You're right." Nathan turned to Hiro, and began to pantomime. "One." He pointed to the mound of dirt that used to be the demon. "Two, three…" He pointed backwards, from where the others had come then held up three fingers. "How many?" Nathan shrugged his shoulders, turned up his palms.

Hiro looked Nathan in the eyes, nodded. "Two more yeow kwai."

"You think he understood?" Donaldson asked.

"I don't know," Nathan said. "Let's go," he ordered. "Column formation. Deacon's on point. Leon, you're on rear. Keep your eye on Hiro. Donaldson, just get in line and keep your eyes open."

In formation they marched deeper into the forest. Hiro requested a hit during the march and Nathan obliged. This time Hiro opted for injecting it then held up the needle to Nathan.

"No thanks," Nathan said, and they continued walking.

Leon stopped. "You sure you're takin' us the right way?"

"Yeah," Deacon said.

"Then why do I hear water?" Leon said.

They all stopped to listen.

"Shit," Nathan said. "Are we back at the river?"

"Did you fuck up the navigation?" Leon shouted.

"No, this makes sense," Deacon said. "The river bends back around on the return. We just intercepted it."

"I don't think that's right," Nathan said.

"I don't know…" Deacon rummaged through his pocket with his free hand. "But since we're here anyway…" He pulled a hand-held piece of electronic equipment free and retracted its antennae. A black screen in the middle of the device blinked intermittently with a red dot.

"The hell is that?" Donaldson asked.

"The tracker," Deacon said. "He's near."

"Who's near?"

"Billy."

"Who?"

"His fuckin' dolphin," Leon said.

"Wait a minute," Donaldson glared. "Wait just a goddamn minute. You didn't drag us back here so you could look for your dolphin, did you?"

"Relax, we're just a few degrees off course."

"Mother fucker."

"It'll only take a minute," Deacon said while orienting himself, sweeping the device left and right. "This way."

"No way," Donaldson said. "We aren't goin' back to the river now."

"You don't call the shots." Deacon started towards the river.

"I agree with the jarhead," Leon said. "We can't fight those things in the water."

"They're right," Nathan said to Deacon. "It's too risky."

"You said it yourself, Nathan. Rob and Billy are part of the team. And they need us." Deacon pointed to the tracking device. "He's close."

"How close?" Nathan asked.

"Less than a klick."

Nathan ran scenarios through his head; it was risky, but Deacon had a point. "All right. Let's go."

"You've gotta be kidding me," Donaldson said.

"You don't get an opinion," Nathan snapped. "You practically begged to come with us. We're doing you a favour, remember? For your brother? Now let's move."

They reoriented and headed back for the river.

"This is a bad idea," Leon said.

Part of Nathan agreed, but he kept it to himself.

Deacon reached the river first. Nathan joined him, signalled all clear, and the others lined up along the bank.

"So where we looking?" Nathan asked.

"There." Deacon motioned with his head. "About fifty meters."

They peered through the hanging foliage. Across the flowing water, the river extended into a large cove of placid water. The bay was roughly circular, dotted here and there with large boulders that were blanketed with water moss.

"He's in that bay?"

"Here, Billy, Billy, Billy," Leon called out, then laughed awkwardly at his own joke.

"So what now?"

"Dolphin whistle." Deacon pointed to a toggle-switch on the tracking device. "Emits a high frequency sound. They're trained to come when they hear it."

"Hold on," Nathan said. "What if those things can hear it, too?"

Deacon shrugged. "There's no reason to think they're around. Besides, what other choice do we have?"

"What other choice?" Leon glared. "We could turn around and get the fuck out of here."

They all looked to Nathan. "Okay," he said. "Do it."

"I got a real bad feelin' about this," Leon muttered.

Deacon flipped the toggle. "It's transmitting now."

"I don't hear shit," Leon said.

"You're not supposed to. It's inaudible high-frequency. Trust me, it's working."

In the bay across the river, the boulders shook, jostled in place, and something huge surged from the water. A giant centipede-like monstrosity, over a hundred meters long. It lifted itself on hundreds of legs, water pouring from between the segments of its body as it rose from the bay.

"Ngu'Tinh," Hiro said.

The gigantic demon turned and snaked towards them through the water. Its legs were a flurry of motion pounding the water, the sound like approaching machine-gun fire.

Nathan froze as the demon charged, then instinct kicked in. "Grenades, rapid," he shouted.

Donaldson threw a grenade; Leon blasted a steady stream with his Stoner. Nathan and Deacon fired high-explosive canisters then emptied their mags into the approaching monster. Three successive explosions rocked the river, sending up towers of water and clouds of vapour. When the mist cleared, the creature was gone, the river silent.

"Holy fuck," Leon shouted. "What was that thing?"

"Where'd it go?" Donaldson said. "Downriver?"

"Hey, guys," Deacon pointed to the tracking device. "Billy's on the move."

They watched the red blip on the screen. It moved perpendicular to them across the river, on to the land, then curved through the forest.

"It's on land," Deacon said.

"That's not Billy," Nathan said. "If one of those things ate the tracker, would it still work?"

"Yeah." Deacon's face fell. "It probably would."

"Weapons ready," Nathan ordered.

There were clicks and shuffling sounds as they reloaded. Deacon placed the tracker on the ground so he could ready his weapon.

"Where is it?" Leon said.

Deacon motioned with the barrel of his M79. "It's closing, slowly. Thirty meters." He read the distance from the device at his feet. "Twenty meters. Ten." He steadied his rifle. "Wait. It stopped."

"Where is it?" Donaldson whispered. "I don't see it."

"What're we waitin' for?" Leon growled.

"For visual." Nathan scanned the canopy. "I think it's in the trees."

The squad was silent, frozen in anticipation. The thing was out there, just ten meters away. They searched, but saw nothing but forest, heard nothing but whispering wind, breeze-blown leaves. The red blip on the tracker was motionless.

Leon screamed.

Nathan swivelled in time to see Leon dragged along the forest floor by one of the mantis-things. It moved so fast it looked like they were flying, and in a split second they were two dozen paces into the brush.

Concealed by the vegetation, Nathan couldn't see Leon, but he could hear the furious slashing of the demon. A few shots rang out, then a scream.

Nathan fired his 40mm. *THUNK. BOOM.* The brush exploded. Nathan was hit in the chest by a chunk of the creature; the rest of the squad knocked over by the shock wave. Nathan landed on his back, ears ringing.

Nathan, Deacon, Donaldson, and Hiro pushed to their feet, shook themselves. They were lightly painted with a mixture of red and green from the casualties.

"Fucking Christ," Nathan said.

"How'd it get over there without us seeing it move?" Donaldson asked, a tremble in his voice.

"It didn't. They're hunting in pairs." Deacon motioned to the tracker. "The other one's still there." The red dot was motionless. Then it darted suddenly.

"It's on the move," Deacon said, glancing between the tracker and the water.

Nathan scanned the water. "Where?"

"The river."

There was a splash, and a faint ripple in the water moving towards the opposite bank. Donaldson fired a few shots of his M1, but the target had vanished.

"Shit. What do we do?"

"I don't know." Nathan bent to pick up the tracker. The red dot had moved fifty meters towards the bay.

Hiro grabbed Nathan by the shoulder, pointed to the exploded bodies of Leon and the second mantis creature, then pointed to his bag of supplies.

"Yeah." Nathan nodded. "Go ahead."

Hiro retrieved the iron knife from the bag then ran to the bodies.

"C'mon," Nathan said to Donaldson and Deacon. The three of them followed Hiro to where a small crater had been blasted into the ground, ringed with the carnage.

"Head," Hiro said, pointing to his own. Then he scoured the area. Nathan joined in the search, brushing aside leaves, and the others followed his lead.

"Got it." Donaldson shouted, and kicked the green demon skull like a soccer ball. It rolled to Hiro, who promptly knelt and stabbed it. The head gave way with a crunch then turned to dirt.

Hiro stood, stared at Nathan. "One more."

Nathan nodded then pointed across the river.

"Wait a minute," Deacon said. "We're not really goin' after it?"

"There's one left, and we know where it is." Nathan pointed to the tracker. "I'm done being hunted. We're doing the hunting now."

"Opium." Hiro pointed to sac on Nathan's shoulders.

"Sure," Nathan said, opening the bag. "Go ahead."

"Now? But we're about to go after that thing." Deacon said.

"Better for him to be relaxed than itching."

Hiro heated the spoon, prepared the syringe then injected the liquid into his arm. He held out the needle to Nathan.

"No thanks. I'm working."

Hiro pushed the needle forwards, insistent. "Ngu'Tinh," he said. "No eyes."

"No eyes?" Deacon raised an eyebrow. "The hell does that mean?"

"I don't know. Doesn't matter." Nathan took the drug para-phernalia from Hiro, then put it in the bag and swung it over his shoulder. "Let's go."

Hunt or be hunted. Nathan marched into the river, trudging through knee-deep water. Cool wetness soaked up into his clothes, a welcome relief from the humid air. He was gripped suddenly with fear of what might be lurking in the dark water. But he had a monster to kill. Nathan pushed forward, deeper into the river. *Hunt or be hunted.*

"Shit." Deacon edged into the water. "We're really doin' this?"

"Yep," Nathan said.

The ground dropped out below, and Nathan started treading. Donaldson was spitting up water, struggling to keep his head above. "How you fuckin' swim like this?" he shouted. "My shit's weighing me down".

"We're SEALs," Nathan said. "It's what we do." In training they'd tied his hands behind his back and threw him in a swimming pool, blindfolded, weights on his ankles. He made it through that hour-long test, so this river crossing would be a breeze. Unless any of those creatures came back.

Hiro reached the bank first, then climbed up and headed towards the bay.

"Slow down," Nathan called out. "You don't even know where it is."

Nathan felt the river bottom with his foot, then stood, dripping wet, and rushed to catch up with Hiro. He hopped into the bay alongside the man, and the two of them stood in the placid, waist-deep water. The top was caked with algae, and the pool was littered with moss-covered boulders, oddly round.

Hiro moved to one of the boulders with the ornate iron knife in hand.

"What's he doin'?" Deacon asked as he joined Nathan.

"I don't know."

Hiro thrust the knife and punctured the boulder. There was a hiss of air followed by a green cloud of gas. Hiro turned his head and closed his eyes, then reached his hands into the gash and pulled it apart, groaning from the effort.

"Egg," Hiro said to Nathan.

"Holy shit." Nathan looked again at the bay, littered with dozens of the mossy eggs. "It's a nest."

Donaldson caught up and hopped into the bay with a splash. "Jesus. There must be a hundred of 'em."

"Let's just hope their mom doesn't come back."

Hiro had torn the shell open wide enough to see inside. Nathan eyed the contents with horror and disgust. A creature was curled up inside, wrapped in what looked like a bag of snot. Hiro dug into the goo, clutched the head with one hand, and thrust his knife. The whole mess turned to dirt, which dissolved into the bay. Then Hiro walked to the next closest egg and punched a hole with his knife.

"So what do we do?" Deacon asked.

"We help." Nathan drew his KA-BAR combat knife.

The four of them worked their way through the nest. Donaldson spearing the eggs with his M-series bayonet, Nathan and Deacon hacking with their KA-BARs, tearing open the shells, and Hiro delivering the killing stroke with his iron knife. They were halfway through the nest when Nathan stopped suddenly. Something didn't feel right.

"Stop," he yelled. "You feel that?"

The algae was vibrating, the water subtly sloshing, the eggs shaking. A crack formed on one of the shells, and a green limb emerged.

"They're hatching," Nathan shouted. "Hurry."

Hiro moved quickly, splashing through the water, slashing the embryotic mantis-things as they pushed free from the eggs. But the dog-sized demons were popping out faster than Hiro could catch them. The bay was quickly teeming with the demons, and the water erupted into splashing as they thrashed and swarmed.

"They're comin' straight for us," Deacon shouted. Nathan and Deacon sprayed on full-auto, sweeping left and right across the hatchling demons, but the swarm closed on them.

Deacon let out a scream as serrated arms ripped through his legs. Nathan grabbed Deacon by his shoulders, felt the body go limp as Deacon's legs gave out.

"I got you, buddy." He yanked Deacon from the thrashing creatures, their green arms now adorned with fresh ribbons of human flesh and ligament. Nathan backed up a few steps and heaved Deacon to dry land beside the bay. Hiro was in the middle of the chaos, leaping from one demon to the next, plunging his knife into their skulls.

"Hey, over here," Donaldson shouted from a dozen paces away. He took careful aim then fired. One of the creature's heads exploded from the shot, and the body fell. The swarm rushed in Donaldson's direction. He took out two more before they closed on him. Slashing arms took out his Achilles tendon, and Donaldson crumpled. He dropped his rifle, started fumbling with something he pulled from his pocket, and the swarm enveloped him.

An explosion ripped through the cluster of demons. Nathan instinctively shut his eyes, shielded his head. The blast knocked him back, and he was pelted with chunks.

Nathan took advantage of the distraction provided by Donaldson's grenade and dragged Deacon deeper into the forest, three-dozen paces from the demon-filled bay, then turned his attention to the wounds. Deacon's lower legs were missing, bones exposed. The thighs were half-butchered. Deep-red blood was pouring out, and Nathan could see a trail of blood from where they'd come.

"My legs." Deacon looked down at himself. "My fucking legs."

"You're alive." Nathan pulled two field tourniquets from his jacket pocket. "Now let's keep you that way." Pulling out his KA-BAR, Nathan sawed away the pant leg, tore the fabric away, and exposed the gashes. He wrapped the tourniquet strap around Deacon's right thigh, and tightened it. "Stay with me, buddy." He tightened the second tourniquet above the deep gouges in the left thigh. "How you doing?"

"I've been better." Deacon groaned.

"This should help," Nathan said, injecting Deacon with a syrette.

A rustling in the brush behind; something coming towards them. Nathan's grip tightened on his weapon. The leaves brushed aside. Hiro stepped out with a smile.

"Holy shit," Nathan said. "I think he got the rest of 'em."

"No way. That's not possible," Deacon said, his voice slurred.

Hiro walked towards them calmly. "Opium," he said. "Ngu'Tinh, no eyes."

"I think..." Nathan paused. "I think he's saying they can't see him when he's high."

"Bull-fucking-shit." Deacon's voice stronger this time.

"How the hell else did he kill all those things? And with nothing but a knife?"

Nathan tossed the bag to Hiro, who fished out the metal spoon, lighter, a vial of brown liquid, and a syringe. He heated the drugs into a bubbling brown liquid, filled the syringe, injected it into his arm then smiled.

"All right, Hiro." Nathan rolled up his sleeve then held out his arm. "Hit me."

Deacon watched with wide-eyed disbelief.

Hiro nodded; prepared another dose. Nathan clenched his fist and Hiro aimed for a vein on Nathan's inner elbow. He felt a pinch as the needle went in. Then Hiro pushed the plunger.

Calm. That's what Nathan felt. The high wasn't mind altering or disorienting. He was wide awake, just suddenly happy, mellow. Then he remembered the mantis demon. Nathan quickly checked the tracking device.

"That thing is still out there," Nathan said. "I'm gonna go kill it." Then he turned to Hiro. "Protect him," he pointed to Deacon. "I'll be back."

Hiro nodded, and Nathan walked into the forest.

On the tracking device, the red dot was slowly circling the bay. Nathan gauged its path, positioned himself for intercept, then crouched in the brush and waited.

A twig snapped.

Leaves rustled.

The creature was there, a few paces away, slinking through the trees.

It edged closer, within arms-reach. He'd seen how fast it could move. He'd get one chance. Nathan steadied his CAR-15. *How did I get myself into this shit?*

He pulled the trigger.

Click.

The creature turned towards the sound. A stabbing fear ran through Nathan's spine as he realised the weapon misfired, and he found himself staring face to eyeless-face with the demon. Heart pounding, breath caught in his throat, the stare-down seemed to last an eternity.

You can't see me, can you? He tossed his rifle to the side. It landed among some reeds with a splash, and the demon swivelled to face the sound. Then it lurched towards the water, slowly stalking the source of the noise.

I've got you now. Nathan drew his KA-BAR then followed the creature. It had a plodding gait, rising and falling a full meter with each lurching step. Nathan stepped carefully behind, slowly, matching its rhythm. The creature bent to the reeds, probing with its serrated arms. Then Nathan leapt.

He landed on the back of the creature and wrapped his legs around the torso. It stood, thrashed its limbs. Nathan struggled to hold on, sawing at its neck with the KA-BAR. The two of them spun in place, the demon thrashing wildly, whipping its body left and right. Nathan's knife tore through the last strand of the neck, severing the head, which dropped and thudded to the ground. The creature fell, and Nathan with it.

He landed, picked up the head, and ran back to Hiro.

"Here." He tossed the green head. Hiro caught it, placed it on the ground, and stabbed it with the iron knife. The head turned to dirt.

"Hey," Deacon said with concern. "The tracker. Is it still transmitting?"

"I don't know," Nathan said, amazed Deacon was coherent considering his injuries, but the man loved his dolphins.

"Check the switch."

Nathan examined the device. The toggle was still in the on-position. *Shit.* He flipped it off just as another blip moved into range. It was coming down the river.

"Another one incoming," Nathan said. "Where's your gun?"

"Dropped it. Where's yours?"

"Fuck." Nathan closed his eyes. He'd left his weapon in the reeds. It was jammed, anyway. "All right, here we go." He bent his knees, combat ready, and held out his KA-BAR. Hiro followed his lead and readied his own blade.

"Thirty meters. Twenty. Ten. It's right next to us," he said. "Sittin' in the river".

"What do we do?"

"You sit tight," Nathan said, and he stalked towards the river. He approached slowly then peered over the edge. There was a large shape in the water. Nathan leaned closer, KA-BAR raised, and a smooth, blue-grey snout broke the surface.

Nathan laughed. "Holy shit. Rob the dolphin." The small tracking device was still strapped over the dolphin's right fin. A second dolphin appeared, minus the tracker. Nathan laughed again. "And Billy." Nathan bent and patted the dolphin on the head. "Jesus, am I glad to see you two. Wait right there." He rushed over to Deacon. "You've got to see this."

"What? What is it?"

"Come on." Nathan heaved Deacon up, lifted him over his shoulders and carried him towards the river. Hiro followed them to the bank.

"Rob! Billy! But how? I thought for sure…" Deacon wiped his eyes. The dolphins chirped, and Deacon laughed.

"You okay?"

"Yeah, I'm okay. Sorry, just happy to see them." He shook his head. "Now lower me into the water."

"What?"

"They're trained for riding," Deacon said. "And they know the way back to base."

"Are you telling we can just ride 'em back to base?"

"That's what I'm telling you."

Deacon was acting remarkably calm for someone missing both his legs. Nathan wondered whether it was because of the syrette or the dolphins. "You sure?" he said.

"Yeah," Deacon answered. "Let's go."

With Hiro's help, Nathan lowered Deacon into the water. Deacon gave Billy a pat on the head, then grabbed onto a fin, and the dolphin took off back towards base, shrinking into the distance downriver.

Nathan turned to Hiro. "Thank you".

Hiro nodded. "I stay."

Nathan handed Hiro his bag, then lowered himself into the water. He took hold of Rob's fin, and the dolphin started back to base. Nathan held tight to the rubbery grey handhold, and looked back to see Hiro standing on the bank, iron knife in hand. Somewhere out there was the demon mother, Ngu'Tinh.

Deacon and Nathan made it back to base without incident. They never had to explain themselves to General Cain as they were immediately moved off-base. First the shit hit the fan, then intel' verified what they could. Six months later, after things had settled down, a handful of medals were awarded, most of them posthumously. Nathan was given a promotion and offered command of a new team, SEAL team-X, clandestine operators tasked with hunting the things they'd found in the forests of Vietnam. The team was equipped with new weapons, NGX series: 40mm iron frags, iron KA-BARs, iron-tipped stoner rounds. Each operator also got a handy pack of epi-pen opioid injectors.

Nathan never liked hunting animals. But hunting demons was another story. Ngu'Tinh was still out there.

WARM BODIES

An Alpha Unit story
Kirsten Cross

"Taints are, without doubt, the biggest threat facing us today. As a result of our ignorance, our arrogance, and our misguided sense of scientific endeavour, we have created a serious threat to the safety and security of this country and its people. This committee therefore recommends the immediate formation of a specialist unit made up of elite members of Her Majesty's Armed Forces with the expressed duty of combating this threat above all else. We also recommend that the unit include experts in the field of science, military tactics, and Vampirism. May God help us all."
Professor Edward P. Glaston, Chairman, COBRA Emergency Committee Report, August 2015.

The trouble with night-vision goggles is that the slightest flash of any bright light and you're effectively 'blasted out'. And when you've got some dirty little bastard Taint intent on chowing down on any soft tissue it can find about three feet from your arse then being blind, even for a split second, is not an option.

"Jesus, Mary, Joseph and all the little saints, these sons of bitches are fast!" Robbie Moore, trying to find his bearings in the eerie green glow of a room seen through NVGs, aimed the adapted M4 Benelli pump action shotgun straight at the snarling face of the Taint. He fired. And missed. "Fuck!"

"Seriously? From six feet away? Who taught you to shoot? Your grandmother?" Terry Warner screamed abuse at his oppo and fumbled with his own M4. As inanimate objects are wont to do at the most inopportune moment, the damn thing stubbornly refused to co-operate. "Shit! *Shit!*"

"Okay, ladies. We all knew this was coming. Breathe." The calm voice of Colby Flynn cut through the screaming and mayhem. "Terry, stop panicking. Safety off. Rob, prime and *squeeze* the damn trigger, don't yank on it. You're shooting a Taint, not giving yourself a hand job." Colby wanted the newbies to get their first kill for themselves this time, rather than having to step in for them yet again. And preferably before the rest of the pack of slathering, wild-eyed Taints came barrelling through the door and tore them all to pieces, if you don't mind lads, thank you *very* much.

An M4 blasted out a cartridge filled with liquid, spraying a fluorescent pale-green mist into the air, like someone had shaken a can of soda and pulled the tab. Colby checked the two men. It was Robbie Moore who had finally got his shit together and managed to fire off a second shot. "Adda boy." He melted back into the corner of the room and watched how the two men handled a close-quarters confrontation with one of mankind's most terrifying creations, a second-generation Taint with an appetite and an attitude. After the initial god-awful fumbling and general fuck-uppery, the two men started to get themselves organised. Their training – if it was ever truly possible to 'train' for your first full-on Taint attack – finally kicked in.

The Taint recoiled as the fine mist drenched it from the top of its oozing scalp to the large hole the M4 projectile had punched through the middle of its chest. It took a few microseconds for it to realise it had been hit. The Taint looked down at its chest, and then back up at Robbie. "In three… two… one…" Colby counted down, ticking the seconds off on curled fingers. "And…"

The Taint went rigid and splayed its arms out. Orange lines snaked through its body, visible under the surface of the skin, like rivers of lava flowing through its veins. Its skin started to bulge and blister. The Taint threw its head back and let out a wail. The incensed creature started to convulse and dropped to the floor. The spasms grew increasingly violent, and there was a loud crack as it twisted so savagely its spine snapped. It thrashed on the floor, screaming like all the souls of Hell were crying out as one voice. The creature's fists smashed into the concrete floor and its heels drummed violently. The orange rivers became a tsunami of fire roaring through its body.

The explosion, when it came, was a bit of a relief to be honest. All that thrashing and screaming always gave Colby a headache. The liquid-filled projectile finally did its job, but it was more of a wet fart rather than a proper 'boom', rather like a damp feather pillow splitting. A shower of sparks and ash mushroomed upwards and filled the room.

"There ya go!" Colby grinned at the two men. It was their first close-quarters incendiary. They'd done decapitation, which was shocking enough, but relatively drama-free. Decapitating didn't cause all that noisy thrashing about and exploding. But a blast from a M4 adapted to deliver a deadly organophosphur payload was a whole different story. It was always interesting watching the newbies react to their first full-on, heel drumming, concrete punching 'party popper', as the lads called them.

The two men stared at Colby. Through their night vision goggles he looked like a very muscular, very menacing green goblin. This particular grinch, though, wasn't interested in ruining Christmas. He was focused on training the new kids to stay alive beyond their first sortie.

Flynn's relaxed posture and nonchalant expression verged on the 'seen it, done it' arrogance that all the veterans of Alpha Unit had. But both newbies knew he was perfectly entitled to at least a certain level of arrogance. After all, the guy had, in fact, both seen it *and* done it. For real.

Colby grinned at his charges and pointed to the open door. "Um, incoming?"

Warner and Moore spun around. "Ah, crap…" In the green landscape created by their NVGs the men could see a set of long, sinewy fingers curling around the doorframe. Ragged, razor sharp nails that no French manicurist could ever redeem tipped off the insectoid-like digits. They dripped with venom. The latest generation of Taints had evolved yet again, developing tubes that ran underneath the skin and ended at the base of each nail bed, delivering a toxin that would paralyse the victim in seconds.

This new development meant that getting 'up close and personal' with a Taint had a whole new level of risk. Q division was working on clothing made from a Kevlar-mesh cloth that would protect the teams from accidental scratches, including gloves, full combats and balaclavas. But they were still a few weeks from going into production. Right now, all it took was one slash, one tear through the outer layers of skin and into the subcutaneous tissue beneath, and you were flat on your backside, paralysed rigid but still fully aware as Taints started to rip into your flesh. Never had the term 'keep the buggers at arm's length' been taken so literally.

Right behind these toxin-laden fingers emerged a face that only a mother Taint could love. The skin on its face was lacerated into tramlines, and every wound was infected. A glimpse of white bone shone behind one particularly broad slash that stretched from its eye socket to the corner of its mouth. A mouth that, as to be expected, was filled with needle-sharp teeth also dripping with toxic juices.

It locked its gaze onto Terry Warner, two eyes filled with hate, vitriol, and probably even more damn venom. These second-gen Taints weren't just mutant vampires – they were walking chemical factories as well.

Colby waited to see how Warner would react. Eye contact was one of the toughest tests anyone wanting to join the Unit would face. That whole thing about vampires having the ability to mesmerise their victims wasn't a myth. The Old World vamps had it, and now, so did the Taints. That blood-curdling, bone-chilling gaze could stop even a fully trained member of the Unit in their tracks. It froze your soul. It coursed down your veins and nerves like crackling ice. It touched a primeval fear that every human being carried in their subconscious. That 'look' could crash though centuries of evolution and turn the most hardened, fully-trained and combat-experienced soldier into a gibbering, pitchfork-waving idiot villager in a second. It was the same cold fear that a human feels when they stare into the eyes of a wolf. That realisation that guess what, buddy, you're no longer the apex predator. However, the bugger in front of you with the golden eyes, snarling face and big, fuck-off fangs most certainly is.

But the look that froze your soul and turned you into a dribbling, compliant moron could be beaten. Its power lay in convincing you that you were helpless in the face of this hellish horror. As in any combat situation, resisting the urge to freeze would be the only thing that would keep you alive. If you were getting the 'look', it meant that the Taint was within a few feet. And that was never a good place to be.

The newbies had been warned. What was commonly referred to as 'getting a dose of epic stink-eye' was right there in week-one training. But in all the fury and confusion of a hunt, Warner had done what all newbies do on their first outing – forgotten everything that really mattered. He flipped up his night vision goggles and gazed into the eyes of the Taint. His arms went limp and the M4 dropped to his side, his finger still curled around the trigger. If he it squeezed now, he'd probably shoot his own damn foot off.

"Terry! Terry, you idiot, snap out of it! *Terry!*" Robbie tried to get through to his oppo, but the mesmerised berk simply stood, gawping at the slathering, snarling Taint. Robbie cursed, swung his M4 up and blasted wildly at the creature. He didn't miss this time. The Taint's head exploded, closely followed by the rest of him.

Then came more. So many more. A writhing avalanche of snarling, slathering Taints poured through the door, screeching and slashing those venom-laced talons towards the two men. Within a heartbeat the Taints were all over them. To their credit, the lads went down fighting. But underneath a rugby-scrum's worth of Taints, they didn't have a prayer. Their own screams joined in with those of their devourers…

Colby Flynn watched the Taints overwhelm the two men. "Damn it!" He glanced up at a corner of the room and made a cutting gesture across his throat. "End program!" A loud buzzer sounded.

The Taints melted away.

All that was left were two whimpering men, lying in a foetal position in the middle of the floor, their M4s abandoned at their sides.

"Well, *that* went well…" Colby sighed and let out a sharp whistle between his teeth. "Upsy daisy, ladies!"

"*Real enough for ya, Col?*" A voice crackled over a tannoy, followed by a nasty little chuckle.

Colby glanced up to a corner of the room and spoke back to the disembodied voice. "Cox, you're a sick, twisted son of a bitch, you know that? A damn genius, granted, and obviously a serious gamer with a Resident Evil addiction, for sure. But sick and twisted nevertheless. Loved all the thrashing and the drumming, though. Super real. When did you upgrade the VR programming?"

"*Ah, there was nothing on the telly last night. So, ya know. Idle hands, devil's work and all that shit…*"

"Remind me to make sure you stay busy, you bloody lunatic." Colby glanced at the newbies, who were slowly starting to uncurl and get back up to their feet. They both looked utterly embarrassed and brushed the dust off their combats, sheepish looks on their faces. Colby turned back up to the corner of the room. "One thing, Micky, that second one? Too slow, fella. Way too slow. We're not dealing with zombies here, mate, we're going up against genetically-altered, batshit-crazy vamps. Speed 'em up a bit. Make it more realistic."

Terry Warner flipped his NVGs up and glared at Colby. "More realistic? More fucking *realistic*? Are you actually kidding me?" A blank stare from Colby reminded him he was talking to a superior officer. "I mean, are you actually kidding me, *sir*?"

"Corporal Warner, you are currently standing in a puddle of your own piss after having been well and truly freaked out by a virtual-reality Taint that, if I'm honest, has some flaws that need to be ironed out–"

"*Hey! I thought you liked Binky!*" Micky's voice crackled over the tannoy again, interrupting Colby mid-rant. He sounded mortally offended.

Colby paused, and looked straight at Warner, who responded with a shrug and a '*Yeah, I heard that too…*' look of wide-eyed astonishment.

Both men looked up at the tannoy and spoke together "Seriously?"

There was a short pause before an indignant voice responded, "*What's wrong with Binky?*"

"What's wrong with *you?*" Colby shook his head, and returned his attention to Warner and his interrupted rant. "Listen, fella. This?" He waved an arm around. "It's a simulation. Nothing more. It's designed as a cold-body experience to get you used to facing a Taint up close and personal before we assign you to a unit. This is just like any other kill house, Warner. A training exercise. Nothing more. Okay, granted, it's a kill house with a truly astonishing level of technical wizardry and the latest in virtual reality immersive training, courtesy of that nutjob up there," he jerked a thumb towards the tannoy.

"*I can still hear you, you know!*"

Colby ignored the hurt, disembodied voice. "But that's all it is, *just* a training exercise. So if you find this disturbing then, trust me, mate, facing a warm body is a whole 'nother level of crazy shit. And in that situation you can't just yell 'player one out!' and hope Micky turns the VR off before you go all pant-pissy and foetal again." He drew a breath and studied the shocked Warner. "Look. Be honest, okay? If you can't cope with this then just say the word and we'll RTU you. Nobody will think any less of you. This gig isn't for everyone, believe me–"

"No, sir! No, that's not what I meant. I… shit. I've got nothing here…" Warner glared at the floor. "Ah, bollocks. You're gonna RTU me anyway, aren't you?"

Colby shook his head. "We don't return someone to their unit just for one fuck up. Everyone fails their first kill house. But if you are selected to join the Unit then bear in mind that, out in the real world? Facing real Taints?" Colby shrugged. "Yeah, you only get one shot at that, mate. So fail in here, survive out there." He pushed himself off the wall and stood a few inches from

Warner. The newbie was still breathing heavy, and the slightly acidic tang of ammonia wafted up from his damp combats.

Colby's normally jovial look melted away, and Warner faced Flynn's own heavy-duty version of epic stink-eye. The big man's pale green eyes were hard, and the hint of a smile that usually pulled at the corners of Flynn's mouth had vanished. "But screw up a second time, or give me any indication that you could end up putting your oppos' lives in danger and I promise you, mate, I *promise you*, you'll be back peeling spuds in the Catering Corps before you can say Dauphinoise potatoes."

"I was with the Guards, sir."

"Same difference." Colby sniffed, and wished he hadn't. "Go and get yourself cleaned up." He threw a glance at the silent Terry. "Both of you." They paused, looking awkward and apologetic. Colby glowered, his eyes narrowing even further. "And you're still here *why*, exactly?"

Without another word, the two newbies turned and trudged out of the room. Their body posture spoke of defeat, dejection and a mortal fear that an RTU order was in their future at some point.

Colby watched the two men shuffle listlessly out. The frown was still etched on his face, but now he focused it up at the corner where the speaker and camera were hidden. He jerked a thumb towards the door. "You get all that?"

There was a click and a woman's voice – soft, authoritative and well spoken – responded. *"They're on their first run-through, Col. It's a beasting nobody expects the first time around. Give them a second go at it and we'll be able to make a decision from there. They'll either get their shit together, or they won't."*

Colby sniffed, rubbed his nose and nodded. "Yeah. Guess we all pissed our pants the first time, huh?"

"Speak for yourself, Mister Flynn!"

"Uh-oh!" Colby laughed out loud. He was in for a smack around the ear later from Yolanda for that one. He could tell – the only time she called him 'Mister Flynn' was when she was going all Sandhurst on his arse. "Okay. Get Micky to do a reset.

We'll go again at oh-two hundred. Zero warning. I want this to be as realistic as possible."

"*Copy that. I'll get him to speed Binky number two up a bit as well.*"

Colby rolled his eyes and sighed. "Seriously, Yol, Binky? Fucking *Binky?*"

"Honestly? I have no bloody idea. I think Micky's a Discworld fan or something."

The tannoy crackled then went silent. Colby flipped his NVGs down and scanned the room. It was too empty to make things realistic. If these guys were to become competent Taint hunters, then they needed to be pushed. Hard. He made a mental note to get some furniture put into this room. It could be an obstacle or a weapon, depending on how the guys reacted.

In the distance, four pops sounded in rapid succession. Colby frowned. There shouldn't be anyone else in the kill house when they were training, so who was shooting? He thought for a moment and then shrugged. "Meh, probably one of the lads on the range." Sound tended to travel in funny ways sometimes, thanks to the topography of the surrounding hills. He forgot about the gunfire and glanced at his watch. "Ooo! Chow time! Thank Christ for that, I'm starving!" His stomach let out a strangled gurgle and he pressed a hand on his abdomen to still the beast. "Yep. Deffo chow time."

As he trotted out of the room and made his way down the corridors and stairs towards the ground floor, Colby mentally assessed the two lads. Terry Warner lacked confidence, but had shown real potential up until the most recent debacle. Leaving the safety on was unforgivable in a sweep-through of a known or even a potential hot zone. And he had frozen when he encountered Binky's stink-eye act. Robbie Moore's aim was atrocious. The lad needed at least a fortnight on the range and another week or two in the live-ammo kill house to get up to standard. But he had reacted according to his training, and saved his partner. So okay, both had messed up, but out of the two, Moore was probably worth a second chance...

"Whoa!" Colby threw an arm out to balance himself as his foot slid away. There was something greasy and viscous on the floor, as slippery as engine oil. The air had a strange metallic tang, mixed in with pungent top notes of shit and opened bowels. The hairs on the back of Colby's neck rose, and he glanced at the floor. A smear, like a sauce flourish on a top-end restaurant plate, formed a crescent where his boot heel had skidded. The liquid was thick, dark, and in the iridescent light of a full moon Flynn could see vapour rising off it. So it was warm, then. And fresh. Very, very fresh.

He crouched, flipped his NVGs up and out of the way, and dipped a finger in the liquid. He rubbed it between his finger and thumb. As he pulled his thumb and finger apart, the liquid formed a hair-fine connection before snapping and creating two globules, one on each finger. Colby scowled. "Damn..." He knew that consistency. Only one fluid in the world felt like that – blood.

He pressed the button on his radio with his left hand. His right instinctively curled around the butt of a Glock 17 that sat in a holster strapped to his thigh. He flicked the safety off and disengaged the coiled lanyard that the Health and Safety lot insisted on attaching to the gun for no apparent reason other than that they knew it annoyed the *ever living shit* out of him. He cradled the butt in his hand, ready for a quick draw if necessary. "Micky, I'm in corridor two. Confirmation please, mate."

A voice crackled in his earpiece. "Go ahead, Col."

"I've got blood here. A lot of blood. Is this part of the simulation?"

"Blood?"

"Yeah. Blood. Ya know, blood. That sticky red shit that's quite important for the whole living thing. I know you have a passion for realism in these simulations, you mad bastard, but does it stretch to chucking a gallon of pig's blood on the floor as well?"

"Negative, mate. Negative."

"Then we have a problem. Scan for heat signatures. I think we might have a live one on our hands here, fella."

"Copy that. The captain's getting Alpha and Bravo teams ready."

Colby pressed the squawk button again. "That's reassuring. Arm up for warm bodies. I've got a really bad feeling about this…"

Colby stood, the Glock now cradled in his hand. His Blackhawk combat knife pressed against his left hip. He had seventeen hollowpoint rounds and six inches of precision ground D-2 steel with a wickedly sharp edge. He patted the knife for reassurance. You might run out of bullets, but you never run out of knife.

He flipped his goggles back down. The NVGs allowed him to see clearly in that weird, mottled-green monotone, but like any soldier he knew full well that they could distort things, especially depth perception. Objects seen through a pair of NVGs could be closer than they appeared, a bit like a police car in a wing mirror. And when you were talking about getting the jump on Taints, that was not a good thing. You wanted Taints to be as far away from you as possible. And preferably dead.

Instinct kicked in. Since his first encounter with the granddaddy of the undead back in Turkey a year earlier, Colby Flynn had gone toe-to-toe with vampires of both kinds on numerous occasions. As part of the elite Alpha Unit, it was his job to keep London free of the man-made monstrosities that constituted probably the worst ever national 'science project gone bad' that the public didn't know about.

Taints.

He thought about the first time he'd been briefed by Yolanda about the damn things. It had been quite possibly the single most bizarre PowerPoint presentation he'd ever sat through. And if it hadn't have been for his experience with Micky Cox and Gary Parks back in that Turkish castle, he wouldn't have believed a single word about vampires or any of that supernatural shit. But Flynn knew now there was a big dollop of fact behind the myth of Vampirism. It was real. It existed, and it sure as hell didn't 'sparkle' like those Hollywood idiots portrayed it in the movies. It bit. It tore flesh. It devoured. And it was loose on the nighttime streets of London.

Yolanda had explained to the team that the Old World vampires were bad enough. But these mutant vampires – these 'Taints' – were a whole different level of crazy. They'd been created in a lab, not in some draughty castle full of bats and bad memories. Taints had emerged from a single lineage – a 'Lucy' whose DNA had been tainted by a rogue gene – hence the name. A hiccup in a single piece of coding had produced a vampire with all the fury, the strength, speed and blood-lust of the Old World version. Only much, *much* worse.

Lucy had been accidentally created by some stupid, science-y type morons who might have had PhDs in being bloody clever, but they had never apparently watched any horror film *ever*. They also didn't stop to think that just because you *can* do something doesn't necessarily mean you *should*. So they'd happily wandered off down the road paved with good intentions and grant cheques, sciencing as hard as they could. They'd isolated a gene known as K307B they thought acted as a blood coagulant stimulator, and spliced it into a strand of vampire DNA they'd acquired as a result of Flynn and the boys' expedition to Turkey. Then, ignoring every red flag, every internal 'WOOP!WOOP!' warning siren and that glimmer of common sense that kept pounding on the door of their consciousness shouting: "This is a really, *really* bad idea!", they injected a willing volunteer with it.

It didn't end well.

Within minutes the serum containing the mashed-up gene, which was meant to be a breakthrough cure for haemophilia, had sloshed its way up through the circulatory system and into the brain of the volunteer, simultaneously turning on every primeval 'kill' command at once. It also gave Lucy an unquenchable thirst for blood that would never, ever be sated.

Nobody knew where Lucy had gone once she'd torn the throat out of the nearest scientist and then jumped out of the window, landing feet first like a cat forty feet below. She'd let out a scream that announced her existence to the world, then vanished into the night.

The hell had begun.

The PowerPoint picture showing a screaming, slathering Lucy up close in the camera lens just before she jumped was one of the most disturbing images Flynn had ever seen. In the blurry, freeze-frame shot he had seen the bloodlust and madness in her eyes. And behind that madness the terror too, as the woman felt her last shred of humanity being obliterated. Colby felt sorry for the lass. Nobody should have to endure that.

"We didn't think this would happen," was the only excuse the one surviving scientist could come up with at the emergency COBRA meeting two days later. He'd wrung his hands, nervously cleaned his glasses and muttered some hollow apologies about what was a 'salutary experience'. Sorry about that. They had people out looking. They never found her.

Lucy's lineage had spawned a whole new generation. The gene had carried on mutating away merrily, turning those with the tainted blood not just into vampires, but into raving lunatics as well. Lunatics with super-human strength, speed, agility and an insatiable desire to feed constantly. The 'off switch' in their brain hadn't just malfunctioned – it had disintegrated completely. So they'd gorge themselves, unable to stop until they slumped unconscious onto a heap of desecrated corpses and shredded body parts.

The next part of the presentation had made Flynn and the lads want to throw up. Lucy had started breeding. The first time was a vile, disturbingly bloody echo of a normal pregnancy – a process that turned her into a cross between an insectoid egg-laying machine and a very angry woman with appallingly bad parenting skills. Initially, Lucy was so confused that she ate the first batch of Younglings she produced, reabsorbing their toxins back into her own body. Slowly, she developed less cannibalistic tendencies as the tiny part of her brain that still worked reminded her that, in order to reproduce successfully, it might be advantageous to avoid snacking on your offspring. She let batch two live and develop into fully-grown Taints – the first generation of their kind.

The Old World vampires of the 'Five Families' had been

furious. For centuries a relative peace had existed between the two species, again, largely unknown to the general populous. Now, thanks to mankind buggering about with genetics and generally screwing up in epic style, all bets were off. The Old World vamps had upped sticks and sodded off back to Europe, leaving the military and the Taints to battle it out on the blood-soaked, nighttime streets of London

And then, of course, just to add a little extra spice to the dish, there was Vlad.

Supposedly turned into pink mist when Gary Parks blew ten colours of crap out of both him and Tokat Castle a year earlier, the granddaddy of all vampires had in fact managed to avoid being obliterated by being remarkably quick on his feet for an old fella. That news came as a shock to Flynn and the lads. Yes, Yolanda had explained, he'd been seriously injured, but not, as they'd first thought, killed. After spending several weeks recuperating in the labyrinth of Tokat Castle, he had eventually managed to chew his way through enough local villagers to replenish his severely injured body with new cells, and then proceeded to snack his way across Europe. The Unit had tracked him. It wasn't hard – they'd just followed the screams and the trail of dismembered body parts. Eventually he landed in Dover. The carnage he left behind in the Channel Tunnel took a week to clean up.

Now, after a meeting of minds and – somehow – bodies between Lucy and Vlad (which was a sex tape *nobody* wanted to see, and thankfully there was no PowerPoint slide to reinforce that particularly disturbing mental image), the second-generation Taints had a much more elaborate set of skills. Not only were they demented killing machines thanks to mummy, but daddy had also given them the ability to use tactics. Up until that point Taints were pretty moronic. They had one thing and one thing only on their minds, and that was the dinner gong. Once Vlad's genes had blended with Lucy's, the second generation Taints were intelligent enough to use some pretty advanced military tactics too.

Any questions?

Flynn and the lads had sat in silence, before Micky slowly raised a hand and asked, "Um, how do we kill 'em?"

All of that was academic, though.

Right here, right now, in the winding, crumbling corridors of the kill house, if Colby really was facing a warm body, a real-life 'Binky' instead of Micky's VR version, then he was in trouble. A shit-load of trouble…

He glanced around. The blood trailed off into a side room, like a grotesquely sticky trail of breadcrumbs. Colby had that twisted, knotted sensation in the pit of his stomach. Warner and Moore weren't armed up for warm bodies. The M4 shotgun capsules they carried were full of coloured water, not the organophosphur compound that would send a Taint into a heel-drumming, party-popping frenzied death throw. This was meant to be a relatively safe environment, so live ammo wasn't issued to the candidates.

Colby, however, never went anywhere without a full clip and one in the pipe. And the Blackhawk. Obviously.

Like Dorothy following the yellow brick road but minus the ruby slippers, he padded silently alongside the body-width smear of blood that led into a side room, his heart sinking further with every cat-like, crossover step. He kept the snout of the Glock up, ready and waiting to spit out a swarm of adapted hollowpoints packed full of organophosphur at the first bastard that moved. If it was human, it would cop a bullet wound accompanied by a pungent garlicky odour, which would probably disinfect the wound on contact. If it was a Taint, though, there'd be the whole blowing up shit with a side order of heel drumming and screaming, even if he only winged the bastard.

A mess on the floor made Colby stop in his tracks. "Damn…" He crouched and saw straight away that the mess was what was left of one of the newbies. Which one wasn't clear on first inspection. There was very little that was still recognisable as human. It looked like an explosion in a butcher's shop. Trails of intestines were laid out like strings of sausages, while all that remained of the man's liver was a few tattered shreds clinging to a flack jacket that had been sliced into ribbons. Colby scanned the room for movement and pressed the squawk button on his radio. "Man down. Kill house is hot. Repeat, kill house is hot."

Yolanda's voice answered instantly. *"Bugger. Casualty ID?"*

"Moore." Colby glanced down at the remains and grimaced. "I think." He saw a glint of metal in the mincemeat that was left on the floor and gingerly extracted a set of dog tags from the detritus of the Taint's feeding frenzy. He squinted at the blood-smeared discs. "Yeah, confirmed. It's Moore. *Shit.*" He curled his fist around the dog tags. The bobble chain draped between his fingers, skimming and jiggling across the surface of what used to be a lung.

"Damn it. Colby, get out of there. We've got sweep teams coming in."

"Not yet, Yol. I've still got a man in here. I'll tie up with the lads when I meet them. Give them a head's up that there's at least one friendly in here, hopefully two. I don't want them friendly firing my arse into the morgue, okay?"

"Copy that. You're armed?"

"Always."

"Live ammo?"

"Of course. Get those teams in here, Yol. Fast. This needs to be contained. Get Bravo team to check the grounds and secure the exits. We don't know how many we're dealing with here." Colby stood. The derelict old manor house that doubled up as the training 'kill house' had five floors including the cellars and the attics, a warren of corridors, dumb waiter lifts, rooms, and at least three 'secret' passages they knew about. Add to that the crawl-spaces between the walls, and you had a whole heap of places a smart Taint could hide out.

They had nothing. No intel at all. This wasn't a carefully planned operation. This was a blind bug hunt. And somewhere in this labyrinth was a man with no ammo and a very low opinion of himself who may or may not know that he was being hunted by a real Taint, and not just a VR simulation.

Colby swore quietly, pocketed Moore's dog tags, and slipped out of the room, leading with the business end of the Glock. If he called out to Warner, he'd give his position away. This was going to be a bitch of a job. Warner didn't have a radio. *Note to self; give the bloody candidates comms in future!*

Man, the debrief (if he got out of this alive) was going to be epic. Number one, how the hell did a cold kill house become red-damn-hot in the space of ten minutes? Number two, how the hell were Taints getting access to secure areas, and number three, what the actual, living *fuck?* Colby tried to suppress the feeling of guilt over Moore that threatened to wash over him. He didn't have time to beat himself up right now. That would be the colonel's job later on. He was the newbies' training officer, so he was responsible for their safety. *Yeah. Bang up job so far on that, Flynn.* Colby gritted his teeth and tried to focus back on the job at hand, and not on the desperately sad meat puzzle that lay in the room behind him. He was fervently praying that he didn't come across Corporal Warner in the same condition…

• • •

Terry Warner was scared.

More scared than he'd ever been in his life.

Shit, this was worse than watching his mates and their supposedly indestructible Mastiff get vaporised by the mother of all IEDs in Helmund. It was worse than walking into that pockmarked, mud-brick hovel and finding the decomposing bodies of an entire family of ten rotting away into putrefying slime puddles. It was way, *way* worse than the sandflies, the heat and the hell of an Afghan tour. And this particular terror was right here. Not in a faraway land, well away from the people he loved, but on their damn doorstep. His wife. His young son. They were just a couple of miles away in the soulless brick semis of the garrison's married quarters. This horror was just *two fucking miles* away from his family! It was creeping around in the leafy, tranquil surroundings of Hampshire, and the crumbling old manor house that had been re-commissioned as the unit's training centre. In a place that was supposed to be 'safe'.

Up until two weeks ago, when he'd reported to the old barracks for 'specialist training', the thing that was chasing him through the dilapidated corridors had, as far as Terry was concerned, been confined to the pages of penny dreadfuls, and the blood-soaked landscape of nightmares. Now it was hunting him through the same corridors that were supposed to act as a training ground to turn *him* into the hunter.

When Terry and Rob had first come across the Taint as it snacked on a rat, they had believed it to be part of Micky Cox's training VR program. So, in an effort to redeem themselves to the faceless watchers who they believed were spying on them through CCTV cameras, they'd played along. Both men had pumped two rounds each from the M4s into the beast. They fully expected it to do the whole 'party popper' routine in front of them. It should have dropped to the floor, thrashing and screaming. There should have been drumming heels and crackling skin. It should have died.

It should have.

It didn't.

It dropped the half-eaten rat. It glanced at the minor four flesh wounds the projectile casings had inflicted on its sinewy body. And then it stood slowly, flexing its venom-tipped talons. A slow, evil smile oozed across its twisted face, giving both men a dazzling display of a mouthful of needle-sharp teeth. Massive muscles and snaking veins made its elongated arms seem even more out of proportion to its emaciated body. This was a second-gen Taint, and a fully grown one at that.

And it was real.

Very, *very* real.

This was no VR simulation created by the evil genius that was Sergeant Michael Paul Cox, ex-REME and SAS lunatic. *This* 'Binky' was the real deal.

Terry was the first to snap out of the trance. The damn thing couldn't mind-fuck them both at the same time. But poor old

Robbie Moore stood limply staring into its hideous yellow-gold eyes, utterly mesmerised. In the training exercise it had been Robbie that tried to save Terry's arse from this exact same scenario. Now it was Terry's chance to return the favour. He swung the M4 up and pointed it at the thing's head. The capsule may not have real organophosphur in it, but he was betting a dollar to a doughnut a shot between the eyes would at least give the thing a nasty headache, and them the chance to exit stage left and run like hell.

The M4 misfired.

The click was enough to attract the Taint's attention, and it snapped its head towards Terry. Warner dug deep and his training kicked in. He was a seasoned soldier. He knew now what he was facing. And he knew what this son of a bitch was capable of doing to a human body. Warner snarled. "Oh, *hell* no!" He spun the gun around, hoisted it up to shoulder level and pounded the butt straight into the face of the grinning monster once, twice, three times. A series of sickening cracks indicated that at least two nasal bones had shattered. The creature let out a yelp and recoiled from the makeshift battering ram slamming into its face. It was enough of a diversion to break the hold it had over Robbie Moore, and the man let out a gasp. "Jesus!"

"Fuck religion, mate, just *run!*" Terry grabbed his friend and pulled him towards the door.

If they had been running from a normal opponent, they might both have made it out. But this was a Taint. A big, ugly and *very angry* Taint. And Robbie Moore was just one step too close.

"Terry, go! For fuck's sake, *go!*" Warner heard Robbie gasp as the Taint's venom-filled talons grabbed his neck and curled around his friend's throat. The tips of the talons punctured the man's skin. One slid like a needle into his carotid artery, pumping toxins directly into Robbie's bloodstream and straight up to his brain. His eyes rolled in their sockets and his oppo slumped straight into the welcoming arms of the Taint.

There was nothing Warner could do. The Taint started

tearing into Robbie. Warner watched, utterly stunned, as the creature disembowelled his best friend right in front of his eyes. He had no ammo. He had the Blackhawk, though. A mix of adrenaline and pure rage kicked in. *"You mother-fucker!"* Terry slid the knife out of its sheath, spun it in his hand and primed to launch himself towards the Taint. Go for the neck. Go in hard…

"No!" Through a froth of blood and bile, Robbie spluttered his last words. "No, mate, run! Get out! Ru…" An explosion of foaming blood poured out of the dying man's mouth and he went limp. His feet jerked and twitched for a few seconds, and then stilled.

The Taint slowly looked up at Warner, a blood-smeared monstrosity – a creature from the worst possible nightmare imaginable. A slow smile spread over its face and it scooped out a handful of stuff that should have really stayed inside Robbie's stomach cavity. The gurning creature held out the handful of intestines towards Terry and in a rasping, guttural voice, spoke two words, *"You. Next."* The creature's grin widened and he recoiled his sinewy arm and stuffed the blood-soaked intestines into its maw.

There was nothing more Terry could do for Robbie. The Blackhawk suddenly seemed about as useful as a penknife. And as much as he wanted to attack the creature right here, right now, he knew it was suicide to do so. A good hunter hunted. They didn't become the prey because they got all emotional and unnecessary.

Get out.

Regroup.

Find Flynn.

And then come back in with a *shit-load* of guns and hunt this bastard down before it escaped beyond the boundaries of the kill house and out into the community.

He let out a scream of rage and glared at the Taint. "You and me, Binky! This ain't over! This *ain't fucking over!"* Warner took one last look at the remains of his oppo, turned, and ran…

* . *

Terry Warner crashed his way through the door of yet another dilapidated room and skidded to a halt. Damn it, the house was huge! He'd got completely turned around and had a Taint, a *real* Taint, looking for him that apparently regarded him as the dessert course. Outside, a full moon had risen to its apex, shining a ghostly white light through the floor-to-ceiling windows. He slumped down, breathing hard and with his back against a crumbling plaster fire surround that, a couple of centuries ago, would have been downright regal. Having it pressed against his spine meant nothing could creep up behind him. So that was a start. He ran a shaking hand through his short hair and tried to get his breathing under control. This was worse than his first ever combat mission. At least that time he'd had some *real fucking bullets!* This time, all he had was a useless M4 that kept doing a Bob Marley on him and jamming. He checked his leg holster – he still had the Blackhawk, but using that would mean getting up close with a Taint. Much closer than Terry wanted to be. Ever.

He pulled his head up off his chest, sniffed hard, took a deep breath and looked around. Okay. Freaking out wasn't going to help. He could do that later at home, in Claire's arms. Right now, he needed to survive long enough to make it out of the house in one piece.

But to do that, he needed to turn from hunted into hunter.

A soft click made every muscle in his body tense.

He brought the M4 up to his shoulder then remembered that it was nothing more than a fancy stick, thanks to a jammed trigger. He dropped the useless weapon and slid the Blackhawk out of its sheath. "Right, you bastard!" he muttered. "Ding fucking ding. Round two…"

Terry let the image of his friend being torn to pieces crash into the front of his mind. He let all the blind, white-hot anger, and all the choking rage pile up, and concentrated it into a single pinpoint of fury. *'Use it. Control it. Focus it. Then unleash hell on the son of a bitch!'* Colby Flynn's words came back to him. Day one.

Combat tactics. Damn, that guy might be a hard-arse T.O., but he sure as hell knew his stuff.

Terry braced, ready to explode up and launch a deadly attack with the Blackhawk on the first Taint that showed its ugly face through the door...

"Whoa!" Flynn slid effortlessly into the room and, thanks to lightning reflexes, years of training and battlefield experience, and a healthy sense of self-preservation, just managed to spring back in time to avoid getting sliced and diced by Warner's Blackhawk.

"Sir!" Warner immediately retracted the knife and spluttered an apology. "Shit! I'm sorry! I thought you were Binky! I... shit, did I miss you? Tell me I missed you! Did I miss you?"

"It's okay, you missed. But nice backswipe." Colby flashed a humourless grin at the man. "Bank that one, Warner. We may need it again before the night's out." He put a reassuring hand on the man's shoulder. "You okay?"

"Yes, sir." Warner's voice trembled slightly, but his jaw muscle twitched and his stance was solid. He might have failed the VR simulation, but he'd come through his first encounter with a real Taint with added fire in his belly. "How did you find me?"

"Fella, you're leaving a trail a blind man could follow." Colby pointed down at the man's boots.

"Shit. Sorry." Warner examined the bottom of his boots. They were still wet with his friend's blood. "Sir, Robbie–"

Colby's voice softened. "I know, mate. I found him." Flynn reached into his pocket and pulled out Robbie Moore's dog tags. He looked down at them for a moment, and then held them out to Warner. "He was your oppo, Terry. You should hold onto these for him until we get out of here."

Warner closed his hand around the tags and cleared his throat, choking back his emotions. "Thank you, sir."

Colby sniffed sharply. "Right then." He pressed his radio squawk button. "Yol, I've got Warner. He's alive. Sound's like we've got..." He paused and looked at Warner, who held up a single finger. Colby nodded. "Yeah, we've got a single Taint that we know of. We're on level one, the old drawing room in the north wing. The Taint is…" Again he looked at Warner, who pointed up, held up two fingers, and then rotated his flattened hand from side to side. Colby responded with another nod and carried on talking into his radio. "We think he's two levels up. Get the team to come in through the side entrance and meet us in the back stairwell."

"Copy that."

"And bring guns. Lots and lots of big, shiny guns." Colby released the button and looked at Warner. "You and I are going to meet up with the rest of Alpha Unit. They're going to give you a live payload for that M4–"

"This bloody thing's defective, sir. Misfired on me. I had to use the other end to hit the Taint in the face." Warner shrugged. "It seemed like a good thing to do. Ya know. Therapeutic."

Colby raised an eyebrow and grinned. "Adda boy. Okay, so we'll get you a damn gun that actually works, and then how about you and me go find Binky and blow its head off? Ya know. For Robbie. You up for that, mate?" As pep talks went, it wasn't Colby's finest. But he knew it would appeal to the lad and his desire to get even with the Taint.

Warner's face hardened. "Yes, sir!"

"Good on ya. Righty-ho, let's go and find the lads."

"Sir?"

Colby stopped and turned. "Yes?"

Warner looked thoughtful for a moment. "When we first got briefed about Taints, the implication was they were pretty non-communicative, right?"

"Yep, they're not known for their sparkling after-dinner conversation skills and witty repartee. Why?"

"Binky spoke to me."

"He *what?*"

"He spoke to me."

"What did he say?"

Warner did a quick impression of how the creature at pointed at him. *"You. Next."* He lowered his arm. "A bit like ET. Only with teeth." Warner sniffed. "That kinda surprised me, sir."

Colby nodded. "It kinda surprises me too, Terry." Colby scowled. "Right now, I'm not intending to debate with the bugger, just kill it. Shall we?" He pointed at the open door, and Warner nodded.

"Yes, sir."

The two men jogged out of the room and into the corridor, Colby leading with the Glock 17 held straight out, and Warner bringing up the rear...

• •
•

"I have never been so damn happy to see your ugly face, Micky! And Gary. Good-o. Where's Dan and Sean?" Colby hopped down the last two steps and into the open space of the stairwell. Warner followed and stood quietly, waiting to be introduced to the legends that were Alpha Unit.

"Covering the exits with Bravo team. Good to see your flabby arse in one piece too, boss." Micky grinned and clapped his friend on the shoulder.

Colby jerked a thumb back at his silent partner. "Mick, this is Terry Warner. Give him a gun. A big, honking gun with a shit-load of ammo. He's coming with. And he gets first shot at Binky, okay?"

"Oh, so now *you're* calling him Binky?"

Gary Parks, a huge, hulking, ebony-skinned man with a passion for killing Taints and blowing things up, frowned. "Who's Binky?"

"The Taint." Colby shook his head and pointed at Micky Cox. "Mate, don't ask me. Ask that daft bastard."

Gary grinned. "Hey, you can call it whatever the hell you want. All I know is we've got a live one. The guv'nor is scanning the CCTV from the control room. If she picks anything up, she'll shout." He handed Warner an adapted C8 carbine. "Live jackets. Make 'em count." He put a huge hand on the lad's shoulder and gave him a sympathetic look. "Sorry about your oppo, mate"

"Thanks. And it's a real honour to meet you, sir." Warner slung the C8 over his shoulder and held out a hand. Gary Parks gave him a firm, brief handshake and then grinned again.

"Save the fanboy stuff for later, kiddo." He looked at Colby. "Boss?"

"Hold up." He pressed his radio. "Yol, we're ready. Anything?"

"Movement on level two. Looks like it's making for the central stairwell and the main exit. No other heat signatures, so you're right, you've got a solo."

"Copy that." Colby turned back to Mick and Gary. "Okay lads, let's tag-team this one. He's just eaten," Colby threw an apologetic look at Warner and then immediately carried on, "Sorry, fella – so he'll be slow. These second-gen Taints have a metabolism issue, so after feeding they slow down for about half an hour."

"I'm like that after a NAFFI steak and kidney pie. Takes me a good hour to digest it." Micky sniffed.

"Mick, for Christ's sake, show a bit of respect!" Colby smacked Micky around the ear. "Oh, and one other thing. Apparently, this one can talk."

"You're shitting me!" Gary raised an eyebrow. "Seriously?"

"According to Warner here, yep."

"Okay then. Let's see if we can get the fucker to say 'please don't shoot me in the face' before you blow it to pieces, how about that?"

"Sounds good to me." Warner nodded and then looked to Colby for orders. "Sir?"

Colby grinned. "Lead on, Warner. You're on point. Gary, bring up the rear. Eyes on."

The four men threaded their way out of the stairwell and into the main corridor that ran from the North Wing to the central section of the house. Warner knew that he had three of the best Taint hunters in the country behind him. And that made him feel a whole lot better about his chances of surviving his first live hunt.

● ● ●

Terry Warner held up a fist and the four-man team stopped dead. He turned back to Colby, pointed at his eyes and then flicked his fingers forward. He then held the flat of his hand back at Flynn, and Colby – grim-faced and serious for a change – nodded and adjusted the grip on the Glock.

Alone, but knowing the team were just inches behind him and ready to back him up if things got serious, Warner stalked into the centre of the main entrance hall. To his right a grand staircase flowed up towards a landing, where it split into two. Carved balustrades that once formed the perfect backdrop to the grand entrances of debutantes in swirling taffeta dresses now stood peeling and battered by time. Through the huge glass windows the moonlight shone in, turning the whole world into a monochrome checkerboard of stark black shadows and illuminated silver-grey patches.

Warner stood in the middle of the house's once-grand entrance hall and scanned the shadows. He rotated three-sixty degrees, the C8 pushed hard into his shoulder and the safety most definitely off this time. His finger lay alongside the trigger housing, ready to slide effortlessly onto the curved steel and squeeze as soon as he saw Binky's snarling face. He stared along the barrel and muttered. "C'mon, c'mon, where are you, you ugly bastard?" He sang softly, "Come out, come out, wherever you are…"

A voice called out softly and Warner glanced back at the team. "Stairs!" Colby pointed up to the staircase's landing.

Bathed in moonlight and looking like a ghastly silver wraith, the Taint slowly raised its head and stared straight at Warner. On either side the stairs curled gracefully away into black shadows. But the landing, which faced the huge windows of the entrance, was drenched in a soft, silvery glow. The Taint gave Warner that poisonous, vicious smile once again and raised a sinewy arm. A single talon pointed straight at Warner and the Taint hissed. "You. Die. Now."

"Oh, ya think, motherfucker?" Warner smiled back. It wasn't a nice smile. Visions of his friend's violated body crashed into his mind and he felt that white-hot anger boiling back up again. *Focus. Use the anger. Focus…* He aimed the snout of the C8 straight at the creature, which let out a gurgling, rasping laugh.

"Broken!" It pointed at the gun. "You. Die. *Now.*"

The Taint let out a howl and leapt, clearing the stairs in one bound and hitting the slippery, black and white floor at a flat run. It hurtled towards Warner, a murderous look on its face and venom-laden talons outstretched.

"Boss!" Gary and Micky threw Colby frantic looks. "Col, the kid's a candidate! He's not trained for this!"

"Wait out. This one's his." Colby watched, but the Glock was trained on the Taint, just in case. He wanted Warner to take this bastard down, but if the damn thing got too close…

In the centre of the hallway, Warner held his ground, legs slightly apart and knees bent. He watched the Taint get closer… closer… *closer…*

Warner slid his index finger into the curl of the trigger. "Broken, huh? Well, guess what, arsehole? *Wrong gun!"*

The C8 let out two shouts as Warner squeezed the trigger twice for a double tap. Both bullets, laden with organophosphur, slammed into the Taint's chest, sending it flying backwards, its grotesquely muscled arms flung outwards and its head back. The mouth was still open and the damn thing was still screaming blue bloody murder.

Warner slowly lowered the C8 and watched the fireworks, his mouth set in a grim smirk.

The Taint hit the bottom stair and spasmed. The organophosphur sent spiders of fire crawling up underneath his skin, a vivid gold that looked even brighter in the muted, silver half-light of the hallway. The Taint squirmed and thrashed as the liquid fire reached its neck and face. Its back arched so hard that the creature's heels almost touched the back of its head. It writhed and thrashed in agony as its skin started to bubble. Finally, the spiders-web of fire underneath its skin filled every vein and artery, and it went into a violent, bone-breaking, heel-drumming fit. With a last ear-splitting howl, the creature exploded. Grey ash filled the hallway, coating every surface with a thick blanket of dust.

Warner watched the creature's violent death throws and its explosive demise impassively. As the dust motes danced in the moonlight and floated down, he smiled. "That's for Robbie." He opened his hand and looked down at the dog tags, still encrusted in his friend's dried blood. While the creature had been thrashing and screaming, he'd slipped his hand into his pocket, clutched the round metal discs into his hand and held on to them tight, feeling the edges pressing into the palm of his hand. Now, he slipped them back into his pocket for the last time and turned to Alpha Team.

Colby emerged from the shadows and walked across the floor, his footsteps making the softest of sounds and the Glock still in his right hand, just in case Binky had friends. He stopped in front of Warner and put his left hand on the lad's shoulder. "You okay?"

"Yes, sir."

Colby gave him a gentle smile. "You did good there, fella."

"Thank you, sir."

"Think you could do that again?"

"Yes, sir. All day long."

"I was hoping you'd say that." Colby's face split into a wide grin and he looked back towards Gary and Micky. "Looks like we've got ourselves a new team member, lads. Waddya say?"

"I'd say he did pretty good." Gary grinned and rested his M4 over his shoulder. "Mick?"

"Anyone who can face down a Taint in full yah-hoo mode is good in my book." Micky nodded and gave Warner a thumbs up.

Colby turned back to Warner. "Looks like you passed, fella. If those two oiks say you're good to go, you're good to go." He holstered the Glock. "Right then. Get Bravo team in here to do a sweep. Top to bottom. I want this place locked down until we're absolutely sure it's clear, okay?" His face darkened for a second. "And get a detail in to retrieve Corporal Moore's remains."

He looked at Warner. "We all lose friends, mate. That's the way this gig works. You know what you're signing up for now. You've got a missus and a kid. Are you absolutely sure you want to do this?"

Warner took a last look at the pile of ash that was all that was left of 'Binky'. A draught blowing from underneath the broken front door was already dispersing the fine ash. In seconds, it was as if the creature had never existed.

Warner looked straight back at Colby, a determined look in his eyes. He was damned if his little boy was going to grow up in a world where these… *things*… existed. He'd seen what they could do first hand. His first hunt had gone from VR exercise to horrific reality in seconds. And if it could happen here, it could happen on the streets where his boy played, and where his wife walked.

No.

No, he couldn't let that happen.

He would hunt these damn things until the day he died.

Terry Warner swallowed hard and nodded at Colby.

"Yes, sir. I'm *sure.*"

THE BANI PROTOCOLS

Rose Blackthorn

Vida waited, crouched low to hide her silhouette. She leaned against a tree trunk, ready at the slightest warning to surge up or forward. Around her in the early pre-dawn darkness, leaves whispered in a fitful breeze. Insects had fallen silent, and songbirds had yet to begin their morning chorus. Still, breathing silently through parted lips, she waited.

Her heart thumped slowly, solidly in her chest. From a few yards to her right she sensed movement but didn't react. Tighe was hidden there, as silent as she, impatient at the enforced delay. There was no point in rushing things; he knew that as well as she.

Something rustled farther back in the black shadows beneath the branches. Cautious steps moved closer, a nearly invisible figure slipping between the slender trunks. Vida closed her mouth and breathed slowly, tuning out the sound of her heart while she listened for the other's approach. Her hands tightened on her weapon, but she didn't arm it yet. In this preternatural quiet, even the slightest hum of its activation would warn their prey.

Stealthy but complacent, the 'ponera weaved through the underbrush on its way to the rift they'd tracked down. Glimmers of pale light glanced off its hard surfaces, and Vida followed its progress with only her eyes. Draped over one pair of the 'ponera's long arms was the limp form of a child.

Vida clenched her jaw, nostrils flaring. How many had it brought back here?

As it neared the site of the rift, Vida heard a rustling from Tighe's direction. The 'ponera heard it too, and twisted around more quickly than seemed possible. It dropped the unconscious child and charged, amazingly fast. A jagged line of bioelectricity crackled between the prongs of its jutting mandibles, allowing her to see its completely alien and hideous face. A bolt of energy came from Tighe's position, which the 'ponera dodged.

Fast; it was so fast! Vida was up on her feet, her hands moving to complete the circuit that armed her rifle. The hum was low, but still caught the monster's attention. Dodging Tighe's shots, it jagged toward her. Vida threw herself sideways, twisting her left palm on the tech etchings. She rolled as the 'ponera launched at her. Tighe's last shot glanced off the creature's carapace and ricocheted past Vida's head. The 'ponera fell toward her, two sets of serrated limbs reaching to rip at her. She pulled the rifle up and fired point blank, a dozen projectiles hammering at and then into its broad thorax. The rounds were hot, cauterizing as they passed through; but such rapid fire in such close quarters meant she got the messy end of the blowback. The 'ponera's momentum carried it past her and it crashed into the underbrush and moved no more.

"You okay?" Tighe asked, his gun still held at the ready as he stared down at her.

"Yeah," she said, turning her head as she spat. "Bug guts are my fave."

His grin was wide and white. He didn't comment, just reached out a hand to pull her up. "Nice center mass."

"Huh." Vida slid her hands on the tech etchings, matching her techtatts to the corresponding designs. In response, the rifle powered down and fell silent. "Hard to miss that close." She turned from the dead 'ponera and back to the limp form of the child. "Medic?"

"Here." Rakehall appeared and knelt near the unmoving kid. He dropped a satchel on the ground beside him and turned the child over, revealing the slack features of an unconscious boy no more than nine years old. "Heart's beating, and he's still breathing," he said softly as he checked the kid out.

"All clear." The voice on the comm was Bronze, calling out from the rear.

212

"We'd better check the rift."

Vida nodded, leaving the kid to Rakehall's capable hands. She and Tighe continued to the site of the rift, where the 'ponera had been headed with its prize.

"You got it?" Tighe asked.

Vida knew what lay behind the question; closing a rift was big juju, and they'd been on the move for two days with no rest and little food.

"Absoliman," she said, answering in her mother's language. *Absolutely.* She let her rifle hang on a strap over her shoulder and faced the thin spot in the fabric of reality. They had tech to find it, define it; but she could *feel* it, with the senses she'd inherited from both mother and father. Still and silent, she measured her breath and slowed her heart. When she was ready, she played origami with her fingers, meshing and rearranging her digits to line up the corresponding lines and geometric designs of the techtatts that covered her browned skin from fingernails to shoulders. When the proper channels were matched, the tech implanted within the designs glowed unearthly blue.

Before her the rift became visible, a ragged rip in the world appearing like a tear in thin silk. Vida moved, her hands dancing in slow-motion gestures, her tattoos sliding against then matching up with each other in odd ways that reminded her of a puzzle box she'd once seen. With no sound or fanfare, the rift shrank and sealed itself. When the last unearthly blue faded away, the sky had begun to lighten.

Vida turned back to Tighe. "Fini," she said, and tiredly rubbed her palms against her dirty trousers. *Finished.*

"Let's get back, and get some sleep. We've all earned it." Tighe touched her shoulder lightly, and Vida saw him flinch, expecting but not feeling a shock of electricity.

"The boy?"

"Rakehall's got him."

She nodded, so exhausted she could have dropped right there and fallen asleep. Instead, she began the two-mile hike back to where they'd parked the trucks. She could rest when she reached them.

* . *

Warm sunlight like golden syrup poured through the open door, pooling on the plain wooden floor. Soft humming and the sound of waves filled the otherwise silent room. The rich tone of the voice made Vida smile, and her mother said, "Reveye pitit anvi dòmi." *Wake up sleepy child.* "Your papa will be home soon."

Vida opened her eyes, not to the small familiar house near the sea, but to the warehouse where the Bani were currently headquartered. The cot she lay on was hard and uncomfortable, but she knew she'd slept for several hours. She sat up, rubbing her face tiredly. Not far from her, Tighe and Bronze were consulting maps on a large display. The area around their current location was clear, but there were blinking lights in at least three other places Vida could see from where she sat.

"You're awake." Aio appeared with a cup of coffee, which she held out. Her bright red shirt and the multicolored flowered band in her long hair was a contrast to all the drab greys and greens everyone else in sight was wearing. "I was starting to worry."

"How long?" Vida asked, taking a cautious sip of coffee. It had obviously just been poured, and was scalding hot.

"Twenty-six hours, give or take." Aio sat on the cot beside her, and slid her fingertips along the intricate tattoos on Vida's arm. "You're pushing too hard."

"Had to," Vida replied, enjoying the gentle touch. "Did we save the kid?"

"Yes." Aio moved her hand from Vida's arm to her cheek, and gazed at her seriously. "You're pushing too hard. I thought you'd sleep for a week."

"We do what we do." Vida's mantra and her only explanation to those who questioned her actions or her motives. We do what we have to do, what we need to do, what we want to do… Any and all of the above.

"We're heading out tonight," Aio said, pulling away. "Tighe said we're getting reinforcements."

Vida nodded. After losing Chen on the last job, and Jensen and Sant a month before that, they were seriously short-handed. "When?"

"Any time now."

"I need a shower." Vida handed the coffee back to Aio and stood, ignoring stiff muscles and assorted bruises. She leaned over and pressed a light kiss to Aio's temple then headed for the bathroom.

• • •

Nate Harris walked into the open bay door of the rundown warehouse without being stopped or challenged once. He gritted his teeth, irritated at the lax security, and wondered again if he wanted to get involved with this off-the-books unit.

Inside, he halted to get a good look around. Several well-used vehicles were parked on the right side of the large open space. At the back of the room were cots and makeshift dividers for some semblance of privacy. To the left stood tables loaded with computer equipment and other electronics. Two men, both in their late twenties or early thirties, were engrossed in the display before them. Behind them were two women, both seated and bent over one's outstretched arm. As Harris crossed toward the ersatz command center, he watched the women, curious as to what they were doing. The thinner one with her arm held out was absolutely still, allowing him to see the intricate black tattoos that covered her brown skin. The other woman, more voluptuous and dressed in bright clothing, used some kind of device to lift and insert a glowing blue filament into the first woman's outstretched forearm.

"I'm looking for T. Lane," he said, and both men at the table looked up.

"Good, you're here." The man who spoke had a red tinge to his hair and beard, and direct blue eyes. "I was starting to wonder if you'd gotten lost." He glanced at the man beside him, adding, "Get Rakehall on the line. Tell him we're loading up."

215

He came around the laden tables then and said, "And the name is Tighe. You go by Nathan?"

Harris shook his head, nonplussed at the way this unit was run. "Nate, actually. You realize I got in here with no one even noticing."

Tighe grinned. "Not likely." He nodded back toward the open bay door as two cats sauntered in. They were similar in size to a leopard or cheetah, standing two-feet tall at the shoulder and over five feet in length, but resembled short-hair domestic cats. They were both sleek and muscular, the color of burnished pewter. When they looked at Harris, he saw their eyes were a vivid clear peridot in color. "Esfir and Faina, our sentries. They let us know you were coming when you were still half a mile out."

"What are they?" Harris had worked some strange operations in his time, which was why he'd been recruited to this top-secret and autonomous unit; but he'd never seen anything like these cats.

"Special breed, out of far-eastern Russia. They're called Cobalts, and they're probably as smart as you and me." While Tighe spoke, the two enormous felines padded toward the back of the warehouse where they were met by two girls. "Kai and Tchaz," Tighe went on. "They're with the Cobalts. You can get a formal introduction later."

Harris nodded, dropping the pack he'd held on a strap over his shoulder. "So, where do you want me?"

"We're heading out tonight, so don't waste time unpacking," Tighe said, leading him over to the two women who were still intent in their strange occupation. "This is Vida and Aio," he said, and the women looked up. "Aio's our biotech specialist. You have any problems with any implants she's the one to talk to."

Aio smiled, looking Harris up and down once with what might have been appreciation then went back to what she was doing.

"Vida's our secret weapon. Stress on weapon," Tighe went

on, and laughed when the woman made an obscene gesture with her free hand. Her other hand gripped the arm of Aio's chair tightly, muscles bunched in her arm as a glowing filament was carefully fed into her skin.

The blackline tattoos were stylized and intricate, and different sections glowed or faded with electric blue as Harris watched.

"As soon as they're finished, we'll start loading gear," Tighe said. "Until then, you can read up on the mission. Questions will have to wait until later." He pointed to a tablet lying on a table past where the women sat, then left Harris to his own devices.

"Rakehall and Sig are on their way back," Vida said, her words directed to no one in particular. "That gives you less than half an hour." She might have meant Harris's reading assignment, or Aio's delicate work on her arm.

As predicted, less than thirty minutes later the rest of the team arrived at the warehouse. Harris had skimmed the info on the tablet, making an effort not to make sounds of disbelief – it read more like science fiction than operational orders. From his peripheral vision he'd studied the women, Vida in particular. She appeared to be average height and weight with medium-brown skin between the multiple tattoos. Her black hair was braided to one side, revealing that it was shaved above her left ear. More of the ubiquitous tattoos traced the skin there. Her eyes, when she looked up, were a pale blue-grey, almost the same color as the Cobalt cats. Harris wondered what the ink and implants were for; he'd seen nothing about them in the document he was reading.

As soon as the last of the group arrived, everything changed. The computer equipment was packed up and loaded in the trucks, as well as food supplies, clothing and weapons. The two younger girls were busy tending to the Cobalts, but everyone else lent a hand to the grunt work. By the time dusk had begun to steal the light from the sky, they were ready to leave.

"You can ride with Sig," Tighe called to Harris, and now he rode shotgun with the big Scandinavian.

The vehicles, fully loaded with all their equipment, pulled

out of the warehouse single file and headed to their next destination.

"Welcome to the rabbit hole," Sig said with a wide, white grin, "Things'll just get weirder for you from here on out."

"Great," Harris replied, wondering again why he'd agreed to this assignment.

• • •

Their next temporary base of operations wasn't nearly as spacious or comfortable as the warehouse. Instead, they set up shop out of the transport trucks themselves. Makeshift tents were erected, and bathroom facilities consisted of portable chemical toilets concealed in dappled canvas lean-tos. Electronics and computer equipment was set up inside the box truck once supplies were moved out to make room. Rather than a generator, the power source was an enigmatic suitcase-sized container with strange etchings unlike anything Harris had seen before. Until he saw Vida checking her weapon.

"What is that?" he asked, pointing to the matte black etchings on the stock.

"Didn't read the mission files?" she asked, but the corner of her mouth twitched, and he realized she was giving him a hard time. "Tech etchings. The latest sci-apps coming down from research and development. Next best thing to voodoo."

As she spoke she stroked the rifle, and he noted the way her tattoos matched up to the markings on the stock. There was a soft *click* and then a low hum. Electric blue glimmered from her implants and the weapon before fading again.

"Handy," he said, immediately seeing the benefit. The rifle couldn't be fired until it was activated; due to the tech, the only one who could activate it was Vida. Even if someone took it from her, they wouldn't be able to use it. "So which came first, the tech or the tatts?"

She laughed, a low rich sound that made him smile in turn. "The age-old question."

"Contact."

Vida and Harris both turned to see the young Cobalt handlers reporting to Tighe. Harris had been introduced to the girls, but so far couldn't tell them apart. They were sisters with more than a hint of Asian ancestry, caramel-cream skin and dark secret eyes. Harris wasn't sure if they were twins or just very close in age.

"Where?" Tighe asked, checking the display.

"Here," one of the girls said, pointing at a spot on the map. "Faina is close."

The other girl nodded, adding, "Esfir reports multiple OHs."

"OHs?" Harris asked. He had scanned the files he'd been given, but didn't recognize the term.

"Otherworld Hostiles," Vida answered, on her feet. "How many, Kai?" she called.

"At least three," the girl said, her eyes going unfocused as she accessed her link to the Cobalt. "Possibly more. She's not sure yet. The scent is so strong it's making her nose blind."

"Tell 'em to keep back," Tighe ordered. "We're on our way." He nodded to Bronze on his way out of the truck, "You've got the comms. Vida, Nate, Sig – with me."

"Vida."

She paused in gathering her weapons, and Nate watched as Vida met Kai's dark eyes.

"There's something out there beside the 'poneras," the girl said, a note of worry in her soft voice. "Esfir is confused. She's not sure what it is. She says it smells bad, worse than the usual."

"Stay on the comms, close to Bronze," Vida said, touching the girl's shoulder lightly before motioning Nate to follow the men. "You let us know what the cats see, but keep them safe!"

Nate frowned as Kai went back to the truck and leaned against her sister, their heads together as though they might be whispering.

"What?" Tighe asked as Vida climbed into the SUV beside the man.

"Something bad," she replied, but did not elaborate.

* . *

Harris checked the time. It was just after twenty-two-hundred hours. He shifted, careful not to make any sound. The sky was mostly clear, with only a few thin, ragged clouds scudding across the star-filled vault. The moon had yet to make an appearance, but in the clearing beyond the stand of trees where he waited, it was still light enough to see.

"Report."

The word was softly spoken, the bud in his ear making sure the sound didn't travel. Just as softly, he replied, "Nothing so far."

Sig's voice, deep and pleasant, said, "All clear."

"Movement." Vida's voice was rich, even over the ear-bud.

Harris tensed, looking to where he'd last seen the woman at the northern end of the clearing.

"Never mind, it's Faina." Eyeshine glinted at the edge of the meadow, but the Cobalt's coloring made her virtually invisible in the dim light.

"Damn," Harris whispered, relaxing again. They'd hustled to get here from base camp, but several hours of hiking and then hiding while the sun set and night came was mind-numbingly exhausting. He'd been brought up to speed on the current mission while they were traveling, and now at least had an idea of what to look for.

"Giant bugs," Sig described simply. "Your height or better, slick black or brown carapace, and serrated appendages. Pincers where their faces should be."

"Don't forget the shock," Tighe added, keeping his own eyes on the road as he drove them to where the Cobalts had found more 'poneras.

Sig nodded stoically. "Yeah, they can generate bioelectricity. They hit you with it, it'll knock you on your ass."

"I don't suppose you're making this up, to pick on the new guy?"

Vida held out a cellphone with a photo on the screen. Harris looked at it and grimaced.

Now, like the others he waited to see one of those monstrous OHs in the flesh. He'd been informed these creatures were coming through tears in the fabric of reality. How they were engineering the rifts was unknown, and why was equally mysterious. They entered the world in unpopulated areas then immediately went searching for the nearest human habitation. There, they would attack and kill, or kidnap the people they found. Those killed were little more than shredded meat when the 'poneras were finished. Those who were taken, mostly children, went to an obscure fate. Once transported through the rift, none of them had ever been recovered.

"Heads up," this was Tighe again, a note of tension in his low voice, and Harris scanned his surroundings for movement. "Esfir reports something coming in from the south-west."

One of the Cobalts, little more than a shadow, moved out of the trees and flowed across the clearing before merging into the darkness at the western edge of the meadow. Electric blue flickered then was gone, and Harris guessed Vida had activated her weapon. The wind picked up, tree branches flailing and making peripheral vision useless; everything seemed to be moving.

The fitful breeze brought an acrid smell, and Harris wrinkled his nose at the rank stench. He turned and crouched, facing into the scent, eyes narrowed as he tried to see something moving besides the tossing underbrush and swaying trees.

"Harris, to your right!"

He swung right, disoriented by the dancing shadows. There was nothing to focus on, everything was in motion. Something big seemed to melt into reality, and the stench of acid and rotten meat filled the night. Harris brought up his gun and fired. At the same time, projectiles from another weapon hit the same target. Blue light pulsed, revealing something from a nightmare. Broad as a draught horse and close to seven-feet tall, the thing was neither human nor one of the 'ponera that had been described to him. It had an extra set of limbs and a jutting chitinous jaw protruding beneath two large ellipsoidal eyes. Harris managed to take that in before the projectiles from Vida's weapon exploded.

He ducked away as a spray of gore and viscera erupted from the thing's chest plate.

"You okay?" Vida gripped his shoulder, and he nodded, making a face at the dripping goo that coated his left side. "On your feet, there's more coming."

He stood and followed her, not sure how she could see where she was going. There were more gunshots south of their position, and once the yowling cry of an angry cat. From the ear bud, Harris heard Tighe giving orders between firing.

"Tchaz, Kai, what's the latest from the cats? Sig, check west. Goddamn these sonsobitches reek. Vida, keep an eye on the rift, and keep Nate's ass out of trouble."

"Two o'clock," Vida said to Harris, seeming to ignore Tighe's chatter. "See it?"

He didn't, but waited before saying so. Something moved against the wind and light glimmered on something hard and glossy. "Got it."

"Aim low, it's carrying something," she whispered, and brought her weapon up.

The next few seconds were like strobes through a kaleidoscope. The trees tossed and shuddered in the freshening wind, undergrowth like splashes of ichor in the uncertain light. Things moved, their shapes unfamiliar and difficult to recognize against the natural background. Vida fired, blue light limning her hands and flashing quicksilver designs on her arms and weapon. Harris aimed low, as she'd said, and the flash from his barrel picked out multi-armed alien creatures beneath the trees.

Time seemed to slow, and Harris could count his heartbeats between the recoil of his rifle. In mere seconds it was over, and he followed Vida to check that the enemy was down.

The earbud conveyed Tighe's words as Vida shone her light on the dead monsters. "The rift, Vida!"

She paused only to shoot one of the downed 'ponera between its protruding eyes. "Check the victims," she said to Harris, hooking her thumb at two still forms that had been thrown free when the creatures fell.

He checked on the boys, both in their early teens, who were unconscious but appeared not to be seriously injured. Then he turned to watch as Vida crossed the clearing they'd been guarding. Roughly in the center, she stopped. The moon had risen now, and pale light seemed to surround her.

She set her weapon on the ground then stood straight once more. Her arms moved in a strange, graceful progression of symbols formed with her whole body. As Harris watched, intrigued, her techtatts began to glow. The light flashed and flared in enigmatic designs, and a few feet in front of her, the air began to lighten to the same intense shade of blue. Harris was amazed, as one of these so-called rifts he'd been briefed on appeared in mid-air. The edges twisted, billowing in a different rhythm than the wind-tossed foliage around the clearing.

The blue light, searing the edges of the tear, revealed a different landscape on the other side. Instead of moonlit knee-high grass ringed by shadowed trees, there was wet black stone and steep stairs curving away out of sight. Before the rip began to narrow, he thought he saw two small crescent moons hanging in that alien sky, one bluish and the other with an orange cast. Then the edges closed together, sealing in a burst of searing blue fire.

Harris blinked, trying to clear the afterimage of the rift from his retinas. In his ear, Tighe spoke.

"Vida, hope you've still got some juice."

"What's up, bòs?" she asked.

"We've got a live one."

* . *

Two days later, Harris woke to find he hadn't dreamed any of the last few days. He really was dealing with monster bugs from a different reality, and everyone else in the group seemed to take it all as perfectly normal. The live one they'd captured and brought back to base was a different breed than the 'poneras they usually dealt with. Tighe called it a belos', named after the belostomatid or giant water bug it resembled, just as the 'poneras were named for the paraponera or bullet ant. Like the huge monster Harris had encountered in his first mission with the Bani, it stank to high heaven, and they'd put it downwind from camp as much as they could.

"Is she still at it?" he asked Aio, who was pouring a cup of coffee.

"Vida?" Aio handed him the cup, and poured a second for herself. "Yes. It was difficult for her to link with it, and I don't think she wants to have to do it again. She's trying to get all the information she can before the connection fails."

"How does she do it?"

Aio shrugged, taking a seat at the small table they used for meals. Hot sunlight beat down on their camp, but the awning over the table kept it a few degrees cooler. "Magic and tech. She's equal parts."

Harris raised an eyebrow, his skepticism obvious.

"You think the tech does all the work?" Aio asked, smiling. "She could already do most of this stuff on her own; the tech just gives her a power boost."

"But how?" he asked again. It wasn't like you could take a class for this shit.

Aio shook her head, her flawless coif and bright-flowered outfit a complete contrast to the rest of the crew. She looked as though she should be sitting in a garden somewhere, eating tea cakes or playing croquet. Not in the middle of nowhere with a bunch of scruffy ex-military types, or two doll-like teenagers and their sideshow pets. "She's got a lot of old blood. Descendant of Haitian voodoo, Apache medicine, and Icelandic Seidr; some of it she learned from her parents, some just came naturally."

Harris sat beside her, drinking the strong, bitter coffee. Past the trucks and maybe a hundred feet into the trees, Vida and Tighe stood beneath a hastily-erected canopy. Strapped to a metal table was the belos' they'd caught. Even in the bright daylight, gleaming blue light could be seen coursing along Vida's tech-tatts. She did not move, and Harris couldn't hear anything from this distance, but obviously something was happening. "It's like the origin story for some kind of super hero," he said, grinning.

"She is amazing," Aio said, slanting a glance his direction.

Harris ran a hand self-consciously over his military haircut; he knew it made him seem boyish next to the rest of the men.

"But she paid for it, every bit," Aio said.

"Never suggested otherwise." He pulled his gaze from the tableau across the camp, and looked back at her. "How'd you end up in this madhouse?"

She laughed, eyes sparkling. "Just lucky, I guess."

About that time, Bronze approached. Of the men in the group, he was the shortest, built stocky and muscular. His right leg had been amputated above the knee, and he switched out prosthetics depending on his need. Today he wore a simple recurved blade, which seemed to make his gait more bouncy than usual, although that might just have been Harris's impression. "Aio," he said, nodding to her, "Nate, you ready for duty?"

Harris nodded. He'd had little to do with Bronze so far, but had deduced the man was Tighe's de-facto second-in-command. "What do you need?"

"We're getting some strange signals from where we cleared the rift. Tighe and Vida are still busy with the belos'. I want you to take Kai and Faina back in to check it out."

Harris set his cup down and got to his feet. "Just the one Cobalt?"

Bronze nodded. "Esfir injured a paw, so we're letting her rest. The cats are linked to both girls, so Kai can interpret for you, and Tchaz can keep us informed here. Take the Jeep so you can drive all the way in. Nothing fancy, just a good thorough sweep to see why we're still getting a signal even though Vida shut down the rift."

"Yeah, no problem." Harris didn't dawdle, but by the time he'd grabbed his gear and walked to the small SUV, Kai and the Cobalt were waiting for him. "You go off alone regularly?" he asked, starting the engine after sliding into his seat.

"I'm never alone," the girl returned, smoothing one hand over the cat's broad head. "Plus, you're here. It's a party."

Harris smiled and shook his head. She looked all of fifteen years old, slender and petite, but she was cool and confident with the presence of a queen. He glanced once at the cat, who was gazing at him solemnly, her bright green eyes reflecting his face back to him. Then he put the Jeep in gear and headed back down the rutted dirt road.

As he drove down the rough track, the cat put her head in Kai's lap and purred loudly. The girl lightly dragged her nails through the Cobalt's thick blue-grey fur, her eyes on the way ahead. After they'd turned onto a narrow paved road that would take them closer to their destination, she said, "So why did you volunteer for this outfit?"

Harris glanced at her sharply, before facing forward again. "What makes you think I volunteered?"

She chuckled softly, gazing down fondly at the feline head lying heavy on her leg. "We're all volunteers. Tighe and Vida agreed at the very beginning, there would be no member of the Bani who didn't want to be here."

"The Bani?" he asked. He'd read the term before, but didn't know what it was supposed to mean.

"Bane. We're the curse on the dark, the downfall of those things that hide in the shadows."

He snorted. "A little melodramatic."

She laughed, a sweet tinkling that made the cat open one eye. "Yes, but still true. We hunt the things that wish to do us harm. But we are all hunted, too." She turned to study his profile, her dark eyes giving nothing away. "What hunts you?"

He didn't turn to look at her, but could see her quite clearly in his peripheral vision.

"Someday, if you want to talk about it, Faina and I will listen."

His mouth twitched; he was going to confess his secrets to a cat?

"We're very good listeners," Kai said.

Harris turned onto another dirt road, this one little more than a couple faint tire tracks through the high grass. He slowed to squeeze past a fallen tree and started as the cat got up and leapt out of the still-moving vehicle. Faina landed squarely on the downed trunk, tail high and twitching, then raced along the rough bark and disappeared into the trees.

"She'll go around and meet us at the meadow," Kai explained.

"So why did you volunteer?" Harris asked, continuing to follow the rough track.

"There were three of us," she replied in her light, breathless voice. "Tchaz, Nikki, and me. Nikki was taken from us. We hunt for the thing in the shadows that took her."

He thought about saying he was sorry, but what good would it do? "Was it one of these things? A 'ponera, or… or the big one, a belos'?"

She was looking out the windshield again, her face composed and emotionless. "No, not one of them. But something like them. It came through a rift, like they do. Someday, we will see it again, and it will pay."

They both fell silent then as Harris guided the vehicle down the winding trail through the trees. Eventually he had to pull off the almost nonexistent road, following the coordinates on the GPS unit attached to the dash.

"Faina is rounding the northern edge of the meadow," Kai reported, her eyes vague as she accessed her link to the Cobalt. "She can still smell the OHs. When she is across the clearing from us, she'll enter to investigate."

"Don't let her jump the gun," Harris said, fighting to hold the wheel as they bucked over the thick undergrowth. "Tell her to wait for us."

He parked when they had driven as far as they could; they had to walk the last few hundred yards. The sun shone, spangles of golden light through the trees, and dense underbrush made for slow going. Ahead, he could see brighter light through the trunks where the meadow opened up. Beside him, moving as silently as her cat, Kai alternated her attention between their surroundings and her link to the Cobalt. She surprised Harris by producing a handgun, which he hadn't even known she carried. Despite her slim stature and young age, she was obviously well versed in its use.

"She's straight across from us," Kai whispered when they reached the edge of the clearing. The smell of the belos' lingered, making her wrinkle her nose. "She's nervous. We're not alone."

"People? Wildlife? Or an OH?" he asked.

"Something she hasn't smelled before."

The answer made Harris nervous, too. "Can she pinpoint where?"

"Upwind." Kai pointed south-west, which was closer to their position than the Cobalt's.

"Is the rift open again?" he asked, glancing into the meadow. He'd been unable to see it before, until Vida worked her tech-magic to close it. It could be open now, and he wouldn't know.

Kai pulled a cellphone from a clip at her waist. For a moment Harris had the idea she was going to try and call the camp, but instead she held it toward the clearing and watched the screen. Expressionless, she whispered, "I can't tell if it's open, but it's still there. That means it can be opened from the other side at any time. Vida didn't seal it."

"Or, maybe they opened it again after we left. Shit."

"It's moving," Kai said, putting the phone away.

"The rift?"

"No." She cocked her head, apparently listening to Faina. "The OH – it's coming this way."

It had been bad waiting in the dark for something monstrous to appear. Harris had figured good light would make it better, but it didn't. He still didn't know what was coming, and found himself wishing the rest of the crew was here. He could hold his own with a man, hell, several men! But he didn't like going up against an unknown, even with Kai there.

"Can she help?" he asked, searching for any movement in the woods. At least there was no wind today; any movement would be easily spotted.

Kai smiled, and there was something of the predator in her dark eyes. "Yes."

Harris took her at her word, and proceeded south along the edge of the meadow, alert for any sign of what they hunted.

* . *

"Vida! Damn it, Calder–"

"Tighe," Aio warned. "You're not helping."

"Sa ki lanfè a…" Vida whispered, brows drawn together as she rolled her head to the side. *What the hell…*

"Vida, don't move," Aio soothed. With gentle hands she examined the techtatts, wincing when the prostrate woman hissed in pain. "I'm sorry, hun. I'm trying not to hurt you."

Vida opened her eyes, grimacing as bright sunlight stung. "What happened?"

Aio shook her head, worry clearly etched on the woman's features. "Overload. I didn't think it was even possible, the way you're grounded."

"The belos'?"

"Dead," Tighe said flatly. "And I don't give a shit, as long as you're okay." He paused. "Are you okay?"

"Yeah." She was disoriented and in pain, but otherwise… "Did you kill it?"

Tighe exchanged a glance with Aio. "You did."

Vida closed her eyes, and let her head fall back again while she tried to remember. She had been linked to the belos', minds and nervous systems aligned with the help of her implants. She'd been fishing through its alien thoughts, trying to read its mind when she didn't even understand its language. Perfectly still and apparently tranquil, it had fought her all the way. When she'd finally found a way through the labyrinth of its synapses, there had been one moment of clarity – and then agonizing backlash. "When it overloaded me, I did the same thing to it, didn't I?"

"It's completely burned out, Vida. Still smoking."

At Tighe's comment, she sat up, ignoring Aio's admonishments, and looked over at the table where the OH still lay strapped to the surface. Tighe had been literal; smoke was wafting from the edges of the belos' chitin armor.

"Did you get anything?" he asked, and she followed his gaze to the burns on her arms from where her implants had fried.

Exhausted, she nodded and pulled away from Aio's ministrations. "We have to go back to the clearing. Something else came through." As she accepted Tighe's hand to get to her feet, Tchaz arrived at a lope.

"It's Faina," she said, wearing the porcelain doll mask that she and her sister had so perfected. But there was a note of worry in her light voice. "They're hunting something at the rift-site. It's not like the bugs, it's worse. They need help."

"Bronze!" Tighe yelled. "Sig! Rakehall! We're rolling out!"

Esfir limped out from the tent where she'd been resting and leapt into the nearest truck where Tchaz joined her. The look on the girl's face brooked no argument. Bronze rode shotgun while Sig took the driver's seat and followed Tighe's truck out of camp. While Tighe drove and Rakehall smoothed antibacterial salve over Vida's burns, she told them what she'd seen.

"It's not random," she said, gritting her teeth as the medic worked on her burns. "There's a plan behind where and when the rifts are opened. They're looking for kids specifically, so they can take them back and raise them."

"For what?" Tighe asked, slamming around a corner and skidding across the narrow blacktop lane before straightening out.

"I don't know," she growled. "I didn't get enough time, just flashes. As soon as I hit pay dirt the damn thing blasted me! All I do know," she said, her voice as set and angry as she felt. "Is that they have someone like me. That's how they're getting so good at opening the rifts."

"Someone like you?" Rakehall asked.

She nodded, pulling her hair back into a quick braid to keep it out of her face, baring the tattoos that arched over her left ear. "A human. A woman who knows the conjuration, to affect the aethyr and achieve Kalfou. Crossroads."

"Crossroads?" Tighe asked, not taking his eyes from the road as he floored the accelerator.

"The rift," she said.

"Shit."

At the rate they were traveling, Tighe nearly overshot the turn onto the overgrown track. Expertly he downshifted and turned the wheel, rocking the truck onto two tires before sliding off the pavement and onto the new trajectory. Sig followed in the second vehicle, managing not to be quite so reckless and so fell behind a bit.

"Where are they?" Tighe called into a radio.

A moment later, Bronze replied. "Tchaz says they're at the far southwest edge of the meadow."

"Got it."

While Tighe drove as fast as he could through the rough terrain, Rakehall handed Vida her rifle and readied his own weapons. As soon as the truck slid to a stop, they were both out and headed toward the clearing. Sig slammed to a halt behind them, and Esfir raced by the humans, a silver-grey streak amongst the trees. Bronze caught up quickly, his blade prosthesis making his gait uneven but fast.

"There," Tchaz called, and Vida caught a glimpse of Kai through the trees. She veered, heading for the girl with Tchaz and Sig on her heels. The other men all went past, spreading out and aiming to reach the edge of the meadow at different places.

"Where's Nate?" Vida asked, crouching low beside Kai when she reached her. The young girl was shaking, and there were scrapes on her hands that oozed blood. Two gashes raked her right upper arm, but she held her pistol at the ready.

Kai nodded toward the clearing just beyond where they'd met her.

The man stood near the middle of the meadow with his weapon seated against his shoulder. There was blood on his arms and upper back, and Faina held her ground beside him with her shoulders hunched and tail lashing. She wailed; a high-pitched warning to something they couldn't see. Behind them on the ground was the misshapen corpse of something that had no right to have ever been alive.

While they watched, something pulled itself through an invisible rip in the air. It wasn't a 'ponera or belos'; it wasn't like anything they'd seen before. It was sinuous, moving as though boneless, and three sets of appendages gripped the edge of the rift as though for purchase.

"What the—" Sig breathed, and then the shooting began.

Harris fired repeatedly, but the thing coming through the rift only moved faster. It squeezed through, casting to the left as another behemoth began to pull itself into the world. Tighe, Bronze and Rakehall came out of the trees then, maneuvering around Harris to fire at the monsters emerging from the portal. Esfir raced to her sister, and together the two Cobalts launched themselves at the first creature. Like dancing smoke, they evaded its tentacle-like arms, biting and clawing at its dappled black hide.

Kai and Tchaz leaned their heads together for a moment, and Vida wondered, not for the first time, if they could communicate with each other through their links to the Cobalts. Then the girls entered the clearing, obviously going to the aid of their feline charges.

The second thing had completely emerged, and a third was on its way through when Sig and Vida joined the others in the fray. The battle seemed like a fever dream, held as it was in the pristine meadow beneath a vault of cloudless blue sky. Vida moved her hands on her weapon to activate it, and caught back a cry of pain and frustration. The damage to her implants was greater than she'd thought; she was unable to activate the tech in the rifle. Useless, except as a club, she dropped it in the flower-dotted grass and raced toward the rift. From her belt she pulled a 1911 pistol with her right hand, a double-edged knife with her left.

For her, the day slowed. Sunlight fell like warm golden syrup, a sweet weight against the crown of her head and the points of her shoulders. The Bani moved sedately, flashes splintering the air as bullets erupted from their weapons. The Cobalts, living sculptures of steel and brushed pewter, danced between the wide-flung limbs of the creature out of nightmare. Blood, a deep ichor more black than red, sprayed in sparkling droplets as they bit and clawed their adversary. Tighe and Bronze were shooting at the second beast, aiming for its multiple eyes, while Harris and Rakehall concentrated on the third still attempting to breach the eldritch doorway.

Vida joined them, firing into the rift, hoping to keep the creature from coming through. The bullets seemed to have little effect, and she wished for the exploding rounds from her useless rifle. The monsters were screaming, bellowing, the sound so deep it made the ground shake. Long feet with prehensile toes dug into the floor of the meadow, keeping it from being blown back into its own world.

"Grenade!" Bronze shouted. Harris and Vida dropped to the ground, while Tighe turned away. The metal egg hit the monster mid-chest, and it caught at it with winding pseudo-fingers. When the grenade went off, chunks of purple-black flesh and shredded dermis flew everywhere. But it cleared the rift for a moment, long enough for Vida to raise her head and look through.

On the other side was a vast courtyard paved in rough dark stone. A cloud-covered sky hid the top of a steep mountain looming in the distance. There were more of the squid-armed monsters, and belos', and a cohort of 'ponera. But in the center of all this was a woman. Dressed in deep red, her head wrapped in cloth to hide her hair, she held some kind of serpent-like creature with multiple heads draped over her shoulders. Her face was dark and slender, eyes like clear amber, and she met Vida's gaze directly.

Everything else faded to little more than background noise. The sound of gunfire became distant crackles, and the bellow of the only remaining monster that had made it through the portal was reduced to the hollow boom of a far-off sea. Vida pushed to her feet, never dropping her gaze from the woman on the other side. She drew back, throwing the blade with all her force. It flickered through the rift, nearly hitting the other woman before one of the belos' blocked it with its own armored body.

Her implants were fried, the burns on her arms throbbing in time with her heartbeat. It didn't matter. Vida dropped her pistol, oblivious to the fight between her crew and the remaining invader. She took a deep breath, focused on her heartbeat, the very center of her being. Gracefully, like an exotic dance, she made the forms with burned arms and aching fingers. The last of her active implants, those above her left ear, glowed and seared her as she called more power from them than they were made to deliver.

Across the rift, the woman in red nodded, turned away and disappeared among the disparate monstrosities that surrounded her. The rip in the air burned, first electric blue and then white hot, twisting like a rising cinder from an unseen fire. Then it closed, a scar upon the fabric of reality, and was gone.

The last creature fell, only yards from its fellows, and rank fluids from its dying body soaked the clean earth of the meadow. Vida saw it fall, saw that the Cobalts and their girls were still whole, that the rest of the crew had survived. Then the darkness that had filled the other side of the rift drifted over her, and she knew no more.

• . •

The world was soft and warm, and rumbling. Vida opened her eyes, feeling as though she'd slept for a year. She was stiff and immobile, for a moment thinking she'd been restrained. But no, it was the Cobalts. One lay on each side, wedging her between them, and their contented purring made the camp bed she lay on vibrate.

"She's awake." The light voice belonged to one of the girls. Vida wasn't sure at first which one, until Tchaz leaned over her. "Welcome back."

"Where?" Vida asked, her throat dry and voice hoarse.

"Hope, Idaho," Kai said from the other side of the bed. She smoothed her hand over Faina's flank, and smiled at Vida. Her right arm was bandaged from shoulder to elbow, and a colorful bruise was just beginning to fade from her jaw. "We've been here three days."

Rakehall appeared then, bringing her a cup of water. "How are you feeling?"

"Like death warmed over," she replied, taking the cup gratefully.

"Slowly," he advised. "I've had you on IV fluids, but there's nothing in your stomach. Don't push it."

"How long was I out?" She forced herself to sip the water, instead of guzzling it the way she wanted.

"Six days," Tchaz answered. "You sealed the rift without any tech. Aio was afraid you wouldn't recover."

Vida glanced at her arms. The burns were well on their way to healing, but she could feel that the implants had been removed. She felt... lighter. "Why here? Idaho?"

"It's a good, quiet place to regroup," Rakehall said, taking her now-empty cup and filling it again with fresh water. "No new rifts since that day. No sign of any OHs. Tighe decided to take advantage while it's clear."

"The calm before the storm," Vida mused, and pretended she didn't see the way Tchaz and Kai exchanged looks.

Later, when she'd managed to talk her way out of bed rest, and eaten a little to fill her empty belly, she sat in a camp chair on the shore of Lake Pend Oreille. The air was calm, the sun low above a bank of clouds, and birds flew over the water on perfect curved wings. She sat in the quiet, listening to the soft slap of wavelets on the narrow rocky beach.

"Mind some company?" Harris asked, joining her with a second chair.

Vida shook her head, but didn't look away from the lovely view.

"How are you?"

She took a deep breath, let it out slowly. "Alive. We're all alive. So, good."

"I wanted to thank you."

That surprised her, and she turned to look at him. There were thin scratches along his temple and cheekbone, more on his neck that disappeared beneath his collar. He'd had blood on his back when last she saw him, in the clearing fighting the 'nychoteuth – that was the name Tighe had assigned to the latest monstrosities they'd encountered. Nate had certainly proved his mettle, and his ability to be a member of the Bani.

"You saved my life. All our lives." He reached over, and very lightly touched her hand. "You're a hell of a woman, Vida Calder."

"Maybe," she said, and she didn't return his touch, but didn't pull away from it, either.

He was silent beside her. She could tell by the way he pursed his lips that he had questions, something he wanted to say to her. But perhaps he felt this wasn't the time, because he kept the words to himself.

"Do you know why I volunteered for the Bani?" she asked after a while. The sun had fallen behind the clouds, and bright ribbons of topaz and saffron streamed across the sky. "When I was a child, my father was away. And one day, a doorway opened into the world between our house and the sea, like the air was a curtain and it was pulled aside. Something, some horrible *thing* came through and reached for me. But my *manman* intervened. She stopped it from getting me, and so instead of taking me, it took her. I was eight years old, and a monster like something from a nightmare stole my mother."

Harris nodded once, understanding in the movement.

"And now, I have to figure out what to do," she whispered, closing her eyes on the tears that welled and slipped down her face.

When her hand turned to hold his, he returned her firm grasp; she was sure he could feel her trembling.

"Because regardless of how they originally broke through to our world," she went on, "They have someone else to open their doorways for them now. Someone who can do it almost effortlessly. I saw her through the portal, and I recognized her."

"No," Harris breathed.

Vida knew he'd seen through the opening before she'd closed it by sheer will, but had he seen the woman's face?

"I don't know why. I can't imagine any reason good enough. But my mother is helping them. I have to stop her."

Harris squeezed her hand, and she turned to look at him. Already the light was fading from the sky; from behind them the lights from base camp were shining. When her eyes met his gaze, he gave her a promise. "I'll help you."

HUNGRY EYES

-A Valducan Story-
Seth Skorkowsky

15 July, 2009

T he second one is coming up now," I said into the radio. From my vantage point, crouched behind a rooftop wall, I watched an orange basket stretcher emerge from the manhole. It stopped as it reached the tripod straddling the opening and swung there, dangling above the pit. Blue-uniformed officers carefully pulled it out and began unstrapping the black body bag secured inside. Colored lights flashed atop the response vehicles, parked to shield the grisly work from the view of onlookers pressing against the nearby barricades. Shouts in French echoed up from the crowd and the police trying to contain them.

Nick's voice came through my ear bud. "Colin, you in position?"

"Aye," Colin answered.

"Mal, keep us posted, but stay out of sight," Nick ordered, his Armenian accent muddling the words.

"Roger that." I wiped the sweat from my forehead, wishing a cloud might block the summer sun. Below me, the men lifted the bag and set it down on the concrete beside the first.

"They're going for the third one." I tucked lower behind the wall as the men sent the now empty stretcher back down into the abyssal hole. In the distance, the distinct *nee-noo-nee-noo* of a police siren echoed through the Paris streets. The line running from the tripod stopped.

Two minutes later, a worker flipped the tripod's winch and the spool began to coil.

"They're reeling it up," I radioed.

"Let's get ready, people," Nick said.

Nervous excitement tingled across my shoulders as I watched the spool grow larger and larger. Finally, the orange stretcher emerged from the catacombs sixty feet below. "It's up."

"Distraction coming in fifteen seconds."

I tightened my jaw, fighting the urge to ask, but knew better. Nick loved his surprises as much as he loved reminding me that I'm the new guy.

"Ten seconds."

The workers pulled the stretcher onto the ground. The crowd behind the barricade pushed harder, cameras flashing as they strained to see. Police stepped between them and the body, forming a human shield.

"Five."

I held my breath.

A loud boom thundered two blocks away. Car alarms erupted, accompanied by screams. Another boom sounded a moment later.

The police and medical workers shot upright, peering in that direction like startled meerkats. White smoke billowed from the direction the sounds had come, filling the narrow street.

Several police and paramedics charged in that direction as others ordered the crowd to disperse. It didn't take much to persuade them, and then the police ran after their companions. One stopped, just beyond the far barrier, his back to the bodies and ear to his radio.

"Clear," I said. "Still one nearby."

"Keep an eye on him," Colin said. He slipped out from between a pair of emergency vehicles and hurried to the bagged bodies, his copper hair hidden beneath a dark ball cap.

Licking my lips, I watched the lone policeman. I stole a glance to Colin to see him peel open the first bag, recoil at the unleashed sight or stench, then lift his camera.

Shouts continued down the street as the thickening white cloud spread. What the hell had Nick done? Was anyone hurt?

"One." Colin zipped the bag and moved to the next.

The lone officer shifted back and forth on his feet but hadn't turned. One by one the shrieking car alarms began to silence.

"Two." Colin said. "These things are weird."

"No commentary," Nick ordered. "Mal, how we look?"

"Some of the officers are headed back," I said. "Block away."

The lone officer started toward the trio jogging out from the smoke.

"Colin, be quick," Nick said.

"Just a few more seconds."

The policeman slowed as he met his companions. They spoke with wild-moving arms, pointing toward some unseen thing down the street. Two of them broke off and headed toward the vehicles.

"Get out of there," I said, my voice a whispered yell.

Colin looked up from his camera. Quickly he zipped the bag and hurried away before the police noticed him.

I blew a long breath, a wash of relief pouring down my body. "He's out."

"All right," Nick said. "Extract. Meet at the hotel."

•••

I sat on the bed, laptop before me. Scouring a map of the catacombs, I marked where the bodies were discovered and the best places we might gain access. Colin sat at the small table across the room working on his own computer. He hadn't spoken much since he arrived, only transferring his photographs over and giving the occasional grunt as he scrolled through the images.

The room door clicked and Nikoghos Tavitian stepped inside, his trimmed black beard framing his ear-to-ear smile. His olive knapsack rattled as he dropped it beside the door. He nodded to Colin. "Doctor," and then to me, "Doctor." With a flourish, he set a paper bag on the bed between us and withdrew a brown bundle. "Dinner is served."

Colin, who isn't actually a doctor, having joined the Order before completing med school, never liked being called that.

Nevertheless, Nick always addressed us that way when he was in good spirits, and terrifying an entire city appeared to have pleased the Armenian immensely.

Nick underhand-tossed a bundle to me. "Good work, Malcolm."

I caught the crinkly roll, feeling the warm bread inside. "What the hell did you do?"

"Distraction." Nick removed his own sandwich. "Needed something big enough to get everyone out of there. Just a pair of flash bangs and a smoke grenade in an alley. No one was hurt. Though…" He chuckled. "I think one woman did shit herself."

"You realize this could wind up on world news?"

He shrugged, his smile dimming. "Back page stuff. They'll write it off as a bad prank."

Colin nodded to his monitor. "It'll make the front page if police see what did this."

I stood and peered down at Colin's screen. The image of a mottled purple corpse; its teeth and cheekbones gleamed out through ragged holes. Blood-caked lashes framed the pits where its eyes should have been.

The image flipped to another – a girl with curly blonde hair. Her throat was torn out and grimy bite wounds covered her bare shoulders. Blue eye shadow crested the black pits of her empty sockets. I no longer wanted my sandwich.

Nick took a bite of his. "So what do you think?" he asked around a mouthful.

Colin unwrapped his own sandwich, unleashing the smell of fresh bread and meat, completely inappropriate for the horrible images. "Look to be cataphiles."

"Cataphiles?" Nick asked.

"People who explore the catacombs," I answered. "The old mines are strictly off limits, but people still go down there to explore, or party. Several even live down there. Three hundred kilometers of tunnels and chambers. Plenty of room for everyone."

Nick shrugged. "Not for them it seems. So, Mal, you're the Librarian. What do you think got 'em?"

I looked back at the screen, this time a young black man with his face mostly chewed off, his grisly skull framed in jagged skin. "Ghouls. Archives show they've made their home down there several times before. Last known infestation was during the war."

Colin nodded. "I agree. Blood wasn't drunk. Bite marks correspond."

"What else does it tell you?" Nick asked me.

"There's at least four of them, either ghouls or ghouls and their undead familiars." I answered, resenting this thinly veiled pop quiz.

"Why?"

I looked away as the image changed to a close-up of the black man's mouth. His tongue had been torn out. "Ghouls only attack if they outnumber the victims or if the victim is injured or ill."

"What about the eyes?" Colin asked.

"What about them?" I asked.

"They're gone."

"Ghouls must have torn them out."

"I don't think so." Shaking his head, Colin scrolled to a close-up of the girl's face. "You can't pop an eye out without tearing the skin around it. At least not without tools. But the skin is unmarked. Same with all of them. It's like they were sucked right out."

Nick leaned in over Colin's shoulder. "What could do that?"

Colin shrugged. "No clue. Something else? Took the eyes and left the rest for ghouls to eat, maybe?"

They both looked to me.

I studied the picture, and then the next. "I don't know."

"Don't know?" Nick asked. "Your job is to know them."

I shook my head. "I don't recall any demon that sucks the eyes out."

Colin gestured to my laptop still open on the bed. "Then search the records."

"Only ten percent of the Valducan Archives are digitized. I'd have to go back to the chateau and search the books."

"We don't have time to go to HQ," Nick said. "The author-ities are going to be scouring the catacombs for whoever killed these people, which means they'll probably get killed them-selves. We have to eliminate the threat now. So *think*, Doctor."

A sharp spike of anger shot through my gut at Nick's scolding. But he was right. I was the team's Librarian. This was my job. Closing my eyes, I searched my memory for anything that targeted eyes and didn't leave a mark. Even beyond the Archives, my experience as an anthropologist gave me a wide knowledge of folklore and supposedly mythical monsters, the main reason I was selected for the job. Other demons ate eyes. Wendigos loved eating them. But surgical removal? "I can't think of anything."

Nick frowned, but only for a moment before his grin returned. "A holy weapon will destroy them, regardless."

"We're in Paris," Colin offered. "Maybe the eyes are French cuisine to ghouls."

We laughed as Nick pulled his duffel from the closet and dropped it on the bed. "We guess ghouls from the initial report. So, Mal, what harms ghouls?"

"Obsidian," I answered.

"Good." He withdrew a box of ammo from his bag and pulled out a round. "If things get hairy, these will drop one." He held up a nine millimeter with a black-gem nose, prongs holding it in place like a goth girl's engagement ring. "We don't want to be shooting much down there," he said, continuing his digging. "Yes, the glass tip will cut down on ricochets, but closed-quarter shooting is always dangerous. I ever tell you about that vampire nest we rooted out of the Moscow Metro?"

"Every time you drink vodka," Colin answered.

Nick paused. "I do, don't I?" He shook his head. "Don't answer that."

"What about my sawed-off?" I asked. "I have some obsidian shells."

"You and that fucking sawed off," he said. "Yes, it'll work. No, don't shoot it. The other problem with shooting down there will be report. Give us all some permanent hearing loss. We'll need to run suppressed and even then, it'll still be loud as hell."

"Then why bring guns?" Colin asked.

"Cause I'd rather be deaf than dead," I answered.

Nick nodded in approval. "That's my boy."

"So what's the plan?" I asked.

"Three hundred klicks leaves a lot of room for them to hide. The sooner we begin the better. I say 2200 hours we go in. So rest up."

• • •

The night was still and humid as Nick and I exited the van, gear in hand. My sacred charge, *Hounacier*, a bone-handled machete, hung at my waist. Nick's holy nadziak, a Polish war pick named *Ozkareen*, clanged from the black plastic ring at his belt. Colin drove off the moment the door was closed, leaving us alone on the empty street.

We stopped at a metal door set into the sidewalk and lit by a single light post orbited by moths. We heaved up the door and a caged screen beneath, revealing a landing four feet down and steel rungs descending into the darkness below.

Nick drew a milky plastic tube from his vest pouch and cracked it in one hand. Orange light ignited within like liquid fire and he dropped it. The glow stick fell and fell, tumbling past more steel rungs until finally bouncing out of sight twenty meters below. He stabbed a finger downward and I swung my legs through the opening and dropped onto the landing. Nick handed me a heavy pack, which I set at my feet before moving to the rungs.

I clicked the lamp affixed to my caving helmet, unleashing a beam of crimson light. With a final nod to Nick, I started the climb down. Dizzying patterns of multi-colored spray-paint and marker covered every inch of the walls. Symbols, names, professions of love, and illegible slogans scrawled in dozens of different languages all stating the unspoken truth – *I was here before you.*

The heat of the summer night quickly vanished, the temperature dropping with each rung downward. The sweat on my neck grew colder, bringing a chill. Colin's whispered voice sounded above me as he returned, the van now safely parked. I looked up to see his silhouette pull the door shut, sealing us in with a metallic thud.

The shaft around me opened up, revealing a long passage, the floor peppered with cigarette butts, spent batteries, empty wrappers, and burnt matchsticks. Nick's glowsitck burned at my feet, casting its light across the graffiti-etched walls. I shone my light either way up the passage, seeing only a short way down each before the darkness swallowed the red beam. Dust rained down from my companions' descent and I stepped aside. I brushed the grit from my face, a pointless endeavor, I knew, as there would soon be so much more to wipe over the next few hours.

Nick was grinning as he reached the bottom, his white teeth glowing red in my light. "Reminds me of Moscow," he said with approval.

Colin's voice echoed from above. "Reminds me of a carnival house into hell."

I glanced over at the giant pentagram spray painted beside me, its disproportionate goat's head leering out from the inverted star. I knew that Colin, the ever-devout Irish Catholic, was going to hate this hunt.

He reached the bottom and curled his lip at the painted symbol.

"Welcome to hell," Nick said. I wasn't sure if he was merely being dramatic, or translating the French words scrawled above the goat's image.

Colin snorted and touched *Saighnean*, the holy anthropomorphic Celtic sword at his waist. "Fuck this place."

"Which way?" Nick asked, turning to me. Joviality was gone. Only the cold steel seriousness of a Valducan knight remained. He was a different man when he hunted.

I pointed down the eastern passage. "Bodies were found that way."

Nick drew his torch, clicked on a bright red beam, and started down, taking point.

We followed the winding tunnel past small chambers littered with spent candles and empty beer cans. One room was still lit with burning candles, but there were no other signs of the occupants. The air was still, completely unmoving, and when we did stop, the absolute silence was more unsettling than I cared to admit. More than once, the low passages forced us to crawl like worms to continue and I was grateful for the helmet as I banged my head into the rock above.

After two hours, the smell of decay tickled my nose. We turned into a small room. Dark splatters, almost black in our red lights, marred the pale limestone walls. Dried, bloody mud covered the floor, broken and dusty under booted footprints. The stink of ammonia prickled my nose somewhere deep below the stench of dried blood and spilt intestines.

"Here we are," I said. Taking a moment, I removed my water bottle and washed the dirt from my mouth with a healthy swallow. My left hand burned from the numerous nicks and scrapes, and I wished I'd worn a glove on it. But the warding eye tattooed on my palm would be useless if covered and taking the time to remove a glove might not be an option if I needed it. The tattoo, one of several on my body, was a gift from Hounacier, a blessed medal to commemorate a special kill.

Nick walked into the center of the dried stains and looked around, searching the ceiling and walls for some hidden secret.

"Wish we could have seen what it looked like," Colin said. He ran a gloved finger around one of the sharp holes left by tripod feet dotting the cracked floor, remnants from where the workers had recorded the gruesome scene before moving the bodies.

"So, Malcolm," Nick said, his headlamp's light falling on me. "Where to?"

I removed my tablet and winced as the screen came on, shining in my eyes like a floodlight. My night vision, previously preserved by the crimson lights, was gone in a painful cinching of pupils. Through slitted eyes I studied the catacomb map and highlighted the path we'd covered. I pointed to an arched doorway. "That will lead us to a lower level. My guess is the nest is deep."

"All right," he said. "You be sure to keep track of where we are. I don't want to get lost."

I flipped off the tablet and stored it away. "Follow me."

We headed down the passage, gradually sloping deeper beneath the Earth. Once we had to climb down a near vertical stretch until reaching an arched passage. Standing water filled many of the halls, forcing us to wade thigh-deep through it to continue and leaving us cold and wet. I imagined unseen hands grabbing us from below the murky surface, yanking us down to be drowned and eaten. I wanted to rush, but the threat of unseen pits hidden beneath the water forced us to move slow. More than once I felt what I was sure to be a bone crack under my boot.

Eventually we stopped in a room with benches hewn from the stone walls and I checked the map. Five hours, and we'd barely begun to cover the catacomb's length.

"I think this is good for tonight," Nick said around a mouthful of cereal bar. His coating of chalky dust left his beard gray, giving him the appearance of a statue come to life. "We should head back. Continue tomorrow. I don't want to stay down here."

"I completely agree," Colin said. "But let's find these bastards soon. I don't want to spend all summer crawling around in this shit."

"Let's hope the next hunt is somewhere warm and sunny," I said, flipping off my tablet and returning it to its plastic bag.

We headed back, Colin taking the lead. The journey felt longer than it should have, my perception of time warped by exhaustion and the impatience to breathe fresh air. While I frequently turned to check behind us, I couldn't help but shake the feeling we were being followed. Unseen eyes watching us from the blackness. Once, I even stopped the others, convinced I'd seen a shadow move at the edge of my light, but there was nothing there.

"You're tired," Nick said. "Just stay alert. Never assume it's in your head."

The paranoia continued to mount until we finally crawled back up that painted shaft and out onto the streets and into sunlight.

• • •

16 July, 2009
We headed down at 2100 hours from a new location, a locked and rusted gate along the Seine. This time I wore rubber waders and carried dry socks stuffed into bags. Three hours later, we reached the room we'd stopped at the night before.

"Look here," I said, shining my light onto the dusty floor. A bare footprint – its long toes resembling a hand with their length and positioning – marked the very center of one of our own old boot prints. "I knew I heard something behind us."

"They knew we were here," Nick whispered, his hand moving to the war pick at his belt. "Biding their time for an opening. Stay sharp."

I sympathized with Theseus, hunting and being hunted by the Minotaur in Minos' labyrinth. I sniffed, a faint and familiar smell tingling my nostrils.

"Ammonia," Colin said, reading my face.

We continued on, searching the tunnels for any signs, that tickling at my nape that we were being watched now fueled and unstoppable. Three times we wheeled around, believing something behind us, but there never was.

We'd rounded a corner when Colin, in the lead, brought up a clenched fist, telling us to stop. He motioned to his ear.

Holding my breath, I listened. Only silence. I opened my mouth to whisper a question when a distinct grunt, like from some large rooting animal, echoed from the darkness ahead. Then the sounds of splashing water followed by another grunt.

Nick looked back at me, his hand lowering to his war pick. I drew Hounacier and we moved forward, silent as we could.

The passage sloped downward, turning twice before opening into a long, vaulted room, its floor completely submerged in milky-brown water. Nick's bright torch reflected off the surface, throwing its shimmering glow across the ceiling.

Another splash brought the light down onto a vaguely human shape twenty meters away at the far end, standing before an arched doorway. The ghoul's eyes reflected the light from their deep sockets. Wild black hair crested its simian head and down its hunched back. Wet rags, the remains of whatever clothes the owner had worn when the demon had taken them, hung in shredded tatters, dripping on the landing on which the creature stood. The ghoul's lips curled back as it growled, long and steady.

Colin began swinging his sword beside him, the blade quickly gaining speed. He took a step forward.

"Stop!" Nick hissed.

Colin looked back, but kept Saighnean spinning.

Nick nodded to the floor. "We have no idea how deep that is."

As if in answer, the ghoul let out a howl and slammed its fists into the floor.

"He's right," I whispered. "It's not coming at us." I scanned the water, searching for any sign of a floor or movement beneath. I didn't know if ghouls even needed air, but their undead familiars wouldn't.

The ghoul roared and hopped, but didn't advance.

"Just keep at it, asshole," Nick said. He dropped his holy weapon into his belt loop and drew his pistol. The black suppressor made it look like a cannon.

The ghoul slapped at the water and took a step forward, obviously unconcerned by the gun.

The shot cracked through the room, louder than I would have expected. The round caught the demon in the thigh. It howled, stumbling back, blood pouring down its leg. Nick fired again, this time blasting a hole in the wall behind it.

The ghoul scrambled back through the doorway. The obsidian-tipped slugs couldn't harm the demonic spirit, but they'd definitely kill the possessed body. It leaped for cover as Nick's third shot rang out.

We stood there for a solid minute, listening.

"Cheap trap," Nick said, holstering his pistol. "Lure us into some sunken pit. Let us drown and eat us." He turned to me. "Is there a way around?"

Giving the water a wary glance, I stepped back into the passage before sheathing my machete and opening the map. "Yes. Take us about an hour."

We headed back and circled our way around, eventually making it back to the flooded chamber from the other side. The ghoul's blood still spattered the ground, but didn't lead us far before ending at another submerged hallway with no way around.

After nine laborious hours, we returned to the surface, tired, bruised, and frustrated.

* . *

17 July 2009
"We'll get them tonight," Nick promised as we started down the manhole on our third night. "I promise."

"You said that last night," I said.

"But tonight they'll get aggressive. Their trap didn't work, so they'll make their move. We just have to beat them to it."

"If you're wrong," Colin said, his voice echoing up from below. "You owe me a drink."

Metal and concrete grinded above as Nick slid the manhole cover into place. It thudded, pinching off the light from above. "Deal."

The ladder ended in a circular brick chamber. Shards of broken bottles gleamed from a mound piled along one side. Three arched doorways led from the room. Above one, stenciled in metallic paint, read Dante's immortal line, *Lasciate ogne speranza, voi ch'intrate*, the words framed with winged skulls.

"All right, Doctor," Nick said as he reached the bottom. "Which way?"

I nodded to Dante's door, "Abandon all hope, you who enter here," and we headed through. We followed the passage past several antechambers, each decorated in its own style. In one, a support pillar had been carved into that of a long-haired maiden, a rotted green blanket wrapped over her shoulders like a cape, and a hundred empty tea light cups laid out on the floor before her. I took comfort that none of those candles were burning.

The passage continued on, shrinking lower and lower until we had to crawl. Nick cracked another glow stick and hurled it ahead. It skittered and fell into a room at the far side. "Is there another way around?"

I shook my head. "No. Not unless we doubled back three kilometers. That should empty into the hall we want."

He shined his light onto the ceiling, revealing a wide crack running the length. One good bump might easily bury us forever.

"Stay low," he said, and continued forward.

Something moved past the light ahead, casting a shadow. Icy fear shot down my spine. There was no way to draw our weapons and fight in this tiny space, and whoever crawled into that room would be open to attack, helpless.

Scratching came from ahead, like fingernails desperately trying to dig their way through a chalkboard.

"Back!" Nick whispered through clenched teeth. "Back! Back! Back!"

We scrambled backwards. Colin cursed as my heel nearly took him in the eye, but I dared not slow lest Nick's back-scrambling boots hit me. Heart pounding, sweat ran down my face and into my eyes. Finally, my feet made it back to the opening of this death trap and I nearly screamed as hands gripped me from behind, yanking my belt.

"Gotcha," Colin said pulling me out.

I rolled onto my knees and helped pull Nick from the hole.

I peered down the empty tunnel, seeing an orange glow the far side, but nothing more. "Did you see it?"

Panting, Nick shook his head. "No. But, it… growled."

"Shit." I looked back down the shaft. "You think it's waiting?"

He blew a long breath. "Possible. If it is, whoever sticks their head out of the passage first is a dead man."

"What if we go close to the edge and pushed each other through at the end?" Colin asked.

"Not willing to risk that. Not if there's another way."

"Three kilometers," I said.

"Then we need to hustle." Nick cracked another stick and dropped it on this side of the shaft. "Keep your eyes and ears open. They're hunting us now."

Taking point, I led us back down the passage, past the cloaked maiden, and into another hall. Steps led down into gray water, leaving narrow ledges on either side. Straddling the flooded passage, our backs against the arched ceiling we moved on, our red-hued reflections staring up at us.

Twice we stopped and listened for sounds behind us, but heard nothing. Each time we dropped another glow stick so that we might see any pursuers following us past that point. After two hours, I turned down a passage and saw an orange glow ahead. Cautious, we drew our weapons and crept forward.

The glow stick rested on the floor, nine inches beneath the square passage in the wall. Hounacier ready, I removed a telescoping inspection mirror from my belt and held it out, making sure the tunnel was vacant, then peered through. Fifteen meters down, I could see the light of Nick's second stick. "Clear."

"Look at this," Colin said, kneeling beside me.

More bare footprints, like those from the previous night, marred the dusty floor. They crisscrossed back and forth across the side entrance.

"At least two," Colin said.

"And one in shoes," I added, nodding to a set of sneaker tracks mixed in with the other prints.

"Which way?" Nick asked.

I motioned ahead.

"So let's find 'em."

We marched on, following them as best we could until reaching bare stone. We stopped in a cathedral-like chamber with four other exits. After checking the map, I selected one. Nick left a fresh stick on the floor as Colin and I built a line of empty cans across the passage entrance.

We made it twenty meters down the hall before coming to a chamber with a dusty folding chair resting in the middle before a framed photograph affixed to the wall.

"That's just creepy," Colin whispered.

I nodded, about to move toward it, when a distant sound of falling cans came from behind.

We spun and headed back. Heart thudding, I crept closer to the room, seeing the spilt can-wall cast in red and orange light. I reached it first and looked around the cathedral seeing nothing.

Nick's bright lights swept the room then froze on a lone figure standing before the far wall, with its back to us.

"Bonjour?" I said, stepping closer. My fingers tightened on Hounacier's horn grip as the figure shuffled but didn't turn. I couldn't tell if it was male or female, only a human in dust-caked clothes. "Turn around!" I ordered, raising my holy machete.

The figure didn't move.

Nick stepped up beside me. "Don't get any closer."

Just then, the figure turned toward us. The flesh along the left side of its face was gone. Its single milky eye locked onto us and a hissing growl came from its shredded mouth.

More hissing sounded to the right. I turned, bringing my headlamp's beam on two more staggering corpses coming from another passage. Each only had one eye.

"Behind us!" Colin yelled, his voice booming in the stone chamber.

A trio of ghouls scurried out from another tunnel, moving on all fours like long-armed monkeys.

"Circle up!" Nick ordered. He swung his nadziak at the half-faced creature coming toward us, though it was still a good seven feet away. Yanking the weapon back mid-swing like a cracking whip, a shockwave of compressed air shot like a cone from the war pick's tip. The cone struck the creature's shoulder with a loud *thop*, and blew a hole through it like a high-powered rifle. The creature reeled around, its arm coming free at the motion and landing several feet behind it. Nick lunged forward and slammed the pick into the zombie's chest – heart shot – before it could recover. It fell dead to the ground.

Colin stepped beside me, eyes on the circling ghouls, and swinging Saighnean before him in a figure-eight. The blade moved faster and faster, gaining momentum until it was nothing but a whirring blur.

"Mal, take the minions," Nick shouted. "Colin, the demons."

Hounacier in hand, I threw my left palm forward toward the closing zombies. The tattoo's warding eye stretched wide, feeling as if the flesh might rip. The zombies froze their advance, their growling hisses rising even above the sound of Colin's swinging sword. Seizing the opening, I lunged, driving the machete's blade at creature's heart. It brought an arm up, deflecting the blade so that it plunged into the right side of its chest and missed the target. Unfazed, the creature grabbed my forearm.

I screamed. The bones in my arm bent, threatening to crack under the creature's inhuman grip. Desperately, I tore Hounacier free from the rotting corpse and swung, burying the blade into the zombie's skull but to no effect.

Nick moved past me in a blur and buried Ozkareen in the creatures back. Its chest exploded as the pick came through, showering me with rotted gore. "Go for the heart!" he shouted.

A pair of ghouls charged Colin.

One moved as if to lunge, but dashed to the side at the last moment. The other one leapt toward him, claws raised. Colin brought his blurring sword up as it reached him. The ghoul's arms diced apart, the blows striking so fast they seemed simultaneous. Shrieking, the demon fell, blood spurting from its twin stumps. Colin rammed the blade down into its head.

Golden yellow fire ignited along the slain demon's skin and from the severed pieces scattered about the room.

The last zombie was coming for me. With my wrist still

aching from its near break, I lifted my warding palm, freezing the creature again, then rammed Hounacier up under its ribs and into its dead heart. The zombie fell, nearly yanking me off balance with the sudden weight coming down on the impaling blade.

Yellow firelight danced along the walls. I wrenched Hounacier's blade free in time to see Nick swing Ozkareen in that whip-like fashion, launching another cone of air at a ghoul. The beast dropped to the floor, dodging it. The cone blasted past, dissipating after ten feet.

The demon leaped toward Nick, but he spun out of the way of a slashing claw.

I ran toward it, bringing my warding palm up. The ghoul turned to face me but then froze, shielded its eyes from the displayed tattoo.

Before it could recover, a conical shockwave struck it on the neck, blasting its head nearly off. Golden demon fire sprayed into the wall and the ghoul's corpse fell, its soul burning away.

Colin began swinging Saighnean in another unstopping pattern, its speed quickly accelerating into a blur. The final ghoul raced toward the nearest exit but I ran around to meet it, Hounacier raised and warding palm out.

Without looking at the tattoo, it lurched to the side, but too late before Colin was on it. Spectral flames erupted as the ghoul seemed to come apart into four pieces. Colin grinned as he pulled the sword out from a hunk of burning torso where the blade had finally stopped.

"Looks like you were right, Nick." I turned to see the Armenian standing, pick raised at his side. A figure stood in the passage before him – fat, vaguely feminine, and naked, reminiscent of a Paleolithic Venus. It had no face at all, only a smooth blankness.

Nick stepped closer, nearing the range for Ozkareen's shock missile.

A vertical slit opened along the creatures face like a lipless mouth. The crack lengthened, stretching down its body, between its sagging breasts, and splitting its hanging gut. Then the demon unfolded like a flower and Nick screamed.

Thousands of eyeballs filled the inside like the seeds of a pomegranate. They rolled and moved in swirling patterns, set to some unheard music. A honey-like aroma flooded the chamber, but beneath that, lurked the eye-watering ammonia stink. Nick's screams ceased. His raised arm lowered and fell limp to his side. Ozkareen slipped from his grip and clanked to the floor.

The demon moved closer. Slender tendrils, rooted at the mass' center, wriggled toward him.

"No!" I charged toward it, and raised my warding eye before me, thrusting it over Nick's shoulder.

The rolling eyes all zeroed in on my palm and then seemed to boil along the flower's surface. The demon flew off like a swimming jellyfish, slinging dust as it surged away into the darkness, tendrils trailing behind it.

Nick's head lolled. I caught him as he stumbled forward and vomited. Colin stepped in and helped me move him to a sitting position, my eyes never leaving the dark passage through which the demon had fled.

Nick feebly reached for Ozkareen lying in the dust.

"Here," I said handing it to him. "Are you all right?"

Still panting, Nick nodded. "What… was that?"

"I don't know. I–"

"You're the fucking Librarian," Colin snapped.

Setting my jaw, I pulled off my pack and opened my tablet. He was right, this was my job. They'd killed the demons, while I'd only killed a mindless servant. I scrolled through the record. While the tell-tale smell and resemblance to the Venus were certainly noteworthy, the sheet of eyes reminded me of something I'd read before, something I thought I'd never encounter.

Nick crawled to his feet and stood behind me. Whether real or imagined, I could feel his mounting impatience. It was getting away.

"Here," I said, clicking a file. A crude image of a Japanese screen peppered with eyes filled the top of the page.

"What is it?" Colin asked without taking his gaze from the passage. His free hand touched his chest, surely feeling the rosary beneath his shirt.

I licked my lips, reviewing the scant description. "A mokumokuren."

"Mokuwhat?"

"Mokumokuren," I repeated. "Extremely rare. Thought to be extinct. Last one reported in Turkey 1892. No mention of stealing eyes, but said to... *entrance its prey with hypnotic patterns of eyes*. Lives in dark places, moves in aquatic fashion, and it can strangle you with its hundred tentacles."

"Lovely."

"What hurts it?" Nick asked, peering closer.

"Pure quartz."

He grunted. "I don't have that."

"I have one shell." I clicked off my screen. "Mixed load, but quartz is in it."

"Just one?" Colin asked.

"Better than nothing," Nick said. "Load it and let's get after that thing."

Quickly, I stored my tablet away and withdrew a lumpy, rolled bundle. I unfurled it, revealing a rainbow assortment of hand-loaded shotgun shells. Moving my fingers along the rows I removed a white plastic shell with a red and black band. I clicked open my Remington and switched it out with one of the obsidian loads before putting the bundle away. "Ready."

Nick held out his hand and I gave over the sawed-off. The yellow light flooding the room had begun to wane as the slain ghouls returned to their once human forms. The honey aroma had faded, but the cat-piss stink seemed to have gotten worse. Nick took point, with me behind him, Hounacier in hand.

We moved slow, checking each chamber and crevice before going on. The passage wound its way deeper, angling sharply before leveling out. Fueled with paranoia, my heart pounded and sweat beaded my gritty face despite the cold, unmoving air.

Nick moved toward a pit-like vault, but I touched his arm.

He turned toward me and I pointed down at a low crevice in the wall by his feet. The limestone dust before it was rippled like miniature wind-swept dunes.

Instantly, he moved past to the other side, his holy weapon raised. I drew my mirror and angled it at the hole. A tunnel, no more than eighteen inches high and two feet wide, extended into darkness.

I nodded to Colin beside me and he lowered his torch, shining the crimson beam along the tight passage. It extended a little over a meter before opening into another chamber. Relaying this to my partners, I crawled onto the smooth floor.

Nick cracked one of his last glow sticks, filling our tunnel with brilliant orange light then he hurled it down the shaft before me.

The stick ricocheted off the tight walls, finally bouncing to a stop just a few feet inside the room. The chamber appeared small, but I couldn't see much from my limited view. I extended the mirror's handle to its full length and stretched my arm as far as I could to get a better look.

It wasn't long enough to reach and I had to crawl a little inside, my arm out before me. Rotating the mirror, I saw no exits. I pushed it out a little further for a better view. Black whip-like strands shot down from the ceiling, wrapping around my mirror and ripping it from my grip.

I cried out in surprise, banging my head as I tried to scramble back. More tendrils fluttered along the top edges of my tunnel, reaching blindly. A palpable waft of sweet nectar filled the passage. Colin seized my belt and dragged me back out.

They didn't have to ask what I'd seen.

"Exits?" Nick mouthed.

I shook my head, panting, then pointed upward. "On the ceiling."

"What do we do?" Colin whispered, his mouth so close I could feel his breath on my ear.

"If we try to crawl in we're dead before we can make it," I replied, looking back down the now empty hole.

Nick crouched beside me, silent as he studied the shaft. He shook his head steadily, seeming to run through our few options.

I licked my dusty lips. "I have an idea."

Nick gave me a look and I pulled off my pack and lay on my back. I drew Hounacier. "Give me my gun. Push me through. Fast."

Colin shook his head.

"It's the only way." I mimed firing the Remington, then hacking the machete.

No! Colin mouthed. He looked to Nick for support, but the Armenian nodded instead.

"It'll work. But I'll go. I'm senior knight."

"You don't have this," I said, opening my palm. "Bang," I whispered, miming pulling the trigger, then dropping the gun and rolling my empty palm before me. "I'm the only one that can do it."

Nick's lips tightened. He handed me the sawed-off. *I'll push you through,* he mouthed. *Then you,* pointing to Colin, *push me. One, two.*

I nodded.

Colin looked at Nick, then to me. Finally he nodded. "You need earplugs."

"Ah." I reached for my pack and drew out the yellow foam plugs Nick had given us. With those firmly in place, I returned to position, gun and Hounacier against my body and before my face.

"Close your right eye," Nick ordered.

I did.

"Open it after you've fired. Otherwise the flash will leave you blind." He cracked his final glow stick and set it on my stomach then took position at my feet, crouched in a runner's stance, hands on my boots. Colin squeezed in behind him, mouth tight in an unhappy line.

Right eye clenched, I nodded to Nick and mouthed, *three... two... one.*

I launched forward, rocks scraping my back. The tunnel flew past me in a blur. As my head came into the room I extended the shotgun toward the ceiling. I had only a moment's glimpse of a thousand eyes looming above, black tendrils lashing toward me.

I fired.

The brilliant flash burned my vision and the boom was so loud it jarred my bones. A keening shriek filled the room, audible through my plugged and ringing ears.

Without time to think I rolled to my feet, staying low but still banging my head, and slinging the other glow stick onto the floor. The room was no more than five feet high. Opening my unblinded right eye I saw the demon before me lashing and writhing like an enraged manta ray. Thousands of eyes rolled to focus in my direction. I dropped the smoking shotgun and extended my warding palm. The tattooed lid stretched wide and the beast shrieked again.

I lunged, thrusting Hounacier into the heart of the thrashing mass. Her blade buried deep. I yanked it free and hacked and hacked, shredding rolling eyes as slimy tendrils squirmed and whipped at my face and arms.

Screaming, I rammed the machete's blade back into the twisting folds with both hands, and then slashed to the side, splitting the monster nearly in half.

Brilliant maroon fire spilled from its wounds as the demon crumpled to the chamber floor. Panting, and covered in blood, now burning with cold flames, I noticed Nick beside me. Hounacier twisted in my grip moving like a dowser's rod, her blade coated in flickering fire.

Loosening my grip, I allowed the machete to move, to guide me where she wanted to go. The blade bent, moving in circles. Transferring her to my off-hand, Hounacier dipped toward my now-emptied right. I brought it up to meet her, palm flat. The edge met my skin then bit in with sharp pain. Demon fire surged into the wound and the machete's fighting ceased, her newest gift bestowed. An orange and blue half-lidded eye, similar to the one tattooed in my left palm, glowed within the flesh of my cut hand. Then the image faded.

"Thank you," I breathed.

"What was that?" Nick asked, his voice muted.

"Hounacier telling me to get a new tattoo." I turned as Colin scrambled into the room.

"Thank God," he said, looking at the dead monster. "Everyone all right?"

"Yes," I replied, closing my bloodied hand. "Let's get some fresh air, and buy Nick a beer."

THE SECRET WAR

David W. Amendola

Death lurked in the hamlet. A great deal of death. Lieutenant Nikolai Zakharov could feel it. He could not smell it – the temperature was at least thirty degrees below zero so anything that died would quickly freeze solid – but he knew it was there, waiting. Kneeling behind a windfall at the edge of the forest, he observed the cluster of stout log cabins in the clearing through binoculars, watching and listening for signs of activity.

Nothing. Not even chimney smoke. All was quiet.

Black ravens perched in the nearby trees, another indicator of death. He noted that they were strangely silent and kept their distance from the hamlet.

Including Zakharov, his team numbered ten. He and seven others were armed with PPSh-41 submachine guns. The wiry Junior Sergeant Okhchen preferred his Mosin-Nagant sniper rifle with its PE telescopic sight. Private Kaminsky, a giant of man with red hair and fierce eyes, was responsible for the DP-28 light machine gun. He handled it like a toy, shouldering with ease the heavy satchel of extra magazines that normally an assistant would carry for him. Each man also had an RGD-33 stick grenade.

They were dressed for the extreme cold: quilted jacket and trousers, woolen underwear, fleece cap, fur mittens, and felt boots. For camouflage a white, hooded snow suit was worn over everything.

Nervous tension sharpened their senses and attuned them to their surroundings, made them alert for the slightest scent or sound. They knew all too well the nature of their enemy.

Zakharov whistled a bird call to get everyone's attention and then motioned. He and six others emerged from concealment, snow crunching underfoot, and warily approached the hamlet.

The tiny settlement huddled on a river bank was an old trading post and stores that had catered to the local fur trade for nearly a century.

Mere minutes of murderous frenzy had snuffed it out forever.

On the icy, dirt street the soldiers found pale corpses and pieces of corpses lying frozen among stiffened tatters of shredded clothing. Puddles of blood and gore had solidified into dark-red ice. The villagers had been ripped apart: heads, limbs, and entrails were strewn about. All were gnawed and half-eaten, bones split for marrow and skulls smashed open for brains. A grisly feast for scavengers, but as Zakharov expected, none were skulking around. Wolves, like the ravens, were shunning this place.

A laika, someone's pitiful pet, cowered behind a woodshed too terrified to even whimper. What had killed and eaten the villagers did not have a taste for dog meat.

The soldiers surveyed the carnage dispassionately, hardened to such horrors. This was not their first mission. All were *frontoviks* – combat veterans. Each had already been awarded the Medal for Combat Merit and a few had also earned at least one wound stripe.

Zakharov motioned again. Kaminsky lay prone and covered the length of the street with his machine gun. Then three men led by Senior Sergeant Sergei Kravchenko, a short stocky Ukrainian who was Zakharov's second in command, crept up to the rear of the nearest cabin, staying below window level. With a bang the door was kicked in and they rushed inside, fingers on triggers and grenades ready to throw. After verifying the cabin was unoccupied, they moved on to check the next building.

At length the search was complete and Kravchenko briskly strode over to relay the results to his superior, who had remained beside Kaminsky.

"All clear, Comrade Lieutenant."

"I assume there are no survivors," said Zakharov.

"No."

Zakharov nodded at Okhchen, who began inspecting the claw and bite marks on the slain villagers. He squatted to study a footprint in a patch of snow stained pink by blood, viewing it from different angles. Roughly the size of a man's, it had three clawed toes reminiscent of a bird's. He walked around and carefully examined other tracks on the hamlet's outskirts before returning to make his report.

"Comrade Lieutenant, there were ten of them. They attacked last night."

"Which direction did they come from?" asked Zakharov.

"Northeast. They're headed southwest now."

Zakharov nodded then turned to Kravchenko. "Let's get moving. We head northeast."

"We're not following them?" asked Kravchenko.

"No, the other teams will have to intercept them. Our assignment is to locate their hole. Signal that we've found evidence of an attack and they're headed southwest."

"Yes, Comrade Lieutenant." Kravchenko beckoned to a private and barked an order.

The Red Army possessed relatively few radios and the team had none. Laying wire for field telephones was often impractical, so messengers and flares were usually relied upon for communication between teams. The private loaded a flare pistol according to his signal chart, pointed it at the sky, and sent a two-star purple and white flare arching high above.

The Secret War had raged on and off for almost a quarter-century, never mentioned in the Soviet press or publicly acknowledged by Soviet leaders. Matters of internal security never were.

Zakharov remembered when he returned from his first search-and-destroy operation. He had been congratulated by his superiors, decorated with the Order of the Red Star, and then bluntly informed that if he ever told anyone outside the unit what he had seen he would be sent to a corrective-labor camp.

There were lulls in the war, but then the things would return. Just exactly what they were no one knew. In the dead of winter, when the nights were longest, mysterious holes would appear in northern Siberia and the things would come forth, hungry for human flesh. They never hunted animals, only people. And Moscow would have to organize another campaign to eradicate the bloodthirsty creatures.

They had no official name, as they corresponded to no known species. Soviet scientists debated whether they were the wild men of myth – the *almasty* of the Caucasus, the *chuchunya* of Siberia, or the *menk* of the Urals. But legends described all of these as similar to apes or men, perhaps even surviving Neanderthals, and the terrifying creatures that attacked villagers and herders were definitely not human or simian. Unofficially they were simply referred to as *upir*, the generic Russian word for bloodsucking monsters such as vampires and ghouls.

Security operations within the USSR were normally handled by the internal troops of the People's Commissariat for Internal Affairs – the NKVD, Joseph Stalin's ruthless secret police. But these paramilitary units lacked the specialized training required. Hunting ghouls was altogether different from conducting mass arrests and deportations of alleged 'enemies of the people'. After an entire NKVD regiment was annihilated along the Middle Tunguska River in 1936, search-and-destroy operations were taken over by the Red Army.

A unique unit of irregulars was formed: Special Group X – *Spetsialnogo Gruppa X*, often referred to simply as *Spetsgruppa X*. The X was not the Cyrillic letter but the Latin, taken from the mathematical notation for an unknown variable, since the creatures they fought were an unknown species. Composed of soldiers acclimatized and trained for winter warfare, preferably those who had been trappers or hunters in civilian life, its independent detachments were based at Siberian outposts. Whenever a ghoul incursion occurred, teams would hunt down the creatures, eliminate them, and destroy their holes.

But when reports were received in late 1942 of renewed ghoul activity they were given a low priority by the Kremlin. The Soviet Union was locked in a bloody death struggle with Nazi Germany, which had launched a massive invasion the previous year. All available troops and equipment were needed to replace the appalling losses suffered in the desperate battles for Minsk, Kiev, Leningrad, and Moscow. *Spetsgruppa X* was reduced to a token force. Before the war Zakharov's team had been the size of a platoon; now it was a squad.

Zakharov took a sun sighting with a sextant. There were no accurate maps of this area, and he kept a log of their movements and location.

When none of the others were nearby, Kravchenko asked, "Permission to speak freely, Comrade Lieutenant?"

"Of course, Sergei Pavlovich." Despite their difference in rank they were on familiar terms in private. Smart junior officers listened to and learned from their senior non-commissioned officers and Zakharov greatly valued Kravchenko's experience. Almost twice as old as Zakharov, he had served in the First World War and the Russian Civil War.

"The detachment's teams are deployed too far apart," said Kravchenko. "We can't support each other and coordinate patrols to sweep each sector properly. If one team encounters too many ghouls it might be overwhelmed before the others can help."

"I raised that concern."

"May I ask what the major's response was?"

"He said we can cover more territory if we disperse this way. Not many ghouls were reported so he's confident each team can handle any it finds."

"Only a few have been detected so far, that's true, but who's to say there won't be more? We have no way of knowing how many will show up each winter."

"I know."

Kravchenko sighed. "Why did Moscow send us a new detachment commander who has no experience in these operations? It's bad enough we're undermanned."

"We have our orders."

"Understood, Comrade Lieutenant. Did the major at least say something about the planes that were requested?"

"No, and I wouldn't count on any either. Supporting our comrades fighting at Stalingrad is Moscow's top priority right now."

They returned to the forest. The dead villagers were left where they lay. Others would come later to dispose of them. The hamlet itself would be abandoned. No one would want to live here now.

Three soldiers in a nearby gully held the team's horses, the animals' foggy breath rising from frosted muzzles. Much of Siberia was still primordial wilderness, impassable for motorized transport. These beasts were small, shaggy Yakutians, a hardy breed that thrived in this brutal climate and subsisted largely on wild grass.

The team slung weapons, saddled up, and rode off in the direction from which the ghouls had come. Tracks led down the bank and over the flat, slate surface of the frozen river, swept by a whistling southwest breeze. This time of year the ice was thick enough to easily support horsemen. Upon reaching the opposite bank they plunged into the forest.

Okhchen scouted ahead, his dark, almond-shaped eyes picking out signs of the ghouls' passage – broken twigs, scuffed lichen, footprints in the snow. But no droppings. Ghouls left no excrement. The team took care to ride single file alongside the trail, not over it, so as not to obliterate any clues. It was easy to follow: their quarry had made no effort to conceal it.

Zakharov considered himself lucky to be assigned to *Spetsgruppa X*. The nature of its operations necessitated giving commanders in the field more freedom of initiative than was usual in the Red Army. This comparative independence had increased with the recent demotion of the Communist Party political commissars. Reduced to an advisory role, they no longer held dual command with military officers.

Keeping one's command still depended on results though. Failure was never an option in the USSR. Even if you were a marshal it could mean a sentence to a penal battalion or the Gulag, the NKVD's network of prisons and forced-labor camps. Or a firing squad.

Not that results guaranteed safety. Thousands had been imprisoned or shot during the purges. To meet the quotas of enemies demanded by Stalin's insatiable paranoia the secret police could arrest anyone for any reason – or no reason at all. Arbitrary terror maintained his iron rule.

Every division had an NKVD Special Department attached. Fortunately the head of this unit in *Spetsgruppa X* was an alcoholic whose wife had an eye for bourgeois luxuries. The commanding general prudently supplied plenty of vodka and furs to ensure glowing weekly reports.

The team followed the tracks through the bleak taiga. Larches stood gray and skeletal, having shed their needles last autumn. The forest floor had little underbrush, tufts of brown grass poking up through the snow in clearings. Siberia was not only very cold, but also very dry. Many parts actually received little snowfall, although what snow did fall would remain on the ground for at least six months out of the year. The only signs of humanity were small deadfall traps; winter was the hunting season for sable.

This time of year the days were very short, a blue twilight only lasting about four hours. The golden sun did not come up until late morning and struggled to rise just above the horizon before setting again by mid-afternoon.

At one point the team heard a long wail far in the distance. The shrill cry resembled nothing uttered by human or animal. They heard it again from time to time, coming from different directions. The soldiers exchanged anxious, knowing looks.

"Ghouls," Kravchenko muttered.

Zakharov raised his hand to signal a halt. He glanced around at the trees. One nearly fifty meters tall towered above the rest. Handing his binoculars to Okhchen, he said, "Get up there and see if you can locate them."

Okhchen strapped spikes to his boots and shinnied up the trunk until he could reach the lowest branches, then climbed up through the boughs. Sitting in a crook near the top, he slowly scanned in all directions before quickly clambering back down.

"Comrade Lieutenant, twelve are two kilometers northeast moving down the trail towards us," he said. "Ten more are a kilometer and a half southwest, following us and coming fast. The second group is probably the pack that attacked the hamlet. They must have discovered our tracks."

"They're hunting us now," said Zakharov. He rubbed his chin thoughtfully. "We could dig in and summon the other teams."

Kravchenko shook his head. "It'll be dark before anyone can get here. We're too far apart. Then the ghouls will have the advantage since they can see at night."

"Then we'd better attack now while it's still daylight and the packs are separated. Eliminate the ones behind us then destroy the rest."

Kravchenko grinned, revealing a gold eye tooth. "We'll catch them by surprise."

The team wheeled about and cantered back the way they had come. Soon the horses neighed. They had a keen sense of smell and ghouls exuded a disagreeable odor.

Swerving behind a rise, the soldiers dismounted. Three held the horses. Okhchen and Kaminsky crawled up to the crest to over-watch positions while the others, led by Zakharov, spread out in a skirmish line in front of the rise.

Ten ghouls ran through the woods ahead.

They were thin, wiry creatures with gray, leathery skin totally devoid of hair. Running in a forward crouch like apes, each would stand a little over meter and a half tall if fully erect. Long, bony arms almost reaching the ground ended in gnarled hands with curved, black claws. Bipedal, they had clawed, three-toed feet. Narrow heads had pointed ears, slits for nostrils, and slanted yellow eyes smoldering with ravenous hunger. They bared slavering fangs and long, blue, forked tongues flicked out.

Even weak daylight impaired their vision so they did not see the soldiers immediately.

A yellow flare was sent up to alert the other teams that ghouls had been spotted. Then the echoing crack of Okhchen's rifle broke the silence. A ghoul staggered as a 147-grain 7.62 millimeter bullet punched through its left eye, blasting out the back of its head in a spray of black ichor. It toppled backwards.

The other ghouls looked around angrily for the source as a second and then a third were killed in rapid succession by headshots, until finally they spotted the humans. With a bedlam of bloodcurdling howls, they charged. One threw back its head and let out a long, wavering shriek that echoed across the forest and sent chills up the spines of the soldiers.

"Fire!" shouted Zakharov.

The ghouls were fast and agile. The soldiers stood their ground and opened fire – the quick, harsh chatter of their submachine guns punctuated by the slower rattle of the DP-28 above and behind them.

The creatures rushed into a storm of lead. They stumbled and fell, riddled by scores of slugs, their ichor sizzling as it splashed on the ground, instantly melting any snow it touched. A pair veered left, trying to outflank the team, but to no avail. This move had been anticipated and they too were shot down, the last collapsing dead just meters from the soldiers.

The team ceased fire and reloaded, adrenalin slowly ebbing from their veins. Zakharov noticed Kravchenko calmly bandaging a wrist.

"Wounded?" he asked.

"A drop of their blood splashed on me," said Kravchenko. "Burns like acid."

The ghoul carcasses began smoldering and disintegrating. Within minutes all that would remain would be heaps of ashes and a foul reek lingering in the crisp air. No bones. And nothing would ever grow in these spots again. This accelerated decomposition had made it impossible to obtain specimens for scientific study, so details of ghoul anatomy were unknown.

Zakharov collected a little bit of the ash, sealing it in an envelope. He had standing orders to take samples when conditions permitted.

Attempts to capture ghouls alive had proved unsuccessful.

They could not be subdued and were totally resistant to tranquilizers. All anyone had to go on were eyewitness accounts, blurry photographs, plaster casts of footprints, and laboratory analysis of ash residue. Ghouls did not appear to have any type of social structure or leadership. Nothing resembling offspring were ever seen and their method of reproduction was unknown. They all looked alike and there was no visible gender differentiation.

The team hurried back to their horses and rode off to intercept the other pack.

The woods thickened, forcing them to slow as they followed tracks down a slope to a frozen, meandering stream cloaked in shadow, the treetops etched against the orange sky.

Okhchen abruptly reined in and motioned for the others to stop. His eyes darted around suspiciously.

The breeze shifted. The horses whinnied sharply.

"Ambush!" shouted Okhchen.

Screeches filled the air as ghouls suddenly leaped from behind the rocks and scrub brush on the opposite bank where they had been hiding.

One private was decapitated by a single slash of a claw and his headless body, spurting bright-red blood, rode along for a ways like a horrid rag doll before finally tumbling from the saddle. Another was dragged off his mount; his submachine gun and arm were torn away and the top of his head was sheared off. The neighing horse of a third man reared and hurled him to the ground, breaking his leg. A ghoul immediately disemboweled him and bit his throat out.

One sprang into a tree above Zakharov, but before it could pounce on him he peppered it with a burst from his PPSh-41. Several branches broke as the ghoul fell heavily to the ground.

The soldiers recovered quickly from their initial surprise and urged their steeds forward. They managed to ride clear of the ambush and then swung around to open a relentless fire from horseback. The pack was quickly eliminated.

Zakharov jumped down and rushed over to his fallen men along with the team's medic.

Two were already dead. The third, the one missing an arm and the top of his skull, was incredibly, horribly, still alive and conscious. With the usual stoicism of Russian soldiers he did not cry out. But he was beyond aid and there was nothing the medic could do except administer morphine to ease his last moments, cradling him in his arms until he mercifully expired.

Zakharov had a green flare fired to signal that all the ghouls seen had been destroyed. Then he grimly collected the identification booklets of his slain men for safekeeping. The bodies were stripped of weapons and equipment and loose stones were piled over each to erect a crude cairn. The iron-hard permafrost made grave digging a herculean task they had no time for. They paused for a somber moment of silence, then mounted up and rode on, taking the extra horses with them.

Because of the classified nature of these operations the government did not award a campaign medal for participation. Zakharov would not even be allowed to write consolation letters to the families. He could recommend deserving men for posthumous decorations, but the citations would themselves be classified. Relatives would never be told the circumstances of their loved ones' deaths, only that each had died "fighting gallantly in defense of his beloved Motherland."

They returned to the original trail. Night descended, the gloom faintly illuminated by the cold gleam of the stars. The temperature dropped still further, down to fifty degrees below zero. The trail was clear enough for the team to continue following it by starlight for several hours before finally stopping to camp.

A sentry was posted and trip wires for flares were strung around the camp perimeter. Everyone would take his turn standing watch while the rest slept. Zakharov determined their location again using a sextant sighting of Polaris.

First priority, as always for mounted troops, was the horses, which were picketed, groomed, checked for injuries, and allowed to graze. Finally a tent was erected and the team sat inside to eat, huddled around the oasis of warmth provided by a little iron field stove.

Zakharov saw to it that his men were taken care of first before wolfing down his own meal of black rye bread, buckwheat porridge, and hard sausage washed down with hot tea. He made a point of refusing officer's rations and eating the same food as enlisted men. An allotment of vodka was also authorized under regulations, but he strictly forbade it. Back at base the men could drink and carouse as they pleased, but on a mission he needed everyone sober and sharp.

Afterwards they cleaned weapons, oiled them with cold-weather lubricants to keep the mechanisms from freezing, and reloaded magazines. They talked and joked and enjoyed the luxury of a smoke, rolling strong, coarse tobacco in newsprint to make crude cigarettes.

The glint of metal betrayed a little Christian cross one private wore around his neck and kept hidden under his jacket. Zakharov, as usual, pretended not to notice.

He had seen too many good men die needlessly – and far too young – to entertain any belief in God. But like his soldiers he was the son of a peasant and understood their ways – their rough humor, their towering profanity, their taboos and superstitions – and he indulged them whenever possible. He also ignored their occasional grumblings about the regime. Zakharov was a pragmatic Communist. So long as his men fought that was all that mattered.

* * *

Zakharov snapped awake amid the frantic neighing and stomping of the horses. Even as he and the others in the tent fumbled for weapons the harsh, white glow of a trip flare suddenly lit up the camp and two bursts of automatic fire shattered the stillness.

Zakharov darted outside. Kaminsky was on sentry duty, smoke curling from his machine gun's muzzle.

"Over there," he said, nodding in the direction. "Two of them. Got both when the flare blinded them."

The team scrambled to defensive positions around the camp

as the flare fizzled out and darkness returned. They waited in tense silence as their night vision recovered. The dark woods seemed fraught with menace, a gibbous moon glowering above. But nothing happened, and at length the horses settled down and became quiet again.

"I don't think there are any more of them," said Okhchen.

The team relaxed. Zakharov went over to Kravchenko, who was squatting beside one of the ghoul ash piles, deep in thought.

"We were lucky," said Zakharov. "There were only two and the horses smelled them before they got too close."

Kravchenko grunted. "That's what worries me."

"Why?"

"Ghouls don't appear to be intelligent, Comrade Lieutenant, not in our sense of the word, but they're not stupid either. They're cunning like any predator. They've been shrieking back and forth all day, communicating. Communicating about us and the other teams. Our flares pinpoint our locations."

"Unfortunately we can't help it. We have no radios."

"For sure the ghouls know all about us – what we are, where we are, how many of us there are. So why are they attacking us just a few at a time or in small packs? If there aren't that many of them, then why not avoid us entirely and hunt for easier prey?"

"I don't know. When you put it that way, it doesn't make sense."

Kravchenko stood. "No, it doesn't."

• • •

The rest of the night passed uneventfully, but the team slept fitfully and rose before dawn. After a quick breakfast they resumed the hunt by moonlight. The trail turned due north.

As the first feeble rays of sunlight filtered through the trees Okhchen spotted something away from the trail and rode over to take a closer look. He got off his horse and examined the ground. Zakharov went to see what he was looking at. Okhchen brushed away snow to uncover yellowed, splintered bones, scraps of khaki fabric, a few black buttons, and the slashed remnants of boots and accouterments.

"Another ghoul victim?" asked Zakharov, dismounting.

"Yes, Comrade Lieutenant, but this fellow died a long time ago." Okhchen bent and plucked from a frayed pocket an identification booklet, its red cloth cover stained and faded. He was illiterate so he showed it to Zakharov.

Zakharov grunted with interest. "NKVD."

A rusted Nagant revolver lay nearby and he picked it up. Flicking down the loading gate, he rotated the cylinder to check the chambers. All seven rounds were spent. "He didn't go down without a fight." He glanced over the remains and noticed a skull fragment with a small, round hole in it. "Looks like he saved the last bullet for himself."

"He was carrying this," said Okhchen, holding up a map case of brown leather, battered and cracked by the elements but otherwise intact. He peered inside. "It's filled with old papers."

Zakharov took the case and the identification and put both in his saddlebag. "I'll look at them later. We need to move on."

They hurried on. Far to the west a yellow flare arced like a comet above the forest. Shortly thereafter they heard faint gunfire. The flurry of shots intensified.

"One of the other teams has found ghouls too," said Kravchenko, reining in.

The shooting tapered off and ceased. A green flare went up.

"And they eliminated them," said Zakharov. "Let's go."

At length Okhchen halted again, studying the ground. Zakharov saw tracks branching off in the trampled snow. Ahead, beyond this divergence, the trail became wider and heavier with more spoor than before.

"The ghouls split up here," said Okhchen. "Those tracks going west are probably from the pack the other team ran into."

Zakharov nodded. "That means we're following the main trail. Good."

Ahead lay a great swath of taiga devastated by wildfire, likely sparked by lightning last spring or summer and destroying thousands of hectares before finally burning itself out. Isolated tree trunks scorched by flame stood stark and black in a landscape of utter desolation. Hooves crackled and snapped on burned timber buried under the snow crust. They stopped to camp.

After eating, Zakharov examined the papers of the dead NKVD man. He flipped open the identification booklet. The photograph of a stern young man was inside along with the identification number, issue date, issuing authority, his rank and position, and so forth.

"So who was he, Comrade Lieutenant?" asked Kravchenko, rolling a cigarette.

"Junior Lieutenant of State Security Boris Stepanovich Sukhishvili, 13th Rifle Regiment, NKVD Internal Troops."

"Those were the ones massacred on the Tunguska six years ago. Far away from where we are. No survivors. What was he doing way out here?"

Zakharov turned his attention to the map case. Inside was a bundle of loose pages tied together that comprised an old file, the paper yellowed with age and stained from moisture. He untied it and began reading, starting with a hastily-scribbled note on top.

"He was trying to get back to his base," he said. "He was a courier from Vladimir Orlov, the regimental commander. When the ghouls attacked, Orlov realized he was doomed and tried to save this file by sending it off with Sukhishvili."

"What's so special about it?"

"Orlov wasn't just leading a search-and-destroy operation," said Zakharov. "According to this he was also tasked with a mission by Gleb Bokii, a senior NKVD official conducting research into paranormal phenomenon. Code-named Operation Hades, it was an investigation into the origins of the ghouls." He flicked to the next page. "In the village of Turukhansk Orlov discovered this file. It's the testimony of a White officer named Grishin, who was captured and interrogated by Red partisans in March 1920."

276

Kravchenko exhaled smoke, contemplating the glowing tip of his cigarette. "That's shortly after the first reports of ghoul attacks."

Zakharov carefully leafed through the file itself. The original testimony had been taken down in longhand and then a summary typed up. Some sections were so faded and stained they were illegible, but he was still able to read enough to piece together the essential facts.

At length he said, "Grishin was an aristocrat who belonged to the reactionary Black Hundreds before the Revolution so during the Civil War he joined the White counter-revolutionaries, serving on Admiral Kolchak's staff. In November 1919, after Omsk fell and Kolchak's White Army was forced to retreat, Grishin was dispatched on a secret mission."

The men listened in rapt attention as the wind moaned outside like a lost soul. Despite the warmth inside the tent they unconsciously shivered.

Zakharov continued, his gaze scouring the pages. "An admitted occultist, Grishin claimed his assignment had been to perform black magic rituals in the arctic to summon the ghouls, the idea being that the Whites would use them against the Bolsheviks. Kolchak had supposedly discovered evidence of the creatures' existence during the two polar expeditions he participated in before the First World War."

"Well, if that's true it sure backfired," said Kravchenko. "Ghouls can't be controlled and they slaughter everybody regardless of their politics. But if this crazy officer summoned them, why didn't he unsummon them after he realized his mistake?"

"He said he wasn't able to undo what he'd done. Even if he could, he was executed after his interrogation. Kolchak had been captured at Irkutsk a month earlier, but during his interrogation he was never asked about the ghouls, which no one suspected the Whites had anything to do with. Kolchak, of course, was executed too. And for some reason this file was never forwarded to Moscow. It was forgotten and ended up collecting dust in Turukhansk until Orlov found it."

"What about Operation Hades? There was no follow-up by Bokii?"

"He was liquidated during the purges. Paranormal investigation fell into disfavor."

Kravchenko shook his head in disgust and tossed his cigarette stub into the stove. "They shot everybody who could tell us anything."

Zakharov carefully slid the file back into the case. "Well, for sure our bosses will want to read this."

They went to sleep, but Zakharov only allowed his men a few precious hours of rest. Beyond the burned area the forest resumed, but then gradually thinned out. Soon the taiga ended entirely and gave way to barren plains of tundra, in the twilight an empty blue-white expanse stretching to the horizon. Only moss and lichen and grass grew here so nothing blocked the whining, bitter wind that whipped the team.

They encountered a man in a long parka riding a wooden sledge pulled by two reindeer, which he guided with a long pole. He was a Nenets, one of the native tribes living in the arctic. In recent years the government had tried forcing them to give up their traditional nomadic lifestyle, so the man was wary when he saw the soldiers.

Okhchen was an Evenki, another reindeer-herding people, and he rode forward in greeting. Okhchen spoke the man's language and at one point the Nenets gestured towards a distant blue ridgeline with his pole. Finally the man moved on, and Okhchen reported to Zakharov.

"He's from a clan fleeing the ghouls, Comrade Lieutenant. Says their hole is on the other side of those hills."

Zakharov nodded. "That's where the trail is headed."

Dusk came. The northern lights appeared, shimmering green ribbons writhing across the black sky casting an alien glow bright enough to read by. The ground became rugged as it sloped up to the ridge. Zakharov could not see any footprints on the bare rock, but Okhchen still discerned faint traces – dislodged stones, chipped ice, bruised moss – and they followed it up to the crest. The opposite side dropped off sharply in an escarpment, the trail plunging down a narrow draw.

They filed down the draw, the horses picking their way carefully over loose scree at the bottom. Okhchen rode ahead and then stopped. He beckoned and pointed.

Up ahead the trail finally ended at its source – an irregular hole roughly three meters in diameter, ringed by piles of frozen earth. They peered over the rim. A foul odor wafted up from below and the horses became skittish, snorting and recoiling. The soldiers dismounted, unslinging their guns and snapping back the bolts.

"Pogodin!" said Zakharov. The team's engineer stepped forward. "Time to earn your pay. Two of you go down there with him and cover him."

Pogodin slung on two satchel charges from his saddlebags and clambered down into the hole, accompanied by two privates.

"Comrade Sergeant, has anyone ever tried going all the way down one of these rat holes to find out where they go?" asked Kaminsky.

"A team did once," said Kravchenko. "They never returned."

"Okhchen believes they go all the way down to the Lower World, where evil spirits dwell. Says the ghouls spawn down there and then burrow to the surface."

Kravchenko shrugged. "Who knows? His people were living here long before white men showed up. They know this land better than we do."

•　.　•

The demolition team switched on flashlights. The beams revealed that the hole was the entrance to a crude tunnel plunging down into subterranean blackness at an angle, delving past the permafrost deep into solid bedrock. Such geologic features were not unusual in the karst topography found in Siberia, but this was clearly not a natural formation created by erosion. It was too straight, too uniform in appearance. Just exactly how the ghouls dug them out was another unsolved mystery.

Pogodin had been a geologist in civilian life. Chewing on his mustache, he carefully inspected the rough, gray limestone with an experienced eye, noting fissures in the walls, piles of rubble fallen from the ceiling, and other indications of instability. He set down his satchels and began unpacking spools of primer cord and demolition blocks of TNT.

His two escorts stood guard nearby, pensive, weapons ready. They wrinkled their noses: the air was cold and dank, heavy with pungent ghoul smell. Then they tensed.

Far down the tunnel they could hear approaching footsteps – the flat, echoing slaps of bare feet and the click and scratch of claws.

Pogodin worked quickly, hurrying to place the high explosive at critical weak points in the tunnel. No time to drill boreholes; no time to double-prime charges either. He inserted a blasting cap into each block then crimped a short length of primer cord to the cap. The ends of these lines, in turn, he began tying to a long ring-main of primer cord so all the charges could be set off simultaneously by a single fuse.

His guards shined their flashlights down the pitch-black tunnel, but whatever lurked down there was beyond the reach of the light. The footsteps became louder, nearer; hissing could be heard. Then the footsteps sped up. Others joined it. The privates glimpsed the malevolent gleam of unblinking eyes.

"Here they come!" shouted one. "Vasily, hurry up!"

"Hold them off!" said Pogodin. "I'm almost done!"

As fiendish howls echoed the soldiers threw an illumination flare down the tunnel to blind the enemy then opened fire. The hollow roar of submachine guns was deafening in the confines of the passage, bullets spraying sparks as they ricocheted off walls. Empty steel casings clattered on the floor. The howls ceased; the flare burned out. The privates stopped shooting, ears ringing and nostrils filled with the acrid reek of blue cordite smoke.

The respite was only momentary. The running footsteps resumed.

"Fire in the hole!" said Pogodin, yanking the pull-igniter at the end of the ring-main. A thirty-second fuse hissed fiercely as it started burning down.

His companions scrabbled back up the tunnel and out the hole as fast as they could. Pogodin tried to follow, then slipped and fell. The others frantically reached down and hauled him out. Up on the surface the rest of the team had already withdrawn to a safe distance. The trio scrambled towards them.

Behind them a geyser of smoke and debris erupted from the hole with a muffled boom.

• • •

Zakharov waited until the air cleared, then cautiously ventured over to the crumbling edge for a closer look. The hole had collapsed and was completely filled with rubble. He nodded with satisfaction and returned to the others.

"Good job, comrades," he said. "Hole's sealed."

He brought out his sextant. Locations of all known ghoul holes had to be recorded. As he annotated his notebook there was a distant rumble and the ground trembled beneath his feet.

Okhchen let out a cry of alarm, his normally inscrutable Asian features taut with dismay. He pointed north. Zakharov scowled and raised his binoculars. His heart sank.

"What is it?" asked Kravchenko.

Zakharov answered by passing him the binoculars.

Kravchenko looked for himself and swore vehemently in Ukrainian. A few hundred meters away a dust cloud billowed from a huge crater that suddenly yawned open. Crawling from its depths like monkeys were ghouls – scores upon scores of them, a swarm of gaunt figures in the eldritch gleam of the northern lights. He let out a gusty sigh and handed the binoculars back.

"It's a full-scale invasion," he said.

Zakharov nodded grimly. "Like six years ago. After that regiment was slaughtered the NKVD had to call in the air force to bomb the holes with poison gas."

"So that's why the ghouls only attacked a few at a time. They were bait to lure our detachment north, overextend ourselves. We're the only line of defense out here."

Zakharov realized how potentially serious this was. The German Army had overrun much of the western part of the Soviet Union, so vital industrial plants had been dismantled and evacuated to safer locations east of the Ural Mountains. Raw materials for those plants came from Siberia. A major ghoul invasion could threaten facilities vital to the war effort. Many of the forced-labor camps and exile colonies of the Gulag were located there too and a ghoul attack would hardly be liberation for the wretched prisoners.

He swung into the saddle. "Fall back!"

The team retreated towards the ridge. A great clamor of rabid howls rose. The ghouls had seen them and gave chase, their eyes glowing demonically. Zakharov knew they could sprint as fast as a horse and had greater stamina.

This was a race he could not win.

They rode up the draw and when they reached the top Zakharov signaled a halt. Grabbing Pogodin by the sleeve he said, "Ride like the devil! Warn the major!" He thrust into his hands the map case with the file, plus his logbook with the hole's longitude and latitude.

"Yes, Comrade Lieutenant!" Pogodin kicked his horse with his heels and galloped away.

Zakharov turned to Kravchenko, his blue eyes narrow slits of determination. "We have to delay them, give Pogodin a chance to get away."

Kravchenko nodded curtly. He dismounted and turned to the others. "Comrades, we make our stand here. Not one step back."

The others knew what this order meant, but obeyed without question. They did not fight for Stalin, or for Communism, not even for Mother Russia. They fought first and foremost for the same thing that all soldiers have fought for since the beginning of time. They fought for each other.

Swinging down, they hastened to take positions among a jumble of boulders at the head of the draw. They unpacked all their spare ammunition and turned the horses loose; no one could be spared to hold them. The escarpment had cliffs too sheer to scale so unless the ghouls went a dozen kilometers in either direction and circled around the far ends of the ridge, they had to come this way.

A red emergency flare was launched even though everyone knew it was futile. No help would arrive in time. A few soldiers crossed themselves, the old Orthodox custom before battle that many rank-and-file in the Red Army still performed out of habit. The last illumination flare was sent up and it floated overhead on its parachute, the ghouls hissing and gnashing their teeth in anger, trying to shield their eyes from its bright, flickering glare.

Okhchen braced his rifle on a rock and began shooting as fast as he could work its bolt-action, picking off creatures at long range, pausing only to thumb in more rounds to reload.

Soon Kaminsky's machine gun joined in, its pan magazine slowly revolving as he hammered away, spent cartridges spewing out the bottom, red lines of tracers streaking across.

The flare burned out and darkness closed in again like a pall.

"Steady, comrades!" shouted Zakharov.

The screeching tidal wave of death poured into the draw.

"Fire!"

Submachine guns lashed out. The ghouls in front stumbled and fell, but those behind did not waver. Heedless of losses the creatures kept coming, jumping over the fallen. The soldiers shot them down in droves, gagging on the rising stench as disintegrating carcasses piled up on the steep slope. They flung grenades and the explosions sent lethal splinters slicing into gray flesh. The draw became a killing zone as their inhuman foes were funneled into it.

But there seemed to be no end to the creatures: still more scrambled out of the crater, and the team could only hold the frenzied horde at bay for as long as they had ammunition. All too soon, gritting their teeth, they snapped in their last magazines. One by one they ran empty and the slobbering ghouls, shrieking with bloodlust, greedily surged forward.

Two privates blew themselves up with a grenade as the monstrosities sprang onto them, taking their foes with them.

Kravchenko dropped his empty submachine gun and plunged a combat knife into a ghoul's belly up to the handle. He viciously ripped upwards, but no entrails spilled out, just a black gush of acidic ichor. The steel blade melted and he screamed as the ichor ate through his clothing and burned his flesh.

Okhchen sent his last bullet crashing through a leering face, then gripped his rifle by the barrel and swung it like a club to crush the skull of a second enemy with the wooden stock. The next tore his head off.

Kaminsky bellowed in defiance and rose to his feet, holding his smoking DP-28 waist-high as he raked the ghouls with slugs. When it was empty he threw it aside and swept out an infantry spade. One edge of the blade was sharpened so it could also be used like an ax – or as a weapon. Wielding it like a battle ax he hacked and slashed at the ghouls like a warrior of old, laughing and cursing them in Yiddish, splattering their gore on the rocks until finally they overwhelmed and dismembered him.

The magazine of Zakharov's Tokarev service pistol held eight rounds. Seven he pumped into the nearest ghoul, bringing it down. Then, as three more lunged for him, he pressed the muzzle to his temple and pulled the trigger.

• •
•

His gnawed bones, and the gnawed bones of his comrades, could not be seen by the aircrews flying high above the ridge a week later. But they could see the crater in the tundra, and the Tupolev bombers carried full loads.

The Secret War went on.

OUTBREAK

V. E. Battaglia

ook was going to be sick.

He had always been susceptible to motion sickness. Reading in the car made his head spin, storm and wrack violently. Boats jellied his legs and turned his skin to sagging seaweed. Hell, even standing too fast could sometimes throw his head through a foggy loop. His stomach achieved acrobatic proficiency in those moments, all back flips and hand springs and harsh landings.

Now, as he sat tight in his seat with the constant whir of helicopter blades pounding above his head and harsh wind coming in at odd angles from the open hatch to his side, Rook remembered why exactly it was that he had opted out of joining the Air Force. He could barely breathe without a wave of nausea sweeping over him. He tried looking out at the city, tried to focus and found that it was a strange still-frame, a city floating on clouded air. High rises climbed endlessly, their windows blistering bright against the dread darkness of a dangerous night, lights flickering on and off and no inhabitants in sight. Fog had crept down through hollows and alleys, drifting towards street level in poisonous wisps that blanketed roads and dissolved short, squalid, razor-edged buildings into acidic vapor.

Acid. Dissolving. Melting. Decaying.

His stomach pushed up at his throat violently. He choked it back down. Bad idea to look out the window. He stared up at the ceiling with bulging, glassy eyes and started thinking through terms he had learned in training, reciting them to himself in no particular order. *Revenant: angry revenge ghost, destroy remains. Imp: small servant of witches, dragon's breath injected into the heart. EMP: electromagnetic pulse, disrupts poltergeists.* It was the only trick that helped, albeit very slightly, when he felt sick or nervous.

"Looking a little green there, Rook." Mouth's voice chirped through Rook's headset.

"First drop. Definition of green." That one was Cypher. "Looking a little sick too."

"You vomit, then you vomit *outside* my rig, Rook. I'm not cleaning that shit up." Chopper. Definitely Chopper, that one.

"Clean?" Mouth chuckled, slapped Deacon on the arm and gave him a scrunched *what the hell?* look. "Clean what, Chop? My ass has been sticking to the same cum stains since '99."

"Keep it up. I'll leave your ass out here, Mouth."

"Yeah, you promise?"

Deacon shook his head. "God help us."

"Quiet." And that one was the Boss. Sergeant Klinkhammer, but no one called him that. His name was Boss. And his word was law. When he said to be quiet, the he-lo took it down a notch. *First rule of Shadow Team: Boss is God. Second rule: Do as God commands. Third: See Two.* "Cypher. Access the south-side apartment's computers. I want schematics and a guest list with running count."

Cypher instantly went to work, pulling a laptop from her pack. Her fingers moved rapidly across the keys, the tapping silenced by heavy blades cutting the air. In seconds, she was done and had turned the screen towards everyone.

The screen scanned through a rapid-fire set of binaries and registry keys, then bisected into two windows. The top, a rotating graphic of a run-down apartment building with fire escapes running down its sides – a vertical slice of the building had been cut away like a piece of cake, showing a quick layout of the interior. The bottom window showed a running tally of guests currently registered to the apartments totaling 123.

"Alright, listen up and listen well because we're ETA 4 minutes, max. Two weeks ago, during a routine scan of New York, Intel picked up on an anomalous energy spike." Boss' voice boomed over the headset. "PK and EM readings went off the scale for three hours without explanation. Then they stopped. Further scans throughout the day returned no results.

In response, we bumped our alert status from blue to yellow and activated SAR Protocol 1. Leak was sent in the following day with instructions to maintain station for a month, investigate grounds and tenants and check in daily with Intel. Two days ago he missed his scheduled check-in time. Scans showed him still within the building and his vitals were steady. Continuous PK-EM sweeps of the building were ordered. Twelve hours later, he fell off the grid entirely. When he reappeared–" Boss looked to Cypher and she reached around the screen, tapped it. "–this signature surfaced, originating in or near his apartment."

A small, dark mass appeared in the vertical slice on the 6th floor of the building, pulsing like a beating heart and radiating angry, jagged waves of red in all directions.

"This signature has continued since his reappearance. He has still not checked in. The job is simple. Standard SR&R. We are to evaluate current SAR status while inside, but our primary objective is to rendezvous with Leak in his 6th-floor apartment and get him out of there."

Rook noticed that everyone had taken huddled positions by the he-lo doors, weapons strapped and slung. He followed suit, awkwardly bumping into Cypher, who stared at him with disgust. Had he just heard Boss say rescue was priority?

"We go in quiet. That means weapons slung, people. I don't want engagement before we find our man unless absolutely necessary."

"ETA twenty seconds, Boss," Chopper cut in. "Sorry for interrupting, Boss."

"Do not touch down on the roof, Chop. We'll drop in. Stay local and stay in the air. We don't know what's down there and we're not taking chances. This shit goes sour and we may need evac ASAP. When I call for dust off, be ready."

"Boss," Rook said tentatively. "Sir, I'm confused. Shouldn't our priority on a Search, Recon and Rescue be to assess and contain threats in accordance with Supernatural Antagonist Response protocols?"

All eyes set upon him, pinning him in place like a butterfly on display. He could feel the needles in his skin.

"That's what we were taught, Boss," he added meekly.

"Rook, what *I say* is priority in *every* mission. Period. That's what you should have been taught and you'd better learn it quick or we'll all pay the price. We are one body. I am the mind. This is not a democracy."

"We're in place, Boss," Chopper said and, with no more than a nod from Boss, the doors on both sides of the he-lo were sliding open, rappel lines thrown over the edge on either side, clamps attached then Shadow Team was gliding down the ropes towards the rooftop in perfect unison, with Rook trailing a few steps behind.

• **.** •

Rook landed on his feet with a heavy thud. The shock went straight into his knees. It stung. He unclipped from the wild rappel as it snaked through the choppy air.

"Squeeze harder next time or you'll break your leg," Cypher said as she passed him without looking up from her arm-mounted computer. "Entry that way." She pointed to a rusted doorway sticking up from the roof like a festering sore, her MP5 tight to her back.

"We have touchdown, Chop," Mouth said into his earpiece. Then, "Oh, fuck off already, just get back here when we call you," and the he-lo stuttered away in stop motion. Mouth smoothly ejected his mag, checked it and slapped it back in, pulled the charging handle of his short barrel AR-15 and a round chambered with a clean mechanical clank. "I know I'm pretty, but you might want to stop staring at me, Rook."

"Right, sorry, sir," Rook said and checked his AR in turn.

"Mouth," he corrected, and clicked his selector from safe to deadly.

"Right. Sorry."

Mouth walked away, a pistol-grip Mossberg pump shotgun on his back.

Rook tested his tactical flashlight, flicked it on then off, then slapped at his foregrip. It jiggled slightly. He pulled a knife from his belt and tightened the screw.

"On me," Boss commanded and the crew scrabbled around him, boots scraping on the rocky rooftop.

"Deacon, give us some protection."

"Boss." Deacon nodded and let his weapon fall to the side. Then he locked his hands together and they all bowed their heads in prayer.

The night was eerily silent, filled with nothing but the soft sounds of their uneven breathing and Deacon's rumbling, arcane verse. Not even the passive swishing of cars on the street could penetrate the fog that separated Shadow Team from the world. It was like the city had become nothing more than a tomb, a new age Roanoke Colony, an abandoned sprawl of hidden sarcophagi with decrepit mummies awaiting discovery within. Rook shivered at the thought. It had made him uncomfortable, this long settled silence. That and what Boss had said.

They were trained. They were strong. They were armed to the teeth. What more protection did they need?

"*In nomine Patris et Filii et Spiritus Sancti,*" Deacon said.

All eyes opened.

* . *

"Let's move." All eyes fell on Boss. He flashed a determined finger at the rusted door and the team made huddled moves towards it and stacked around the frame, first he and Mouth, then Deacon and Cypher just behind. Rook lagged a moment before stacking behind Deacon.

Boss thought it over a moment; he didn't want Rook at the back. Not a good idea.

"Rook, move up." Deacon let him pass. The kid's eyes were wide, he was breathing heavy and he looked like the mouse that saw the hawk. "You stay with Deacon. Watch his back. He'll watch yours."

"Yes, Boss."

Deacon patted Rook on the shoulder. "And you watch Boss too, Rook. We watch our front *and* our back in this crew."

Boss wasn't sure that this one would last, but he did know Rook would be fine with Deacon. He had no doubt about that.

With that settled, Boss tested the door knob. Locked.

Mouth looked to Boss; placed a hand on his Mossberg.

Boss shook his head in answer to the silent query. "Cypher, you're up."

She pulled a small drill from her vest, attached a drill bit and stripped the lock. The door popped open slightly, fragments of metal falling from the holes where tumblers once rested. She fell back in line.

Boss pushed the door softly and glanced through the opening. He shook his head and opened the door fully, waiting for his eyes to adjust. Its metal hinges squealed their complaints and the red flakes of rust and decay that had set in was soon lost in the gloom of the night.

They moved into the darkened stairwell together, Mouth and Cypher shadowing close behind him, and Deacon covering the rear. Rook was lost somewhere in between. Boss popped his flashlight on and looked over the railing. Stairs spiraled jaggedly down the corrupt walls of the building and into the fast-approaching darkness below. He could see no living thing on the stairs, but that didn't mean he believed the façade. He had been here before, a few too many times in fact. He knew the difference between still air and dead air. That kind of quiet that was *too quiet*. Too quiet because something had *made it* too quiet.

This was dead air. And the whole damned city seemed to be filled with it.

"PK-EM is strong here, but no heat signatures, Boss," Cypher said, hovering her arm over the stairwell as if reading his mind.

"You trust that?" Mouth blurted.

Boss raised a fist. Talking ceased. Then he signaled to move forward.

They spread out along the stairwell, moving down step by step, flashlights bouncing on wall and stair alike. As Boss spiraled downwards, he watched the dingy walls for any bad signs. He didn't see any recognizable writing amongst the symbol-laden scrawl – well, nothing more than the standard, illegible, black spray-paint graffiti that should be expected of a shithole New York apartment – or any signs of struggle. No blood. No scratches. No charred marks. No holes that seemed to have tunneled themselves open out of nowhere and lead on and on and on. Just the usual grit, grime and decay of a needle-supported residency.

Floor after floor, they continued down towards a growing question mark, and on every landing Boss looked to Cypher who checked her computer.

"We just went down five floors and you're telling me you haven't picked up a single signature?" Mouth whispered hoarsely.

"Not one," she said icily.

"And that doesn't strike you as fucked up?"

"Not one? Not even like a cat or something?" Rook chimed in, the kid's voice wavering.

"Nope." Cypher gripped her MP5.

Boss could see the nerves setting back in on the kid. Normal. But he needed Rook to have his head in the game, not in the clouds. That's the tough part of the job. Stopping the *what if* to focus on the *what is*.

What is kept you alert. *What if* could get you killed.

"Cut the chatter. Now. We're moving."

When they reached the 6th floor, Boss took to the doorframe and signaled to stack up once more, realizing now, for the first time, as he turned and looked back up the stairs just how dark it had become on their descent. He watched his team slowly materialize like ink blots out of the solid black that had swallowed them. All except one.

"Where is Deacon?"

Rook looked back over his shoulder. "I-I don't know, Boss."

"What do you mean *you don't know*, Rook?" Mouth growled. "Everyone watches the man to his front and back. Always."

"I'm sorry–"

"Quiet," Boss said. He listened closely. The stairwell seemed to rumble gleefully at him. The air felt heavy, different. Almost leaden. His head was buzzing, and the gentle hum behind his eyes that shook his teeth told him he was being watched. "What's that sound?"

"No signatures still, but PK-EM is off the charts, Boss." Cypher said. "Could be auditory distortion as a result of the waves."

"Could that also be blocking heat signatures?"

"It's possible. The radiation is definitely strong enough. It's unbelievable, Boss. There's only one thing strong enough to produce this."

"A Sink Hole." The words fell heavy from his mouth.

"Seriously? Oh, that's good. We got a party on our hands and *he* lost D. Fan-fucking-tastic," Mouth said with a mocking chuckle.

Rook winced, but the kid had the good sense to stay silent.

Boss placed his foot on the first step and watched closely, expecting a Rorschach test named Deacon to spill from the black, backing down the stairs with his AA12 Automatic Shotgun poised and ready.

Waiting for it.

Hoping for it.

Come on, Deek.

Nothing but the steady thrumming that bounced through the stairwell. And it sounded louder. Hungrier. No more time to wait.

Boss stepped back from the darkness and pressed himself to the wall once more. Then he signaled for them to stack on the doorway.

It was time to move.

• • •

The team slid through the door effortlessly, fanning out, flashlights flicking every which way, casting their disfigured shadows over the walls and doors like prowling hunchbacked creatures.

The hallway was long and untended, dirt and painted scribbles similar to those in the stairwell leading like breadcrumbs to a central lobby where the desiccated bodies of wilted plants draped over a stained and torn sitting area.

Rook watched as Boss flashed a light down each corridor then signaled empty. Cypher shook her head – no signatures. Then Boss pointed down a hallway and they were moving in.

A Sink Hole. Rook couldn't believe it – no, he didn't *want to* believe it. First field drop and he might have to deal with a Sink Hole. His anxiety welled up again.

It could have been anything else. Why that? Why couldn't it be something simple? Ghouls would be fine or goblins; yeah, goblins would be perfect! Doppelgangers, vampires, a poltergeist or two. Anything but a goddamned Sink Hole.

Rook stayed close behind Boss, checking his front and his back constantly. He wouldn't make that mistake again. One brief lapse may have already cost someone their life. He hoped that one time he would look back and see Deacon rushing down the hallway to catch up. It didn't happen.

Cypher was behind him, Mouth following her. As they moved down the hall, the sound from the stairwell swelled in volume, pumping its thick tones through the halls into the very heart of the building. Only now it had changed. This was no longer the inarticulate clearing of a throat but a deep growl that streaked discordant high-pitched squeals throughout its roaring bass. The screeching was fast and long, then short and slow and all the while it was pained, bleeding agony in the air that shot through Rook in electrified spears and brought them straight to room 613 – Leak's room.

The door was covered in scratch marks, embedded with fingernails and painted with streaks of blood. Black muck oozed from the door frame with every agonized pulse that emanated from within.

"Ectoplasm," Cypher said. "Someone is angry."

Boss signaled and they formed an arc around the door, all arms shouldered and ready. Boss tried the knob. Locked. Mouth stepped forward, pulled his Mossberg 590 and waited for the signal.

Rook dug his weapon into his shoulder, heart racing as he started rifling through his training.

Ghouls: flesh eating hell beast. Cut out the heart.

Cypher sat machine still.

Poltergeist: nasty ghost-human attachment. Exorcism.

Boss was trained on the door, his eyes locked and ready.

Revenant: already went over that one. Shit.

Mouth aimed at the lock.

Sink Hole–

Mouth fired.

• • •

The lock splintered into shrapnel and Boss booted the door, leading the charge into the dark room. He wanted this procedure to go by the numbers, even envisioned it all. He kicks in the door, the team files in behind, splits off into the adjacent rooms in a flurry of feet and reflex, all uneven gallops and sudden squeaking stops as corners were checked and rooms called "clear" until they found whatever had taken Leak – whatever ghost or goblin or ghoul – and they would blast it straight back to whatever hellhole it had clawed its way out of and Leak would be fine and they would pull out. That was the plan. It was a good plan. Solid. Perfect.

Except they had already lost Deacon. And there were 123 residents unaccounted for in this apartment complex. And there seemed to be a Sink Hole somewhere nearby, which meant *someone* had to open it. And that someone would be dangerous, yes, but not nearly as dangerous as the Sink Hole.

So, as the splinters floated in mid-air and he shined his light into the apartment, Boss was in no way surprised to find that his plan had gone all to hell.

The living room was a crimson massacre delivered in flashes of white light. Blood soaked the walls in angry splashes beside deep, hateful scratches that were adorned with hunks of fatty flesh. Chunks of bone and sinew were strewn about the hallway like a child's toys. The kitchen sink was filled with red and bubbled with putrid black sewage. The room smelled of shit and vomit and putrefaction.

Someone gagged behind him. Boss knew that was Rook.

"What the fuck?" Mouth stepped forward, accidentally crushed a bone and hopped back. "Shit. Sorry, guy."

"Boss." *Cypher.* And for the first time since he had known her, she sounded nervous.

"We're finding Leak then Deacon and we're out of here." Boss shouldered his weapon. "No one goes off alone. In ninety seconds, we're out the door either way." He pointed to the lone hallway in the apartment. "Move."

• • •

Rook couldn't think of a single term to calm his nerves. There was no definition or explanation or measure of focus that could possibly push the images that were flashing in front of him from his mind. From the moment the door flew open and they had crossed the threshold, he knew these moments would be forever imprinted on the forefront of his memory.

He was living a nightmare and he knew it. There was no way to escape, not until they had seen their mission through. And that's exactly what he wanted to do. See this through, get the hell out of here and never look back.

Rook fell in line behind Boss, his head now on a permanent swivel. He could feel uneven sprinkles of fluid dripping on him as he stepped carefully through the ruined apartment. He didn't need to flash his light to the ceiling to know that stalactites of wet flesh were dangling above him, didn't even want to, but the sight of this apartment served not only as a shock but as a warning. Something could be hiding up there in the darkness. So, he flashed the light upwards and discovered how bad it truly was.

They reached the first door. Boss kicked it in.

There were bodies – more accurately, *pieces* of bodies – in every possible position. Some were twisted and contorted in spider-like mockery of the human form. Others were dangling from chains that sunk deep into their skin, stretched out and posed like bleeding, disfigured marionettes, strung up and splayed out with parts from other broken bodies shoved into their abused and ruined orifices. Rook glanced in only briefly; just long enough to be sure it was safe.

"One hell of an orgy," Mouth said, moving past the door. "Are we sure Leak is alive?"

"Yes," Cypher said. "And that's more troubling to me than if he were dead."

Boss threw a grave look over his shoulder, and Rook didn't need to ask why. A Sink Hole didn't just open. Someone had to open it. And if that was the case, and all of these dead *weren't* Leak... Well, it didn't take a rocket scientist to put two and two together.

The next door led to the bathroom. That one, Boss didn't have to kick in – it was held ajar by another shredded corpse.

Then they had reached it, the last door on the left. The spectral sounds coming from behind it blasted straight through Rook's chest.

All weapons were raised, trained on the door and, for the first time, Rook felt like he was part of the team.

He wished desperately that he wasn't.

Boss kicked the door in...

•   •   •

Inside, a squat shirtless man with a sharp Neanderthal face hovered over a gaping hole in the floor, circling it erratically with a wild-eyed smile. His gnarled hands were bunched like claws, and he was entirely oblivious to the fact that anyone else was there. Boss signaled for the others to hold position and stepped into the doorway. The hole seemed to be growing out of the floor, pulsing its impossible flesh with a respiratory rhythm, blowing putrid air and tortured sounds at him with every powerful contraction.

It was a fresh, fully formed Sink Hole.

"Leak," Boss said, taking one step over the threshold of the room.

The man stopped suddenly with his back to him, as if hearing a human voice for the first time. His body twitched and jerked rapidly, and he turned. Eyes blackened like burnt out coals, mouth dripping salivary red, he snarled then let out a horrid screech that shook the room.

This was Leak, or what was left of him. What he had become. A Reaver. A man possessed by demon sickness. And there was only one way to deal with him.

Boss put a bullet into the man's brain, the hollow-point round blowing the back of Leak's head onto the wall in a crimson fireworks display and sending his body tumbling down the moaning hole.

The room stilled, silent but for the sounds of the living hellhole before him. Boss noticed the walls were covered, once more, in scribbles and scrawls – ones that matched those in the hall and the stairwell. He had a sinking feeling that he had made a mistake and overlooked something.

"Boss," Cypher said and he immediately recognized the apprehension in her voice. "I've got signatures. A lot of them. And they're coming right for us."

Boss approached the hole, shined a light down and what he saw shook him, knocked the words from his tongue.

Reavers.

There must have been a hundred of them.

And they were scrambling up the walls of the Sink Hole.

•   •
•

A shrieking blast of anger shot out from the Sink Hole, shaking the building to its very foundation. The force was so strong that

Rook lost his balance and fell on his ass, then sat there mouth agape. Frozen. Terrified.

Mouth had braced himself against a wall. "What the fuck was that?"

The writing on the walls glowed fiery red and Boss fired his rifle down the hole, backing out of the room and screaming, "Fall back! We've got Reavers incoming. Fall back to the rooftop and shoot anything that moves!"

"Guess we know where all the people went," Mouth said, grabbing Rook and hauling him back.

Rook caught a glimpse of a corrupted claw reaching over the hole as he was helped to his feet then the door slammed shut.

Boss led the charge back through the human wasteland. Rook's eyes were locked onto the man's back, no longer checking around carefully. He had seen enough. He just wanted out, wanted to go home. He needed to leave and fast.

Lights bounced in every direction. The walls cracked and shook as they raced through the apartment, all too aware of the savage screams of hell beasts beating at the door behind them. When they reached the hall, they heard the wood splinter.

Rook was halfway down the hall when he finally turned around and the first of the Reavers showed themselves, rushing out of room 613, their skin scarred, meat peeling off their bones in slabs. They were rabid, ravenous, and coming fast.

Mouth stopped, dropped to a knee and let loose with his AR-15, sending a burst of 5.56 mm ammunition into the first black-eyed psycho that came his way. Then the second. Then the third.

"Mouth, Chopper," Boss called out, firing at his own set of takers as they ran from the doorway in stuttered bursts.

Cypher ran up, slapped Mouth's shoulder and started firing, her MP5 rattling off rounds savagely.

Mouth fell back from the gunfire. "Chop. We need evac ASAP, we're knee deep in shit creek here."

All the while, Rook hadn't fired a single round. He stood back, watching this unfold through the buzzing static that had invaded his vision, his muscles, his brain. From the moment the shooting had started, he felt like he was watching a movie in slow motion. And as the bloodlust-frenzied creatures closed in on them, part of him had expected to be suddenly sitting on his couch at home, waking up from some immersive dream state.

Fast running people, *former* people, rushing straight at him. Straight at his screen. Claws, teeth, bone showing. Bad horror movie. Bad movie. That's all it was.

And then one screamed, shrieked right through him and he knew it was no dream. It was coming straight for him. He shouldered his AR and squeezed off a round into its shoulder. It ran through as if nothing had happened. Rook squeezed off another and another as he fell back, and before he knew it they were in the central lobby and bodies had hit the floor. How many he didn't know. He felt no relief, no sense of calm, but for once, he didn't need to think. He only needed to act.

That was when he noticed it.

"Boss," he screamed against the rattle of gunfire. "The walls!"

Boss turned; a frown there and gone. "Shit. Move, people, move!"

The graffiti-covered walls glowed a searing red and cracks had begun to run out from the sprawling text forming small charred, fleshy, pulsing circles. More Sink Holes. All around them.

And now the enemies were pouring in. Not only Reavers but other monstrosities. Ghouls, Ghasts, Arachmonae. They were clawing their way out from the Depths, skittering out of their holes like so many swarming insects – some taking to the floor, others to the walls – and they had the team trapped in the central lobby, so close to the stairwell, to escape.

"Hold them back," Boss commanded, swapping a mag.

"We don't have the munitions to keep this up!" Cypher pulled her Colt M1911 and squeezed off a few shots into a leaping Arachmonae's parasitic underbelly. It fell at her feet, its many legs chittering wildly, only to have a few more rounds pumped into its elongated humanoid skull.

Mouth was stalking down a group of rushing Reavers, lighting them up with his remaining bursts of 5.56 ammo. One of them broke through his fire and took a swipe at his leg before it bought it. Mouth clutched at the leg, yelling something unintelligible as he retreated, letting rounds go one-handed.

Rook's heart pounded. *Bang. Bang. Bang.* Louder than the sound of the gunfire around him. *Bang. Bang. Bang.* He turned his fire to the spot Mouth had vacated while the man stuffed his leg with a Quick Clot pad and tied off the wound. *Bang. Bang. Bang.*

It wasn't until he heard the screaming that he realized the sound he was hearing was not his heart at all. It was the sound of an AA12 automatic tearing down the hallway, clearing the way for their escape.

"Move it!" Deacon called, blasting a hole into a decrepit Ghoul's chest.

Rook felt a moment of relief at seeing the man, a brief moment of reprieve. He had thought his earlier lapse had gotten Deacon killed. It was freeing to know he wouldn't have to live with that guilt. Even more freeing to know they now had a chance, a chance to escape, a chance to make it back home. Things had been looking bleak, but now, what if . . . What if they could really make it?

He almost wanted to smile.

In that moment of relief, Rook had been distracted for a moment too long, had seen Deacon's face change, twist and contort a moment too late, had heard the man call a warning but couldn't make out the words in time.

If he had, Rook would have known a Reaver had ripped through a Sink Hole beside him. He would have stopped it from digging its claws into his soft abdomen. And he wouldn't have been dragged screaming down into the Depths.

• • •

"Rook, watch out!" Boss called, spun and aimed true. Right at the head. *Click.* Dry. And he knew then that it was over. Rook had been torn into before Boss's spent mag could even hit the floor. Nothing more could be done but to save his team.

"Cypher, Mouth, we are leaving now!" He ran up and hoisted Mouth's arm over a shoulder, pulling his Beretta 92FS.

They galloped down the hallway together to the beat of Deacon's AA12 pounding away, broke into the stairwell and shut the metal door. They bolted it shut just in time for the beasts on the other side to slam into it. It would hold for a short while.

"We should move fast. More of those things are going to open up in here, Boss, and we got no room to fight," Deacon said. Blood and sweat oozed down his arms.

The walls were glowing all the way up the stairwell. The team rushed upwards while the hell spawn slammed the door below.

"Where the hell were you, Deacon?" Boss demanded.

"Reaver clocked me a few floors up, Boss. Got lucky. He wanted to use me to open a Hole. I woke up before he could do it. I came as soon as I could. No bites. Don't worry."

The downstairs door slammed open sending a shockwave through the stairwell. Boss knew they had maybe a minute before the Reavers caught up. Maybe less if the Arachmonae pushed through first and took to the walls. He turned and started to hoist Mouth up the steps. "We need to move fast."

"No, Boss," Mouth said and pushed himself from Boss's shoulder. He leveled his Mossberg pump. "You guys move fast. I'll hold them."

Boss waited a moment. "Deek. Trade."

Deacon handed over his AA12 and took the Mossberg. "Do God's work, my friend."

"God? You know that's not my style." Mouth pulled open his tactical vest. Boss could see a single grenade dangling within. "I've got a one-way ticket and I'm taking them straight to hell with me. Get out of here."

"Move," Boss ordered and they took flight up the steps.

Three floors up, they heard the pounding start and all the while, Boss watched the walls glow, hoping they wouldn't open up another hole ahead of them.

When they reached the top, the pounding stopped.

Then a powerful blast rocked the building.

• • •

Boss, Deacon and Cypher burst out onto the rooftop. Boss turned on his heel, slammed the door then wedged his empty AR against the handle. Chopper had already touched down. Three bodies lay face down between the roof entrance and the chopper.

The Reavers crashed into the door as Boss loaded into the he-lo.

They took off in time to see the door give way, Reavers and hell spawn filling the rooftop almost instantly. And through the sickly fog that encased the surrounding city, a familiar red glow spilled out, breaking free.

Boss strapped into his seat and pulled on his headset. Deacon and Cypher were already settled. Cypher sat with her computer in her lap. She looked a little shaken, but okay. Deacon had his hands clasped together in prayer. Blood dripped from between his fingers.

"Cypher, we need to organize a strike team ASAP," Boss said, thinking of Rook and Mouth – he wouldn't let them die for nothing.

"Already on it, Boss. I'm reporting in now to HQ and requesting Emergency Response Forces."

Boss nodded; he had no more to say.

"What the hell happened down there, Boss?" Chopper's voice blared strangely over the radio. "We got reports of PK-EM readings popping up all over the city."

"Leak betrayed us, Chop. He opened a Sink Hole down there. A whole network of them."

"Shit. That would explain the Reavers on the roof. Came out of nowhere, Boss. Four of them. Took care of it though."

Boss frowned. "Did you say four? I only saw three bodies, Chop."

Chopper took a moment, spoke slowly, methodically. "Yeah.

One got up close and personal. Took a bite out of me. I kicked him off the roof."

Cypher's head shot up. Deacon stopped his prayer. Boss struggled to unstrap himself as the helicopter lurched forward without warning, slamming him back into his seat. Cypher's computer flew past his head like a missile as the he-lo's emergency alarms blared.

The chopper had lost stability. They were going down.

Boss tried once more to free himself, fighting the erratic movements of the helo. And as he fumbled desperately with his straps, the cabin door flew open with a savage scream.

Droch-Fhola

Brad C. Hodson

The bars of the cage rattled and knocked together as the cart rolled deeper into the forest. The construction was shoddy, hastily thrown together to carry slaves across the isle. He contemplated kicking it until the wooden bars shook loose, but that would make too much noise.

The two legionaries with him were still unconscious, each covered in crusted blood and swollen bruises. He was surprised they were even alive. This was his fault, no way to deny that.

Flurries of snow whipped through the cage and he hugged his knees to his chest, shivering against the cold and willing himself to stay awake. His fingers and the soles of his feet had already lost feeling. The bastards could have at least left them with their clothes. It would be difficult to sell slaves missing limbs from frostbite.

Shadows stretched over the forest as the sun died. They played tricks on his eyes and for a brief moment he thought he saw men crawling between the trees on their bellies.

One of the barbarians said something in their garbled tongue and the cart creaked to a halt. He maneuvered over the legionaries and pressed against the bars as they set up camp, hoping he would see some way out of his predicament. A fire soon raged, the smoke thick and sweet, and the men gathered around it. A wineskin was passed about as they erected some kind of wooden cabinet off to the side. He didn't know what he had hoped to see, but whatever it was never appeared.

When they had finished piecing together the slabs of wood, one of the men went to another of their carts and removed a black stone. It was thin but large enough that he had to hug it to his chest to carry it. He placed it atop the cabinet and it shimmered in the firelight.

Three of them came to remove him, the others standing nearby with swords drawn in case he ran.

"Come, boy," a one-eyed old man said, his Latin accented but clear.

They grabbed him with rough hands and jerked him from the cart. He fell face first into the snow and they laughed. The urge to sprint into the woods was strong but he fought against it, knowing that if they didn't kill him the cold would.

One of the larger ones pulled him to his feet. This close, they smelled musty and sour. His stomach churned. The legionaries were carried from the cart next and he was brought with them over to the fire. Standing in front of the cabinet, he could see it clearly. Strange circular braids were carved into the wood. The doors were open and a wooden statue sat beneath the stone slab. It was of a skeletal figure with long arms crossed over its chest. The head was upturned and a wide, mangled mouth open. Dark stains covered the statue, and he finally understood they were not going to be sold.

He turned to dart from the campsite, but the one-eyed man kicked him hard in the stomach and he collapsed, tears in his eyes and the knowledge he'd piss blood tonight evident in each piercing breath.

If I live that long.

He couldn't fight the tears that burned his eyes. The barbarians laughed at him as he curled on the frozen ground, his cheek already numb against the snow. What would his father have thought if he saw him like this? Silanus hadn't even known a woman yet, and here he was crying in the face of death. He imagined the decorated Centurion would have spat on him and told him to stand up, that it would be better to die fighting like he had done. But Silanus was no soldier, merely a thirteen–year-old boy playing at being a man.

"I'm just a cook," he said through the tears. "Please."

His plea was translated and the barbarians laughed all the harder.

One of the legionaries was dragged to the cabinet and smacked in the face. The man groaned, coming to just as he was slammed chest-first onto the stone. Fighting to stand, he was too weak and easily held down.

Looking up, the legionary's eyes were wide with fear. They focused on Silanus and then the cutting began. The man screamed as the knives peeled the flesh from his back in long strips, blood dripping from the slab and into the statue's hungry maw.

One of the Ordovices, large and bearded, stepped up. Draped in furs, he looked more bear than man. In one hand he held a chisel. He placed it against the legionary's back then swung a hammer. The hollow crack of the man's ribs breaking away from his spine echoed through the woods.

Silanus could no longer watch. He stared at the ground, the smoke stinging his eyes and throat. The man's screams did not last much longer.

This is the end. I never even got to see Rome.

A whistling sound cut through the air. Silanus looked up in time to see a pila slam into the hammer-wielder's chest. The man staggered back, eyes wide, and crashed to the ground.

The other barbarians whirled and pulled their swords as more pilum struck their targets. Three more of them went down, two dead and one wheezing bloody foam onto his lips. A fourth had managed to raise a shield and catch the spear that came for him. The soft metal head bent from the weight of the shaft, just as it was designed to, and pulled the man's shield down. He stomped on the pila but it held. Dark shapes erupted from the trees but his shield had been made useless.

Roman soldiers rushed in. Silanus almost cheered as they cut down his captors. The Ordovices were fierce and met their enemy head on, swinging their long swords and crashing against the Romans with abandon. They were met by sturdy shields when the legionaries crowded them, rendering their long swords useless as sharp gladii stabbed with almost mechanical precision.

Silanus scrambled over to a cart and away from the fight, searching for something he could defend himself with. He found another hammer but tossed it aside when he saw the hilt of a Roman short sword. Knowing it likely belonged to the soldier he'd seen sacrificed, he clutched it tight and crouched behind the cart.

The Romans made quick and vicious work of the Ordovices, blood steaming as it spattered the snow. Silanus could not place what legion the men were with; he'd never seen soldiers dressed in indigo and charcoal armor before, but he didn't care. He would live because of them.

Bodies littered the small clearing, twitching and moaning. There had been over twenty barbarians when they had stopped here; now only the one-eyed old man and two of the younger ones lived. Scanning the Roman soldiers, Silanus was surprised to count eight of them. It had seemed a full legion descended upon the clearing. How could a single a contubernium take out so many? He hoped there weren't other bands of Ordovices nearby.

The three survivors dropped their swords and fell to their knees, hands behind their heads, and begged in their tongue for what could only be mercy.

One of the Romans stepped forward, wiping his gladius clean on his thigh before sheathing it. His hair was gray and a scar ran from the corner of his mouth to his ear. He must have been the unit's Decanus.

"I can only assume you're begging for your lives," he said. "Where is the Droch-fhola?"

Silanus didn't understand what the soldier had said. *Droch-fhola?*

One of the barbarians spat on the ground and the other two glared.

The Decanus sighed. "Then you're useless to me." He turned to his men. "Open them."

The soldiers stepped forward.

"Wait," Silanus said and stood. They turned as he walked toward them, his voice trembling as much as his freezing muscles. "That one speaks Latin."

The old man turned his one good eye to the boy. "You bastard."

The Decanus pulled a thick cloak from one of the fallen barbarians. The dying man weakly clutched at the cloth, and the Roman brought his boot down onto the man's face as he jerked the cloak away and tossed it to Silanus.

The commander nodded to his men and they went to work stabbing the bodies on the ground to make certain they had all been killed in the fighting. Most had.

Kneeling, the Decanus asked his question again. "Where is the Droch-fhola?"

"Killing more Romans," the old man said, "if there is any justice in the world."

Nodding as if he'd expected that answer, he grabbed the barbarian to the old man's right and pressed a thumb into his eye. The barbarian squirmed and fought, but the Roman's grip was iron and blood soon ran down the man's face.

The other barbarian scampered to his feet and ran. He made to shove one of the soldiers out of his way but the soldier pivoted and brought the edge of his shield down onto the man's knee. There was a loud snap and the barbarian fell to the ground squealing. Looking to his commander, the soldier received whatever confirmation he needed and brought the edge of his shield down again, this time on the barbarian's throat. The squealing stopped.

"Please," the old man said. The color had left his face. "I'm sorry. Please."

The Decanus released the man, who fell to his side and held his face as he sucked sharp, trembling breaths.

"Have you seen the Droch-fhola?"

"Promise you will show us mercy."

"As you have shown your prisoners?" He motioned to the legionary on the slab, his body limp and eyes empty.

The old man shook his head. "That was an offering. It's not the same."

"I'm not here to debate the merits of cruelty. You will die – you and your friend. Tell me what I want to know and it will be quick. Refuse and I'll cut your tongues from your mouths and remove your feet and leave you here for the wolves."

"All right," the old man said, his voice weak. "I'll tell you, then. It is in these very woods."

"We know. Have you seen it?"

He nodded. "We spotted it last night. Only the sacrifices would have kept us safe."

"And how does one kill the thing?"

The old man's mouth twisted. "Kill it? How does one kill the wind?"

"I am not hunting the wind."

Scratching the scar tissue where his left eye had once been, the old man said, "You Romans. There is no creature or spirit that you don't think should roll over and bleed for you. I'll tell you this thing, and it isn't much, but is all I know. When I was a child and the Droch-fhola killed our sheep, my grandfather built a hut of yew and we slept there for seven days and seven nights."

"That is all you know?"

"That is all."

"Thank you." The gladius flicked his wrist and opened the old man's throat.

That one eye went wide and the barbarian fell forward, gurgling and sputtering until his twitching ceased. Another soldier did the same for the remaining barbarian.

The Decanus turned to Silanus. "What's your name, boy?"

"Decimus Junius Silanus, sir."

His brow furrowed. "The Younger?"

"Yes, sir."

"Your father was a Centurion?"

That took Silanus off guard. "You knew my father?"

He waved the question away. "That was a long time ago. I suggest you find some clothes and shoes." He walked over to the remaining captive, the legionary that had not been sacrificed, and placed his fingers to the man's throat. "Who were these men?"

Silanus hurried to him. "Soldiers from the Second Legion."
"Augusta?"

He nodded. "I'm a cook in the legion, apprenticing to be a soldier." He swallowed and thought quickly. "We were on leave, the three of us," he lied. "In a village east of here. The Ordovices crept in at night and the villagers betrayed us."

"If they were soldiers then we shall give them a proper funeral." He stood. "Gather wood for the pyre."

Silanus saluted. "Yes, sir."

"But find your clothes and shoes first. Your feet may be frost-bitten by now."

He did so, finding his things in the same cart that had held the gladius. He also found the soldier's belt and sheath, wearing the weapon on his hip as he went to work gathering wood. The clothing and thick cloak helped warm him some but the cold had wormed its way deep into his bones and he couldn't shake it.

The legionaries' bodies were burned and prayers given. The soldiers searched the wagons for anything of value but there wasn't much, barely two saddlebag's worth, most of it taken from the soldiers they'd murdered. Silanus had not known either of the soldiers but still felt a twinge of sadness at the idea they'd been reduced to loot. Scanning the dark wood, he did not relish the trek ahead of him. The Second Augusta was scheduled to march east tomorrow at sunrise. It would be impossible for him to catch up with them, even had he wanted. Better to put as much distance between them and himself. And what if he were to come across other bands of Ordovices? His stomach twisted at the thought.

"Let's be off, then," the Decanus said.

Silanus approached him. "May I travel with you, sir?"

Cold eyes bored into him and he couldn't tell if the man was going to agree or cut him down where he stood. Freezing, starving, his abdomen still throbbing from the kick he took, Silanus refused to look away.

"With that thing out there," one of the other soldiers said, "the boy won't last the night."

Silanus didn't know to what they referred but didn't care. There were a thousand ways for him to die in this forest. What was one more?

"Keep pace with us," the Decanus finally said. "If you fall behind, we will not wait for you to catch up."

"Thank you, sir."

"At the next village, you're on your own." He turned to his men. "Move out!"

As one, they rushed into the forest, Silanus trailing behind.

• . •

They made camp an hour later inside a small cave on a hill side where two soldiers pulled brush in front of the entrance. The Ordovices had a hunk of cured boar in one of their carts and the men sliced ribbons from it and ate around the fire. They seemed uncomfortable with Silanus there and did not speak much.

The Decanus handed him a slice of meat. "Here. Eat."

He took it and ripped a massive bite away. It was salty and tough as leather but he was glad for it. When he had finished, he asked what legion they were with. The men looked to one another. One of them grunted.

"The Hundredth," their commander said.

Silanus laughed. "There's no Hundredth Legion."

"There is." The older man handed him another ribbon of meat. "You won't find it listed on the Senate rolls. But it exists."

He couldn't tell if the commander was playing him for a fool or not. He looked to the other men but they simply watched the exchange, no smiles or laughter among them.

"What's the legion called, then?"

"Ex Nihilo," the commander finally said.

"Now I know you're having me on, sir. Why would anyone name a legion 'The Nothing'?"

The Decanus stared at him and drummed his fingers on the owl emblem adorning his breastplate. "Do you know why you were to be sacrificed tonight?"

He nodded and swallowed another chunk of pork. "To appease their barbarian gods."

"No. To appease the Droch-fhola."

That word again. "I don't know what that is, sir."

Reaching into a pouch, the commander removed a small trinket. He tossed it to Silanus. It was smooth and a dingy white.

"Nine days ago, Senator Paulinus and his entire caravan were found butchered in the forest near the River Medway. Their backs had been opened and their lungs removed. The attacker had not left so much as a footprint in the snow."

Examining the trinket, Silanus was certain it was made from bone. It was of the same figure the Ordovices had placed in their sacrificial cabinet. Long, spindly arms were folded over the chest and a jagged mouth turned upward.

"The attack matches one that occurred a month ago at a trading outpost. A dozen Romans were killed. A slave, an Ordovices woman everyone called 'Mama', was the only survivor. They found her in the stables. She had cut open a lamb there and painted sigils on herself with its blood. The governor's men thought she had conspired with the attackers but, when tortured, she said it had been the Droch-fhola. She'd gone mad and kept raving about how the thing would kill us all and so they put her out of her misery.

"Upon consulting the records, we discovered that Romans had been killed in the same manner since Julius Caesar first landed here. The Ordovices and the Cornovii claim it has been stalking them every winter for centuries."

Silanus looked at the men around the cave, hoping one would be laughing. None were. "You believe this thing is real and you're what? *Hunting* it?" he asked.

"That's what the Hundredth does, lad," one of the other men said.

"We do the dirty work no one else is suited for," the man beside him added.

The commander pointed to the trinket in Silanus's hand. "To the average Roman, these things are superstitious myths and barbarian legend. But we've seen what the night spirits can do." He tapped the scar on his face. "Seen them up close and personal. This thing is responsible for the deaths of nearly two hundred Roman citizens over the years and Orcus alone knows how many Britons. We're here to put an end to it."

Outside the cave, the cold wind howled.

• • •

The snow fell in heavy flurries from a sky the color of dead flesh. The morning had done little to brighten the forest and even less to dispel the cold. The soldiers kept a steady pace despite the biting wind, following some trail that only Crito seemed to recognize.

He had learned little of the men aside from their names. Crito, a short but stout Gaul with red hair and a nasally voice, had some kind of gift for tracking beasts like the Droch-fhola, and Decanus Marcellus had set him to the task at first light. Antonius, the tall African and only soldier who wore a beard, served as Marcellus's second. He'd made Silanus into a kind of pack mule for the group. Weighed down with provisions, he struggled to keep pace with the unit. At least the sweat he worked up warmed him some.

There were horses, Antonius had explained, but the poor beasts refused to travel anywhere the Droch-fhola had been so they'd stabled them at a village several miles back. His breath quick and legs heavy, Silanus wished desperately they had the animals now.

Crito raised his hand and the unit stopped. The wood was silent aside from the roaring wind and they stood motionless, Silanus holding a hand over his mouth to muffle his breathing. He would have been thankful for the break but his sweat-soaked tunic quickly turned freezing. The scout eventually moved again and the unit followed.

They continued like this for most of the day, hurrying along until Crito raised his hand. They took a break around mid-day and Silanus fell asleep with his head on a saddlebag. Crispus, a handsome Roman who laughed like a horse when something struck him funny, woke Silanus by kicking him in the shin.

"Let's get going," Crito said. "The thing covered a lot of ground last night."

Silanus threw the bags onto his shoulders. "How is he tracking it in this weather?"

"By its decay," Crispus said.

"What?"

"I'm not entirely sure myself, but the way I understand it, these things corrupt what they touch in small ways," Crispus said. "Rotted twigs, blackened pine needles, that sort of thing. Crito knows what to look for. He's also able to smell the thing, who knows how. Says it smells like rot."

Silanus took a deep breath but could smell nothing.

Crispus shoved a saddlebag into Silanus's chest. "Now, get a move on."

They continued on, following Crito until Silanus thought he would pass out from exhaustion.

As the sun set, they came across a farm. It was little more than a small house, a shed, and a fence. The structures cast long shadows onto snow red from the dying light.

The soldiers drew their weapons. Marcellus made a motion with his hand and the unit crouched low, fanning out around the fence. Crispus motioned Silanus toward a barren tree, its trunk stout and limbs reaching low like thieving hands. He hurried behind it and crouched, watching as the men approached the farm.

A man was slumped over the fence, blood frozen on his face and hanging in gruesome icicles from the wooden slats. Antonius made his way to the corpse. He took one look at its back and nodded to the rest of the men. One by one they hopped the fence, as silent as the night creeping in, and made their way toward the farmhouse. Silanus lost sight of them.

The falling night was still, the only sounds the wind and his heart hammering in his chest. He waited, sweat trickling down his spine despite the cold, and hoped they would hurry.

A twig snapped off to his right.

He turned, hoping to see Crispus coming to fetch him, but saw only snow and barren trees. Something waited in those trees. He wasn't certain how he knew but he did. It waited, watching him with sinister hunger, and he thought he should run. But he couldn't.

Wind shook the thin, gray limbs of the trees and then he saw it. It was tall but hunched over, head cocked to one side, stick-like arms brushing the ground. It seemed brittle from here, hidden perfectly among dead trees that looked so much like itself, and he again knew he should run.

It stepped from his view and he was again afraid to move.

Maybe it didn't see me. He pressed against the tree and closed his eyes and prayed it would pass him by.

A sickly sweet smell hit him, faint but unmistakable. It was the smell of carrion left to rot.

Snow crunched a few feet from him and this time he did run, turning so quickly he tripped on a low lying branch, tumbling over it. His face smashed into another limb, stars exploding behind his eyes, and he rolled onto his side, the strap of a saddlebag catching on a bulbous knot. Panic flooding through him, he fought to a crouch and almost cried when he realized he was in a gnarled tangle of limbs and dry brush. Something hot ran down his face, stinging his eye, and he wiped it away, certain it was blood.

The thing paced around him, its quick changes of direction suggesting irritation.

Why aren't I dead already?

Ducking its head low, Silanus caught sight of its face and cried out. Its sockets were empty – gaping holes as dark as graves. The skin was black and leathery, the mouth a jagged maw of blood-stained stones. It pulled away and scrambled to the other side of the tree on all fours.

A hand shot between two branches, long talons scraping through the snow-dusted earth as it reached for his foot. He kicked the hand and it jerked up just enough to scratch its thin forearm on a twig.

The scream that erupted was loud enough to send pain radiating through Silanus's head. He covered his ears until the shrieking faded into the forest.

Another hand grabbed at him and he kicked it furiously.

"Boy," Antonius said. "It's us."

He scrambled from the tangle, shoving the saddlebags off rather than fight with the straps, and fell to the snow. The Roman soldiers surrounded him, swords drawn, staring off into the night.

Marcellus took a knee and asked him what happened. He related his ordeal, ashamed at how the panic made his voice sound as high-pitched as a child's. When he'd finished, the Decanus stared at the tree for a long while.

"I think you've found what we've been looking for," Marcellus said as he stood.

"I saw an axe in the shed." Crispus took off across the farm.

"I don't understand," Silanus said.

The Decanus grabbed a branch and shook it. Snow fell from it in clumps. "What tree is this?"

Standing, Silanus wracked his brain to identify it. When he did he couldn't help but laugh. "Yew."

* . *

Marcellus woke him at dawn. Silanus followed to the shed where they had stored the bodies. The children had been the worst and he had emptied his stomach when they were carried from the house.

"Our time for watch, sir?"

"Lepidus and Gaius still have half an hour or so," the Decanus said.

They had used the blankets in the house to cover the family. The four bodies were pressed together on the floor, their shapes visible under the cloth. The little girl's hand had slipped from beneath and lay pale against the dark earthen floor.

"What will we do with them?"

"Burn them," the commander said. "But not yet." He scratched his chin and the white stubble that had grown there. "I'm going to ask you something and I want the truth from you. Can you do that for me?"

"Yes, sir."

"Good." He glanced at the bodies and then back to Silanus. "The legionaries that were with you. They weren't on leave, were they?"

His throat went dry; he tried to swallow, but it was difficult. "They were."

Marcellus's gaze was intense.

Silanus looked away. "No. No, they weren't."

"Why were they in that village?"

"To retrieve me."

"You're a deserter?"

He nodded and thought he was going to be sick. "When my father died, he left me to the legion. Wanted me to be a soldier like him. My mother had died in childbirth and we had no other family. The cook they placed me with, he… Well, he tried to do things with me. And so I ran. Those soldiers had been sent to drag me back. And now they're dead because of me."

"Yes. They are." Marcellus leaned against the wall and crossed his arms over his chest.

"What will you do with me, sir?"

"The punishment for desertion is crucifixion."

Silanus lowered his head and nodded. After everything he had been through, it seemed wrong he would die this way. His knees trembled and he thought he might fall, but he didn't. That was something, he supposed.

"I said I knew your father," Marcellus said. "What I didn't tell you was that we served together in Spain. He saved my life a dozen times over and I saved his nearly as many."

Silanus looked up, hope suddenly within his reach.

"When we have killed this thing, you will take a day's worth of rations and go into the wilderness. You may live out your life there. You may even marry some barbarian girl and have

317

children. But if you ever set foot in a Roman settlement again, you will be crucified. Is that understood?"

Hope faded. "Yes, sir."

"Good. Now go wake Crito and the two of you get started carving up the lumber we brought in."

• • •

Dark clouds hid the moon and only the torches they had placed around the farm's perimeter provided any light. They danced in the wind and Silanus thought for certain they'd blow out, but each one held. He was stationed inside the house, the door open and snow gathering on the floor. Pieces of yew had been carved into rough weapons, one end pointed and the other hacked into a grip – Silanus held tight to his. Marcellus had insisted he sit there in the dark; *am I some kind of bait?* If so, the position wasn't undeserved.

The house creaked against the wind. Or was that Lepidus and Crispus shifting their weight on the roof, faces painted black with soot? He wasn't sure.

The other soldiers were out there somewhere in whatever positions Marcellus had placed them. If he had to guess, he'd say there were two more men atop the shed. As to the other four, he couldn't imagine where they might be hiding.

A tickle in his groin told him he would need to empty his bladder soon. Would the Decanus be angry if he stepped outside to do so? He could just go in here, he supposed. It's not like anyone would be living in this room anytime soon.

One of the torches winked out.

Silanus blinked. Rubbed his eyes. He hadn't been mistaken. *Must have been the wind.* The only light now visible was the orange flickering onto the snow from the next torch over.

That, too, went dark.

He crept to the door, fear flooding him as, one by one, the torches died.

Then he saw it.

A dozen yards away. Little more than shadow. It stood tall and stretched its arms high. If he hadn't known better, he would have thought it a tree.

It vanished.

It was coming for him. He had hurt it and it came to pull his lungs from his back and drink his blood.

Knowing he shouldn't but not caring, he slammed the door and ran to the corner of the house. Piss streamed down his leg as he pressed his back to the wall and gripped the yew tight. He trembled in complete darkness for several minutes, waiting for a thud against the door or a scratching on the walls. How disappointed his father would have been.

The rough scrape of bone against wood.

Silanus's breath caught and he slid down onto the floor. It was in here. With him. How was that possible?

The noise came again, frenzied now. Something brushed his foot. He ran. Colliding with the door, he tumbled out onto the snow.

The clouds had parted and the moon shone brightly on the farm. He rolled onto his back and looked into the house. The Droch-fhola was pulling itself free from the wall as though it had always been a part of the wooden structure. Those empty sockets locked on Silanus as the thing's feet snapped away from the house and came after him.

It was out the door before he could get to his feet. *I'm going to die here.*

A dark shape dropped onto its back. The Droch-fhola buckled but did not fall as Lepidus wrapped an arm around its throat. The soldier raised his yew dagger as the creature stood to its full height, thrashing and bucking like a rabid stallion.

Lepidus fell from its back.

It turned to him as Crispus slammed into its side. The two crashed to the ground, snow dusting the air, and the soldier brought his dagger down into the Droch-fhola's thigh. It screamed that same awful scream and bent its head backward at an impossible angle, clamping its jaws onto Crispus's face and rose.

Crispus punched it twice, two solid blows that sounded like an axe striking oak, and then it shook its head viciously from side to side. A loud snap and Crispus fell limp to the ground.

The snow exploded around Silanus as the others erupted from the ground. Crito and Antonius charged its flank as Marcellus and Gaius circled to its front. The two other soldiers, Titus and Lucius, charged toward its side, surrounding it. It crouched low, its head darting back and forth between the three groups. Crispus's dagger was still sunk into its thigh but no blood flowed.

Lepidus leapt from where he was thrown and jabbed it with his dagger. His retreat wasn't quick enough and the thing's claws gashed his leg open. Antonius made use of the distraction and stabbed its ribs. It whirled to strike but Gaius had stabbed its other side. Neither wound was deep but something flowed from each and danced in the wind. Titus made a quick jab – missed. Crito, Marcellus, and Lucius repeated the maneuver and some of what escaped the Droch-Fhola landed in front of Silanus. He hesitated a moment before snatching some and rubbing it between his fingers. It wasn't blood. It looked like dried, crumbled leaves.

Antonius stabbed it again but it spun as Gaius followed, slipping by him and rushing toward the house. Lepidus tried to roll out of its way but it hooked the back of the soldier's armor and dragged him as though he weighed nothing.

"After it," Marcellus shouted and the men rushed the house.

Silanus couldn't make himself follow. A voice whispered in his head that he should run, that he owed these men nothing, and to stay here would be his death. It was a voice he had struggled with for a long time and he fought hard to ignore it.

Rushing to the door, he saw the thing toss Lepidus against the back wall hard enough to shake the entire house. The soldier crumpled to the floor. Whirling on the others as they entered, the creature was a blur of limbs. For a moment Silanus could only see the indigo armor of the Hundredth and then, one by one, they fell. He would be next.

He backed away from the melee.

It roared, a sound of victory that reverberated like thunder, and then Marcellus was tossed from the cabin. Blood covered his face and Silanus was sure he was dead.

The Droch-fhola ripped the door from the hinge as it stepped from the house. It roared again and leapt for Marcellus.

The Decanus squirmed onto his back and brought up his gladius. The Droc-fhola fell on it. The blade pierced its chest, but the monster didn't seem to feel it. It pushed itself down the iron, dry leaves crumbling from its mouth and onto Marcellus's face.

"Go on, then," the Roman said. "Send me on my way, you bastard!"

It roared and jerked forward.

Without thought, Silanus rushed forward. He slammed his yew dagger into the Droc-fhola's back. It shrieked as the wood sunk deep and Silanus pressed harder, pushing it in further. It thrashed but he would not let go.

Yes, he thought, ecstatic to bring it agony. *Die you miserable thing!*

It shrieked louder. Something like a thin branch whipped up into his face.

Everything went black.

* . *

When Silanus woke, the smell of smoke was thick in the air. He struggled to sit and almost threw up.

"Slow down," Marcellus said and placed a hand on his shoulder.

Silanus lay back on the bed. They were still in the farmhouse. "Did it get away?"

"No." The Decanus leaned back in his chair by the bed. "You saw to that."

He didn't know how to respond. For a moment when he woke, he thought everything had been a nightmare. The knowledge it had been real should have driven him mad. Instead, pride rose within – he had been the one to kill the Droch-Fhola.

"We'll be moving on soon. Likely tomorrow."

Silanus nodded and tried to think on which way he should travel from here; of what life held for him now.

Antonius barked orders to the men outside as Marcellus watched them through the door. "You're welcome to come with us. If you want."

"As a prisoner?"

The older man laughed. It stretched the stitches in his face. "As an apprentice. Not every man can be a soldier in the Hundredth, boy." Marcellus turned to him and slapped a hand onto his chest. "Not every man belongs to this life. There's no shame in saying no. You've seen how we live." He coughed once, a wet sound deep in his chest echoing it. "And seen how we die."

Silanus struggled to sit again. The room spun but he willed himself to steady. That voice again whispered that he owed them nothing, that he should leave here and run far from them. The voice was much easier to ignore this time.

BONKED

Patrick Freivald

Four bonks?" Lieutenant Washington ran a hand over the wispy stubble on his dark-skinned head. "Are they stupid?"

Matt Rowley tried not to sigh, and for the most part succeeded – the resulting noise more of a dissatisfied grunt.

Conor Flynn, just as bald as Washington but pale as milk, grinned at Matt across the giant conference room table emblazoned with the eye-and-thunderbolt logo of the International Council on Augmented Phenomena, the elite organization founded through UN-NATO cooperation to combat the threat of Jade and unregulated Gerstner Augmentation. "FNG got an opinion?"

Jeff Hannes froze in his thousand-dollar suit and glared at all of them, his thumb over the 'advance slide' button. "Are you implying there are non-stupid Jade users, Washington?"

"Point, sir. But they have to know they're playing with fire. I mean, look what Gerstner Augs did to the Russian military. A gang's not going to have that kind of firepower."

Flynn spoke without taking his eyes from Matt. "Maybe that's what the other three are for. One goes bonk, the other three take it down before it wrecks the neighborhood. Somebody else Augs up; lather, rinse, repeat."

Washington pounded a fist on the manila folder that contained his mission briefing. "Are we equipped to deal with that kind of oomph?"

While avoiding Flynn's unwavering gaze, Matt replied. "Yeah, we are, according to the analytics. If they don't know we're coming." Matt turned to Jeff. "They don't know, do they?"

Hannes threw up his hands. "Unless they've got a mole in this room, they're clueless, just another Jade gang hopped up on power. The biggest, sure, and they've seized way too much territory, but they're just a gang. And besides, to have a mole they'd have to know we're operating on American soil."

Flynn quirked an eyebrow at Matt. "Dibs for fun on the pointy one, New Guy." His Irish mumble would have been incomprehensible if not for a decade's friendship, which made the 'New Guy' treatment all the more absurd. Their units had fought together in overseas operations and they'd kept in touch in the years since. That Flynn had signed up for ICAP two years before Matt didn't erase that history, so shouldn't change their friendship.

Matt glanced from Flynn to the photo jacked from a nightclub security camera, splayed large across the white wall that served as a screen. The largest of the four bonks had augmented himself beyond anything Matt had seen before. At least ten feet tall with hands the size of Christmas hams, he loomed over the scene behind giant sunglasses, massive arms crossed over his naked chest. In lieu of hair, steel studs protruded from the top of his skull in a regular grid. Metal spikes protruded from his forearms, ending in cruel barbs sharpened to a razor sheen.

Flynn stroked his chin with an air of too much theater. "He's prettier than me. I can't let that stand."

Turning to Jeff, Matt tapped the picture. "How has he not bonked out already? Nobody can tolerate that level of Augs." Bonks had gotten their nickname – which Conor found particularly funny – from the inevitable psychosis that overtook chronic Jade users, the superhuman threat that ICAP had been founded to confront. The more you took, the bigger and badder you got, until the whispers drove you into a killing frenzy you never come out of.

And Jade is addictive, with a recidivism rate over ninety-nine percent.

Psychotics are bad. Psychotics that can shrug off bullets and throw cars are rather worse. The Russian military wouldn't be a threat for at least a generation.

And now it's a street drug.

Hurya al-Azwar answered with a roll of her pale-blue eyes. "It's a matter of time, Rowley. You know it, I know it, he has to know it. Which just makes him that much more dangerous." A scar ran from her left temple back into her short blonde hair. It, and the missing quarter-inch off the top of her ear, spoke of a life on the streets of Detroit before two tours as a Marine in the sand box, before Jade and augmentation and ICAP, before the regenerates that would heal any damage short of death without mark or scar and in seconds or minutes instead of months.

Five years his senior in ICAP, she'd seen dozens of her colleagues bonk out, had to put far too many of them down, and her first-generation regenerates put her at a higher risk than any of them. Augmentation protocols had improved as scientific understanding increased, but everyone in the room ran the risk of psychotic, ravening insanity. Everyone but their boss.

Jeff's constipated grimace pulled them away from the picture. "Look, we've got four heavily-augmented threats and at least sixteen who might be normals, or might just not be showing. I'm bringing in Platt and Karle," he raised his voice over their groans, "and giving Karle operational discretion on this one."

"Why do you hate us?" Flynn asked.

Jeff ran his tongue over his teeth. "Karle's got a better success rate than any of you. I want you all back alive, and there's something about this," he waved his hand at the scattered pictures, "I don't like at all."

Washington sighed without looking up. "Feel the love, man."

* . *

Matt eyed the sunglasses in Flynn's proffered hand and shook his head. "Those make me look like a cop."

"You are a cop. Were a cop. Pretending to be a cop. Whatever you did in Tennessee."

"No need to advertise it."

"Eat your bones." Flynn tossed the shades into the back seat and fastened his seatbelt, then ran his hands over the fake leather dash above the late-model Impala's glove box. "Brilliant. These American-made autos really spice up the sex life, Rowley. We'll fit right in."

At two hundred and forty pounds and one percent body fat, Conor Flynn looked every bit the cop, or ex-military, as Matt. His skin-tight gray t-shirt did nothing to dispel the effect, and his square sunglasses screamed, 'I am a Government Agent. Do not speak to or trust me.'

Flynn raised an eyebrow at the naked appraisal. "What?"

Matt just shook his head and put the car into gear.

They cruised through the suburbs, past an endless stream of one-story ranches and dingy, sun-faded plastic swimming pools. The smells of the city filtered through the air conditioning, street food and salt water and sweat and garbage rotting under the blazing summer sun. Matt considered grabbing the shades from the back seat, but wouldn't give Flynn the satisfaction. Chain link replaced white pickets, and vinyl siding blurred into graffiti on decaying brick.

They pulled up to a stoplight and idled next to a cluster of young men, baggy street clothes and wary brown faces sweltering in the midday heat. This far south it took a special kind of stupid to wear pants if you didn't have to, which might explain why half of them hung on their thighs or even lower. The pale yellow bandanas around foreheads, necks, wrists, or ankles identified them as Camino Reals. Heroin dealers and thieves, they lay outside ICAP's jurisdiction even with their new domestic operations protocols.

Flynn held a hundred-dollar bill up with two fingers, but no one approached the car, their lack of attention as conspicuous as staring.

"Oy, boys." Flynn waved the folded bill in the air. "I could use some information." They glowered at the ground, at the sky, the telephone poles, anywhere but at the car. "Brilliant, lads. Thanks for nothing." The light turned green and Matt pulled away, eyes on the mirrors, watching them watch him with wary eyes.

"No love from the South-Side Banana Hammocks." Flynn chuckled and slipped the money back into his pocket. "Told you we look like cops."

"If you're so worried about it, why are we the ones going?"

"I didn't say I was worried. It's just going to be hard to pick a fight if they know we're the law."

"We're not here to pick–"

Babbling whispers slithered through his mind, a mad cacophony of thoughts bent on murder and pain, the worst side effect of Gerstner Augmentation. Matt took the warning from the Late-Second Precognition but ignored the lurching desire to tear Flynn's face from his skull and stuff it into his mouth. Jerking the wheel, he hit the brakes then the gas to bring them around ninety degrees, then floored it before the jeeps rounded the corner behind the run-down convenience mart.

Flynn laughed and reached down, but stopped when Matt shook his head.

"You won't need the pig-sticker, they're just running us off." He down-shifted to pick up speed, then jammed the car into higher gear, gas pedal to the floor. The motor whined, a cicada with an internal-combustion mating call.

Flynn took his hand off the hilt of his katana, leaving it on the floor between the seats. The titanium and carbon nanofiber blade had yet to see use in combat, but Matt had watched Flynn dice up a car in the practice arena without breaking a sweat. Why an Irishman fought with a katana Matt would never understand.

Flynn jerked his thumb toward the back. "You want me to get the trunk?"

Matt shook his head. The REC-7 carbine and Auto-Assault 12 combat shotgun could stay where they were, in the trunk under lock and key. If worse came to worse he had his personal Glock 9mm in the glove box. But it wouldn't. They'd been made as cops in a no-go zone, but hadn't done anything to justify a murder, even from a gang as vicious as the Camino Reals.

They blew through two red lights, the jeeps swerving and honking behind, but as they passed from one turf to the next the pursuit broke off and didn't return.

"You sussed those out pretty fast. Precog, yeah?" Flynn asked.

Matt nodded without taking his eyes from the road.

"Brilliant, brilliant. They wouldn't clear me for it, said I'd had enough. I'm thinking what's the harm, right?"

"The harm is you go bonk and kill everything around you until other people like you put you down."

Flynn chuckled. "That's what I mean, right? The side effect is 'fun.'"

"Just keep your pants on."

"Aye, Sergeant."

Ten minutes later they rolled past the Marquee, a modern glass-and-steel structure at odds with the dilapidated neighborhood. The fading day washed the neon lights to a pale glow but did nothing to hide the ultraviolet paint across the front windows, a cartoon shark swimming through a golden crown that would be invisible to unaugmented eyes.

"See that?" Matt asked.

Flynn nodded. "Fancy. You think the Shades don't have blacklights?"

Matt shrugged. "One cop in fifty might have augged vision, maybe. Not like the Mako Kings don't know the police know where they hang out, anyway. As long as they think we're just cops, we'll–"

Flynn popped his handle and stepped out, the car still rolling at fifteen miles an hour. He hooked a parking meter with his right hand and used it to spin himself around, stopping with a flourish with his toes balanced on the edge of the curb. As Matt slammed on the brakes and swore under his breath, Flynn took a bow to the wide-eyed onlookers. Flynn waited behind the car for Matt to pull over, put on the brake and get out.

People milled the streets, heading home from work or out for a Friday on the town. As one they gave the car a wide berth, eyeing both newcomers with open suspicion or naked hostility.

Matt stepped up to his friend with his jaw clenched in frustration. "Dammit, Conor, we're supposed to be scoping the place, not painting bullseyes on our heads."

A seven-foot tall bouncer, rippling with muscles impossible through normal exercise, eyed them from the front door across the street. Taking in the sea of Hispanics, all either staring or trying too hard not to stare, Flynn ran a hand over the stubble on his pasty scalp. "See, we fit right in, sunnies and all." He put on his shades and sauntered across the street.

Music trickled out behind the double-doors, Latin horns over a hip-hop beat, death-metal Spanish growling from a microphone. They approached, cop-casual, Matt two steps behind. The bouncer moved to intercept them. His voice rumbled an octave lower than a normal man's, his accent a blend of Mexican and south Florida. "Can I help you, gentlemen?"

"Yes," Matt said. "We–"

"Looking for a drink and twirl is all." Flynn spun, an elegant pirouette that ended in a curtsey. He held the pose and looked up under his brow into the bouncer's eyes. "Heard the Marquee had it happening, am I right?"

"You're not our target clientele, ese." The bouncer put his hands on his hips so that his massive frame blocked most of both doors. Matt winced as Flynn's eyes flashed, an almost imperceptible twitch that showed not the slightest hint of fear. The bouncer put his hand on Flynn's chest, fingers splaying almost to his shoulders. "You're going to have to leave."

"What, because I'm white? You discriminating here? You think the Irish haven't faced–"

Matt put his hand on Flynn's shoulder. "We're not here to pick a fight, Conor."

"–their share of discrimination, you racist prick? Why don't you make me leave, big guy?"

To his credit, the bouncer didn't take the bait. Much. He extended his arm, slowly, forcing Flynn several steps back on the sidewalk. "Move along, little man. This isn't the place for you." He extended his fingers and Conor stumbled back two steps.

Matt moved between them and Conor rebounded off of his back. "We're sorry, sir. We'll be on our way." He stepped back, bumping Flynn toward the street, then turned and backed him off the curb and into the road. Through gritted teeth he mumbled, "The point was to maintain surprise, moron."

Flynn almost frolicked toward the car, locking eyes with anyone and everyone who dared challenge his right to be there. "Nah, there's no fun in that, and he thinks we're cops or feds or something anyway. The point was to size that meathead up. You see what I saw?"

Matt recalled the scene, his eidetic memory enhancements bringing to crystal-clear focus details he hadn't seen in real time. "Tracks?"

"Right is right. He's on the H, not just Jade. We follow him home, wait for him to snow out, bangers and mash," he mimed tossing a flash-bang grenade. "Black bag over the head, voila. New toy for the intel department."

Matt tried not to smile as he gunned the engine. "Call it in."

"We could just–"

"Call it in, Conor." He pulled away from the curb and took a left toward the expressway.

The dash shook as Flynn banged his fist on it. "Karle's a pussy. We've got an opportunity here, and you know he'll–"

Matt sighed. "Twelve years a Royal Marine, decorated six times for valor, awarded the Victoria Cross for insane but admirable stupidity in the Kandahar valley. . . What rank were you when you left the force to join ICAP?"

Flynn mumbled.

"Say again, Corporal?"

"Cor-por-al." He emphasized every syllable. "And you know it."

"And why not a Sergeant? A Warrant Officer? Lieutenant?"

They said it together. "A history of unpredictable behavior and violent tendencies uncurbed by disciplinary measures."

"ICAP wanted a killer," Flynn mumbled again, "so they can't complain when they get one."

"Right. But right now we need to be smart. We're on US soil, and have limited mission parameters. If Karle sanctions the move, we–" His eyes widened as the whispers shrieked blood-soaked charnel houses into his brain. Before it happened a shadow separated from the wall, crushing the Impala and tumbling it end over end into the sidewalk grocery.

Late-second precognition made Rowley and a select few other Augs impossible to surprise, at least while awake. The whispers gave warning, but not much. Matt swerved, taking the bonk head-on.

He squeezed his eyes shut as the airbags deployed, gritted his teeth against the impossibly loud crunch, and yanked the 9mm from the glove box. Two pulls of the trigger deflated the airbag and caused the massive shadow dwarfing his vision to stagger. His eardrums healed as fast as the explosions shredded them, and the car lurched sideways. Gasping in a breath of chalky white dust and the tang of gunpowder, he tore off his seatbelt.

Flynn had disappeared, his door hanging ajar on a crumpled hinge.

A monster lifted the car by the front, a wall of muscle and spikes with jet black eyes, teeth filed to cruel points, threaded steel studs protruding from its head in a regular pattern. The bonk roared and Matt's world overturned, the roof imploding as it impacted the asphalt. Neck tilted almost to ninety degrees, he fired twice out the spider-webbed windshield.

Hot red blood exploded from the bonk's enormous black sneaker, a chunk of leather torn free from the glancing shot. Matt pushed with his legs, straining against the seat as massive fingers gripped the hood under the car and lifted. If the bonk had felt the gunshot, it made no sign of it. Matt's stomach lurched as the car raised up. He pushed harder, bracing his hands on either side of the steering wheel for leverage.

The seat snapped and he fell back, his face sliding across the upholstered roof as the car smashed into the ground again, trapping him in a sandwich of crumpled metal.

* . *

Conor Flynn rolled right as gunfire peppered the sidewalk. His heart soared as civilians screamed, the adrenaline rushing through his veins in an orgy of pending violence while his augmented heart beat at a steady seventy beats per second. He hit the facade of the brick building at a full sprint and ran straight up it, using his momentum to gain traction on the vertical surface.

Twenty feet up he grabbed the roof lip and jerked, sailing over the top in a graceful arc. One knife had already left his hand, sinking to the hilt into his first opponent. Conor ignored the dead man as he drew and threw the second knife left-handed.

Shooter number two held his HK53 like a movie gangster, the stock collapsed, relying on arm strength to bring and hold the weapon to bear. He jerked as the knife hit, glancing off the gun instead of finding purchase in his flesh.

Conor landed, crouched low, grinning in the thrill of battle. Bullets zoomed over his head as the gangbanger's weapon jerked high. Three steps brought Conor in range, so he drew the katana and spun. The ancient bone fragment hidden in the hilt sang to him, urged the blade forward, thirsted for the death that it had brought in life. He resisted and pulled back at the last second. The monofilament blade took the man in the bridge of the nose without the slightest resistance, a spray of red gore joining the near-silent steel breeze. Stepping in as the man dropped the weapon to bring his hands to his face, Conor shouldered him off the roof.

He fell with gurgling wail that cut off in a wet thump on the pavement.

Picking up the carbine, Conor looked down at the overturned car and the giant bonk slamming it into the pavement. "Oh, Matt, you silly boy. I called dibs."

He dove sideways as the roof access door banged open, bullets tearing through the air where he'd just stood. Three men armed with ARs fanned out as Conor scrambled behind an air conditioning unit. They moved with an uncoordinated, nervous energy, to make room for a dark-skinned bonk in a black trench-coat, like Wesley Snipes's Blade enlarged on a photocopier.

A sharp itch shot up from his ankle, and he looked down to find his cuff darkening with spreading blood just above his boot.

The pain hadn't hit him, and wouldn't before the wound healed.

"Brilliant, lads. Let's play."

• •

Automatic weapons-fire punctuated the mind-rattling crunch as the bonk beat the car into the ground. Matt squirmed to the back, popped down the latch to access the trunk, and pulled the case containing his AA-12 combat shotgun into the back seat. His stomach lurched as the car lifted and he ran his thumb over the biometric lock.

The car slammed down and a searing, white-hot pain shot up his leg into his spine.

He popped open the case and slid out the weapon, the drum magazine already loaded with fin-stabilized fragmentation rounds. He turned, his left leg making a sloppy ripping sound as it tore free from the jagged chunk of metal that used to be the gearshift, and took aim.

The car came up, and in the four-inch space between the dash and the remains of the roof the bonk's abdomen came into view, rippling muscle barely contained in a baby-blue t-shirt. Matt fired, the roar deafening in the confined space.

He held the trigger as the bonk whirled to the side and only one microgrenade found its mark, the others deactivating automatically as they missed the intended target. As it exploded the world disappeared from view and the car crashed down onto the pavement with a final crunch. Matt squirmed back and crushed the latch on the trunk with a knife-hand, tearing it free with a wince. Ignoring the bloody mess he'd made of his fingers he launched himself out, weapon raised toward the rooftops.

He fired and swept right over three targets, wishing for his tactical helmet with its Friend-or-Foe identifier and smart projectile guidance system. A man's head exploded, raining bloody brains and chunks of skull from the rooftop before pitching back out of sight, but the other two took cover, unharmed. Shots rang out from the roof across the street, though at what target he couldn't tell.

Footsteps rang behind him. On his back, he rolled his head to take aim at the charging bouncer, eight-hundred-plus pounds moving at twenty-something miles an hour. He triggered the rounds to explode 'downward' toward the sky and pulled the trigger. The weapon barely recoiled against his shoulder, and a dozen shots flew in two seconds. The depleted uranium-tipped rounds punched into the bonk's legs and abdomen and then erupted in a bloody mist. The massive thing stumbled mid-stride, left femur and part of its hip exposed by the rapid disintegration of intervening flesh.

Matt fired twice more, punching up under the fused bones of its ribcage to pulp the heart and lungs. With any luck the trauma would be enough to bring it down.

The whispers tittered in hateful glee and he jerked his legs up, but his injured left knee didn't respond. The shredded remains of his Impala came down on top of it in an explosion of wet red pain, erasing everything below his lower thigh in a gory smear across the concrete. Black spots formed in his vision, but he jerked up the shotgun – and found no targets. Blue sky and scattering civilians filled his vision over the demolished car.

As the arteries pumping life from his body closed and meat formed around undeveloped bone, he lay back and panted, trying to circumvent the unbearable, itching agony of bleeding, knitting flesh. His vision darkened, but he forced his eyes to remain open and trained on the rooftop. His view remained empty, devoid of targets.

In the distance, sirens wailed.

He slid to a sitting position, his right hand on the stock of the AA-12, and looked down at the tattered remains of his leg. The muscle writhed, ropy masses weaving together only to split, bleeding, as the bone grew between them.

A shadow crossed his vision. He looked up.

Conor shook his head, frowning, every inch of him covered in bright red blood. He smiled, white teeth glinting like the metallic sheen on his sword in the fading sunlight. "You let him get away. You going to do your job or what?"

Biting back his vulgar reply, Matt allowed his head to drop to the sidewalk, filling his vision with clear blue sky. "Call it in. And put that damned sword away – the cops are en route."

• • •

Hurya al-Azwar stepped down from the helicopter and surveyed the carnage wrought by Conor Flynn. Five dead men sprawled across the rooftop, policemen already marking evidence with little yellow tags – shell casings, severed limbs, discarded weapons. Red stains marred the gravel in an expanding spiral that ended in the shredded remains of a giant black man, a third of his head three meters further away, remaining eye wide open in unending shock, mouth open to reveal serrated steel teeth bolted into his jaw.

"How many did they get?" She nodded toward the corpse.

Sergeant Karle frowned down at the dead bonk. "Two, plus nearly a dozen normals. All fatalities. Conor's unhurt, Matt will be fine in an hour or so if we stuff enough food in him."

"This was recon. What the hell happened?"

Karle held up his hands. "Conor Flynn happened. Matt said he picked a fight."

"Remind me to never do that." She nudged the dead bonk with her toe. "Intel didn't even know about this one. What's a big black guy doing Augging-up in a Latin gang?"

Karle grunted. "Tell Platt and Washington to make nice with the locals. I'm going to see if we can't get Conor and Matt out of custody."

"Aye, sir."

• • •

The map appeared on Matt's HUD as Karle spoke in his ear piece. The Mako Kings controlled a nine-block area just outside of downtown, and ruthlessly crushed any and all opposition regardless of whether or not they were law enforcement, rival gangs, or even the cartels. Pioneers in nationwide Jade distribution, they'd partnered with Dawkins's organization to spread like a virus from Chicago to both coasts and everywhere in-between. With an irresistible product and superhuman augmentation they destroyed their competition and carved out an empire from the ashes of burning ghettos.

A network of Dragonflies gave Matt real-time data of the Mako Kings's turf, the quad-copter drones blanketing the area with sonar, visual, and infrared surveillance. Coupled with his own infrared and ultraviolet vision, the HUD removed the fog of war and replaced it with stark, robotic clarity. The overlay projected an image that saw through brick walls and even assessed the likelihood that any particular person was a target or a civilian.

Pointy, as Conor had taken to calling him, had left a blood trail from the wreckage of Matt's rented Impala through the back alleys to an abandoned shopping plaza now known as 'Spanish City', a lawless haven for derelicts, junkies and people who didn't want to be found. A wall of wrecked vehicles surrounded the parking lot and included a crude gate made out of the burned-out carcass of a double-decker bus rigged to an old crane.

The reek of unwashed bodies, burning garbage, and urine combined into something not unlike ammonia-soaked charred bananas left to rot in the sun. Matt couldn't imagine what it smelled like in the midday heat and humidity.

Dozens of people wandered the asphalt, or warmed themselves at fires set in rusted steel drums. Junkies lay on the ground, or on each other, sharing needles and pills and body heat in the midnight chill. Sentries wandered the rooftops, armed with long rifles and binoculars that may or may not be night-vision capable.

Too many civilians. A squad of Augs could make mincemeat

of the hostiles without the use of heavy ordnance, but the civilians would pay a heavy toll. Besides, if Jade wasn't involved it wasn't their purview, and while some Jade dealers found their way to Spanish City it was not, according to their intel, a pipeline worthy of ICAP's attention. Yet.

Karle had operational control – former rank meant nothing in ICAP – but ultimately the plan came from Washington. Washington, Karle, and Flynn would storm the gates, loud and proud, with flash-bangs and drone support to crack a hole in the wall. As the civilians ran and the guards engaged, Rowley, Platt, and al-Azwar would eliminate Pointy. Conor had complained, citing "dibs" which Washington ignored, mollifying him with a chance at the fifth bonk the Dragonflies had pegged near the gate.

Mission parameters authorized deadly force for the bonks and anyone identified as a Mako King. Between the baby-blue bandannas and facial recognition, the quad copters had added eleven human-sized targets in addition to the two bonks. Matt's HUD outlined them with double red triangles, the suspected civilians with orange triangles, and his own team with green circles. In the age of Jade, collateral damage had become a price of law enforcement, and the DHS hoped the joint UN/NATO strike force would bring so much firepower to bear that they could minimize or at least contain the destruction . . . but this somehow wasn't a 'military operation'.

Peace through superior bureaucracy.

The timer hit zero, and the bus-gate disintegrated in a roar, the fireball rising skyward as the drone banked toward home.

Screams. Panic. Weapons-fire pinging off the wreckage from jittery, untrained gangbangers wasting their ammo—and precious time reloading.

Pointy's hulking form, bright yellow on the infrared, bolted from his mattress in the abandoned Macy's sales floor, joined by several others. The huge blob raced through the open space toward the loading dock a hundred feet from their position.

Platt charged, screaming, before the bay door had opened.

Matt opened his mouth to countermand, and closed it, angry. Platt came to a halt inches from the unmoving metal.

Pointy's blob faded, then disappeared.

"What the hell?" Platt put his fist through the loading-dock's side door, pivoted, and ripped it off its hinges. Staccato pops sounded from inside, and chips of cinderblock lashed into Platt's face.

"Hold position!" Matt moved up, his HUD tracking for targets simultaneously on the Dragonfly feed and the helmet camera, the 'Identify Friend or Foe' lighting up at several weapon profiles sticking out from around pillars and decrepit, half-burned display cases.

He fired three times on approach, eschewing the Groucho technique he'd learned as a Tennessee police officer in favor of a thirty-mile-per-hour sprint and superhuman strength to keep the recoil-suppressing weapon aimed true. The fin-stabilized microgrenades auto-aimed toward the identified targets, skimming past the makeshift defilade and exploding downward and sideways. Men screamed. A pair of legs kicked out from behind a cracked marble pillar, the IFF fading from red to black as a pool of blood spread across the filthy tile.

He grunted as a round rocked his shoulder back, the gel under the dragon skin hardening to dissipate the energy before turning soft again. Behind him, al-Azwar's NATO-issue REC7 chattered, spitting ceramic composite 'bonk killer' rounds with unerring accuracy.

Matt's visor automatically dimmed over the continuous muzzle-flash as Platt fired full auto and swept inside, following the bullets through the doorway with a roar that carried over the intercom. Matt and al-Azwar came in behind, al-Azwar keeping their targets pinned down with tight, controlled bursts while Matt killed them with the directional grenades.

Seconds later the room fell quiet, the FoF indicating no living targets.

"Here!" al-Azwar cried, flipping up a metal access hatch with her boot. Without waiting she stepped in and dropped out of sight, carbine pointed down as she fell through the hole.

Platt and Rowley whirled as a pair of men ran in, gaped wide-eyed at the carnage then fled in panic. Matt stepped up and looked inside the hole. A series of rebar handles led into the darkness, which in the UV spectrum resolved into a ladder descending several stories to a concrete floor. IR signatures showed faint signs of passage, but the tunnels glowed too warm for much more.

Platt nodded at the hole. "You first."

Matt stepped inside, pressing his boots against the walls to slow his descent enough not to break his legs when he hit the ground. Above him, Platt stepped in and grabbed a rung.

Platt hissed as his fingers separated from his hand in a flash of silver. He turned, groping for his carbine left-handed. Another flash and his helmet toppled down the shaft, his head still inside, neck spurting steaming red blood. A block of plastic bricks followed Platt's dead body down the hole, a red light blinking in the darkness.

Matt fired a burst up the shaft and pulled his feet back, falling the last twenty feet before impacting hard on the concrete floor. He leapt. With a spin he just managed to pull himself behind a metal door before the room erupted.

Heat washed over him in a deafening, blinding white, crushing him between the wall and the door. His armor crackled, the HUD went dark. He held his breath for as long as he could, then gasped in air that seared his throat, scorched his lungs. Gagging, he stumbled to his knees and tore off his helmet. His hair shriveled in the fading heat, and he kept his eyes squeezed tight.

A moment passed, and a breeze tickled his skin as more air rushed back into the room. He gasped in a breath, cleaner now, and opened his eyes.

Flecks of blackened skin fell from his hands, the only part of his body exposed to the explosion. He flexed his fingers as the skin knitted over and through the damaged tissue – he'd have to cut it away later to let blemish-free skin grow. If there was a later.

Dust and smoke obscured his vision, but from his vantage point he could just make out the pile of demolished concrete that had once made up the shaft, and next to it the smoldering remains of one of Platt's boots, a chunk of bone sticking out of the ruined meat. Matt stood and looked down at the bandoleer of drum magazines for the AA-12. The smoking leather had protected the munitions just enough. Had they detonated, he'd be a dead man.

He rounded the corner, weapon up, and left the room, his useless helmet lying next to Platt's boot. "Hurya, do you copy?"

Static burst through his ear bud, intermingled with what might have been al-Azwar's voice.

"I'm on your six. Platt's dead."

"–ay again, Rowley." Karle's deep voice reverberated through his ears. "Y– king up."

"Karle, Platt's dead, hostile unknown. We're underground." He rounded a corner and snarled at the uselessness of his IR; the floor and walls glowed a uniform red, an afterimage from the explosion, or perhaps from a subterranean heat source. "al-Azwar, I'm on your six, copy."

The indecipherable noise that followed left him no idea whether or not they'd understood, or if Hurya had heard him at all.

• • •

Bullets pinged off of the bus-gate as Conor leapt through the holes left by the trio of AGM-176 Griffin missiles, the drone-capable, candy-ass little brothers of Hellfire missiles designed to limit collateral damage. His ears filled with the melodious sounds of rifle shots and screaming panic, and in his mind his katana sang of unending bloodshed as he drew it from its sheath.

He ignored the scattering civilians, and the whispers' nagging encouragement to cut them down. They didn't tell him anything he didn't already know, and there were bigger, more challenging prizes to pursue.

Karle and Washington took position behind the gate and fired short, controlled bursts from their M4s, letting the IFF targeting system guide the electronically-controlled flechette rounds to their targets. They couldn't shoot around corners, but in Conor's opinion, 300-meter shots without bothering to aim just scoured all the joy out of combat.

Conor leapt, taut muscle launching him twenty feet in the air and straight at the bonk charging their position.

Smaller than Pointy, the nine-foot monstrosity wore full body armor, matte black carbon fiber over enormous metal plates, and wielded a battered stop sign like an axe. A mane of black hair flowed down her back from a topknot that gave her a vaguely Mongolian look, though she bore the extended brow and thick facial structure of bonks everywhere. Enormous claws extended from her left hand, the gleaming metal bolted to or through the bone and stretching half a meter from her fingertips.

Conor swung, two-handed, but without purchase he couldn't put enough force into the blow to threaten such a creature. She didn't take the feint. Faster than he believed possible, Scratchy sidestepped and swung. He twisted to take the blow on his hip as the stop sign swatted him from the air. He took the landing on his left hand, cartwheeled, and came up swinging.

The monofilament blade sparked against the sign inches from his head, skittering up the handle to bite into the reflective sheet metal. Scratchy twisted, tearing the blade from Conor's hands, and swiped low with her claws.

Laughing, Conor stepped into the swipe, using her elbow for a foothold to spin-kick her in the face. The steel toe caught her in the temple, the shock of metal on thick bone reverberating up Conor's left leg as the blow arrested his momentum. The reinforced steel in his boot crumpled with the impact, crushing his toes.

Scratchy dropped the sign and stumbled back, shaking her head like a dog.

Conor dove into a roll, grabbing the hilt of his blade on the way by. The metal shrieked as he wrenched the sword free. He spun, weapon up, and gave her a nod of respect.

"C'mon, lassie. You've got some fight in you."

Scratchy swept up the sign and advanced, makeshift axe and claw whirring almost too fast for his augmented eyes to follow. Metal clanged against metal as he backpedaled, limping, sword flashing to deflect the blows before either crushed or sliced him to pieces.

His back hit the wall. Scratchy swung.

• • •

Hurya al-Azwar closed her eyes, but heard only the soft trickle of water in the distance, the echo washing it out to white noise in the sewer tunnels. She muttered a soft prayer of thanks that sanitation services had long-since failed in this part of the city, and only the ghosts of odors remained to haunt her senses. All said, the sewers smelled much better than the mall above.

Her COMMs produced nothing but occasional static, like her GPS and the IFF linked through the network of Dragonflies, though because of intervening metal or deliberate jamming she couldn't say. Pointy – despite Conor's childishness, a lack of known identity had ensured that the name stuck throughout operational planning – had vanished down the twisting corridors, and the heat from the walls kept her from tracking him with IR vision.

The tunnels had rocked a few minutes earlier, in what she'd hoped had been a deliberate explosion set by Platt or Rowley, and since then her world had condensed to long, dark corridors rendered bright by augmented eyes, dripping water, and the desiccated memories of ancient shit.

She waited. Rats squeaked in the distance, their feet scrabbling across the stone-and-mortar hallways, too far and too quiet for human ears to hear.

Something Pointy's size couldn't move through these corridors without making noise, and her augmented ears could pick up a pin dropping at ten meters. A scrape of boot on the floor, a shoulder brushing against the wall. If he moved, she'd hear it, and she'd have him.

A bead of sweat trickled down the back of her neck, tickling from her hairline until it hit the collar of her undershirt, the white cotton soaked under her armor in the oppressive heat. She tightened her grip on the carbine, textured handle proof against her sweaty palms, and took one careful step, rocking from the ball of her foot to her toes. Silent, she regulated her breathing to the barest motion, letting not even that betray her presence.

Her ears pricked at a soft scrape. She turned, rotating soundlessly on the balls of her feet, breath held. It came again, closer, from a hall on the left. She lifted the REC7 and crept two careful steps back. The FoF highlighed a potential target, blue for an unconfirmed type. Another step back, and–

She jerked up, too late. The giant shape landed on her, thick, sinuous muscle crushing her arms to her chest. Pain exploded in her trigger finger as it snapped sideways in the guard. Hot runnels of fluid streamed to the floor as serrated barbs sank deep into her flesh. She stomped with the strength of a dozen men, driving her heel down onto the foot below.

Pointy only squeezed harder. Her ribs, fused as part of augmentation, cracked. Slamming her head back, she hit thick muscle instead of teeth or nose. She gasped in a breath, but her lungs wouldn't inflate. Held in the air, she found no purchase. The grip tightened, and the fire in her chest strangled hope. Bones shifted, her infrared vision blurred.

Her fingers walked along the black leather of her belt to the loop holding the grenades. She fumbled for the pin, the spoon, any part of it, something she could drop and kick behind them, shred the monster from the back.

She groaned out the last of her air.

Her finger touched metal.

Blood and organs vomited from her mouth as her ribcage collapsed, the hot, meaty taste her last sensation before the world went black.

* * *

Conor spun right as the wall next to him disappeared in a puff of concrete dust, Scratchy's claws reducing the brick facade to chunks and powder. He slashed downward, and the sword's psychic scream pumped energy into his exhausted muscles. It drank deep, pulling blood and life from the bonk's thigh, cutting through muscle and bone with an ease that technology couldn't account for.

What ICAP didn't know wouldn't hurt them.

He danced away in a hot arterial spray, Scratchy's muscles already knitting in ropy, purple masses. One mass formed a lump-like, writhing tentacle. Conor smiled. First Generation Regenerates had their own set of problems, so he decided to have some fun.

She charged, a limping rhinoceros's trundling attack, brute force and sharp steel at forty miles an hour.

Eschewing the sword, he drew his 9mm pistol and fired, emptying the fifteen-round magazine into her face and arms in a series of little red holes and streaks of shredded tissue. Small caliber rounds wouldn't do anything but annoy a bonk of her size, but it would tax her system just enough for his next–

–she slammed into him, carrying him to the ground in a gridiron tackle that blasted the air from his lungs, but he kept his blade pointed out and maintained his grip. She bit down on his shoulder. The armor absorbed the brunt of her iron hard teeth. The increase in pressure didn't restrict his movements any more than her arms already had.

Fabric tore. The pressure increased.

He let her squeeze, and worked the katana back and forth across her exposed wrist. Even without leverage the razor-sharp blade sliced through the meat without effort. His teeth clenched against the growing pain in his shoulder; Conor worked the katana up and down in a rough sawing motion, the best he could manage with his arms pinned to his side.

She grabbed his thigh with her claws and squeezed. The bone gave way with a burning rush of endorphins and heat, and Conor fought to remain conscious through the unbearable, itching agony. He slid the blade up, and then down.

Up. Down.

Muscle parted. Metal scraped against bone. Scratchy dragged her teeth free then slammed her head into Flynn's helmet, again and again, stars exploding across his vision. Something cracked, and cracked further, then white supernovas streaked through his skull. Still he sawed.

Her grip slackened against the blade, just enough to free his arm. Conor pulled a combat knife from his belt and jammed it between metal plates, through carbon fiber and meat into the junction between her leg and groin. He propped the pommel against the metal plate on his abdomen and used her leverage to shove it farther in. Hot, sticky fluid gushed over his hand.

Her squeeze became a squirming, frantic push, but he straightened his good leg to lift against her weight, jamming the blade deeper until it met bone, and then a little further. As the knife sank between the ball and socket he twisted with every ounce of his augmented strength. The joint popped free.

Roaring, she let go and rolled off of him.

He stood.

Tearing off his helmet and letting it drop to the ground, he whirled, blade slicing through the air and her mid-spine without slowing. Her claws tore into the asphalt, desperately scrabbling across the pavement, limp legs trailing behind.

Conor hobbled after her, unable to put much weight on his left leg. The sword bit down, slicing armor and meat once, twice, three times, tracing deep gashes across her shoulders and upper arms. Purple masses writhed across the wounds as she dragged herself away from him, legs twitching as her spine began to knit.

She rose to all fours.

He cut across the back of her knee, severing tendons and ligaments, the wound welling black under the sodium-vapor sky. As she fell he drove the blade into one kidney, leaning in to punch it through to her armor on the other side. He pulled it out and did the other.

She swung, an ineffectual batting with her claws that he hopped way from. He took several of her fingers. They fell to the ground in a gush, and as she reared to her knees he took her right ear. The contrast highlighted the difference between first and second-generation regenerates: his thigh itched as muscle and bone knitted under his armor, but it still wouldn't take his weight. She healed much faster, but the unstable flesh molded and twisted her body into something less than human.

He stabbed her again, avoiding her heart to target her right lung. Once. Twice. Then her stomach, just to the left of her spine.

No reason to keep you down too long, darling.

She fell back to her hands and knees. He took the time to slice the side of her neck, just enough to prick the artery. Blood gushed in erratic spurts across the decaying asphalt, and she collapsed to her face, shaking, as the wound slithered and squirmed.

Her whole body shuddered, and a mad, keening growl erupted from her throat.

"There it is."

The whispers slithered through his mind, calling to their sister, entwining her, embracing her in an unending maelstrom of madness and carnage. She thrashed on the ground, a half-ton child in a temper-tantrum, denied her favorite toys.

He glanced up long enough to see Washington and Karle advancing toward the mall without taking fire, then looked back down at Scratchy's transformation. First-generation bonks made for the best bonk-outs. *Tee-hee.*

Tentacles oozed from her shoulder, and a mouth gnashed with serrated teeth from the wound in her neck. He limped back with too much theater for the benefit of the Dragonflies and took shelter in the shadows by the wall, his smirk hidden in the shadows.

Scratchy erupted in a mountain of writhing flesh, suckered tentacles and ropy masses of muscle almost obscuring her humanoid form. Her scream couldn't come from human lungs, an animalistic rage purer and more potent than the worst that men could devise.

And better than most, Conor Flynn knew what men could devise.

Karle and Washington turned and opened fire as the bonked-out mountain of flesh charged them. His voice admirably calm, Karle called for air support and then addressed Conor. "Flynn, you alive?"

He coughed for effect. "Barely. Be a minute."

"Well, step on it. We've got company."

"Aye, sir." From the shadows, Flynn smiled, and watched.

Washington drew a pair of combat knives and took the charge head-on. He disappeared in an avalanche of psychotic, ravening meat. Blood fountained up from the hideous abomination, though from his squad-mate or the monster Conor couldn't tell.

He tried his leg. An electric jolt shot up his spine, but it held his weight and didn't get any worse. Satisfied, he limped right, around the side of the building. Karle bellowed in the distance, and staccato gunfire echoed across the parking lot. Conor found a manhole, popped it up with his foot, and cocked his head.

Far beneath him, a bloody mess stained the ground, just hotter than the walls and floor. In what little streetlight hit the bottom he could just make out the remains of an ICAP uniform, too small to be Rowley or Platt. Organs and steaming chunks of viscera spilled out of the helmet, a viscous glob of jellied entrails that crisscrossed al-Azwar's unmoving chest in a pattern his mind had to and wouldn't recognize. The eldritch symbol lanced through his head, seeking a foothold he would never allow it to find. He snuffed it out and opened eyes he hadn't realized he'd closed.

Overhead, streaks of orange fire lit up the sky. The earth rocked a moment before the explosions hit Conor's ears, and Karle's bellow of triumph brought a small shake to his head.

What's your hollering about, big man? He'd never understand the valor in a drone strike, the glory in killing by remote control. The warriors of antiquity wouldn't recognize this dispassionate barbarity. The bone shard hidden in the hilt of his sword cooed its agreement. He laughed, and it took that moment of empathy to attack.

Daggers of black thought lanced into Conor's mind, seeking dominance and control, freedom from the eternity of death and the enslavement of soul. It surged forward, triumphant, exultant in the ease in which it invaded his mind. Instead of fighting, Conor let it in, deeper and deeper in its orgiastic triumph, until it came at last to the center of his being. He laughed at the panicked retreat from what it found there, then cut it off and strangled it with his will.

You serve me. And you will serve.

Cowed, the sword mewled in his mind, but it would find no mercy, no sympathy in its new master. A tremor of despair vibrated through the blade, and turned to a single, pathetic, razor thought: *Hungry.*

Conor patted the blade, a reflexive gesture with no emotion behind it. He grabbed a rung and climbed down, careful not to mess his boots any further on the slippery, stinking remains of Hurya al-Azwar.

• • •

Ten minutes after he found al-Azwar's shattered body, Matt stopped with a mental grunt. Pointy's bloody tracks marked the floor in the ultraviolet spectrum like highlighter, disrupted only by spotty patches of urine – rat or mouse by the look of it – and the acrid smell of the place. Pointy's tracks led into a small room made of dark brick, and then straight under the steel door on the far side, a bulkhead-type monstrosity with a gasketed rim and a rusty, wheeled, double-bar lock.

Pointy had gone inside, so it couldn't be flooded, but Matt doubted he'd be able to open it without giving away his presence. He sniffed the axle and detected no trace of WD-40 or grease, nothing to keep it from screaming like a banshee if he tried to open it.

If you're going to be loud…

Matt pulled a fist-sized wad of C4 from his combat pouch, split it into two pieces and pressed it into and around the latching mechanism on either side of the door. The detcord came next, clothesline-like material impregnated with PETN that burned at four miles a second, not so much a fuse as a linear explosive. He pushed the nylon-like material into and around the gasket, as well as through the wads of C4. Last, he added a blasting cap and set the detonator to radio signal.

Sixty feet down the hall he rounded the corner into a side passage. He set the detonator's remote on the floor twenty feet from the intersection, gripped his shotgun in both hands, and backed up. Then he ran.

A typical ICAP Aug could maintain a three-minute mile indefinitely, and run a hundred meters in eight seconds. Matt's personal record topped out at seven point seven-two. Legs pumping, he tried to beat it.

The impact as he stepped on the red button rocked the world sideways, and the shockwave buffeted him back just before he reached the main hallway. Legs pumping, he ran halfway up the far wall, muscles straining to turn him ninety degrees at such speeds, and fired a three-round burst of fragmentary projectiles toward the remains of the door and anything that might lie behind it.

Still glowing from the aftermath, chunks of shredded metal and broken brick littered the small room, and the resulting hole opened up not into a sewer tunnel but a metro line. A pair of tracks led left and right, and hazy orange sodium-vapor lights dotted the walls amid generations of overlapping graffiti.

The whispers chittered in anticipation of the slaughter. *As Matt rushes through the door, Pointy drops from the arced ceiling, a thousand pounds of muscle and brute force crushing him to the floor and pulping his head with one double-fisted crush.*

Matt tucked into a roll as he flew through the doorway, pulling the trigger as Pointy's gigantic form came into view. Two slugs impacted on the ceiling. Three found flesh.

Gore spattered Matt's face as he finished the roll and spun, firing again. Pointy slapped the shotgun out of the way and punched, telegraphing the move without the slightest bit of finesse. Matt rolled with it, taking the impact on his shoulder. His armor stiffened with the blow, reducing the punch to a solid hit with a Louisville Slugger.

He backpedaled as Pointy advanced, the hole in the bonk's leg knitting closed even as he picked up speed. A center-of-mass burst failed to penetrate skin, and the fragmentary rounds shredded Pointy's pectoral muscles to expose a gore-covered solid mass beneath. Half-blind, face streaming blood from a thousand gouges, the bonk dove, arms outstretched to catch Matt as he tried to flee.

Instead, Matt dropped prone and rolled left. He screamed as Pointy stomped, crushing his knee to the ground right through the ceramic composite. Matt fired, and two rounds caught the bonk in the stomach before he slapped the AA-12 hard enough to dent the barrel and send it flying from Matt's grip.

Chunks of meat and organs sprayed them both.

Matt scrambled back, his shattered knee a bonfire of itching, squirming flesh. He drew his official-issue pistol, a .50 caliber Barrett WildStang with ICAP-custom SLAP rounds. The depleted uranium core and tungsten carbide tip combined with a nanofiber composite sabot and fifty grains of powder to produce a bullet that would go through just about anything. It kicked like a mule, and took superhuman strength to fire with any accuracy.

Two shots took Pointy in the bloody meat over his heart, and another two ricocheted off of his forehead.

Pointy charged, strings of intestines flopping out of his abdomen to trail behind him.

Matt fired four more times as he rose to his feet, and two more before the bonk crushed him against the wall.

Blood erupted from Matt's mouth as his ribs imploded. A giant hand smashed the gun against the wall, denting the metal in a shower of brick dust.

Pointy stepped back for another body check. Matt let his knees buckle, dropping to the floor, and tore at the exposed viscera, fingers digging into slippery organs, wrenching them out to splatter on the ground.

The dark tunnel exploded in stars as Pointy's knee caught him in the side of the head. Deafened by the ringing in his ears, he scrambled to the side and whirled, pistol raised. A six-car double-decker train shimmied down the tunnel at forty or so miles an hour, its light catching Pointy's right side, washed in bright red gore.

The abomination's abdomen had closed, cutting off the dead intestine and sealing over with fresh skin. It took a tentative, wobbly step forward. The train's horn reverberated through the tunnel, too loud.

Matt took inventory: three combat knives, two 32-round magazines for a broken gun, no functional firearms. His knee no longer itched, but Pointy stood moments from full health.

As the train flashed between them, Matt bolted alongside, grabbed a handle and jerked himself aboard. He landed with his toes on the lip of the entry, pried the door open left-handed, and stepped inside. A half-dozen shocked faces gaped at his blood-spattered face and body armor.

"Go to the front car." They stared, wide-eyed, but nobody moved. "NOW!"

The train lurched.

"GO!" Matt tore a stainless steel pole from the car and ran toward the back of the train. Ignoring the squeals of panic behind him, he stood alert, ready for bear.

Pointy's head appeared in the rear window. Matt moved to dive forward, and the whispers chittered their approval as his body crushed into the rails, his brain splattering into the ground. Instead he backpedaled, shouldered open the door between cars, and gripped the handle to the coupling mechanism. The back door came off in a shriek of twisted metal, and Pointy threw it to the side.

Matt heaved, and the cars separated with a lurch.

The bonk pulled himself up onto the trailing car, quickly falling away into the distance, an almost quizzical look on his blockish face. Matt sighed in frustrated relief, alive but without his quarry.

And then the train braked, hard.

Matt shifted his weight to maintain balance as the other car gained ground, momentum carrying it forward as the train slowed to a stop. If the conductor didn't have the sense to keep going, Matt would have to lead the bonk from the civilians on the train. He looked down at the pole, the best weapon he had, and suppressed a grimace. *Better than nothing, but not by much. Not against that.*

As the train ground to a halt he leapt out the back then darted left toward a side tunnel.

• • •

Miguel Salido watched the man in black armor fade into the distance, wielding a metal pole like a Ninja Turtle. He growled in curious frustration.

The high pitched squeal of brakes brought a low tremor to his throat; a laugh. The whispers rejoiced, a slithering, pernicious cacophony of psychotic bloodshed that got harder to ignore with every passing day, and though he couldn't understand them, they urged him to slaughter every man, woman, and child on the train.

He crushed them to a disappointed mewling, forced himself to think like a rational person.

The man in black armor, the woman he'd crushed, Miguel had never encountered anyone like them. Through years of street fighting, standing guard over drug deals, rising in the ranks of the Mako Kings despite being Cuban, not Mexican, Miguel had always been bigger, tougher, more of a *cabron* than any bastard around. When Jade hit the streets and everyone started getting bigger, Miguel pushed the limits of musculoskeletal enhancement and backed it up with surgically-added barbed spikes in his wrists and titanium alloy plates under his skin.

But this man, not much bigger than most, had almost taken him down. One crazy gun and some kickass bullets helped balance the score, almost too much.

Since growing up in the shantytowns of Arroyo Naranjo, swiping fruit from stalls at the mercado to stave off scurvy and starvation, he'd come to appreciate the big things in life. In coming to the United States, his time with the Mako Kings had given him almost everything: a bachelor's degree in Business Administration from the University of Miami – despite his size he'd never had the team spirit for football – a mansion, three cars, all the gold, drugs, and pussy he could ever want. But since Jade, since augmentation, they couldn't give him a challenge.

Sometimes it took the little things to bring a smile.

Miguel took off at a run. At twelve hundred pounds he couldn't sprint much faster than your average Olympian, even with no body fat. But he knew these tunnels, had operated in Spanish City for two years, and his prey hadn't. That had to count for something.

He slowed, approached the train at a jog, and cut left at the smell of the man, subtle deodorant and gun oil and blood tinged with an underlying spice he couldn't quite place, like Jade but not. He followed the scent until it reached an access door, and stopped. Sized for normal men, it would constrict him, keep him from using his reach or bringing his full strength to bear. A perfect place for an ambush.

* * *

Conor Flynn watched as Pointy approached the doorway. The hulking monstrosity moved with a smooth grace at odds with its blocky form, silent in giant, almost comical basketball shoes. It cocked its head and waited, one hand on the door, listening or feeling for vibrations or something.

Stepping to the side, it pulled open the door, which squeaked on old hinges. It winced, waited again, and after a long, long pause, went inside.

Conor followed through the open door, sword drawn. Darkness swallowed him.

* * *

Something thrummed through the floor and walls, a breathing shudder too low-frequency for even Matt's ears to hear. He drew a mental map to al-Azwar's body. Her REC7 carbine didn't pack the punch of his AA-12, but it beat the hell out of combat knives, and he wasn't likely to beat Pointy with his fists and elbows.

He jogged down the dark hall until it ended at a T intersection, on a hunch took a right, and a few minutes later when the hall took another right, farther away from al-Azwar, he backtracked to the intersection and headed left.

• • •

Miguel paused. The man's scent tracked in both directions.

The right-hand path led back to the railway, and past that, deeper into downtown. The left-hand path led to Spanish City, the Mercado Royale, and a warren of smaller access tunnels under the city's west side.

Where are you going?

He chuckled, a low rumble with more growl than mirth. A smart man would try to get back to his allies, back to whatever blew the gate to the parking lot, back to guns and backup. With a shrug, he turned left – if Miguel caught him before he got out, it wouldn't matter.

The scent grew in intensity, the sharp tang of Old Spice, the underlying notes of blood and gun oil. He froze at a realization. In the chemical miasma that permeated his enhanced nose he noted the lack, the utter absence, of anything approaching fear. Running, hunted, through unfamiliar tunnels, the man smelled of predator, not prey.

A tingle of excitement ran up Miguel's spine, a shiver of apprehension. *How are you not afraid?*

• • •

Matt knelt over al-Azwar's shattered body, ignoring the pungent reek of shit to rifle through her kit. Someone had stripped her of her carbine, pistol and combat knives, but had left her first aid kit, which all ICAP agents carried in case an innocent or suspect needed saving. That it had soaked with urine when her system had let go had probably discouraged close inspection, and he gladly took the morphine autoinjector.

He looked up at the ladder embedded into a short tunnel that terminated in a round steel hatch. Heaving on it bent a rung on the ladder but did nothing to budge the portal.

He tried the COM again. "This is Rowley, come in."

Nothing. However they built this place, it made far too good of a Faraday Cage.

He climbed down, listened for any signs of pursuit then hatched a plan.

* . *

Conor Flynn let Matt creep off, waited a full minute then approached the body. Matt had hidden the tripwire under Hurya's exploded viscera, a clever move that would reduce detection but make it less likely that Pointy would trip it in the first place. Matt had wrapped his remaining det cord around the magazines for his ridiculous shotgun, thirty-two-round drums loaded with smart, direction-triggerable microgrenades, enough raw explosives to make mincemeat out of anyone who tripped the switch.

He knelt, ran his finger just above the wire, and pulled the detonator from the cord.

"What the hell are you doing?" Matt's whisper clawed down his spine like fingernails down a chalkboard.

Conor plastered on a half-grin, the charming mask he'd worn for over thirty years. Matt gave him a slack-jawed stare, trust and suspicion warring in his eyes. The sword begged him to cut Rowley to ribbons, and the whispers cajoled their elated agreement.

"Not now," he growled.

Matt hesitated. "What do you mean?" His wary stance

betrayed too much caution, and Conor suppressed a chuckle at the misunderstanding.

He whispered back, "I called dibs. Not my fault you blighters don't listen, is it? So let's kill this thing."

"Are... are you insane?"

Conor hid the truth behind the truth. "That's why they hired me, am I right?"

* . *

"Put it back," Matt said. He took a step toward his friend, for the first time wary around the enthusiastic psychopath.

"Oil of palm, Rowley." Flynn replaced the detonator, though Matt had no idea what 'oil of palm' meant in these circumstances. His wife, Monica, had said that rhyme slang was much more of a cockney rather than an Irish thing, but either way Matt had yet to find Conor's flippant word games particularly comprehensible.

"Are you–" he cut himself off from asking the same question again. "Get over here and watch our six. These bastards killed Platt and al-Azwar, and I'm not about to let them get away with it."

Flynn sauntered over, thumbs hooked in his belt loops, katana slung at his waist in exactly a non-Japanese manner.

"What have you got for weapons?"

Flynn pulled his pistol, identical to Matt's. "Just this and the sword. Couple knives. Here, take it." He held it out grip-first.

Matt took it and holstered it.

Flynn smiled, but kept his voice at a barely audible whisper. "I'll go up. You can be bait." Before Matt could argue he'd scampered up the ladder to crouch in the darkness overhead, wedged in place like a movie action hero, left palm pressed against one wall, feet against the other. He drew his katana and winked. "Run along, little birdie. And tweet a little, would you?"

Chirp, chirp.

* . *

The scents mingled, the man's combining with someone else's, sharper, a cold, metallic bite reminiscent of dentist's offices and morgues. Miguel hesitated, then peeked around the corner. The body still lay where he'd left it, though her weapons were missing. Nothing moved, and nothing registered in the infrared.

He stepped out, approaching the body in a silent walk, and the cold smell grew stronger, more dominant. An infrared glow filtered down from the access hatch, normal in the daytime but out of place at night. Miguel tried not to roll his eyes at the soft scrape from the end of the hall.

There had never been a time, not since puberty, that people hadn't underestimated his mind. Only Calloway had seen through the lump of meat, lifted him up and made him a true player in her organization. The Mako Kings had no idea what they'd gotten themselves involved in, and she kept them rolled in enough cash to keep them blind, but she trusted Miguel, and used his shrewd mind to cement her ties with the Latin gang.

If you want a bull...

Miguel charged, as they'd expect him to, but at the last second leapt, punching into the overhead tunnel, driving his massive fist and barbed metal spikes into hard armor and soft flesh. The hidden man let out a strangled grunt as his abdomen imploded, and as Miguel tore away he went slack. Miguel's foot came down, slipped on the body, and the world went white.

* * *

The whispers cooed their disapproval as Matt rounded the corner too late for the explosion to shred his flesh. The bonk had stumbled to one knee, a mass of charred skin smeared with red where the mass of fragmentation grenades had sheared through. Pale metal shone through the injuries, an enhancement Matt hadn't expected.

Conor dropped from the shaft, hairless skin golden and shiny from the intense heat, and hit the ground on his knees and elbows, too hard. And stayed there, gagging.

Matt fired, a single round straight to the forehead. The bonk jerked sideways and the bullet ricocheted off, gouging the skin but otherwise doing no damage. As burnt flesh knitted over metal, it looked healthier than when they'd started.

Holy shit.

The bonk leaned forward and drove a fist down, crushing Flynn to the floor. His pelvis shattered and his legs twitched, but he didn't scream.

Matt charged, firing, as the bonk raised his fist again. The impacts should have driven it back, but instead it lunged forward, rising to its feet in an athletic leap. It stumbled as Flynn lashed out. His composite blade caught it in the knee, slicing through the meat to lodge in the joint.

Flynn held on, two-handed, as it dragged him another half-step and then fell, unable to drag its other leg underneath it.

Matt stepped forward and aimed, point-blank, at the top of its head. The single shot rang out and the bonk dropped, hot red fluid pulsing from the hole. He let out a breath, pointed down, fired twice more into the fractured skull.

Kneeling, Matt put his hand on Conor's shoulder. "You alive?"

Conor's hand twitched, and his thumb extended.

Matt patted the top of his head. "Sorry about the dibs. You maniac."

* . *

Six hours later they landed in D.C., Karle and Flynn still on stretchers, al-Azwar, Platt, and Washington in body bags. Matt shook Jeff Hannes's hand on the tarmac, Jeff's tie lashing in the downwash from the propellers.

Jeff pinned Flynn with his eyes and spoke as the chopper lifted off. "What the hell was that, Flynn?"

Karle held up a hand. "We already discussed it, sir. Flynn thought he'd taken down his target, so once he'd recovered from his injuries he'd redirected to assist in the hunt for, um, for Pointy."

Jeff looked from Flynn to Karle, his anger fading to his familiar grimace. "We lost three Augs taking down four, with drone support. How did that happen?"

Matt licked his lips. "We're still not sure. Something ambushed us on the way down, killed Platt and isolated al-Azwar so that Pointy could take her out. We looked at the Dragonfly feeds, and IR picked up a signature, but not much of one, and it disappeared into the crowd before we'd finished the sweep."

"What are you saying?"

Karle answered. "We... we don't know, sir. Alpha, Bravo, and Charlie squads came in on cleanup, and we vetted everyone before we released them or turned them over to metro PD for warrants. Nobody flagged, not even as suspicious, though way too many tested positive for Jade – nothing serious yet, just junkie-level cut crap."

Jeff looked at each of them in turn. "Well, in that case, I think you have a new mission."

Thanks for reading SNAFU: Hunters.

We hope you've enjoyed the book as much as we did putting it together.

Please consider leaving us a review if you see fit.

Any and all reviews are gratefully accepted. If you have any questions, or want to quote from the book, please contact us at any time.

Thank you.

* * *

Geoff Brown - Director, Cohesion Press.
Mayday Hills Lunatic Asylum
Beechworth, Australia

Amanda J Spedding - Editor-in-chief, Cohesion Press
Sydney, Australia

www.ingramcontent.com/pod-product-compliance
Lightning Source LLC
Chambersburg PA
CBHW031944260626
47157CB00017B/2312